I0783814

Book 1

by Dungeon Ducky

ISBN (print): 979-8-88993-043-3

ISBN (e-book): 979-8-88993-042-6

Written by Dungeon Ducky

Published 2025 by MoonQuill

Arlington, VA

www.moonquill.com

Table of Duckness

THE HIRO IS A RUBBER DUCK

Chapter 1

I Am a Rubber Duck!

Today, like most days, I floated.

Bobbing up and down, I drifted along the waves of vile, disgusting sludge that filled the sewer pipelines. Unable to move, I remained but a helpless victim of the tides—a mere passenger—forever trapped inside the shell of a small, yellow rubber duck.

To understand my pitiable predicament and current rubbery duckness, I'd have to take you back to the day it all started, when Truck-kun magically appeared and ran me over.

Yes, the Truck-kun from that ONE anime.

Now, you might be thinking: 'Wow! What a silly premise!' or 'How cliché! There's no way anime's #1 serial killer found you!'

Alas, I kid you not. Truck-kun exists as a vengeful spirit, and it takes no prisoners.

I remember that day fondly, despite my inevitable demise, as it was one of my last moments of autonomy and, in turn, a precious memory of a life before this one of perpetual buoyancy. It was dark and raining, and I had just picked up a cup of large fries from WacDonalds—a little salty goodness to celebrate my new job as an office worker, away from the stress of my army career.

Then, it happened.

Straight out of an alley.

I never stood a chance.

Once again, my imaginary friend, you might have more questions: 'How do you know Truck-kun doesn't take any prisoners?' and 'Why did it target you?' Well, I'm glad you asked!

Simply put, I DON'T KNOW! As driven as it was to mow me down, then and there, it wasn't clear as to why I was its 'chosen one.'

And I didn't die from the initial impact!

As a kid, I ran track, practiced martial arts, worked out, and spent my days cleaning houses to pay for college. So I was fit and had a strong constitution. Or at least I think I did. Maybe I'm confusing myself with the kid next door.

Anyway, when Truck-kun's headlights flooded the narrow alleyway and marked me on its war path, I instinctively tried to dodge. My futile attempt to save myself, however, only prolonged my suffering as my body slammed into its radiator, flying over the truck's dark hood instead of beneath it.

Hitting the ground with an 'oof,' I started to crawl. Though my aching limbs screamed at me with each agonizing drag of my crippled form across the pavement, my mind was firmly tethered to the squelch of potato mush beneath me—my reward, my comfort. Despite everything, I found myself helplessly lamenting the loss of my salted french fries, even as I desperately tried to get to safety.

Funny, I was on death's door, yet all I could think about were those fries.

It was then that Truck-kun came back into view. Its headlights sliced through the pouring rain, illuminating my broken body beneath a night sky swirling with thick, oppressive clouds, with the moon completely hidden from view. There was a palpable ferocity in those fluorescent beams, flickering with a blinding fury from the fact that it had failed to one-hit KO me. I could feel it: an all-consuming rage that its perfect streak had been broken.

It honked, revving its engine as I lifted a broken arm in futile defense and pleaded for it to spare me. Yet, my pleas fell upon deaf, metallic rearview mirrors.

It sped over me, mercilessly crushing me under its weight.

But it didn't end there. By some cruel miracle, I was still alive.

So, Truck-kun put it in reverse and backed over me, driving my mangled flesh further into the pavement. Again. And again, until I was nothing but a fine, bloody paste on the weathered cement.

Yeah.

That's how I originally died. I had read stories about things like this, watched shows, and hell, I'd even heard rumors of Truck-kun appearing with monsters, emerging from portals in Mexico, the US, and Japan, and people gaining RPG-esque systems. But it was all quickly dismissed as mere hoaxes.

Fast forward a bit, and I met a red-haired man who claimed to be a god, all while petting his adorable white cat. He apologized about his apostle's behavior before telling me that I'd been summoned for a grand purpose: to defeat the Demon Lord and save a world on the brink of disaster.

You know, generic isekai stuff.

I recruited and led my party of heroes, gathered skills, fell in love, and, in the end, had my grand stand-off with the Demon Lord, just as it had been ordained.

A heroic tale as old as time, right?

Except, in this story, I didn't win.

I lost against the Demon Lord. The bad guys won, my party disbanded, and my skills were sealed away. To add insult to injury, my soul was condemned inside that of a rubber duck, intended as a gift for the emperor's daughter.

The very daughter who, in a stroke of unfortunate luck, accidentally flushed me down the toilet.

And... that's pretty much my entire life story. Oh, and did I mention it has been a hundred years since then? A hundred years of isolation—just me, the sludgy water, and the slimes.

At least, I think it's been a hundred years? It's kind of hard to tell when you're a rubber duck, particularly one without access to a smartphone, a watch, or even, a sundial.

Or... sunlight for that matter.

Or ears.

Or eyes...

That's right. I can't see! But I can squeak. Taking in air through my mouth, I can expand and compress my body, forcing air through a squeaker in my beak. After a hundred or so years of experimenting, I eventually developed a nifty echolocation ability.

That's it—the ins and outs of my woeful condition. I float and I squeak, existing aimlessly through the putrid sewers that I resignedly called home.

Speaking of home, the underground waste network was built in a strange circular pattern that seemed to stretch on forever. Or so I thought. Every now and then, I'd experience a sudden drop, as if I were falling, but upon using my **Squeaker-Location** (an apt name, I know), I discovered I was simply being teleported. There was some kind of magical effect that bound me in place, tethering me back to the middle of the sewer, where I'd land with a splash and continue my never-ending voyage.

Up and down, up and down.

Forever.

And ever...

And ever...

An endless cycle of drifting.

Please, help me.

Experience has reached MAXIMUM level!
Core Accumulated!

Huh?

Standby for Integration...

What?

Integrating...

What's going on?

Integrating...

What the hell is this?

A spark. Something stirred within me, like a rumbling in the void at the hollowed center of my squishy prison.

Core Connected!

Who is this? Who are you?!

Dungeon System... Activating!

Wait, what the fu—

Dungeon Core: Active!

Suddenly, for the first time in ages, I felt something.

It felt like a surge of energy, like electricity, or an explosion of power that kick-started my long-since dulled senses. I could feel the broiling water beneath me, the warm caress of steam, and the smell...

Oh. Oh, God.

Oh, God! OhGodOhGodOhGod!

My squeaks echoed throughout the sewer channels as I convulsed and gagged on the inside. I attempted to will my body to twist, to shrink in on itself, or to cut off my ability to smell altogether, to no avail. The hysteria only worsened my situation, forcing my body to involuntarily gulp volumes of the foul odor.

I was unprepared. The rancid stench of my home overwhelmed my reclaimed senses.

NOOOOOOO! KILL ME! PLEASE!

What is your name?

Words, once again, began forming in my mind—a welcome distraction, to which I could only respond with a single, *What?*

Confirm Name: What?
Y/N?

What? No!

What is your name?

Name, name, name! I had a name once, but what was it? I racked my nonexistent brain, thinking, sorting, and sifting, trying to uncover the traces of my past. I struggled to maintain my sanity amid the sudden bombardment of stimuli and the glaring white text forced into my mind.

My name...

It started with an 'H,' this I knew, but I couldn't recall. It was like there was a fog blanketing my inner thoughts. I could envision glimpses of people as they spoke to me, addressed me, called out to me, and cheered for me, but for the life of me, I just couldn't remember. So, I went with the two things I knew about myself.

One, I was a rubber duck.

And two, I was a hero.

Confirm Name: Hiro
Y/N?

Yes.

Processing...

I focused long and hard on those words, placing them at the forefront of my mind to prevent my psyche from collapsing from the wretched smell that permeated the space around me. It was disgusting, and what I had thought was water from a septic conduit in the sewer turned out to be bubbling, toxic sludge.

Disgusting! Disgusting! I tried to focus on the words engraved in my mind's eye, yet the smell triumphed over all!

Clean! Clean! LET ME CLEAN! I raged.

It was the first emotion I'd ever felt in hundreds of years, and it was the desire to purge the filth from this world.

Dungeon Registered: Hiro's Dungeon!
Dungeon Core Skills Unlocked!

Congratulations! Please see your system handbook for instructions on how to run your dungeon! Good luck killing heroes!

The mysterious words left as quickly as they had come, leaving me alone once again. But now, I was angry and confused, driven by an overwhelming compulsion to OXICLEAN the world of its stains.

Rolling... Starter Skills

The system was back, but this time, it was different. Less intense and more focused, its interface was easier and more comfortable to perceive within my thoughts. I felt a tug, as if my very being was being shifted, until suddenly it stopped, leaving me with a plethora of messages in the void that was my inner consciousness.

Water Affinity Detected!
Obtained: Squirt Water Lvl.01
Obtained: Bubble Blow Lvl.01
Obtained: Acid Immunity Lvl.??
Obtained: Striking Resistance Lvl.06
Obtained: Slashing Resistance Lvl.06
Unique Skill Detected!
Integrating... Squeaker-Location
Obtained: Squeaker-Location Lvl.02
Soul-Bound Skills Detected!
ERROR! 404! Skill Page Not Found!
Troubleshooting...
Soul-Bound Skills Sealed!
Attempting Seal Break... 1 of 146

Suddenly, a weighty pressure wrapped around my sense of self, like a complete and utter vice around my soul.

Pain.

For a lack of a better word, that's what I felt. Having been numb for so long, I relished it—madness in my soul, as something I thought I'd never miss sprang forth: happiness, of a degree I never knew I could achieve!

I squeaked in jubilation, instantly regretting it as the sewer's gaseous toxins assaulted my innards once more. My lamentation, however, didn't last long, as the next message I received froze me to my rubber.

Seal Break: Successful!
Soul-Bound Skills Unsealed!

Immediately I could feel another change occurring inside, a cataclysmic adjustment in my core.

Reclaiming... Soul-Bound Skills

Was this it? Was I going to reclaim my heroic stature, my skills, and my position as the strongest hero? Even as a rubber duck, just having a fraction of my old skills would be a start! I greedily waited, anticipating that with this power, I might one day regain even a semblance of my former glory.

Skills Reclaimed: 2

Eh?

Obtained: Summon Rock Lvl.01
Obtained: Impart Instruction Lvl.01
Curse Feedback Detected!
Permanently sealing soul-bound skills to protect the user from curse feedback!

What?!

Sealing Skills...

NO! NO! NO!

It wasn't fair! I could see them—my skills—foreign yet familiar and grayed out on a list that was rapidly disappearing!

Please! No! No! NOOOOOOOOOOOO!

Squeaks of agony bled from my permanently gaped beak. This was it; my hopes and dreams were eviscerated within a matter of seconds. Memories I had once thought lost had just begun to resurface—memories of all my time, effort, and tears I had shed in pursuit of power.

And just like that, it was all gone. Once again, it was locked away, and there was nothing I could do to stop it as the skill list vanished. The tragic reality hit me as harshly as Truck-kun had stolen me from my peaceful one.

I was a rubber duck, and my time as a hero was truly over.

Chapter 2

Please Stop Eating Me...

U p and down, up and down, the emergence of new skills did little to obscure the futility in my still, pitiable existence. My body, stiff and unwilling—as it had been so cruelly designed—remained captive to the unyielding churn of thick, dense muck beneath me. This time, however, anger swelled in my veins as every fiber of my plastic demanded freedom from the accursed smell.

My metaphorical veins.

As a rubber duck, I obviously lack the anatomical framework of the average human. I don't have blood vessels, or a circulatory system, or—well... organs. But you get the gist. Of course you do.

Wait...

Do I have organs? Functioning organs? If I can smell, I must have olfactory receptors, right? If so, why? I'm a rubber duck! What kind of sick, twisted sadist would do that, and in the sewers?

Is it you, God?! Are you messing with me? Even after all these years?

I SWEAR I'LL DESTROY THE VERY WORLD YOU TASKED ME TO SAVE!

-1 HP

Ow! What the hell?

Something pricked me, causing me to flinch internally.

-1 HP

Wait, what?

-1 HP

Okay, I get it! That's starting to get annoying!

-1 HP

HEY, STOP THAT!

As an attempt to identify the threat, I squeaked loudly and forcefully.

I regretted it immediately. My soul burned as the stench violated my senses anew, but it was a necessary trade-off to activate my **Squeaker-Location**. The ability revealed to me the image of something amorphous that had latched onto me.

A SLIME!

-1 HP

Hey! Get off me!

-1 HP

OW! What did I ever do to you?

-1 HP

Are you an agent of Truck-kun?! Are you here to finish what it started?!

Yet my tantrum went unnoticed by the soulless creature. Instead, it continued absorbing me, affixing itself to my body and dragging me into its jellified maw. It was lukewarm, like a slimy blanket enveloping my entirety, embracing me like a mother's womb.

In short, it was absolutely VILE and disgusting.

Then, it hit me.

This was happening. After a hundred years, I would finally die. The legendary Hiro, turned into a rubber duck, finished off by a slime. Who would've thunk?

-1 HP

At least the smell was better, but not by much.

-1 HP

Oh, nice. Now I'm tasting it.

-1 HP

How am I tasting it?!

-1 HP

Sitting there, being dissolved, I lamented my life thus far. Back in my prime, I could easily dispatch these low-level monsters with ease. Now, here I was, about to be devoured by a worthless slime of all things.

-1 HP

Oh, how the mighty have fallen, but at least I'd finally be at peace.

-1 HP

I embraced death, waiting for the darkness to take me.

-1 HP

-1 HP

-1 HP

-1 HP

-1 HP

-1 HP

-1 HP

-1 HP

-1 HP

-1 HP

Man, this is... kinda taking a while.

-1 HP

Okay... How many health points can I possibly have? I'm a rubber duck for duck's sake!

At my command, a menu suddenly lit up, materializing in my mind's eye and dispelling the usual darkness.

Dungeon System Interface
Name: Hiro Dungeon
Level: 01
HP: 6999/7000
MP: 0999/1000
EXP: 000/500
Tamed Monsters: 00/10
Pending Quests: 1

Wait, what the hell is this?!

Why is my health pool so damn high? And why isn't it decreasing?

HP: 7000/7000

-1 HP
HP: 6999/7000
HP: 7000/7000
-1 HP
HP: 6999/7000

Then it suddenly hit me: I was regenerating faster than I was taking damage. For every two health points I lost, I would recover five. *Great.*

-1 HP

Just great! I groaned. My one shot at ending this nightmare, and of course, I was too strong to be slain.

-1 HP

What's this about a pending quest?

-1 HP

Focusing on the quest icon, it suddenly expanded into a smaller box of text.

Quest List
Mark Your Territory!
Reward: +100 EXP

Mark my territory? It seemed as though the system was prompting me to set up my dungeon.

There was just one problem.

How the hell am I supposed to claim territory when I'm being dissolved?!

-1HP

Alright hold up, I've got skills right? Let's try using those.

SKILL LIST
Bubble Blow Lvl.01
MP Cost: 5

Create a bubble of charged mana. When it pops, it releases a light burst of magic.

Squirt Water Lvl.01
MP Cost: 5

Create and squirt water from your beak.

Summon Rock Lvl.01
MP Cost: 10

Summon a small rock. That's it. It summons a rock.

Squeaker-Location Lvl.02
MP Cost: 1

With a squeak, send out a pulse to map your surroundings and form a vivid image in your mind.

Impart Instruction Lvl.01

Teach skills and share experience with minions or selected creatures.

*Well. How useful... Not! What kind of skill is **Bubble Blow**?!*
Wait. What's this?

Amid the flood of system messages, something drew my attention. Hidden behind the sea of glaring, internal text was another tab labeled "Dungeon Core." I homed in on it, opening it to reveal a wealth of interesting new talents.

Dungeon Skills
Domain Expansion: 0/1
Sustained
MP Cost: 500

Radiate your will and designate a nearby area as part of your domain. If there are other competing claims to the area, the strongest will prove victorious.

{Locked} Designate Minion Lvl.01: 0/10
MP Cost: 20 (Per Minion)

Creatures you target must make a wisdom saving throw against you. Upon failing, the creature is forcibly placed under your command.

Huh... Half my mana to mark my territory. Why not?

I gave it a try. Almost instantly, I could feel my awareness extending, my essence radiating around me like a weird out-of-body experience. My will, my mana, crept outward in a sphere about fifty meters wide—a boundary that stretched my consciousness to everything within it.

I became aware of everything around me that I had already known: the slimes, the bubbling acid, the grime on the smooth, mold-covered pillars that supported this shrine of filth and decay. Yet somehow, there was more. For the first time in an age, I felt ownership. I was able to feel like something truly belonged to... me.

Quest Complete: Mark Your Territory!
Your territory has been claimed! You are now on your way to becoming a great dungeon!
+100 EXP

This was now my home. My Domain. MY CASTLE! It was my filthy, filthy domain that needed to be cleaned!

Unlocked: Designate Minion Lvl.01!
Incoming Quest!
Designate a Minion! 0/1
Reward: +100 EXP

A flood of emotions hit me, but I couldn't let them overtake me. No, there was work to be done. I had tasks to accomplish and minions to gather. I left the quest unaccepted for a couple of moments, reflecting on its objective and my progress thus far, as my health points constantly ticked down and then back up.

It was then I knew, without a doubt, who my first minion would be. Although it wasn't some powerful dragon, necromantic lich, or magical cyclops, it would have to do.

After all, we all must start somewhere if we're going to conquer the world.

Chapter 3

Stop Bullying My Slime!

My sense of self narrowed, twisting to focus on one thing and one thing only—the slime devouring me. I could feel the gelatinous creature tremble, spasming violently as it reacted to my mind infiltrating its red core—the very essence of the monster's life force and being.

'Dissolve, dissolve, dissolve! Intruder, intruder, intruder!' Its thoughts struck my mind, startling me with its intelligence— intelligent enough to think, let alone attempt to resist my authority.

You! Are! Mine! I sent back, demanding it to submit to my will.

In response, the viscous walls encasing my body shook and vibrated wildly until it suddenly stopped, bringing with it a system message.

You have tamed your first minion!
What is this creature's name?

Slimey, naturally.

Name: Slimey

Level: 01
Species: Mutated Cleaning Slime
HP: 10/10
MP: 3/3
Skills:
Dissolve Lvl.01
Slime Shot Lvl.01

At my designation, Slimey shook as a sense of familiarity was established between it and I.

Quest Complete: Designate a Minion! 1/1
+100 EXP
New Quest Available at 10 Minions!

Welp, it was time to get to work.

It wasn't long before I was mobile. With Slimey now tethered to my will, it immediately became my trusted steed—my island, my brace against the sludge. That said, Slimey was quite mobile. The creature absorbed water and shot it out to propel itself around. It was something I hadn't known slimes were capable of.

At first, it was overwhelming—the noises, the smell, the monsters. The life force of every creature rubbed up against my own, within my sphere of influence.

Sitting atop the green slime, I slowly roamed, moving to and fro in my acid-drenched domain as I commanded my minion to shepherd my body.

Why was I touring my domain when I could easily "see" everything within it?

Easy. It was mine—and it was liberating that I could finally move. Well... direct where I went.

For once.

Ah... this feels so good, I recalled thinking. Although, it surely would've felt better if I had legs... or could move at all. What I wouldn't give to be able to stretch!

As we moved through the winding channels, the monsters that dotted my domain began to turn away and flee—all except the slimes. Oddly enough, they weren't running. No, instead, they seemed to be—

Oh. Oh, no.

I could feel them moving. There were roughly a dozen minds, each pressing against the edges of my own expansive consciousness as they drew near. They were clearly drawn to the same thing that had attracted Slimey.

In other words, me.

Trudging toward me from all directions, the slimes moved in concert, each creature chanting, *'dissolve, dissolve, dissolve!'* Not vocally, of course. The rhythmic, mental pulsing of their aggression filled my mind and steadily grew in volume. But my priorities remained as steadfast as ever.

Heh, easy prey, and soon-to-be minions eager to serve a new master!

Foolish slimes. I am none other than HIRO, the legendary champion sent to purge the world of filth and grime! GROVEL BEFORE YOUR EMPEROR, FOR—

Suddenly, my smooth ride became anything but smooth. In just moments, I found myself boxed in and surrounded, with dozens of slimes closing in around Slimey and bashing it back and forth between themselves. My attempt at dominance was effectively disrupted, and all I could do was bob helplessly as they brutally assaulted my underling.

WARNING! Your minion is under attack!

Whoa, hey! Stop that! STOP THAT! I didn't mean what I said earlier! STOP! I yelled, but of course, slimes being what they were, my pleas went unacknowledged.

WARNING! Minion, Slimey's health is below 80%!

Another system message appeared, notifying me that Slimey was getting hurt. My bastion against the wild currents and my only means of transportation wiggled valiantly, fending off the other slimes as they fired slime balls and crashed into Slimey with their bodies.

Slimey! Hang on!

'Wiggle, wiggle,' my slime seemed to reply, losing bits of itself to block attacks aimed at its master.

WARNING! Minion, Slimey's health is below 50%!

Aaaarrrrgh! I just got out of the sludge!

Think, Hiro! THINK! I've got to find a way out of this!

Closing my mind to the chaos, I opened my skill list and reviewed what I had.

Dungeon System Interface
Name: Hiro Dungeon
Level: 01
HP: 7000/7000
MP: 0479/1000
EXP: 200/500
Tamed Monsters: 01/10
SKILL LIST
Bubble Blow Lvl.01
MP Cost: 5

Create a bubble of charged mana. When it pops, it releases a light burst of magic.

Squirt Water Lvl.01
MP Cost: 5

Create and squirt water from your beak.

Summon Rock Lvl.01
MP Cost: 10

Summon a small rock. That's it. It summons a rock.

Squeaker-Location Lvl.02
MP Cost: 1

With a squeak, send out a pulse to map your surroundings and form a vivid image in your mind.

Impart Instruction Lvl.01

Teach skills and share experience with minions or selected creatures.

Bubbles? Useless. Squirting water? Useless. Summoning a ROCK?! I never even used that when I had my human body!

Suddenly, an idea hit me as I glanced over **Impart Instruction**, the solution to my current dilemma.

WARNING! Minion, Slimey's health is below 20%!

AHHHHHH! How do I use a skill?! I screamed in frustration, fumbling around in my mind, searching for its hidden switches.

WARNING! Minion, Slimey's health is below 10%!

IMPART! IMPART! **IMPART INSTRUCTION!**

An interface lit up, an invisible connection seemingly strengthening between Slimey and me, before an option to allocate experience or skills came into view.

You have 200 experience points available to spend!

I fed all of it to Slimey, who suddenly exploded with energy.

To an average human, a hundred experience points was the equivalent to killing a big, angry boar. But to a slime? To a creature that sat at the bottom of the food chain, sucking up filth? It was like a dragon imparting wisdom to an infant child.

Okay, I may be over-exaggerating, but still.

Slimey's core grew bright. The slime's level immediately jumped to three, regenerating its health, which now capped off at a nice twenty-five, and it gained a new skill.

Name: Slimey
Level: 03
Species: Mutated Cleaning Slime
HP: 25/25
MP: 9/9
Skills:
Dissolve Lvl.01
Slime Shot Lvl.01
Solidification Lvl.01

Solidification! A slime's natural defensive ability against prey and predators. It was a skill that allowed slimes to harden and protect themselves!

Immediately, I began to beseech my trusty steed, commanding it to solidify so that we would be whisked away from these cretins who dared to impede on my righteous mission to IGNITE THE UNCLEAN!

Heeding my orders like a good minion, Slimey took me into itself, its oozy, disgusting body forming a cocoon around me, and activated its **Solidification** skill.

Aaaaaand we started plummeting deeper into the sewers.

We're just falling...

Oh, there's fish. Neat... HOW ARE THERE FISH HERE?!

NEVERMIND THAT! WHY ARE WE FALLING?! I THOUGHT YOU SLIMES WERE BUOYANT! I screamed, as I left the range of my domain and descended into the uncharted depths of the sewers.

Chapter 4

A God's Oversight

ELSEWHERE, IN A BRIGHTLY LIT CAVE FILLED WITH BOOKS AND SKELETONS...

Sitting on a throne made of bones and endless-night obsidian, a red-haired man with cat ears and golden eyes, dressed in a pink bathrobe, yawned as he petted the fluffy white feline in his lap.

He was called The Bookkeeper, and despite his shaggy appearance, casual demeanor, and furry friend that occasionally fired laser beams at skelly cats that got a little too close to its master, he wielded divine power.

"I wonder what Junith is doing," the man muttered to himself. He scratched his stubble as he opened a blue one-way portal to spy on the cat girl in stylized black armor with golden skull pauldrons. The woman was in the midst of slashing away at the tides of grotesque voidlings with a blue flaming bonesword, its ivory blade bathed in a raging inferno of blue flame. "Seems about right."

The Bookkeeper raised a hand, about to wave the portal away when his attention was drawn to a blip on another screen.

Superior One, an abnormality has occurred.

"Hm?" The archivist arched his brow as his white feline familiar climbed his bathrobe to drape itself across his broad shoulders. "Bring it up, D."

Of course, Superior One.

The second portal swirled into a messy blur of colors, smokey and swimming with ancient magic, until it began to clear again, but this time, zoomed in on a small, yellow duck encased in a rigid slime. Together, they were seemingly falling through a concrete passage lined with grime.

AAAAH! WHY AM I STILL SINNNNKINNNNG?! A voice pierced through the portal, the distressed, high-pitched inner thoughts bouncing off the walls of The Bookkeeper's private dwelling.

"Huh... Well, that's new," he commented with his head cocking to the side. His familiar, Schrödinger, mirrored the movement. "I was wondering what... D, what was this soul's name again?"

Sawano Hiroyuki.

"Wait, the composer? Bragi's avatar?"

There's no relation to Earth Prime's god of music.

"Ah. Hm. Who was this one's sponsor?"

You, Superior One.

"Oh..." The Bookkeeper leaned forward, squinting his cat-shaped eyes. "Wait. Is he a rubber duck?"

Yes, Superior One. His shell is composed of hyper-enchanted, polyvinyl chloride.

"Mhm. Wasn't he sent to kill a demonic entity running amok about two thousand years ago?"

Two thousand two hundred and fourteen days, fifty-two hours, forty-nine minutes and—

"Okay, I get it. Where's the Demon Lord now?"

One moment, Superior One...

Triangulating... Demon Lord Barbaroll

"Meow!" Schrödinger cried, slipping from its master's shoulders and back onto his lap, stretching out over one of his legs as if trying to garner his master's attention.

Analysis Complete
Target Inquiry: Demon Lord Barbaroll is deceased.

"Deceased?" The man frowned, opening a system display and flipping through translucent pages to locate the file. "Cause of death... old age?"

That is correct, Superior One.

The Bookkeeper scratched the back of his head. "Well... mission complete?" He dropped his hand, letting it smooth over the back of his cat as it purred in satisfaction. "Bring him back, D."

As you wish, Superior One.

ERROR!

Unfortunately, I cannot comply with your request, Superior One.

The Bookkeeper narrowed his eyes as a woman in white materialized before him. She was a white-haired cat-woman, clad in leather, with red tattoos adorning her translucent skin.

"What? Explain why not," he queried, irritation lacing his voice at being denied.

This soul has integrated with the world's mana distribution system. Removing the target forcefully from the world system would send a shockwave across the entire planet. Additionally,

the interference required would ignite a rallying cry to the void-beings, signaling them to descend upon the planet.

The Bookkeeper turned his gaze to the paladin tearing her way through swarms of viscous monstrosities, before his eyes shifted back to the rubber duck being torn from his slime's embrace by a pack of spinelings—creatures with elongated bodies and bone-like features.

AHHHHHHHH! STOP EATING ME! OW! OWOWOWOW! SLIMEY! SLIMEY, SAVE ME!

"Interesting…" A smile curled on his lips as an idea slowly unfurled in his mind. "Let's see what I can do with our rubbery friend."

WE RETURN TO OUR PROTAGONIST, HIRO.

-27 HP

-3 HP

-49 HP

-18 HP

-7 HP

-30 HP

-54 HP

-33 HP

-26 HP

-12 HP

-29 HP

-30 HP

-13 HP

STOP, STOP, STOP! STOP! THAT HURTS!

Of course, I finally acquired a sliver of freedom, and now I'm being torn apart by unknown monsters in the dark that were no doubt sent by Adam to spite me!

-24 HP

But... I guess, on the flip side, I would finally be free of this accursed existence...

-17 HP

For real, this time.

-3 HP

Ah... sweet oblivion. I can already see the light.
Wait. See? I can't even squeak under water!

Suddenly I could feel myself rising. My entire being seemed to stretch as I was quickly being elevated, with my assailants still affixed to my rubber body.

It felt like I was caught in a vice, like a ball of putty in someone's hands that squeezed me from all sides. I could feel my core, my shell, my very being tremble as I was exposed to the rapid change in water pressure, and my body began to expel what air was trapped inside my rubber shell.

-1872 HP

Without Slimey to take the brunt of the weight, I was easily compressed and my body flattened, a guttural sound leaving my squeaker as I was molded into a tight, yellow ball around my core.

Plop.

I broke the water's tension, bursting free from its depths and resuming my buoyant coasting along the water's filthy surface of green sludge.

Somehow, I made it back. Home. My domain. Except now, instead of being a rubber duck, I was a yellow ball, rolling with the tides.

Great. I'm a ball.

Slimey joined me a moment later. Our connection let me know that my servant was reunited with me—that I wasn't alone.

The green and wounded monster slinked its way towards me, instantly wrapping itself around my sphere. The creature was ready to protect me with what little remained of its little green body.

I'm sorry, buddy, I sent to Slimey. Although it was just a monster, Slimey was mine, and it was all I had. And it had suffered, which made me feel guilty.

It wiggled in response, with no thoughts on its mind other than, *'protect, protect, protect!'* A loyal servant.

Then it happened—a strange popping sound. My body suddenly decompressed as my health points started slowly ticking back up; it unfolded, repairing itself and reforming me back into its original shape as a rubber duck.

"Squeeeeak." The release in pressure pulled a noise from my beak, as I pulled air into my hollow shell. Still, there was this unusual feeling in the pit of my rubber, like something still churned within me, that wasn't my own body caving in on itself. It made me feel almost nauseated at the thought of waste settling within me, and I heaved as if to cough out any trapped debris. That's when black water shot out from my squeaker and hit a nearby wall, melting the acid-resistant stone surface.

Huh?

My spew dribbled down, bubbling the surface and taking the minerals with it, eventually slinking onto the walkway where it did the same. A black odor rose from its aftermath, adding to the pungent medley of smells that permeated through my domain.

HUH?! WHY DO I SPIT ACID?! WHEN COULD I SPIT ACID?!

I prepared myself to activate **Squirt Water**, to see if it was related to the skill or if I was just regurgitating a mouthful of sludge that I'd collected in the chaos.

But why was the acid black when the sewer sludge was green? I was about to fire off another water spurt, but just as the liquid started to pool in my gut, my new friends returned.

Twelve of them, to be exact.

The slimes had entered my domain.

Chapter 5

Round Two!

The slimes... I could sense them. The monsters were coming out of the shadows beyond my territory to intrude into MY domain once more, and those thieving gelatinous monstrosities were out for MY DELECTABLE PLASTIC BITS. They wouldn't have it! No, no, no! Not on my watch!

Activating **Squirt Water**, the black ooze I emitted splashed against the sewer wall once more, turning it into a warped, fizzling mess that filled me with a sense of twisted glee.

If the walls could withstand the muck below me for thousands of years, yet couldn't handle the touch of my corrosive ink, then what would it do to a monster at the bottom of this world's pecking order?

Ehehehehehehe.

An evil feeling blossomed in my... heart? A desire to purge the unclean and subjugate minions to expand my domain resonated from within my being.

It was time for round two.

The slimes were on the move, slinking in a pack and making their way through the water towards a promising free meal.

Okay, Slimey! Turn me around! It's time to make these scum pay! I directed my minion, the injured slime heeding my command without delay and shifting its body to reorient me.

The pack of slimes were nearly upon me, thirty feet to be exact. Fortunately, the strength of the opposing sewer currents staggered their advance, buying me time to formulate my plan.

I steeled my resolve, "observing" the monsters through my domain senses while I sent out a few squeaks to ping the area, despite the revolting smell that would sneak through each breath and strike my soul.

Activate! **SQUIRT WATER!**

After locating my target, I took aim and fired my black acid. Unfortunately, I failed to account for the fact that I'm a rubber duck and my water squirting ability was limited to the design of my body.

In short, my attack fell—well, quite short—striking the restless sewage, where it sizzled and kicked up steam.

DRAT! How am I supposed to hit them if I can't reach them?! Okay! Wait. Just think for a moment, Hiro! Think!

Then it hit me—an idea. An image of a boat sinking in the water, getting ready to strike at its targets from far away. If I couldn't hit the creatures from this range, what I needed was leverage: height, angles, a way to strike from a distance like a catapult!

Slimey! Lift me up! Angle my body up by thirty degrees! My loyal companion immediately began to wiggle and shifted toward the instructed trajectory... Or it tried to.

NO! Thirty degrees, not ninety! THIRTY! Less, not more! ANGLE ME CORRECTLY! THIS IS SEVENTY!

What was I even doing trying to communicate math to a slime?

Down! Lower me down! Down, down, down, down... Stop! Up, up, and a little to the left! Up, down, left, right! Hold it there! **SQUIRT WATER!**

Now perfectly angled, I fired off my corrosive attack, and the water arced through the air where it struck one of the slimes directly.

YES!

Immediately, the monster began to bubble and fizzle, wobbling and caving into itself as the acid that ate away its protective gel and evaporated its outer layer until all that was left was its shiny red core.

+10 EXP

+10 EXP

+10 EXP

+10 EXP

Ehehehehe! DIE! DIE! DIE!

Glee and a lust for victory flooded my senses. Though it was only one slime, for the first time in millennia, I was suddenly not powerless! *I WILL CONQUER THE WORLD!*

+10 EXP

+10 EXP

+10 EXP

+10 EXP

I continued firing the noxious venom, making corrections to my height and firing angles to Slimey, who remained steadfast by my side.

The slimes were getting closer now, only twelve feet, but at least I had managed to splash and eliminate eight of the twelve, leaving only four remaining. However, something was wrong. My squirts were coming out less pitch-black and more of a greenish black, a change occurring in my skill that made my attack less deadly.

Still, I kept squirting, firing my liquid evil at the slimes still persistently inching towards me.

One slime came close—closer than the others—bouncing out of the river and attempting to engulf me into its body. But Slimey wasn't having it. My new companion inhaled a copious amount of water and propelled its body to the side, leaving the assailant to splash harmlessly into the water, where it was then met by my squirt.

+10 EXP

Three left. I had sixty mana points left to dominate them, with ten feet of distance remaining before they would reach Slimey and me.

I reached out, my conscience touching theirs. A chorus of *'DISSOLVE! DISSOLVE! DISSOLVE!'* echoed repeatedly in my mind, driving home how one-dimensional these creatures were. Despite the loss of so many of their comrades, there wasn't an ounce of fear or worry—only the singular thought that propelled the monsters forward in their attempt to purge me from this world.

But that was my job.

Disappointingly for them, I wouldn't go quietly. As if I ever would.

YOU. BELONG. TO. ME. My domain projected my thoughts to the creatures who dared to intrude upon my castle. Through my dominion, I could feel them squirm, wiggle, jostle, as my claim pulsed from wall to wall. The slimes made a pathetic attempt at resistance, even as they were physically battered by the crippling reverberation of my authority.

Yet, without twelve minds assaulting and attacking me all at once, I could clearly assert my will and dominance, forcing the collapse of these small monsters' juvenile minds.

You have tamed a new minion!

Multiple menus blinked into view, each reading a similar set of text and prompting me to declare ownership of the newest additions to my growing horde.

What is this creature's name?

Slime 1, Slime 2, Slime 3. Obviously.

Slimey was my first, so of course it was special.

Upon dominating the remaining three slimes, I could feel a fatigue shoot through my body as the system popped up in the forefront of my consciousness.

Dungeon System Interface
Name: Hiro Dungeon
Level: 01
HP: 4211/7000
MP: 0000/1000
EXP: 090/500
Tamed Monsters: 04/10

Suddenly my mind was besieged by a chorus of *'Protect! Protect! Protect!'* The slime's thoughts of dissolving were overwritten with the directive to accommodate my every whim.

They moved in unison, joining with Slimey to form a viscous island of goop in the sickly green river, propping me up and acting as a sort of throne. As this happened, Slimey slinked out of the pile, asserting its dominance over the newcomers by sitting atop them and forming around me, almost to say, *'I WAS FIRST!'*

Now no longer subjected to the whims of the tides, I smiled inwardly as I processed the rush and excitement of the events that had just transpired.

Although I had nearly died, I now had servants under my command. Granted, they were disgusting, stinky, disease-riddled creatures whose touch made me want to scream, but they were mine. My first steppingstone. I just needed to collect six more stones to complete my stairwell to glory.

Chapter 6

Please Construct Additional Pylons!

In the dark recesses of an old, decrepit castle—long abandoned by the mortal realm and left to stew in its filth and dust—a small green slime wiggled back and forth, attempting to break free from the cocoon of foreign goo wrapped around itself.

Sitting atop Slimey as per usual, I inwardly smiled and watched as a slime struggled within my cage of slimes, which was reminiscent of an old monster capturing game known as **TRADEMARK REDACTED DUE TO LEGAL REASONS**, if I recall correctly.

Be. Mine. The monster's feeble will clashed against my own with me winning out. Its thoughts of *'dissolve, dissolve, dissolve'* quickly turned into thoughts of *'protect, protect, protect,'* just as the others before it.

You have tamed a new minion!
What is this creature's name?

Slime 9, of course, I named the latest slime in my collection that quickly slinked off to join the growing mound of jelly beneath my feet... flippers? My bottom? My big juicy plastic? My ruba-donkadonk? My train of thought was interrupted by flashing words in my mind.

ConCATulations on building your horde!
Unlocked: Pylons!
Incoming Quest!
Construct Territorial Pylons! 0/5
Your defenders have grown, but so too should your territory!
Reward: +New Skill, +Minion Capacity Increase

ConCATulations? What's with the typo? And... pylons? I sat there for a moment, wondering how exactly I was supposed to create a "pylon" with no hands and a bunch of gooey, amorphous monsters under my command that had taken forever to gather.

Suddenly, electricity seemingly shot through my system, like a heartbeat that pulsed and sent a current of energy seeping straight out of my core. In that moment, a sudden rush of euphoria flooded my body as my consciousness seemed to vacate my rubber shell and ascend.

I became keenly aware of my territory—of the space I called my own—not in the sense that I owned it, but rather, it was a part of me, with each inch and crevice containing my will. It was an extension of myself... filled with... FILTHY DISGUSTING PIECES OF CRAP THAT SOILED EVERY INCH OF MY DOMAIN!

I was abruptly thrust back within my shell, my grimy rubber duck body rocking back and forth in anger.

UGH! I WANT TO BE CLEAN! I DESIRE TO BE CLEEEEAN!

Dungeon System Interface
Name: Hiro Dungeon
Level: 01

HP: 7000/7000
MP: 0500/1000
EXP: 110/500
Tamed Monsters: 10/10
Pylons: 0/4

My system updated, showing me that I had reached the maximum capacity for tamable minions, while also displaying a new tab for pylons.

Great. Thanks for the useless information.

There was still no button or tutorial for making a pylon, leaving me frustrated and stewing in stagnation and filth.

For a while, I wandered aimlessly through my territory, allowing Slimey and myself to recuperate before making any big moves.

It was fascinating to watch Slimey repair itself. Unlike humans, whose regeneration capabilities were based on cellular division, the goop that slimes were composed of was actually produced from the filth they collected and absorbed into their body. I suppose it made sense, given that slimes were monsters engineered from recycled monster cores to keep sewers clean.

And, damn, did they do a piss-poor job of that...

Next, my entourage of slimes and I began to move to the outskirts of my domain.

While I could "see" everything within a fifty-meter radius that was my domain, anything beyond that remained enshrouded in black. It was like the fog-of-war mechanic in one of those real-time strategy games I used to play—except the fog didn't clear as I neared.

This is assuming I'm remembering video games correctly. It felt so weird getting glimpses of my past... BUT THIS IS NO TIME TO REMINISCE!

At the edge of the abyss, I braced myself upon the bodies of my slimes, taking in the toxic, moist air before compressing myself to activate **Squeaker-Location**.

Immediately, my sound wave painted an image in my mind, my squeak bouncing off of every surface of the black void, reporting to me what I already knew lurked in the shadows: winding sewer channels and monsters.

There were mostly slimes, giant roaches, bulbous six-legged creatures, and something bumpy pulled back onto its haunches with a massive maw and a tail. I could only surmise it was a bipedal crocodile, because why wouldn't a sewer have a crocodile?

After scanning my surroundings, I had a better understanding of my situation.

I was at the crossroad of a t-shaped network, with a river of slime flowing down to me from two different sides before conjoining to head downstream.

To my right, a giant croc seemed to reign as the boss of the area, as everything would steer clear from its kin casually lazing about. To my left and below, the channels were simply inhabited by slimes, bugs, and various other harmless creatures.

Now resting on the cobbled walkway that bordered the wild streams of sewage, I pondered my situation. Mostly, I continued to wonder how the heck I was supposed to craft things with no limbs, let alone opposable thumbs!

SIIIIIIIIIIIIIIIIIIIIIIIGH. Man, I wish I could just shut my mind and go to sleep... recharge my mental batteries, but nooo—

Entering... HIBERNATION MODE!

Who—What now?

NARRATED IN THE VOICE OF SIR DAVID ATTENBOROUGH…

As Hiro unwittingly placed himself into a coma, the slimes guarding their rubber sovereign stood on alert. The little green, spherical gels composed of acidic filth huddled together to form a barrier around him.

Although none could tell, as neither moon nor sun penetrated the thick sewer walls, a great deal of time ultimately passed with the minions dutifully protecting their emperor—dissolving bugs that wandered too closely or subsuming other slimes to build up their own, already sizable mass.

Eventually, as Hiro rested, the usually docile slimes became far more aggressive as they recalled the guidance of his greater will. They became vicious predators that attacked anything and everything, leaving not even a carapace fragment in their wake.

Three days and three nights, this had gone on, with the gelatinous omnivores bonding together to mend themselves after each bout and run-in with a foreign monster. That is, until finally, something miraculous happened.

The slimes began to harmonize. The red cores of each gooey warrior drew them closer and closer, until they touched, and they began to merge. Now united, instead of ten individual minds thinking the phrase *protect, protect, protect,* it was one. But it was still the will of ten that was resolutely breathed into the thought…

'Protect.'

THE HIRO IS A RUBBER DUCK

Chapter 7

Destruction of Private Property

H uh?
What the— Why is everything so different? What just happened?!

Coming to, I instantly noticed that my surroundings had changed. One moment, I was laying on top of my minions, sitting beside a wall, wanting to sleep, and now I was resting upon a throne made of bricks. Around me, tree limbs and other pieces of disgusting refuse lay strewn about, but my minions were nowhere in sight.

Then it hit me—my complaint about wanting to sleep... It had actually put me to sleep! My minions were without their father to protect them or my authority to guide them! Had they all died? Were they out there fighting? Where could they possibly have gone?!

...Did they abandon me?

These concerns engulfed my mind as I wiggled back and forth, anxiously opening up the system's interface.

Dungeon System Interface
Name: Hiro Dungeon
Level: 01
HP: 7000/7000
MP: 1000/1000
EXP: 110/500
Tamed Monsters: 01/10
Pylons: 0/5

One? ONE?! What happened to all of my minions?!

Immediately, feelings long dead began to kindle—feelings of panic, fear, and anger. Someone or something had attacked my precious employees, squandering all my efforts! Again!

I released a squeak—one of outrage—that bounced off the walls.

Slimey! SLIMEY, ARE YOU THERE?! My mind shouted through the void, guiding my cries through the winding pathways of my domain as I opened the minion's profile. That's when my metaphorical jaw dropped.

Name: Slimey
Level: 03
Species: Elite Mutated Cleaning Slime
HP: 120/120
MP: 20/20
Skills:
Physical Resistance Lvl.01
Dissolve Lvl.03
Slime Shot Lvl.04
Solidification Lvl.02

Bounce Lvl.02
Blend Lvl.01

HUH?!

I suddenly felt the throne of rubbish move beneath me, the various colors of odds and ends falling away to reveal a familiar green bubble nestled among the trash.

SLIMEY!

In response to its name, the slime fully revealed itself. What was once a tiny slime had transformed into a massive glob of green, with multiple red cores swimming around in its ten-foot-tall jelly-like form.

'Protect... Lord Hiro,' Slimey sent back. Hearing my name in its garbled voice, for some reason, brought a deluge of figurative tears to my metaphorical eyes.

Of course! How could I forget?

I could see now what had happened as the large slime wiggled ecstatically as if welcoming back from my deep sleep. My collection of minions had fused—a natural course for slimes that remained in close proximity to one another.

A thought popped into my head as I eyed my minion counter greedily. The system now seemed to recognize Slimey as a single entity. Meaning...

Ha... Ahaha. AHAHAHA! Excellent! EXCELLENT! OH, YOU BEAUTIFUL, DISGUSTING MONSTER!

At my compliment, Slimey wiggled with more ferocity, the monster reacting to my emotions.

Slimey, fetch me more slimes! Ahahaha! HA!

You have tamed a new minion!
What is this creature's name?

Obviously, Slime 19.

Days passed in the sewers, each one spent adding new additions to my collection, all of them intended to be sacrificed for Slimey's ascension.

Oddly, I noticed there seemed to be fewer slimes in the area—fewer than there should have been—as I shuffled around my domain, sending Slimey to encase and entrap more.

Though, no matter how many compressed and kept together, the slimes didn't seem to want to fuse, leaving me frustrated and annoyed. I even tried hibernating again, hoping for a nice surprise of another elite slime, but alas...

What am I doing wrong?

I turned my attention over to Slimey, the ten-cored, big green blob idling beneath me, surrounded by nine other, tiny iterations.

Oh. Oh wait, I'm a dingus.

Of course they wouldn't fuse! I didn't have enough slimes!

UGH! All this wasted effort!

My little rubber duck body deflated.

The only way for me to gain more minions slots was to create pylons and fulfill the quest requirement. Yet, I was stuck. I didn't know how to create a pylon, what a pylon was, or what it would be used for.

*If only I could just look at a space and say, "**Create Pylon**" and be—*

Suddenly, my entire body shook. My senses flickered out for a moment, my domain trembling, as something bubbled up from the ground!

My beak squeaked, and my body quivered at the sight of the glowing pillar that rose from the cobblestone and connected with the ceiling. The new, twisted structure made of brick and decorated with vines reinforced my sense of self and domain.

Pylon Created!
Pylon Cooldown: 59:54

IT WAS THAT EASY?!

I felt the urge to cry. Days of trying to figure this out—what a pylon was and how to make one—was solved in an instant by me simply willing it into existence.

Alright! SUPER SLIME MINION, HERE I—

That's when... An intruder. I could feel it. A monster set foot into my domain and unknowingly revealed itself to me from the darkness surrounding my territory.

It wasn't a slime, and it wasn't a bug. No, it was the bipedal crocodile I had pinged from my earlier scouting mission.

Oh boy... The description of what my **Squeaker-Location** had pinged didn't do the monstrosity justice now that it was within my superior scope of vision. It was hunched, seven feet tall, standing on thick hind legs that connected to a large, scaly green mass of pure muscle. Along its reptilian hide were pustulant bags, infected scales that stretched from its milky eyes to its blackish tail, and a pouch of skin beneath its neck that was filled with some unidentifiable substance.

It was walking towards me, heading in the direction of—

No! My pylon!

Hey! Shoo! Go away, I bellowed at the creature, my slimes already spacing out and forming a jelly wall to defend me.

Yet it ignored me, even ignoring my attempts to dominate its mind as it casually walked by and punched my pylon, reducing it to a pile of rubble.

Hey! What gives?! I squeaked in fury, but the monster continued to ignore me and my slimes as if we weren't a threat—as if I weren't even worthy of acknowledgement! Frustrated, I reached out, attempting to dominate it once more, but it didn't work. An invisible barrier of some kind seemed to keep from doing so.

Eventually, it just wandered off, disappearing back into the shadows, to leave me behind to stew in my anger.

No, no, no. You've had a thousand years of isolation, Hiro. You're fine. Everything is fine. What's an hour of waiting?

I sat there, staring at the pylon timer, counting down the seconds until I could finally proceed with the quest. Despite it only being an hour, each second felt akin to a minute, each minute akin to an hour. In hindsight, I probably shouldn't have been staring at the clock, but when you are a rubber duck, there's not much in the way of entertainment.

Create a Pylon… Ready!

Finally.

Pointing at an area in my domain, I willed the creation of another pylon, and it materialized within seconds.

YES!

The crocodile came back.

NO!

The monster emerged from the shadows, lumbering directly towards my freshly erected pylon.

Slimey! Slimes! ATTACK!

I sent my minions forward, my little green goops bouncing around and shooting toward the creature with determination, but it merely swiped them away in annoyance and continued on its path. With a well-placed strike, two of my slimes were immediately out for the count, their fractured cores staining the sewer walls in red as they slid meekly to the floor.

My heart sank as my minion counter ticked down, one by one. My brave little slimes did no tangible damage against the monstrous beast I classified as a "crocotaur."

Slimey moved, the large slime wrapping itself around the crocotaur, which grew angrier at having to wrestle Slimey from its torso, tearing it in two. The opposition's stride was ceaseless until it finally reached its destination, face to face with my pylon, discarding the remnants of my dearest companion onto the floor.

My pylon...

Oh, come on! What did I ever do to you?! I squeaked wildly as the crocotaur effortlessly destroyed my pylon and slinked back into the shadows once more.

Chapter 8

The Power of the Little Ones!

Sitting in silence, I contemplated my next course of action as Slimey regenerated its lost mass.

Hrrrrn. What should I do?

My main quest required me to make pylons, but every time I did so, the crocotaur would show up again, rudely punching my tower before walking off. And the slimes didn't stack up well against the monster, as it seemed to have an innate resistance to their dissolving ability due to its scales and the corrosive environment it lived in.

Hmmmm...

It was obvious I needed to get rid of this fiend. But the question was: *how?*

Name: Slimey
Level: 03
Species: Elite Mutated Cleaning Slime
HP: 109/120
MP: 20/20
Skills:

Physical Resistance Lvl.01
Dissolve Lvl.03
Slime Shot Lvl.04
Solidification Lvl.02
Bounce Lvl.02
Blend Lvl.01

I eyed Slimey's stats, my champion, wondering how I could improve it. One of the more obvious solutions was to have it hunt and kill things to gain experience. So that's what I did. In the meantime, I redirected my other slimes, ordering them to create a perimeter and defend me as I continually summoned our unwelcome visitor with pylon after pylon.

Each time, like clockwork, its massive bulk would emerge from the shadows, its webbed talon feet thundering towards the spire, which the monster would shatter to bits. Over and over. But that was okay—I wanted that. The real goal here was to observe the monster, study its physiology, and find the chink in its metaphorical armor.

This went on for some time—hour after hour, day after day—of me baiting the crocotaur, and it demolishing my creations... all while Slimey trained.

While I was observing, Slimey was learning.

While the crocotaur was lazing, Slimey was preparing.

While the anthropomorphic reptilian turned its back on yet another pile of rubble, Slimey was growing stronger.

Of course, I also kept my other slimes busy. They were cleaning out the underground—little by little—of other unallied slimes and small bugs but leaving behind their enemies' remains so that Slimey could soak up all of that juicy, succulent experience.

The slimes seemed to catch onto my intentions, after a while, taking it upon themselves to locate and hold off on engaging overgrown critters so that Slimey would solely benefit.

The crocotaur, which I had come to name "Dave," all the while had never ceased. He would always walk by, without much of a reaction, and always ignore me. Day after day. Only once, he paused to sniff the air.

I realized something after several attempts at asserting my dominance on the monster: it wasn't possible because I had reached capacity on tamable minions.

Which was fine. I had other plans for it.

Considering his scale and size, the crocotaur would make an excellent enforcer. Since he wasn't under my command, however, the reptilian only proved troublesome. Wherever he went, he scared off the lesser monsters, which meant less prey and less experience. He would also eat slimes, devouring their cores, greatly interfering with my plans to create a super slime.

I could not let that stand.

Name: Slimey
Level: 05
Species: Elite Mutated Cleaning Slime
HP: 180/180
MP: 40/40
Skills:
Physical Resistance Lvl.01
Dissolve Lvl.04
Slime Shot Lvl.04
Solidification Lvl.03
Bounce Lvl.04
Blend Lvl.01

Constrict Lvl.01

Slimey had gained two levels, with its skill levels rising and a new skill gained as well. Considering there weren't many strong monsters on this layer of the sewers, besides other slimes and a variety of carapaces, it was undoubtedly an achievement—at the cost of hundreds. The new skill was particularly very beneficial to my plan.

Good job, Slimey.

The elite slime wobbled back and forth, clearly happy with my praise.

The time for me to make my move was nearing; I was plotting a large-scale ambush to demonstrate the sheer might of my legion's will. Opening my minion registry, I carefully assessed my forces for the battle ahead.

Minion Registry
Slimey: Elite Mutated Cleaning Slime Lvl.05
HP: 180/180
MP: 40/40
Slime 11: Mutated Cleaning Slime Lvl.02
HP: 15/15
MP: 6/6
Slime 12: Mutated Cleaning Slime Lvl.02
HP: 15/15
MP: 6/6
Slime 13: Mutated Cleaning Slime Lvl.03
HP: 25/25
MP: 9/9
Slime 14: Mutated Cleaning Slime Lvl.01
HP: 10/10
MP: 3/3

Slime 15: Mutated Cleaning Slime Lvl.01
HP: 10/10
MP: 3/3
Slime 16: Mutated Cleaning Slime Lvl.02
HP: 15/15
MP: 6/6
Slime 17: Mutated Cleaning Slime Lvl.02
HP: 15/15
MP: 6/6
Slime 20: Mutated Cleaning Slime Lvl.02
HP: 15/15
MP: 6/6
Slime 21: Mutated Cleaning Slime Lvl.02
HP: 15/15
MP: 6/6

Everyone had leveled in some way. Most of my minions were now stronger than the average slime or any of the monsters that frequented these filthy canals.

It was time.

Setting the initial phase of my plan into motion, I led my slimes to and fro. The near-dozen jellies climbed and crawled along the walls and ceiling of the sewer tunnels, while Slimey used **Blend** to stealthily slip into position behind the spot I designated for my newest pylon.

Create Pylon.

The ground began to shake. Cobblestone bubbled up from the pathway beside Slimey and the earth warped as a spire of tile began to erupt from nothing with twining ropes of green that seemed to follow it all the way up toward the roof.

I mused to myself, my domain senses picking up on Dave's presence as soon as everything stilled.

The scaly monster snarled at the pylon, for once showcasing a clear sign of annoyance. He seemed to walk more swiftly, eager to finish and return home, completely oblivious to my slimes concealed nearby. Within seconds, Dave stood at the pylon's base, balling its three-fingered fist and cocking it back, preparing to strike.

NOW!

Slimey revealed itself, the massive slime shooting forward to wrap around the monster, which immediately tensed as the glob used **Constrict**.

Solidify! The slime then hardened, its goo turning from fluid-like to a high-tensile restraint that kept the crocotaur's limbs from moving freely.

YES!

Phase one worked; next came the hard part. To prevent Dave from running off, I sent several slimes to attach themselves to the creature's feet, ordering them to interlock like a human chain to slow his movements. The rest of my slimes dropped from above, aiming for the creature's face.

Fun fact: crocodiles don't have gills. They breathe and require air just like humans and most mammals do—something I recalled from my previous life. The absence of gills revealed a weakness, and while my slimes might lose in a contest of strength and raw physical power, it wouldn't matter if I blocked his airways from the inside.

From head to toe, the creature was covered, resulting in him falling to the floor with a thud as he squirmed and flopped about in distress. He rapidly twisted his body to try and break free from the sticky slimes that pinned him down, but it was useless.

Ehehehe.

An evil feeling blossomed inside me.

Perhaps the best part: due to the gooey nature of the slimes, they tended to stick to surfaces like a stubborn adhesive. No matter how much Dave chomped and bit with his powerful, jagged-toothed maw, he couldn't shake the slime blocking his airway.

Thirty minutes.

That's how long most crocodiles can hold their breath. Was that the same for an upright, pus-ridden sewer monster that kept annoying me and interfering with my destiny to purge the world of filth? I wasn't sure, but it is always fun to learn new things.

Dave continued to thrash around, the crocotaur futile in its attempts to break free from my slimes, which were slowly dissolving portions of the creature and absorbing his nutrients.

Excellent.

Before I knew it, my rubber body was letting out squeaks—loud high-pitched sounds that were akin to... laughter? Was I laughing? My squeaker was doing something weird, something I hadn't experienced in ages. But even though this feeling was foreign, I knew one thing was certain...

I was happy.

Chapter 9

Constructing Pylons!

Pylon Created!

*F*INALLY.

With those words, I eyed the spiral structure that jutted from the sewer cobblestone, a pillar that represented and marked my territory. The final one I needed to progress to the next quest.

Quest Complete: Construct Territorial Pylons! 5/5
You have successfully expanded your domain!

Almost immediately my sense of self increased, the range and scope of my domain inching out another five feet in every direction, the fog of darkness parting ways to show me unexplored sewers lines I had yet to conquer.

Minion Capacity Increased to 20!

My body shook, a happy feeling of accomplishment washing over me as various notifications flooded my mind.

You have earned a new skill!

Giddiness—that's the one word I could use to describe the feeling blossoming in my rubbery body as I awaited the dungeon message.

Please select a skill!
Unlocked: Purify Lvl.01!

The moment I saw the skill **Purify** I selected it without hesitation. Screw the other skills—even if one of them was something involving a dragon's flame. I wanted—NO, I needed to be clean!

SKILL LIST
Bubble Blow Lvl.01
MP Cost: 5

Create a bubble of charged mana. When it pops, it releases a light burst of magic.

Squirt Water Lvl.01
MP Cost: 5

Create and squirt water from your beak.

Summon Rock LvlLvl.01
MP Cost: 10

Summon a small rock. That's it. It summons a rock.

Purify Lvl.01
MP Cost: 20

Gathering light mana, attempt to cleanse an object or creature of curses, poison or disease. Effectiveness scales by level.

Squeaker-Location Lvl.02
MP Cost: 1

With a squeak, send out a pulse to map your surroundings and form a vivid image in your mind.

Impart Instruction Lvl.01

Teach skills and share experience with minions or selected creatures.

My skill list updated, adding the new ability to my modest repertoire. Naturally, the first thing I did was target myself, activating **Purify** with a desperate desire to be cleansed!

ERROR: Unable to purify!
Please choose a new target!

@&#%!

Of course, it wouldn't be that easy.

But... at least I could still use it on EVERYTHING ELSE AROUND ME!

PURIFY! PURIFY! PURIFY! PURFYPURFPYIPURAOFAYI! PYFARYP! PORYAPRCNAK PURIG—

An unknown amount of time had passed. I say unknown because... it's a bit embarrassing to admit how long I sat there spamming **Purify** to clean the unending sludge.

However, I did learn a few things from my... experiment.

One! It didn't work well on non-soluble surfaces, like brick and stone. It helped purge the gunk, but ultimately didn't do much else.

Two! It works on slimes! Well, somewhat... I ended up striking a slime by accident during my... fit. It left it with a subtly, satisfying gleam, the slime's coloring now slightly paler than the rest.

And lastly! I got an idea for a new project! I'd be able to get to it riiiight... after I took care of the alert that blinked incessantly through the darkness of my mind.

Dungeon System Interface
Name: Hiro Dungeon
Level: 01
HP: 7000/7000
MP: 0054/1000
EXP: 230/500
Tamed Monsters: 08/20
Pylons: 5/5
New Quest Available at 20 Minions!

Speaking of minions... I turned my attention to the slumbering crocotaur, aka Dave, the monster lying on the floor of the sewer surrounded by my slimes. While I had initially wanted Dave dead, I realized something as I watched the humanoid crocodile flounder about, suffocating at the globs of my gooey legion.

It had hands.

Well, three clawed fingers that imitated a human's hand—minus the index finger and pinky. Humans have five fingers, right? It's been so long since I've been human, let alone saw one...

In any case, I revised my initial plan to feed Dave to my slimes. I would make the crocotaur my enforcer, instead, a shield against my enemies. Aaand my getaway. While slimes were neat and all, they weren't fast. Nor were they very strong. If something bad happened, I'd be in a pickle—more than I already am!

Pickle... mmm... pickles... food... I wish I could taste actual food...

Pulling myself out of my thoughts, I redirected my attention to Dave, focusing my will on him. I reached out, my conscience pricking against his own.

Dave's eyes promptly snapped open, immediately entering a rage and thrashing about. Fortunately, Slimey and the other slimes still coated the entirety of his mass, holding firm and pinning the beast down despite his struggling.

Mine! YOU! ARE! MINE! The pulse of my will momentarily stunned him, but the creature quickly recovered from his shock, valiantly attempting to oppose my psionic intrusion. Yet my will was greater, and Dave's mind began to crack open like a walnut, revealing his inner thoughts and most guarded secrets.

My mind was suddenly beset with a vision—one that showed a baby alligator being coddled by a snot-nosed, four-horned wench dressed in gaudy clothes that I immediately recognized!

THE DEMON LORD'S DAUGHTER!

My body shook, a feeling of loathing and hatred overwhelming my senses for a moment as I recalled how this HARLOT had flushed me down the toilet, only for me to spend HUNDREDS OF YEARS in a SEWER!

A SEWER!

But I digress... In the vision, I saw happy memories—memories of a beloved pet, a monster hatched from an egg, held and taken everywhere by the girl in fancy clothes. Up until, of course, one day she decided to try and send Dave back to his people... by flushing him down the toilet.

Ah... I see. Perhaps I judged you too quickly, my friend, for you and I are the same. We are both beings condemned to this acrid, watery grave, abandoned by SHE who we had the disprivilege of being gifted to... Truly, a heart wrenching set of circumstances. But not to worry, I shall take care of you, my orphaned brother.

You have tamed a new minion!

Dave ceased his struggles, and my slimes instantly halted their assault, with Slimey softening and sliding off the crocotaur.

Name: Dave
Level: 12
Species: Emaciated Blighted Crocotaur
HP: 310/350
MP: 50/50
Skills:
Pain Resilience Lvl.02
Minor Regeneration Lvl.01
Swim Lvl.03
Bite Lvl.04
Iron Tail Lvl.03
Endure Lvl.02
Blend Lvl.01

YOUCH! My slimes barely hurt it! And only level twelve? Hmm... I suppose it makes sense, considering I've only encountered slimes and big bugs so far. Things would be different if there were living armors wandering around this layer of the sewers or giga-bats.

Dave sat up, the monster slouched and looked around, his eyes darting left and right as he seemed to be trying to regain his bearings.

Hey! Come here!

Dave obeyed, the lumbering, scaly creature's steps slapping against the cobblestone until he stood before me, where he knelt like some kind of knight.

SHEESH! This is emaciated?! He was built like a metaphorical truck! Up close, I could now see the way his hide seemed to be stretched thin around the sheer size of his muscles. *What would you look like if you were fully fed?!*

Once more, an evil thought entered my mind.

Why don't we find out?

I eyed my minion counter—a total of eight critters and now one sizable beast under my command. Albeit two fewer than I should've had. I mourned the loss of my slimes that had been viciously slaughtered.

May you rest in peace, Slimes 18 and 19... You will be missed for your honorable service.

After a moment of silence for the fallen, I ordered Dave to take me into his three-fingered embrace, and without provocation, Slimey followed suit, wrapping itself around the crocotaur. It was almost like a suit of armor, but it mostly hovered around the beast's chest where I was cradled.

Observing Slimey, it didn't seem to be too thrilled that it was no longer my throne, at least judging from its restless wiggling. But it was hard to tell with an amorphous blob that had no face.

Although... I suppose the words, *'ANGRY! ANGRY! ANGRY!'* coming from the slime was a good indication of its feelings.

Huh. Slimes have feelings.

To placate Slimey, I inwardly sighed, ordering Dave to place me near Slimey, who immediately and rapidly absorbed me, pulling me into its disgusting sludge body that was still attached to the larger creature.

Slimey shuddered, almost like a purr, its goo rippling and making my insides revolt. But at least its thoughts had settled back into the usual *'PROTECT! PROTECT! PROTECT!'*

EHK! It was a small price to pay for my minion's satisfaction, I suppose.

LET NO ONE SAY I WAS NOT A GOOD BOSS!

With my minions in tow, it was time to do a little exploration and finally continue our work on Operation Super Slime.

Chapter 10

It's ALIVE!

**You have tamed a new minion!
What is this creature's name?**

*D*efinitely, *Slime 31,* I inputted, the last slot of my minion capacity being taken as the final slime succumbed to my will.

**Minion Registry
Slimey: Elite Mutated Cleaning Slime Lvl.05
HP: 180/180
MP: 40/40
Slime 11: Mutated Cleaning Slime Lvl.02
HP: 15/15
MP: 6/6
Slime 12: Mutated Cleaning Slime Lvl.02
HP: 15/15
MP: 6/6
Slime 13: Mutated Cleaning Slime Lvl.03
HP: 25/25
MP: 9/9**

Slime 14: Mutated Cleaning Slime Lvl.01
HP: 10/10
MP: 3/3
Slime 15: Mutated Cleaning Slime Lvl.01
HP: 10/10
MP: 3/3
Slime 16: Mutated Cleaning Slime Lvl.02
HP: 15/15
MP: 6/6
Slime 17: Mutated Cleaning Slime Lvl.02
HP: 15/15
MP: 6/6
Slime 20: Mutated Cleaning Slime Lvl.02
HP: 15/15
MP: 6/6
Slime 21: Mutated Cleaning Slime Lvl.02
HP: 15/15
MP: 6/6
Dave: Blighted Crocotaur Lvl.12
HP: 350/350
MP: 50/50
Slime 22: Mutated Cleaning Slime Lvl.01
HP: 10/10
MP: 3/3
Slime 23: Mutated Cleaning Slime Lvl.01
HP: 10/10
MP: 3/3
Slime 24: Mutated Cleaning Slime Lvl.01
HP: 10/10
MP: 3/3
Slime 25: Mutated Cleaning Slime Lvl.01

HP: 10/10

MP: 3/3

Slime 26: Mutated Cleaning Slime Lvl.01

HP: 10/10

MP: 3/3

Slime 27: Mutated Cleaning Slime Lvl.01

HP: 10/10

MP: 3/3

Slime 28: Mutated Cleaning Slime Lvl.01

HP: 10/10

MP: 3/3

Slime 29: Mutated Cleaning Slime Lvl.01

HP: 10/10

MP: 3/3

Slime 30: Mutated Cleaning Slime Lvl.01

HP: 10/10

MP: 3/3

Slime 31: Mutated Cleaning Slime Lvl.01

HP: 10/10

MP: 3/3

I may have had a naming problem...

Buuuut... it's a problem I wouldn't have for long.

I was working tirelessly, sending Dave off to hunt for his own food while I ordered my slimes to separate and test a theory. I started with Slime 31, the latest to my menagerie of green ooze. If one was going to be sacrificed, let it be the newest and lowest of my employees.

Purify! I focused my will on the little green jelly that trembled as my skill wrapped around its tiny mass, bathing it in holy light. The glob jiggled, clearly affected by the skill, its green losing a bit of its luster.

I squeaked in excitement, momentarily forgetting about the sewer stink that hit me in an instant.

What happened next was a long and arduous process—one that involved me, a slime, a dark corridor, and spamming **Purify** so many times that I blacked out on several occasions.

And then, it happened...

Name: Slime 31
Level: 01
Species: Cleaning Slime
HP: 20/20
MP: 3/3
Skills:
Dissolve Lvl.01
Slime Shot Lvl.01
Cleanse Lvl.01

The metamorphosis I was looking for. Instead of a green ball of jelly, what sat before my yellow rubber body was a blue slime—one that gave off an aura of antiseptic and cleanliness.

CLEANSE ME!

Of course, the first thing I did was order Slimey to drop me onto the purified cleaning slime. It lifted me up and lowered me toward the blue glob, but it stopped short, its hold lingering.

Slimey! DROP ME, I ordered, but it refused, seemingly vibrating in agony.

DROP! I'M ORDERING YOU TO DROP ME! I WANT TO BE CLEAN!

The elite slime wobbled furiously, a single thought radiating from its one-track mind: *'MINE! MINE! MINE!'*

SLIMEY! YOU ARE BEING A BAD SLIME! BAD SLIME! A VERY BAD SLIME! DROP ME AT ONCE, MISTER!

At my rebuke, Slimey quivered, the jelly deflating and finally, reluctantly letting me go into the blue slime that reached up and took me within itself.

Aaaaaaaah, sweet relief.

I could already feel the cleaning slime hard at work, the monster using up what little mana points it had to activate **Cleanse** and eat away the muck that sullied my body.

Bliss. Finally, I AM CLEAN!

After my spa day, an idea formed in my head. If I could mush together multiple slimes to create a stronger slime... what's to say I couldn't purify dozens of slimes and make a bigger, stronger, faster CLEANING SLIME!

I quickly went to work.

Placating Slimey's blatant JEALOUSY, I sat atop the disgusting slime. The seconds turned into minutes, minutes into hours, and hours into days, until finally, I had purified all my lesser slimes, and it began...

Fusion.

It was subtle at first, a process that took days, with a few slime cores gravitating slowly toward each other until ten cores were caressing one another. After some time, each slime began to eject their cores, depositing them into a central slime that collected all ten cores—like Slimey... except clean.

Name: Slime 31
Level: 03

Species: Elite Cleaning Slime
HP: 110/110
MP: 20/20
Skills:
Physical Resistance Lvl.01
Dissolve Lvl.03
Slime Shot Lvl.04
Foam Lvl.01
Solidification Lvl.02
Bounce Lvl.02
Blend Lvl.01
Cleanse Lvl.02

Before long, I was focusing on a new elite slime, the creature radiating a firm and resolute *'protect, protect, protect,'* just as Slimey had done when it evolved.

For the next few weeks, I went around collecting even more slimes, purifying them, and gathering them as materials for the final stage of my time-consuming project, until finally, I was surrounded.

Minion Registry
Slimey: Elite Mutated Cleaning Slime Lvl.06
HP: 200/200
MP: 50/50
Slime 11: Elite Cleaning Slime Lvl.03
HP: 110/110
MP: 20/20
Slime 15: Elite Cleaning Slime Lvl.02
HP: 100/100
MP: 10/10
Dave: Blighted Crocotaur Lvl.13

HP: 421/470

MP: 50/70

Slime 25: Elite Cleaning Slime Lvl.02

HP: 100/100

MP: 10/10

Slime 36: Elite Cleaning Slime Lvl.02

HP: 100/100

MP: 10/10

Slime 44: Elite Cleaning Slime Lvl.03

HP: 110/110

MP: 20/20

Slime 56: Elite Cleaning Slime Lvl.03

HP: 110/110

MP: 20/20

Slime 64: Elite Cleaning Slime Lvl.02

HP: 100/100

MP: 10/10

Slime 79: Elite Cleaning Slime Lvl.02

HP: 100/100

MP: 10/10

Slime 81: Elite Cleaning Slime Lvl.02

HP: 100/100

MP: 10/10

Did I say weeks?

I'm exactly sure how much time passed—though it doesn't really matter, considering I'm a rubber duck that doesn't need to eat or drink. I do know, however, that my domain was... oozing with cleanliness!

Cramped, some would say.

Nay! Stuffed! COMPACT! FILLED! BURSTING AT THE SEAMS—

You get the idea. The cavernous walls were spotless, and I even raised **Purify** to level five!

I... may have been a little overzealous in my desire to clean.

At least Dave wasn't emaciated anymore. From what I could glean from the lizard's thoughts, it seemed he was just depressed and lazy.

Dave didn't express himself like Slimey and the other slimes. Unlike their limited vocabulary and single-worded mantras of *'protect'* and the occasional *'dissolve,'* he mostly communicated in mental images and grunts.

And strangely, I understood them.

It was mostly just Dave crying about being abandoned, annoyed that I was ordering him to feed himself, and angry that he was being put to work.

Which, I get, but... *THERE ARE NO SLACKERS IN MY ARMY, FREELOADER!*

So, while Dave was off Dave-ing, I ordered my group of ten elite slimes together, hoping to fuse them as I had with their lesser slime counterparts. After a couple of attempts at piling them on top of each other, starting a mosh pit, and even commanding a round of musical chairs, I realized it wasn't going to happen. Not anytime soon. And I wasn't about to go through another time-skip, so I redirected my efforts.

Slimey was still a goop of green sludge, and no matter how many times I spammed the skill, I couldn't purify it—nothing seemed to have any effect on the monster's slick anatomy.

NEW STRATEGY: BATH TIME.

Slimey didn't seem to like the idea much, especially with my many previous attempts at trying to cleanse it.

ALAS! I HAVE BEEN A VERY GRACIOUS BOSS! NOW GET INTO THE CLEANING PIT!

(Oh, I have a cleaning pit now. One dug by Dave. Thanks, Dave!)

Moving slowly, Slimey reluctantly ceded, the green ooze almost akin to a puddle as it sulked across the floor and entered the scrubbing pit, surrounded by my blue elite slimes.

Do it.

I gave the command, and all nine of my elite cleaning slimes piled into the hole to surround Slimey, activating their **Cleanse** and **Foam** abilities while I spammed **Purify**.

'NO! NO! NO! NO!' I could hear Slimey's thoughts, the overgrown, disgusting slime crying out to be left alone! … TO BE DISGUSTING!

Not on my watch.

In its panic, Slimey tried to flee, to run, but fortunately, I had accounted for such a contingency.

Dave appeared—the now well-fed crocotaur placing a large rock over the pit's opening—while a scream of *'NOOOOOOOOOOOOOOOOOOOOOOOOOOOOOOOOOOOOOO'* echoed throughout my mind.

For three days and three nights, I sat in Dave's hands, my attention on the minion menu, diligently observing Slimey's status. It was truly a creature of the filth. The monster was determined to hold out against the multitude of slimes and my **Purify**, but eventually, the rock atop the pit had ceased shaking.

After another day, my curiosity took hold, telling me that something significant was about to occur.

I ordered Dave to move the rock, to directly inspect with my senses the status of Slimey, and if—

Light. Blinding light. That's what flooded my senses as an air of freshness began to seep out from the pit and overpower the sewer's pungent rankness.

RISE! RISE! RIIIISE, MY BEAUTIFUL CREATION!

Name: Slimey
Level: 10
Species: Elite Super Cleaning Slime
HP: 1500/1500
MP: 200/200
Skills:
Physical Resistance Lvl.03
Cold Resistance Lvl.02
Shape Change Lvl.01
Dissolve Lvl.06
Slime Bullet Lvl.01
Foam Lvl.02
Solidification Lvl.04
Bounce Lvl.04
Blend Lvl.01
Mimic Lvl.01
Duplicate Lvl.01
Constrict Lvl.01
Cleanse Lvl.03
Name: Dave
Level: 14
Species: Blighted Crocotaur
HP: 470/470
MP: 70/70
Skills:
Pain Resilience Lvl.02

Minor Regeneration Lvl.01
Swim Lvl.03
Bite Lvl.04
Iron Tail Lvl.03
Endure Lvl.02
Blend Lvl.01

AHAHAHAHAHAHAHAHAHAHAHAHA!

Chapter 11

Unexpected Visitors

S tanding on a jungled hillside lush with purple and red flora, a group of humanoids gathered in a space untouched by the toxic miasma that seemed to coat every surface of the world.

"It's safe now. The purifier is up," a scaly humanoid wearing thick goggles and a large black mask over its face said as it tinkered with a machine spinning on a tripod and emitting energy. "You can take your filters off now."

The group of adventurers took a moment to check their oxygen boxes, their chief defense against the poisonous smog. Satisfied that the air was now clean, they began to pull down their black masks, each fitted with a built-in air detoxifier. The group of five took a deep breath of the pristine air and let out a collective sigh at its crispness.

"Is this it, navigator?" The question came from a human male in full plate armor that stepped forward, his eyes peeking out from his dented barrel helm, and he stared at the decrepit castle that loomed hauntingly in the distance, overgrown with moss and mold.

"Aye. Looks to be da place... Heroes' Folly," a dwarf answered. The species was named as such due to their incredible height, a stature that dwarfed every other sentient species. The eight-foot-tall, hunched, bearded male nodded, assured in his navigation and the accuracy of the crudely drawn map on tarnished leather that he held gently in his rough hands. "Priestess? Watcha dink?"

A well-endowed woman garbed in the typical black attire of the Church's nunnery responded, "I sense it." Her green eyes narrowed at the structure as she held her holy symbol, a medallion of a cat. "The archdemon's power resides in there; of that, there can be no doubt. Our course is true, guided by the hand of Adam. The One Who Slumbers most surely remains entombed within its walls."

"See? Nottin' to worry 'bout. Da journey's nearly ova!" The dwarf chortled to himself, much to the grimace of the knight leaning on his claymore.

"Be that as it may, Ivanc, when we embarked on this endeavor, we were a cohort of twelve. Now, our numbers have dwindled to only a handful of steadfast companions," the knight commented. The soldier removed his helmet to reveal the face of a middle-aged man who, despite the laugh lines on his tanned skin, was frowning. His stern eyes were fixed on the castle. "Breaching the walls of the archdemon's forefather's home will be the climax of our journey thus far, so pardon my apprehensiveness."

The priestess rested her hand upon the knight's charred gauntlet. "Their sacrifice will have been worth it, Lhikan," she reassured before turning to the other three adventurers who had survived. She had only come to stand beside them at the precipice of their long, hard-fought journey. "It will be worth it. The lord has not yet abandoned this world to tyranny and darkness. Our mission here is holy and true, and our efforts will be rewarded."

"Yeah, well... Let's just hope your god delivers on this messiah, Natalie," a dark-skinned drowthraki hissed. Opening his bag, he shuffled through it until he was pulling out wooden stakes, tools, and dehydrated food—everything needed to camp the night.

"It will. I swear in the name of the Bookkeeper; it will," Natalie stated firmly, her hands grasping the cat pendant tightly.

"GO, YOU GITS! GET OUT OF HErrEk—"

"IVANC!" Natalie screamed. The priestess stopped herself from lunging toward the lanky dwarf that was being ripped apart by a swarm of putrid witherlings—corpses of long-deceased gnolls animated by foul magic.

"Hold on to your lightstones and do not stop," Lhikan barked, picking up the map Ivanc had tossed to the survivors in a final act of heroism before his demise.

"Ivanc..." The priestess fell to her knees as she watched the severed arm of her best friend land nearby, her tear-soaked eyes unable to look away.

"On your feet, priestess!" Lhikan grabbed the battle-fatigued priestess as Zak'naufen, the drowthraki ranger, fired arrow after arrow at the horde pursuing them.

"Damned undead! Die!" Zak'naufen howled in frustration. His innate darkvision allowed him to expertly place an arrow into the rotting skull of witherling, but it didn't fall. Instead, it recoiled before snapping its head back, snarling, and releasing a horrific shriek that echoed through the castle catacombs.

"Conserve your arrows!" Lhikan commanded. "We're heading to an antechamber ahead!"

Running with an inconsolable Natalie under one arm and the map fluttering wildly in his other, he yelled back as his eyes quickly scanned for possible routes. "Do you still have the bag of holding?!"

"Yeah," the archer replied with a nod, turning and falling into a hastened step with the duo.

"Good! Plan Three-Eight, it is!"

Zak'naufen blinked before taking a deep breath through his respirator and rummaging in the blood-stained bag tied to his waist, the container that once belonged to their artificer, a lizardman that went by the name, "Krota."

"Are you sure?!"

"We have no other choice if we are to escape our pursuers!" The trio followed the winding path of the narrow hallway, swiftly reaching and entering a stone-covered antechamber.

The drowthraki spun, chanting the activation phase inscribed on the gems he threw at the chamber's entrance.

The multi-colored gemstones shone brightly, momentarily blinding the survivors before they detonated, collapsing the tunnel entrance just as the undead gnolls began to pass beyond the threshold of the catacombs.

Panting and out of breath, Lhikan finally dropped Natalie, the nun unceremoniously hitting the wet stone floor.

"Great... Now we're stuck," Zak'naufen hissed, readying his bow as he scanned the room, his purple eyes darting back and forth. "How the hell are we going to get out now?!"

Lhikan sighed, glancing down at his gauges on his oxygen box that was glowing red. The mana stone inside indicated it wouldn't last much longer.

"We don't," Lhikan muttered, sitting down to replace the mineral powering his life-support. "We aren't getting out of here without finding what we came for."

"What?" Zak'naufen furrowed his brows in disbelief. "You can't be serious! We've been down here for a month! A MONTH! We have no provisions, half of us are dead after following that priestess, and you want to press on?!"

Natalie flinched at the provocation, curling into herself as she tried to process that she had led everyone to their deaths.

"That's precisely why we must move forward," Lhikan continued, the normally pessimistic knight surprising Natalie. "We've come too far, lost too much, but we're so close. I can feel it."

Zak'naufen's face twisted as the knight's hand clenched.

"Oh, don't tell me you believe in this savior nonsense? I thought you, of all people, wouldn't be foolish enough to buy into the ramblings of a madwoman."

"I had my doubts, but after being down here... the presence I've felt, the traces of holy power. Can you stand there and say you don't feel it as well?" Lhikan's mind was flooded with images of their findings, their recordings, and the discovered remnants of battles that still radiated holy power after two millennia.

"This is a fool's errand. I won't meet my end here like everyone else. You two can go it alone, and I'll find my own way out," the ashen-skinned hissed, his forked tongue flicking.

Natalie looked up, eyeing the man whose hand rested on his scabbard.

"If you're going to leave, give me Krota's bag of holding." Lhikan extended his free hand to Zak'naufen, but his voice stern with no room for argument. The drowthraki, however, simply bared his fangs; one hand gripped his bow tightly while his other gently caressed the feathers of an arrow in his quiver.

The knight brandished his blade as the archer raised his bow. "It doesn't have to be this way."

"I'm afraid it does."

Walking through what appeared to be a sewer, Natalie clutched a light stone to her chest as she hugged the slime-covered wall. Her body was cold, bloodied, and covered in wounds—wounds that were infected and oozing with pus, her mana long since depleted, leaving no energy to heal herself. The soles of her boots were worn thin from the journey, as well, the leather biting into her heels with each step. Despite this, and despite her injuries, the priestess kept moving— one foot in front of the other, slow and as steady as she could manage, as if on autopilot.

A month had passed since she and her party breached the depths of Heroes' Folly. It was a month of torturous trials, endless monsters, and betrayals.

First, Krota, a lizardman engineer and artificer, fell to enchanted traps.

Next, Ivanc, the dwarven navigator, was slain by witherlings.

Then, Zak'naufen, slain by Lhikan's hand.

Now, she was alone... separated from her knight by winding traps and monsters.

Alone to continue the mission she'd received from God.

That had been... two days ago? And, Lhikan had the bag of holding, leaving Natalie down to her last mana cell, her oxygen box depleting with each breath she took.

This was it...

She had come searching for a glimmer of hope in the darkness, searching for a champion to liberate the world from the Demon Empress' tyranny.

She had found nothing.

Natalie looked down as a sound alerted her that her oxygen box was now fully depleted. The green light flickered once more, then it turned red.

This was the end.

Yet, she didn't halt her movements, dragging herself forward with one step after another, until...

Her surroundings shifted, the grim, mold-covered walls giving way to pristine white bricks that seemed to flow, an impossible contrast to the filth she had grown used to. Was this a hallucination? The priestess couldn't tell, nor did she care to try and make sense of it in that moment. All she knew was that her body was weary, her filter had stopped working, and every breath she took now fed her lungs poison.

Her legs gave out first, and she collapsed to the floor. Her hands barely caught herself, stopping her face from colliding with the cobblestone beneath her, but her arms soon lost their strength as well. Her vision blurred, and the light stone she held clattered across the immaculate floor, coming to a stop as it gently bounced against something blue.

A slime... carrying... a rubber duck?

The thoughts left her mind as quickly as they had come, as the world around Natalie began to melt away. It felt almost peaceful to finally shut her eyes, warming her cat pendant in a tight fist.

Chapter 12

A Reward for the Loyal

Squeaking, I sat in my cleaning pit, ignoring my quest objective as I usually did, and worked on purifying my discolored cleaning slimes that had been hard at work scrubbing my domain.

With my **Purify** spam and Slimey's skill as a super elite cleaning slime, "bathing" the other slimes and curing them of their "mutated" status became less of a hassle and more of an autonomous thing. I even sent Slimey out to purify wild slimes, helping to spread the gospel of cleanliness to the heathens living in the darkness beyond my domain.

Of course, I still participated, spamming **Purify** to level it up. Eventually, I made it to level eight, and I was pleased to note the lesser mana cost. Now... if only I could clean the one thing I wanted to clean the most right now...

I turned my attention to the single eyesore in my domain (aside from the flowing sewage, of course): the blighted crocotaur.

Dave was getting stronger and stronger each day, his body filling out, but he was still... so disgusting, with pustules and infected wounds, and his maw occasionally drooling ick. **Purify** cleansed poisons, curses, and diseases, but it didn't seem to do anything to whatever was making Dave "blighted."

Hmmm. Maybe when I level the skill to level—What?!

At the edge of my domain, I felt a presence, an intruder, one that tore me from my daily bathing ritual. My senses, attuned to the expanse of my domain, zeroed in on something familiar—something I hadn't seen in hundreds of years.

A human.

Before I knew it, I was atop Slimey, and the super slime, now ten feet tall and ROUND bounced off the walls at swift speeds to deliver me to my objective.

But wait—STOP!

I reigned Slimey to a crawl, taking a moment to calm my excitement as I realized how bad it would look if a monster just showed up out of the darkness.

I'll just calmly approach it. I don't want to startle it... Nice and calm. NICE AND CALM!

Who was I kidding?

Go! GO! PICK UP SPEED! I sent my thoughts to Slimey, my gooey cleaning friend shooting slipping and sliding across the polished sewer floors.

For the first time in hundreds of years, there was a human! A person! AN ACTUAL—

Aaaaaaand they're dead... Nice.

I urged Slimey closer to the collapsed human, her body convulsing for a moment before it stopped, and from her now limp hand, a glowing rock of some sort rolled free.

Quick! Check for a pulse!

Slimey didn't move, the words clearly lost on the slime.

Ah! Wrap around its neck and tell me if it has a pulse! I tried instead, my blue goo friend holding onto me tightly as a part of it quickly wrapped around the neck of the lifeless body and began dissolving the tissue with a sizzling sound.

NONONONONO! BAD! BAD! BAD SLIME! STOP!

Slimey quickly retreated, dropping the woman's face, which lifelessly fell against the floor with a thud.

Well... if she wasn't dead before...

I observed the blonde-haired woman in ruined nun attire, Slimey moving me to and fro as I inspected the cleric—from her black-stained feet poking out of her shoes to the slashes on her back and abdomen, wounds that were clearly infected. *Who was she? Why was she here? How did she get here? Was there a way out the way she came from? What killed her?*

I didn't know, and upon closer inspection, I could see that her wounds were covered in pus and ick, so similar to Dave's it began to make me wonder.

Were they inflicted with the same disease? Was she blighted? And what was this thing she wore on her mouth...?

Question after question struck my rubber-duck mind until an image of a man wearing forest-pattern clothes and carrying a black staff appeared in my mind, his arm bearing the symbol of the USMC.

Ah! Wait! Uhhh... AHA! A GAS MASK! THAT'S WHAT THOSE THINGS ARE CALLED! But why did she need one?

Summoning Dave, I had him move the corpse to the inner sanctum of my domain and assist me in picking the woman's pockets after hundreds of corrective commands.

Of course, Dave kept trying to eat her, but fortunately, Slimey was there to reluctantly stop him per my instruction.

Now that I think about it, Slimey has been sulking a bit lately since finding the woman. Not quite sure why, but the ten-foot-tall super slime appeared lethargic as I focused all my attention on the corpse giving off a holy vibe and the items that she held on her person.

Outside of the gas mask affixed by a tube to some kind of box on a belt, the woman had scarcely anything in the way of possessions:

A leather bag with bits of moldy breadcrumbs.

A glowing stone that emanated a warm, undying light, likely acting in place of a torch given the fumes in the air.

A drawing, or perhaps a map, etched into leather proved difficult to read thanks to the blood on it.

Her clothes, and finally, an oddly familiar pendant shaped like a... cat?

All in all, after my thorough investigation, it was safe to assume that I knew nothing at all and this cute woman was still a myster—

And then it hit me: the pendant, the cat! Adam! THE GOD THAT SENT ME TO THIS HOVEL!

This was one of his disciples!

My body let out an involuntary squeak, one filled with rage, as all of my minions collectively flinched, reacting to the hatred brewing within me, long dormant until now!

AAAAAAAAAAAAAAAAAAAAAAAAADDAAAAAAAAAAAAAAAAAA AAAAAAAAAAAM!

Was this an agent of his sent here to find me? To finish the job? Or was this a messenger, finally here to apologize for RUINING MY LIFE?!

It took about an hour or so before my bottled-up emotions finally settled, and I ceased my ranting. I'm not proud of it, but it is what it is.

I opened my menu screen, taking a moment to distract myself and observe the quest that I had been putting off until my domain was purified.

Create a Mana Core!
The mana core is the heartbeat of all dungeons!
WARNING! Crafting a mana core will attract rivals!
Reward: New Quest Chain

Yeeeeaaaaah, I don't think I'm gonna do that right this second. The last thing I needed was a thousand monsters descending on me and chewing up my sexy rubber bits.

Now calm, I finally turned back to the corpse at hand. Or flipper? Beak...

I spent days not quite sure what to do with the body. Another interesting idea popped into my mind—to try and raise the woman up as a zombie, to spit in Adam's face—but priests and clerics have that whole annoying blessing from God or whatever preventing them from coming back as undead.

So... that idea is off the table. *Oh hey! Humans do have five fingers!*

Sitting there, I contemplated my options as Dave drooled over the body and Slimey visibly shook in anger, the two monsters towering above my other slimes that loitered around the corpse.

Every slime was jiggling, each monster oozing with a desire to dissolve, viewing the pus and open sores on the woman's body like a cancer that needed to be destroyed.

And they were right. Such filth didn't have a place in my sterile utopia, and every moment that passed was another in which it was rotting away.

Okay, so everyone wanted a piece of the body. Though... I'd rather not have had human juice splattered all over my freshly scrubbed walls.

Sorry, Dave, but you'll have to sit this one out.

Looking to appease Slimey and reward it for its constant and faithful service, I turned the body over to the super slime. The blue cleaning ooze shook off its sulking behavior to pounce on the body, much to Dave's dismay.

Sorry, Dave, but you destroyed three dozen pylons! Consider this your punishment!

Dave trudged off as Slimey absorbed the corpse into its goo, dissolving the woman in a process that was quite time-consuming.

Slimey vibrated in delight, the amorphous cleaning blob compressing and decompressing rapidly—a sign I'd come to learn meant slimes were happy.

'THANK! THANK! THANK!' Slimey overflowed with appreciation and its inner thoughts were akin to that of a child thanking its parent for a Christmas gift.

I turned my attention elsewhere, focusing on the cleaning process of my domain and preparing a few scouts to begin exploring the upper plane—something I had been wanting to do before this unexpected visitor showed up.

Though, if I was getting visitors, it would only be smart to get the lay of the land and set up an actual, grand welcome for intruders. After all, I had been human once, and I recalled the greed involved with smashing dungeon cores—something I had now become!

No, no, no. There would be no dungeon smashing here! If Adam had the audacity to send his minions to me, then it would only be expected that I'd vanquish them!

Suddenly, an explosion of light—a basking glow—pulled my attention away once again, this time from my introspection, towards Slimey as an alert flared across my screen.

Chapter 13

Holy Slime!

A blinding light flooded my senses, a star burning with intense wrath that washed over me in a way that made me almost sick to my stomach. The queasiness was so debilitating, such that it bubbled up from within and made me want to vomit.

Slimey was undergoing some form of 177013—a metamorphosis—a transformation that brushed against my senses as a notification tumbled out of the light, hitting me square in my rubber mind.

Through the devout faith from a truly pious follower…
You have gained the "devotion" status!

Huh?

Dungeon System Interface
Name: Hiro Dungeon
Level: 01
HP: 7000/7000
MP: 0480/1000
{LOCKED} DEVOTION: 100

EXP: 380/500
Tamed Monsters: 20/20
Pylons: 5/5

Neat... I guess? It would be a lot cooler if it wasn't sealed.

Name: Slimey
Level: 13
Species: Holy Super Slime
HP: 1650/1650
MP: 300/300
Skills:
Physical Resistance Lvl.04
Cold Resistance Lvl.02
Shape Change Lvl.01
Mend Lvl.01
Dissolve Lvl.06
Slime Bullet Lvl.02
Foam Lvl.02
Solidification Lvl.05
Bounce Lvl.04
Blend Lvl.01
Mimic Lvl.01
Duplicate Lvl.01
Constrict Lvl.01
Cleanse Lvl.05
Holy Imbue Lvl.01

When the light simmered down, Slimey was still... Slimey. Nothing had changed... at least, not on the surface. Aside from leveling up by three levels and gaining some new skills, Slimey looked no different than before.

All that for the "holy" attribute, huh? And here I was expecting some enormous visible change...

Still, the corpse of the nun seemed like a blessing, adding more abilities to Slimey's repertoire that would no doubt be put to good use in cleansing the world.

Observing my first minion, Slimey seemed happy as it bounced up and down, the nun's remains completely dissolved and her final resting place completely spotless. The only trace of the woman left now was her outfit.

Again... I wasn't really sure of Slimey's thoughts or intentions with not dissolving the dress, but I knew it was clearly garbage that needed to be disposed of.

BUT OF COURSE. Slimey refused to dissolve the dress, the giant jelly repeating *'REWARD! REWARD! REWARD!'* repeatedly in its mind like a child.

Fine. If you want to keep it, suit yourself. But don't just leave it around!

Slimey wiggled, and the creature suddenly embraced me entirely into its gooey being.

Yes, yes, yes... I'm a benevolent leader. NOW BACK TO WORK!

I idly watched the rest of my slimes return to their duties of purifying and cleaning the residual filth of strewn across our home, when a thought occurred to me as I reviewed Slimey's changes and the events that had transpired over the last few hours.

The nun had been injured, unarmed, and weakened. Even at full health, judging from her wounds, there was no way she came into the Demon Lord's domain alone.

Which meant... there were others.

Most likely corpses by now, considering the state of their healer. After all, the cleric was the most powerful asset of any adventuring party's composition! If the healer died... well, it was only a matter of time before the rest of them started dropping like flies.

Other bodies that could be fed to my minions for skills...

Was I a bad person?

No! Of course not! I'm not even a person anymore! Besides, those poor souls would want their bodies cleaned—cleansed of their putrid scum and brought to heel under my banner!

Hmm. But now the question remained: *what lay in the darkness beyond my domain?* I had, of course, sent my minions out to scrub, clean, and evangelize random slimes to restore them to their natural state, but for the most part, I had no idea what lay beyond the sewer or what had even become of the Demon Lord, for that matter.

It was time to change that.

After all, knowledge is power, and I want to be smart.

With every threat around or near my immediate domain gone or subdued, it was time for me to brave beyond the confines of my territory. I need to sally forth into the uncharted black abyss like a pioneer aboard the Mayflower, searching for the New World.

More than half of the pilgrims perished once they had embarked, so... many of my slimes were likely to die, but it was a necessary sacrifice... one I was more than willing to make.

In short, it was time for an expedition.

At the very edge of my domain, I resumed my usual perch atop Slimey, but this time in style, within part of its body that was morphed into the shape of a house with hollowed pockets for windows.

Behind Slimey was my entourage of minions, with Dave situated at the front as the party's tank, holding a rotting tree branch in one hand and a brick in the other. Crude weapons, I know, but we work with what we have.

To protect Dave, I had several slimes draped across the crocotaur. Again, it wasn't much, but each of them had physical resistance, giving the upright crocodile some form of protection, even if it wasn't particularly thrilled with its passengers.

Alright! Let's move!

Bracing myself, I inwardly cringed before inhaling deeply, the grotesque smog filling my insides and settling within me like rancid bile. The smell—and taste! *OH GOD, THE TASTE!* It was like moldy gym socks wrapped in microwaved fish, then smeared with butt chocolate.

Every fiber of my being shook, my rubber duck eyes actually releasing tears as I did my best to ignore the taste on my nonexistent taste buds, letting out a loud and powerful...

"SQUEAK!"

My voice echoed, **Squeaker-Location** pinging an impermanent image of the void that lay beyond my domain. The image was clear, yet not as telling as I had hoped, highlighting faded lines on a black canvas that seemed to fade little more with each passing half-second, until it was just a void once more.

Nothing ventured, I guess.

With a very crude idea of the tunnel directly up ahead, I directed Dave forward, the large reptilian leading my small army of slimes into the unknown darkness of the sewers.

ELSEWHERE...

CLANG! CLANG! CLANG!

Racing through the narrow pipes of the sewer, Lhikan's eyes widened before he threw himself backwards, his body dropping as he slid under a large polearm that aimed to bisect him. The knight swiftly rose to his feet, a veteran on multiple fronts, his breathing even and steady behind his gas mask. He spun to his left, crossing his arms to deflect a rusted blade with his steel gauntlets and throwing his arms to the side, redirecting the sword away from his torso.

Taking a step back, he balanced himself then sent a kick that shattered the skeleton before him, his steel boot reducing it to a pile of bones. He didn't even take a moment of reprieve, however, turning and resuming his sprint, just as the rest of the skeletal horde rounded the corner, the cluster of ivory already reforming.

CLANG! CLANG! CLANG!

"Damn it," Lhikan groaned, leaping over a chasm he had almost fallen into if not for his glowstone lighting his way.

The skeletons weren't much of a threat to the human one on one; the real issue was the sheer volume of reanimated undead. The creatures had formed a crude ball, rolling and bouncing off the sewer's walls in their relentless pursuit to consume him.

He clambered up a pipe, muscles working overtime to bear the weight of both his mass and the steel hugging his body. He made it to the top, where the vertical pipe led to another, larger horizontal one, only to find himself at another ledge—this one leading to a stream of green sludge.

CLANG! CLANG! CLANG!

Lhikan threw a glance to his side, frowning as he saw the sphere of undead still rolling toward him, now on the same pipe he stood on.

"Well... shit," the knight swore before unclipping his plate armor and tossing it aside. He grabbed a syringe from his bag of holding, stabbing the needle into his thigh and wincing as scales began to form on his skin.

Buffed, he leapt into the sludge below.

CLANG! CLANG! CLANG!

He hit the toxic river with a splash, the bubbling acid immediately tearing away at his hardened skin and soft eyeballs. Fortunately, it did little more than irritate him, the serum providing effective protection.

"UHK!" Lhikan choked, the sewage flooding the inside of his gas mask. Each desperate breath only aided in making things worse as clusters of bubbles flooded his vision and effectively blinded him. He tore at the face covering with scaly hands, clutching it as he scrambled for the surface. Once again, it was fortunate that his oxygen box was made to withstand such hazardous environments.

He swam left, avoiding the massive shadow that plunged into the water. The skeleton ball had followed suit, leaving a dozen or more skeletons to sink into the sludge, their red eyes glaring daggers at the knight as they were lost to the depths. It was a silly move on their part, as skeletons weren't known to be good swimmers, much less swimmers at all. Not that Lhikan was complaining. Their density, coupled with their undead traits, allowed him to escape as the acid burned away at the skeletons' fragile ivory.

Free from his pursuers at last, he swam to the surface, breaking through and reaching out towards a slick wall to steady himself for a moment. Blinking rapidly to clear the corrosive liquid from his eyes, the knight retrieved his glowstone, holding it above his head, while his other hand continued to push him through the restless green waves.

Once he found solid ground and pulled himself from the canal, Lhikan collapsed on the wet stone, allowing himself a moment to breathe. He was worn and he was certain he looked it—most of his clothes now tattered, his hair a mess, and his skin red.

He took a couple of deep breaths, steeling himself for what lay ahead, before reaching down into his bag of holding to replace the mana stone powering his oxygen box.

I need to find Natalie... The middle-aged man rolled onto his side before sluggishly rising to his feet. He felt around in the bag once more, checking for the item he fought Zak'naufen to the death for. It was the one thing that would guarantee his salvation—an item Krota cherished but never got to use due to his unexpected death.

A riftstone—a magical artifact used to teleport its user to a prerecorded destination.

The catch? It only worked for one person.

"Damned girl... Where'd you run off to...?" Lhikan exhaled as he clutched his aching side.

He walked for some time, pausing to activate the oxygen box's field function, which projected a field of clean air around him at the expense of its mana charge.

The knight bit into a piece of stale jerky, savoring the taste of what could very well be his last meal. After he swallowed the last of it, he sighed, pulling his mask back over his face, and resumed the search for his charge.

Squeak!

Lhikan froze, his weary eyes darting left and right, looking around for the source of the noise.

Squeak!

It sounded like a... squeak, but the sound was seemingly coated with an essence of mana, filling him with unease. Something was lurking in the dark and it was close.

Lhikan lightened his footsteps, straining to listen for the sound again. He drew his newly acquired black dagger, taken from the fallen, uncooperative drowthraki, while his other hand still gripped his luminous stone in front of him.

Squeak!

There it was again! This time, it was louder, more pronounced, causing the knight to tense just as the ooze of a slime slinked into the edge of his light.

"Just a sewer slime..." Lhikan muttered to himself, throwing the enchanted dagger at the tiny blue slime and shattering its core. The obsidian blade pierced the monster with ease, slicing its red center in two before the weapon magically returned to his hand.

'Odd,' he thought. First time seeing a blue slime. He deftly slid his weapon into its sheath at his thigh as he turned his head—

SQUEAK!

The knight flinched, the remaining hairs on his body rising as he felt a rush of anger directed his way. Then, there was movement— the shift of the wind alerting him that something was on the prowl.

He swiftly rearmed himself, frantically scanning his surroundings, the tension in his shoulders mounting with every passing second. He nearly stumbled back into the river, barely correcting his footing and keeping himself upright.

That's when he saw it: blue ooze—the unmistakable trail of a slime, and suddenly, the tension melted from his body.

"Oh, it's just a..." The human trailed off as a massive blue slime fully came into view, slowly approaching him and threatening to swallow him whole. But that wasn't what made his heart lurch in his chest. No, what gave the veteran pause was the religious attire swirling in the daunting mass of the mutated monster.

Chapter 14

Natalie?

Crawling through the underground, I squeaked, sending out high-pitched, sonar pulses to help me navigate the abyss.

That's when, suddenly, I saw something... humanoid in shape. My **Squeaker-Location** wrapped around what seemed to be a man, hunched over and possibly injured, but I couldn't tell for certain. Outside of my domain, I couldn't see, hear, or feel anything, not even in the space closest to me, my safety was entrusted entirely to Slimey, who held me close. My **Squeaker-Location** was all I had to perceive anything at all, but the ability merely created images through shapes, devoid of feeling or color.

I sent out another squeak, ensuring what I "saw" was correct.

And it was.

There, in front of me, was a living, breathing human. He was surely ripe with experience and skills, and even more, knowledge of the world outside this filthy hell.

I needed him alive.

I quickly concocted a plan, pausing my troops' advance and sending out a single slime to test the man, to see how he would react, and to lure him towards me if possible.

Slime 77, occupying my twentieth minion slot, crept ahead through the darkness where it—

Minion, Slime 77 has perished!

Yeah, that's about right.

I let out another squeak, this one causing the man to flinch and lift his dagger in the air defensively.

Hmmm. Must be a rogue or something.

Slimey began to wiggle beneath me, an odd sensation emanating from the slime and touching my consciousness. It felt sort of... subdued, like a whisper I couldn't quite understand.

No, no time to focus on that. We needed to move. I needed this human captured before he got himself killed, or worse, escaped.

Next, I had Dave double back with a few of my other minions. The canal we walked along conveniently split into two channels, the paths curving until they met again, giving my minions the perfect opportunity to flank. If I was going to catch him, I needed to cut off all avenues of escape and box him in. Since Dave was the fastest out of the small troop, he could even run down the man if he decided to flee.

Maybe I should try and tame some spiders. Silk would go a long way for trapping stuff...

I signaled my minions into action. Slimey was the first to move, spreading its mass to coat the surrounding walls with its ooze, forming a barrier that blocked the entire passageway behind us.

OH! AND NO DISSOLVING OR EATING HIM! I NEED HIM ALIVE! ALIVE!

I squeaked again, but by now, he'd gotten much closer. I could now make out his expression of horror and shock as Slimey slinked out of the darkness, emerging into the light from the luminescent stone he was holding.

LHIKAN

The knight slashed at the massive slime's body, but it did nothing, causing him to scream in indignation. Fury guided his hand as the man continued to hack futilely at the creature's goop, his mind fixed on the image of Natalie falling into its clutches.

In retaliation, tendrils suddenly shot forth from the slime—blue tentacles attempting to seize his limbs—but he easily sliced through them, keeping them at bay.

He was no rogue, but he knew blades well.

Damn it! Lhikan gritted his teeth, turning the glowstone to the path beyond the slime, only to find his way forward blocked. So, he did the only thing he could think to do—he spun on his heel. Taking one last, pained glance over his shoulder at the familiar dress, he ran for his life.

HIRO

Everything was going as planned.

The human ran off... or hobbled off, but I'd obviously expected as much, and I chuckled inwardly. My squeaks trailed behind him as I urged Slimey to follow, my **Squeaker-Location** confirming that Dave was in position, along with the sixteen slimes I'd sent to support him, coating that end of the tunnel from top to bottom.

Assuming the man was a rogue class, and his speed was limited by his injuries, this was an open-and-shut trap, and he would soon be mine to question.

Any time now.

LHIKAN

Lhikan's eyes went wide, his jaw dropping as he came to a halt, his steel boots skidding across the soggy floor. In front of him stood a blighted crocotaur, a ten-foot-tall beast man wielding crude weapons made of rotting wood.

Tsk. He gripped his dagger, eyes moving to what appeared to be a horde of slimes lurking behind the hulking beast.

The knight paused, took a breath, and rolled his shoulders, his eyes narrowing into a glare as he stood his ground and pulled several syringes from his bag of holding.

Empty vials shattered on the floor, and Lhikan took a deep breath as his muscles constricted and his eyes glowed red, his body radiating invisible energy.

Then, he did something unexpected—something even Hiro hadn't accounted for.

He threw his dagger.

Lhikan's blade cut through the air, aimed straight for the crocotaur's throat. The creature narrowly deflected the weapons at the last moment, its scaly arm held in front of its face.

With its vision now obscured, the knight pounced from its blind spot.

Suddenly, the lizard was lifted off the ground, the force of an uppercut sending it several inches into the air. Lhikan kicked, sending the crocotaur crashing into the sewer wall, its large frame smashing into the unfortunate slimes behind it.

HIRO

Minion, Slime 76 has perished!

Minion, Slime 63 has perished!
Minion, Slime 70 has perished!
Minion, Slime 71 has perished!
Minion, Slime 53 has perished!

MY BABIES!

Notification after notification filled my "vision", notifying me that multiple slimes had succumbed to Dave's mass.

The man was now in front of him, the reptilian struggling to wrestle free himself and rise to his feet. Despite my plea for my underling to rise faster, however, it was too late.

The human grabbed Dave by the maw, lifting his scaly snout up before delivering a punch that firmly fixed the crocotaur into the concrete.

WARNING! Minion, Dave's health is below 50%!

It suddenly dawned on me that there was a reason this man was still alive and relatively unhurt in the Demon Lord's castle, as I "watched" him race away from me while effortlessly tearing apart my slimes.

Minion, Slime 54 has perished!

He wasn't a rogue at all! Even my elite slimes were being torn apart as the man reached into their blobs, ignoring the burning of his skin, to grab their cores and shatter them.

Minion, Slime 64 has perished!

"SQUEAK! SQUEAK! SQUEAK!" I squawked in frustration, commanding the human to yield.

GAH! WHY CAN'T I TALK?!

Minion, Slime 61 has perished!

This was starting to stress me out!

SLIMEY, GET HIM! DAVE, STOP PLAYING DEAD!

YOU LAZY BUM, GET ON YOUR FEET OR I'LL FEED YOU TO SLIMEY!

Slimey activated **Bounce**, my chief minion contracting in on itself before launching forward, while simultaneously pushing me deep into its body to shield me as it engaged the knight.

Dave rose from the rubble, letting out a roar, as all my minions converged on the human in the darkness.

LHIKAN

Lhikan ducked under a swipe from the crocotaur, backstepping to avoid an incoming acid bubble that struck where he'd just been.

The reptilian beast huffed as it hunched lowly, restabilizing before charging directly at the human—only to receive three kicks in rapid succession.

One to the knee that bent the lizard.

One to the side that sent it tumbling.

And lastly, the end of the three-piece combo—a kick to the maw that knocked several teeth loose.

As the crocotaur went down, something unexpected happened. Lhikan's foot became stuck, his steel boot clinging to the side of the beast, forcing him to do a double take at the slime armor holding him there.

The knight forcefully lifted his boot, smashing down on the crocotaur's face and the slime, shattering the tiny slime's core. He lifted his boot once more, preparing to finish off the pus-ridden monster, its green blood staining the ground as it lay defeated.

Suddenly, something struck his head—a rock that hit him square in the eye, making him wince.

"SQUEAK! SQUEAK! SQUEAK!"

Lhikan turned to the offender, his bleeding face shifting to the sight of the rubber duck that was squeaking obnoxiously.

"A... rubber duck?" he muttered, his eyes tracking the bath toy perched atop the gigantic blue slime. He clenched his fists, eyes wide at the monster Natalie had no doubt lost her life to, a monster clearly powered by the ball of condensed energy he detected from the duck.

"SQUEAK!"

Lhikan dropped his foot, ignoring the monster at his feet, and walked towards the large slime once more, determined to tear it apart and recover Natalie's remains. Even if she had no body, she still deserved a burial—a spiritual one, at the very least.

HIRO

AHHHH! CRAPCRAPCRAPCRAP!

He's approaching me! This was a mistake!

Reflexively, I had used **Summon Rock** in a pathetic attempt to save Dave, who was broken and bleeding. It had worked, but unfortunately, it also drew with it the ire of the man—the berserker scowling as he approached me with ill intentions.

Aaaaaahhhh! I should have just stayed in my domain!

Slimey shifted, liquid tentacles lashing out at the human, who summoned the dagger back to his hand and severed the appendages aimed at him.

AH! Should I retreat? My instincts screamed at me to run, to flee. But I couldn't just leave my freeloading minion! As much as I griped about how lazy Dave was, he was still one of my employees—one of my minions! To abandon him would make me a bad boss! *I AM NOT A BAD BOSS!*

Stuck between a metaphorical rock and a hard place, there was only one thing left to do—only one thing I could do...

Attack.

Or... at least I would have, if not for something I did not foresee happening from Slimey.

LHIKAN

"L-hi...kin."

At the words, the knight froze, his eyes going round at the distorted blue shape wearing Natalie's robes. It was only for a moment—a brief hesitation—before his fist was compelled to rise and destroy the abomination before him.

"S-sss-top," it gurgled, the "voice" coming from the rubber duck. Lhikan's fist was an inch away from the monstrosity, which radiated holy purity—a light only capable of emanating from a being of divine nature or one who served with absolute piety.

"Pw... Pleas... zeeeeesqueak!" The shape of Natalie bubbled, its form wriggling as its hand reached out and touched Lhikan's shaking fist.

He flinched, retracting his hand—which was... healing!

Instead of burns, his knuckles had been grazed by a healing touch, one that injected holy mana to reverse the effects of the corrosive tissue on his skin.

"Natalie?" Lhikan murmured in disbelief, the slime's form seeming to stabilize, solidifying, with the rubber duck now firmly lodged in the throat of the monster in the shape of the priestess.

"Yesqueak!" Its hands reached out to brush over Lhikan's shoulders, continuing to mend his injuries.

"What... what happened to you?" Lhikan demanded, his eyes narrowing, still suspicious of the monster.

"Isqueeek..." The being wiggled. "Fooound... Herrrooo."

Lhikan's eyes widened. The source of their mission—the impossible quest—had been completed. Their mission was over! But this thing... this creature speaking to him through the mouthpiece of a toy, this abomination... the words of such a being... could it be trusted?

The knight didn't know.

All he knew for certain was that he needed to report his findings, bury Natalie, and take that rubber duck, the source of power directing the monsters to attack him. He had never heard of a dungeon core attempting to communicate, but it was clear that this was tied to their mission, to the hero... something that—

"Uhk?!"

Lhikan looked down, finding a hardened tendril of slime lodged in his abdomen.

"Squuuuueakrrrrrrry," the thing with Natalie's face said before more tendrils suddenly shot toward him and pierced his arms, legs, and torso—all non-fatal attacks intended to pin him down.

"Shit!"

The large slime immediately attempted to pull him in, to cover him, to devour him. Acting quickly, Lhikan tore his arm free from one of the spikes, his flesh splitting open to grab his trump card—his one ticket to safety that he reserved for Natalie.

His riftstone.

Chapter 15

Tactical Withdrawal!

*N*OOOOOOOOOOOOOOOOOOOOOOOOOOOOO!
In a flash of light, the man was gone, the human pulling out some kind of stone that teleported him from Slimey's sticky clutches to a place unknown.

AH! YOU STUPID! STUPID SARAWAK SLIME! WHY DID YOU DO THAT?! The large blue slime immediately deflated from my mental abuse.

Of course, I knew why Slimey had attacked the man, it sensed danger, reacting on instinct to protect me as the human suddenly flared with mana, his fists preparing to strike.

I couldn't blame Slimey for its actions, it had done so to defend me, but at the same time, I was just so frustrated that my quarry had escaped.

All that effort and many of my employees... gone.

And with Dave laying half dead on the sewer floor still bleeding profusely.

Okay, Hiro, you just need to calm down, accept this 'L' and keep pushing, you have a lot of questions but right now Dave needs you and there surely MUST be other humans about.

Ordering Slimey to heal Dave, the large holy slime moved with purpose, almost as if to make up for its blunder. It slithered quickly, pulling the injured crocotaur into its body where it began nursing the injured reptile.

It was time for a tactical withdrawal, and my answers would have to wait.

Minion Registry
Slimey: Holy Super Slime Lvl.13
HP: 1650/1650
MP: 210/300
Dave: Blighted Crocotaur Lvl.14
HP: 103/470
MP: 20/70
Slime 36: Elite Cleaning Slime Lvl.02
HP: 100/100
MP: 10/10
Slime 56: Elite Cleaning Slime Lvl.03
HP: 83/110
MP: 09/20
Slime 79: Elite Cleaning Slime Lvl.02
HP: 100/100
MP: 00/10

Besides Slimey, most of my other slimes were dead, save for three. That left me with a total of five minions to my name, making this a costly venture—so many of my children slain. All around me were shattered slime cores and puddles of blue goop—the remains of my allies, my servants, who had died attempting to fulfill my whims.

But it was okay.

Their sacrifice was not in vain. I was alive, and most importantly, lessons had been learned—lessons that would ensure a catastrophe like this didn't happen again... lessons I would reflect on.

Thus began our journey home.

I turned us back toward the way we had come, with Slimey mending Dave and his own natural regeneration kicking in, improving the creature's... complexion?

Creeping through the tunnels with my entourage of survivors, I took a long look at what had gone wrong.

I was too confident, too sure of my success, and probably still riding on the high of reclaiming and building my skills. However, what I failed to consider was that my repertoire of minions wasn't diverse enough, and the level of threat presented—one human— solidified that. I dove in with limited information, no forward scouts, no traps, or any proper ways to defend myself or protect my minions from a superior foe.

All my hard work had been flushed down the drain, and no one was to blame but myself.

But I'd get it right next time.

I let out a squeak, my weary troops and I slowly slinking our way back home when I uncovered what appeared to be several large spiders. Roughly about a foot big, the tiny arachnids were seemingly docile, not interested in bothering anyone or anything unless it touched their web.

Considering the entire sewer was pitch black and my **Squeaker-Location** wasn't picking up on any eyeballs, it was safe to assume that the spiders couldn't see. Their vision was apparently tied directly to their connection to their web.

Reflecting on my recent failure, I decided now was a good moment to ensure my future victories and diversify my arsenal.

I reached out into the darkness, my mind brushing against the spiders', my will overlapping with theirs.

Something felt... different.

It didn't feel like I was simply forcing it to submit, but more like I was trying to push out something foreign.

You have tamed a new minion!

What is this creature's name?

Spooderman, obviously.

Fortunately, that feeling quickly fell away as the spider quickly fell under my control.

Name: Spooderman

Species: Lesser Tarantula

Level: 01

HP: 15/15

MP: 25/25

Skills:

Spin Silk Lvl.01

Paralytic Bite Lvl.01

Poisoner Lvl.01

Pounce Lvl.01

Blend Lvl.01

The first thing I noticed was that compared to level 1 slimes... THESE SPIDERS WERE SO MUCH BETTER!

Slimey wiggled beneath my body, the giant slime shifting its mass to swallow my newly acquired minion.

HEY! STOP! BAD SLIME! BAD! I scolded, Slimey hesitantly retracting its gooey tentacles from Spooderman sitting on its web.

I then went about dominating the other spiders on my path, the same feeling occurring between them as I named the subsequent Spooders 1, 2, and 3 respectively.

I waited for a moment, pausing in case of ramifications for my actions, yet none came, allowing me to turn my attention back to my new minions.

As my first of its kind, Spooderman obviously deserved its own name.

The four spiders joined my retreating menagerie of monsters, the creatures hopping onto the unconscious Dave being carried by Slimey and using him as a bed.

Oddly, the four spiders were doing a little dance of some kind, shaking back and forth, much to the distress of Slimey, who wasn't happy about others riding on it. But even as small as they were, I got a sense of intelligence that was roughly the same as a regular slime. The only difference was that they didn't communicate in words but rather emotions.

And right now, they were excited. Mostly hungry, but excited that they'd get to hunt prey.

Now back in my near spotless domain, I deposited Dave in a pit that served as his bed before allowing myself to be submerged by Slimey's body.

First things first, a nice slime bath.

Entering my domain, the first thing I noticed was that I was filthy. Not as bad as I had once been, but still dirty after hanging around all those pollutants.

Come to think of it... I had been sitting in and out of Slimey the entire trip. It should have kept me clean, so how was I so dirty?

Never mind that, I was getting distracted! Now that I was in a safe place and out from immediate danger, I needed to review all that had happened!

SLIMEY COULD SPEAK!

Well, not really. It had used me as a mouthpiece, speaking words in a language I didn't understand.

But the man did, enough to lower his guard! That meant that there were changes—abilities unseen—that Slimey had undergone!

Perhaps it had absorbed more than just the affinity from that nun?

Perhaps it had taken her memories?

Or perhaps the soul of that priestess lay dormant inside Slimey up to that point!

I didn't know! And after spending an hour poking and prodding Slimey, I got no answer other than wiggles and jiggles.

Turning my attention to the new additions and survivors, the spiders had already spun their webs, each Tarantula taking a corner of each hallway at the tip of the T-shape of my domain.

I guess it's fine... although it is kind of an eyesore... actually... I don't like it.

Suddenly, Slimey moved, the blue slime swiftly scrubbing the webbing much to the dismay of my spider minions. It was almost as if it were responding to my disgust, acting on my behest despite no orders being given.

Yet despite the eyesore being wiped away, I wasn't happy.

Mainly because my spiders weren't happy.

The emotions they felt from having their webs taken down were nothing but sadness.

Crap...

Good morale is good for the company. What's good for the company is good for me...

I'm a good boss.

I ordered my spiders to get to work setting traps, of course, outside of my domain before I had them line the pathways with strings of silk that led up to a web that clung to the ceiling like a carpet for the roof.

An early warning system to things outside my domain. If anything touched the webs, it would alert my spiders who would then alert me.

After all, one couldn't be too careful.

Spooderman directed the other spiders, as Dave let out a groan.

Perfect.

Now situated within the safety of my domain, I knew what I needed to do next.

The dungeon quest...

Kidding, IT WAS TIME FOR A TRAINING MONTAGE! *TIME FOR PAIN! GAINS! AND NUMBERS GOING UP!*

My monsters were weak! They were torn to bits after their first encounter with a human! What would happen the next time they encountered a human? Or multiple?!

If there was something I knew about mankind, it was that they were tenacious beings, rodents. After all, I used to be one!

If you saw one, it was only a matter of time before they multiplied, their numbers a tide. Adventurers were the worst of them, greedy beings who would no doubt be drawn to my domain with thoughts of treasure and glory!

BUT I HAD NO TREASURE!

But they didn't know that, and I needed to be prepared. Those grubby, money-hungry humans!

Plus, perhaps the secret of Slimey's speech and use of the nun's clothes would be revealed upon the slime leveling up.

Turning my attention to the gelatinous goop, it was just wiggling about, attempting to fill in the priestess outfit it pillaged off the nun's corpse.

ELSEWHERE, THE KNIGHT LHIKAN...

Lhikan gasped, stumbling out of a blast of light that deposited him onto the cold stone floor.

"Huh?! Healer! Fetch a healer! GO! ONE OF THEM HAS RETURNED!"

Lhikan blinked, his breaths coming in gasps as he bled onto the Prior, who held him in his arms.

"Lhikan! Hold on! I've sent a scribe to fetch healers!" The man of the cloth assured, his eyes darting toward the white portal that shut. He frowned, his attention turning back to the veteran soldier, the man tasked with protecting their priestess.

If he was this injured...

The Prior knew that Natalie had fallen. He had felt a severance not too long ago, a feeling of loss that haunted him all day. Now he knew why.

"Nurse Joy is coming!" A scribe yelled, racing down the nearby spiral stairs.

"Hang on, Lhikan!"

"I... I..." Lhikan muttered, his eyes widening as the drugs he'd taken began to wear off, and his body underwent the backlash.

"Save your breath, knight. Conserve your strength!" The Prior demanded before Lhikan firmly grasped the religious man by the shoulder.

"We found him," Lhikan said firmly, his eyes locked with the astonished priest's before Lhikan's gaze wavered and his eyes rolled to the back of his head.

Chapter 16

A Trip Down Memory Lane

Sitting in my domain, I focused on my minions, who were hard at work.

Well... everyone other than Dave.

For Dave, I allowed the large lizard to relax on a bed entirely woven by spiders—one that had been stripped of its stickiness thanks to my slimes partially dissolving the webs.

It had taken some time and experimentation, but now, when he wasn't out hunting, Dave had a bed to lie on—a thank you for his hard work after our recent expedition. After all, he had tried his best and deserved something for nearly dying and having his teeth knocked out.

Since returning to my domain, my list of minions had expanded to include: Slimey, Dave, Spooderman, ten cleaning slimes baptized by Slimey, five other spiders, and now, two skeletons.

The skeletons were something I had found after they wandered into my spider alarm system. The skeletons got stuck in the webs spun at the edges of my domain, designed to ensnare and reveal any intruder.

And it worked—much sooner than I had expected!

Name: Hector
Level: 07
Species: Minor Skeleton
HP: 70/70
MP: 00/00
Skills:
Undead
Name: Chloe
Level: 05
Species: Minor Skeleton
HP: 50/50
MP: 00/00
Skills:
Undead

The skeletons weren't very strong and lacked skills other than the typical undead ability to reform as long as their core remained intact. But what they lacked in strength, they made up for with FINGERS and TOOLS! Both were wielding rusty swords, which made them useful as fighters.

However, unlike my other minions, these undead possessed no thoughts or feelings, at least none that I could discern. There was a will buried deep within them, something to dominate, but it felt extremely muted, dull—like a blank slate awaiting its master to paint on.

So, that's what I did.

Since I had dominated both skeletons at the same time, I decided to name them together.

Hector and Chloe.

The taller skeleton, with a thicker pelvis bone, was Hector. The smaller one, missing a few ribs, was Chloe.

They were named after my companions of old, my original adventuring team—both of whom were likely long gone after my defeat at the hands of the Demon Lord.

I wondered what they would say about my current predicament. Hector would probably laugh, pulling me into the nearest lady's bathroom to describe everything in the most degenerate way possible. Chloe, on the other hand, would likely panic and rush me to the nearest temple with tears (blue, maybe?) in her eyes.

Hmm. It's been so long; I can barely remember their faces. I could picture them, hear their voices, remember the laughter, the campsites, the inns—but their faces... they're just blurs. Gaps in my memory caused by the erosion of time.

An odd sense of melancholy began to take root, a sadness that crept through my rubbery form as fragmented memories resurfaced.

Memories from my former life. Reminders of my failure.

I could see them: shards of memories long thought lost, now resurfacing in a way that was both sweet and bitter. The life I had left behind, the friends I no longer had, the world I had failed.

And now that same world had moved on without me.

It hurt.

But I pushed that aside. I couldn't influence the past—only look to the future.

And right now, the future I envisioned was one of purity, cleanliness, peace, and prosperity! One ruled by my hand... err, beak?

To make that happen, I had to ensure my minions were up to the task! They couldn't lose to a single human! No one, and nothing, could threaten my freedom again!

So, I watched my minions grow, observed their mannerisms, and tracked their levels.

It was a slow process, but I guess that's why they call it grinding.

And it would all be worth it if I could rise from this filth and ascend to heights that even the gods who sent me here would never have expected!

Hours passed. My minions gained skills and experience by scouring the floor.

But despite all the time spent, it didn't seem like they were truly getting stronger. In three days, Slimey had only leveled up once, while Dave had reached level fifteen. My other employees were doing alright, but my two champions seemed to have hit a bottleneck, stifling their growth.

That was a big problem.

Now, I faced a dilemma... should I continue at this slow and steady pace? Safe? Or should I send them out again to face stronger foes? Could we even handle stronger enemies?

It was all about balancing risk and reward.

I didn't want my precious minions to get hurt, obviously, but if there was no pain, how could I expect them to gain?

I knew what needed to be done. Of course, I knew. But I was reluctant after my last encounter.

Sigh.

Hesitation is defeat. I knew that. And procrastination was the death of time. My enemies wouldn't wait for me to grow stronger, nor should I expect them to.

I turned my attention to Slimey, who was happily playing with its black dress, and Dave, who was munching on a monster core fed to him by Spooderman.

It was time for another round.

Chapter 17

Into the Catacombs

Slinking through the darkness of the cavern, I rode atop Slimey while my minions marched in a perimeter around me.

Dave, my tank, stood at the front of the pack, wearing a cuirass crafted from hardened spiderwebs, with a few slimes stretched over it for added protection.

Behind him, my skeletons, Chloe and Hector, were similarly covered, albeit in sticky webs that wrapped around their rib cages, skulls, arms, and legs. In a way, they almost appeared to be mummies, thanks to how thick I had the Spooderman and the spiders weave their webs.

In the center were Slimey and me, with a trail of arachnids sticking to our rear and leaving webbing in their wake—meant to alert us of any potential stalkers and slow down attackers.

This time, I wasn't going to take any chances.

Every few paces, I would squeak, mentally mapping out the sewers as I traversed the filthy walkway.

Fortunately, resistance was light, with most of the monsters already exterminated and turned into experience for my army as they passed through. Occasionally, however, I would encounter wild slimes—ones that I had already forcefully cured of their mutation, turning them into slimes that worked under me without being directly in my employ.

Of course, they moved to attack me, but against a super holy slime like Slimey, their meager attempts to reach me atop my moving mountain were all but futile.

Is this what it feels like to be a king?

I have to say it does feel quite nice.

Wait. What's that?

My next squeak picked up something—multiple somethings—humanoid shapes in the distance, clutching weapons. Skeletons, I made out, judging by their lack of flesh and the creatures having the same blank signature my skeletons originally had.

Dave, you're up.

Of course, the ten-foot-tall crocodile wasn't happy. I could feel it through our bond, but he'd done enough relaxing and needed to be put to work! After all, the best rehabilitation after severe physical trauma was rest, recovery, and then exercise!

Now we were in the exercise stage, and my lazy minion needed to move!

Dave stomped his feet, striking the stone floor with his scaly tail, which slapped against it repeatedly before he released a mighty roar—one that sent a vibration coursing through Slimey and into me.

Immediately, Slimey shifted, coating me head to toe in its gooey body, save for my beak, which it knew to keep unrestricted for my **Squeaker-Location**.

Like an angry bull, my crocotaur charged. The skeletons answered Dave's challenge by turning and rushing him, their bony hands cradling dull weapons that did little against the monster who landed in their midst.

Thanks to the hardened silk and slimes coating his body, Dave resisted the damage, performing a 360-spin that immediately shattered the undead forms as his tail smashed through the fragile bones.

But the battle wasn't over yet. The problem with fighting undead was that they revived if their cores weren't destroyed. Like the stories of liches from the fantasy novels of my home world, all undead in this world operated with a phylactery—the source of their animation and power.

Ghosts and spirit types tended to have theirs in their physical bodies, their corpses buried somewhere. Zombies and skeletons usually kept theirs in their skulls, while more advanced undead had theirs tied to items, relics, or even spouts of mana given form by intense emotions, like drowners or penitents.

Dave had only broken their torsos, and the skeletons, churning with magic, had already begun to reassemble themselves, their bones already moving to resemble their previous forms.

We quickly put an end to that.

Ordering Dave around, my champion quickly disposed of the skeletons, stomping on their brittle skulls and immediately ending their threat.

Of course, there was barely any experience to be gained, BUT! There were weapons!

Crusty, brittle, probably rusted weapons—but weapons, nonetheless. They were weapons Dave could use, material for potential tools, and traps!

I paused my menagerie, ordering Dave to pick up the tools. The giant crocodile huffed but followed my orders.

Using the slimes that coated him, I had the monsters hold onto the weapons like little holsters and sheaths. Whatever didn't fit onto Dave's impromptu backpacks, I had Slimey pick up the rest.

Metal was metal, after all, and RUST is deadly! Even if I couldn't wield the blades and axes as intended, I could find a way to break down the material for other uses.

All in all, I collected four shortswords, two axes, a spear, and a mace—most of which were stored inside Slimey, with explicit orders not to dissolve them, much to its displeasure.

Carrying on, I kept squeaking, searching for the source of the skeletons to procure more metal now that I knew I was on the right track.

Eventually, my search led me to a large drain—one roughly twenty-by-twenty feet—jutting from a wall, with nearly two dozen skeletons loitering around the tail end of the pipe.

After dispatching the horde and collecting their loot, I sat on my slime, pondering whether I should ascend, its innards swirling with dozens of weapons.

Judging by the trail of scattered bones, it was clear they had descended from wherever this pipe led, which, to my best guess, was either a dumping ground or a catacomb.

Right?

Should I chance it? What do you think?

...

I really need someone to talk to.

Squeaking into the pipe didn't do much of anything, as my sound bounced upward and didn't return, telling me nothing of what lay beyond.

Perhaps that was the exit? Or a way toward one? I didn't know, but the only way I would find out was by taking the first step.

I ordered an elite slime ahead—my number 99. If anything happened to it, then I'd know it was dangerous. If not... well, still dangerous, but probably less so.

Slime 99 detached from Dave, the gooey fiend crawling its way up the pipe to be my scout. The simple orders: crawl to the exit, wait, then return.

I waited.

And waited.

And waited...

99 returned!

I let out a squeak, ordering my monsters forward while mentally mapping my path and leaving behind webs in case I got lost.

Turning my attention to Chloe and Hector, I ordered Slimey to swallow them up, storing them in its mass so that we could all go together.

Huh?

Oddly, the skeletons—without minds of their own—backed away from Slimey's tendrils as they reached out.

Slimey attempted to grab Chloe and Hector again, but just like before, they backed away.

Weird.

Get in the slime. I ordered, yet the pair of undead were reluctant.

Ugh, we don't have time for this! GET IN THE SLIME!

At my command, the skeletons both took a step forward into Slimey, their bony appendages clicking against the floor as they stepped into the slime—only to SUDDENLY COMBUST INTO FLAMES.

WHAT? HUH?!

Dumbfounded by the unexpected heat, the pair of skeletons were immolating themselves just to follow my command!

GET OUT OF THE SLIME! GET—OUTOFTHESLIME! GET OUT!

So… after that fiasco, I learned something I had completely forgotten:

Undead are naturally averse to holy attributes… so much so that they disintegrate or burst into flames when exposed to righteous light.

Now, I had two lightly charred undead with half health and no way to heal them. I didn't possess negative energy, nor did any of us have milk, so I had permanently crippled two of my minions just because of a lapse in memory…

Sigh.

Sending Chloe and Hector back to base with my newly procured armory of weapons, the rest of us eventually made our way to the top, where I entered a winding tunnel of decrepit catacombs.

At least, judging from the structure of the walls, the bones, and the skulls littering the area, I assumed it was a catacomb.

My body shivered. Odd, because I wasn't cold—no, this was a different sensation. Something that made me uneasy.

I let out a squeak, pinging the nearby surroundings. My sound washed over the bones and weapons scattered about, many of them broken, with no undead rising in response.

Judging from the carnage and the lingering holy energy in the space, it was a safe assumption that Priestess Slimey had come from this direction.

It was also a safe assumption that the warrior from earlier had come from this way too—the man who had tried to find his companion only to run into me.

Cautiously, I ordered Slimey and Dave forward, deeper into the unknown, as a sense of foreboding—and, curiously, excitement—took hold.

I had never been this far before, never "seen" this place. A whole new area to explore! New minions! New loot! OH, HOW I MISSED THE FEELING!

No! Don't get too excited! Every time you do, something bad happens! Better to just play it safe—smooth and calm...

After rallying my wild emotions, my army and I marched forward into the catacombs, with Slimey leading the way. The skeletons lingering about weren't a threat at all. In fact, most of them attempted to flee, and those that didn't... Well, let's just say they weren't a problem after Slimey ran them over. Plus, I now possessed enough weapons to outfit a small village.

Eventually, after much crawling, many squeaks, and copious amounts of undead turned to dust, my gang and I made it into a large chamber. A collapsed section of wall most likely led to another entrance.

Inside, I squeaked, my sound bouncing off each wall and registering something that made me giddy.

A body.

Chapter 18

Cursing Elves

Huh...

Hovering around the corpse in the center of the room, I was astonished to find a humanoid body—not because it was humanoid in nature, but because of the ears.

It was an elf of some kind, or at least I thought so. I'd have to take it back to be sure.

The corpse had pointy ears—long, from what my Squeaker-Location could tell—but without the actual sight provided by my domain, I couldn't know for sure.

What was an elf doing so far from Valesgrand? As far as I knew, the white-skinned tree huggers never bothered to leave their homeland of waterfalls, lakes, and rainbow-vomiting narwhals. They even refused to fight the Demon Lord, claiming it wasn't their problem because life was so perfect for them with their crystal-clear lakes, vibrant flowers, and copious amounts of sugarweed they ground into cigarettes. OH! And their stupid "peace for the world" nonsense, how I should try talking to the murderous psychopath known as Barbaroll.

IN FACT! NOW THAT I'M THINKING ABOUT IT! THOSE UPPITY HIPPIES STILL OWE ME FOR SLAYING THE JABBERWOCKY!

But I digress... Let me stop before I go on a never-ending rant about my hatred for elves...

Like, I'm not racist, but did I mention they had the gall to boast to my face about being able to beat the Demon Lord anytime? And that a hero class like me wasn't needed because they were all super-duper gifted in magic, even—

Okay. I'm stopping. I promise...

Did you know—

Minion, Dave has reached the level cap!

Huh?

I let out a squeak, a tidal wave of anger hitting me as the corpse on the ground disappeared, with Dave munching away despite Slimey trying to pry his mouth open to get the overgrown reptile to stop.

DAVE! NO! BAD CROCODILE! BAAAAD!

But of course, Dave didn't care. Instead, he laid down, ignoring my pestering squeaks and commands.

GET UP!

Nothing. No response from Dave, the monster's status updating.

Name: Dave

Level: 20

Species: Hibernating Blighted Crocotaur

HP: 550/550

MP: 100/100

Skills:

Strong Body Lvl.01

Heavy Constitution Lvl.01

Pain Resilience Lvl.03
Minor Regeneration Lvl.02
Swim Lvl.04
Bite Lvl.05
Iron Tail Lvl.05
Endure Lvl.02
Blend Lvl.05

Hibernating? HIBERNATING?! YOU LAZY REPTILE, GET UP! GETTTTT UPPPPP, OR I'LL FEED YOU TO SLIMEY!

Of course, Dave didn't wake up. Out in enemy territory, and now I was down one of my strongest fighters because he was hungry...

... Great.

Damn elves. Somehow, even in death, they still managed to annoy me!

AAAAAAAAAAAAAAAAAAAAAAAAGH!

Carrying Dave on the back of Slimey, I had my minions guide me around the room, exploring the location, poking and prodding. It was some kind of burial chamber. There was a circular opening in the ceiling that led somewhere I couldn't reach. Below it, a round plate of some kind rested, cracked tiles beneath it from the impact. It seemed like it had originally blocked the hole.

My assumption was proven correct a few moments later when a few skeletons fell from the hole as my entourage neared. They landed in Slimey, immediately being purified in the holy slime's body.

Beyond that, this antechamber was barren, save for the collapsed entrance on the other end, filled with rubble and the copious amount of skeletal remains.

Taking a moment, I compiled all the clues and events that had transpired involving the humanoids to reconstruct a theory on what had happened.

From what I could deduce, the adventurers had been fleeing something, making their way to this chamber where they collapsed the entrance to cover their escape. Judging by the state of the priestess and her lack of food when I found her, it was a safe assumption that the adventurers' supplies had been low, and they were in desperation mode. A tale as old as time.

A tale I knew all too well, as a former hero.

With her condition, the sealed exit, and the situation at hand, there was a good chance the adventurers had devolved into infighting—the elf fighting the nun... no. Her injuries were infested, more akin to a monster attack than an arrow or dagger from an elf. If there was one thing the elves were good for, it was their unparalleled accuracy with pointy objects. Especially throwing ones.

So, the warrior versus the elf.

They got into a fight while the priestess ran. Then, judging from the round plate on the ground, the fighting had triggered a trap of some kind, releasing skeletons from above.

The warrior capitalized on the confusion, killing the elf before making his way to pursue the nun, possibly in a bid to hunt her down for her supplies, so that he...

No... That didn't seem right either.

He had talked to Slimey, hesitated in striking me down as Slimey took on the form of his former companion.

He was her guardian, possibly a paladin charged with keeping her safe as his charge, which would explain his absurd strength and fury in combat!

Yes. The pieces of the puzzle were coming together, but now that left me with more questions than answers.

Who were they?

It was clear they weren't just an adventuring team but rather a group on a mission—one of great importance if it involved one of those uppity hippy elves.

What was their mission?

Where had they come from?

Was the church they belonged to the same church I had woken up in when I came to this world?

More importantly, what were they running from that even that powerhouse of a paladin and elf couldn't deal with?

I wouldn't have my answers lazing around like Dave.

With only one entrance, this place would make for a nice base setup. Of course, I'd have to dismantle my old base and get rid of the pylons. *Is there a way to move my domain?*

Would you like to abandon your current domain?

I guess there is.

Hm... should I? Then again, I know the sewers—at least most of them. The monsters there weren't much to deal with, and I still had the project of cleaning out the sewers.

I'll table it for now, at least until I'm stronger and level up. There's no telling what threats lie beyond that sealed tunnel, and if I went to the next stage of my dungeon questline, it might endanger me.

No, it's better to have a buffer—floors to separate me from the stronger monsters that lurk above.

Right?

You agree with me, right? Sure you do, friend. Thanks for coming to my Duck Talk...

I really need someone to talk to...

Dragging Dave behind us, I gave the order to my menagerie of monsters to return home. Despite not being able to bring the corpse back to my domain, the journey itself hadn't been fruitless. By my estimation, at least forty various weapons had been obtained. Slimey proved to be a natural enemy to all enemies on the second level, and despite Dave's appetite, he had hit a level cap and was undergoing some kind of metamorphosis.

Hopefully, he would evolve into something less lazy, but considering my luck, that seemed doubtful.

The return trip home wasn't too bad. Thanks to the string of webs Spooderman and my tarantuals set up, finding our way back through the winding tunnels was a piece of cake!

Eventually, I re-entered my domain, dismissing my companions while depositing Dave onto his bed and having Slimey deposit all the weapons it had picked up into the cleaning hole. While the adventurer side of me told me to keep the rust on the weapons, the "duck side" of me demanded they be cleaned. Purging them of their filth, there was no reason I should allow or tolerate uncleanliness in my domain.

After all, a clean home is a happy home, and if I was going to have guests, they should be greeted with the best "welcome to my domain" package I could muster.

Somewhere, in the darkness of the sewers, several blind spiders lay at the edge of Hiro's domain, surrounding a larger tarantual with glowing red eyes. The monster stood on six legs, observing the horde of slimes and creatures gathered around a yellow source of mana.

The creature rubbed its hairy front legs together, plucking at the web trailing behind it, a web that belonged to none of Hiro's dominated spiders. The high-tensile web vibrated, sending a message that traveled along the string for several hundred feet, reaching something in the dark that brandished a hungry smile.

THE HIRO IS A RUBBER DUCK

Chapter 19

Dave Is Dav... ette?

NARRATED IN THE VOICE OF SIR DAVID ATTENBOROUGH...

In the darkness of Dave's mind, a small mote of light ignited, synapses connecting as it mind-melded with its master—an event spurred on by its recent meal of a sentient being.

Sad. Hungry. Sleepy.

Memories—dozens, hundreds—not belonging to itself, but rather Hiro's and the catalyst in Dave's stomach. An unheard-of event was occurring between it, the consumed soul, and the thing trapped in the shell of a rubber duck.

The human soul.

Minion, Dave has a Species-Advancement available!

The word appeared to Dave, not as a voice or tangible letters, but rather as a feeling to its non-sentient mind.

Sad. Hungry. Sleepy.

Human feelings, human thoughts. The soul of a higher being brushing against its own, the life experience forgotten in the shadows of time by one infecting the other, propelled forward by the catalyst.

Sad. Hungry. Sleepy.

Dave shifted, knowledge unbefitting of its status touching its monster core, warping it, changing it. The unique status of Hiro influencing a change that should not have been possible—and would not have been if not for the monster's master being a human.

Sad. Hungry. Sleepy.

Sad. Hungry. Sleepy.

Sad. Hungry. Sleepy.

Sad. Hungry. Sleepy.

Eeepy. I sleep...

But hungy. Hungy much hungy. Uuugh. Hungry! HUNGRY! But sleeepy.

As if waking from a long slumber, a spark was ignited.

The emotions twisted, merging with the knowledge of the souls and Hiro's desires—to be free from his shell, to be human again, to speak with another person—spurring an event unique to the sentient dungeon that allowed a 177013 to occur.

Species Path Selected!

The message played, words in the awakened soul.

"Errrrh." Dave let out, the crocotaur feeling strange, mostly hungry. Its mind racked with pain as it blinked repeatedly, wiping its eyes with a slender green talon. It yawned and sat up.

"Hrrn." It let out, its mouth feeling odd, its top teeth clacking loudly against its bottom. Had it broken another tooth? Dave didn't know. The crocotaur ran its talons through the long green fur on its head. Weird.

Dave opened its eyes fully, coming face to face with a menagerie of monsters staring at it.

"M'hurnkry." Dave slurred awkwardly, the evolved crocotaur speaking to the rubber duck, which let out a squeak in response.

Congratulations! You have created a new species!
What would you like to name your new species?

As the blinding light faded in my domain, I was left flabbergasted by what I was "seeing."

Name: Dave
Level: 01
Species: ???
HP: 500/500
MP: 30/30
Skills:
Human Potential
Strong Body Lvl.01
Heavy Constitution Lvl.01
Pain Resilience Lvl.03
Minor Regeneration Lvl.03
Dark Vision Lvl.02
Swim Lvl.04
Bite Lvl.06
Iron Claw Lvl.01
Iron Tail Lvl.05
Endure Lvl.02
Blend Lvl.05

After nearly a week of training my minions, dissolving weapons, setting up traps, and using bones scavenged from the catacombs to build a "fence" around my domain, Dave had finally woken, a notification striking my mind as I was in the process of having my spiders reinforce the walls with their webs.

Dave had evolved! And Dave wasn't a "Dave" at all, but a Dave... let? Davetta? Davida? Davina? Davinia? Davella? Okay, enough of that.

DAVE! I sent, the monster jolting at the mental command.

Dave blinked, the reptile cocking its humanoid face, its black-spotted eyes staring at me. Dave was now a green-skinned humanoid, with the face of a woman and long green hair. Its scales had receded greatly, with its once-elongated jaw now replaced by a human mouth attached to a human face, complete with human-like green pupils.

The scales that had coated its body now only dotted its face and parts of its naked, muscular, and toned green body, two massive mountain peaks facing me.

Huh...

Suddenly, I was on the floor, dropped by Slimey, while Dave was on the move.

WHAT? HEY!

The ten-foot-tall green woman was abruptly snatched up by Slimey, the blue holy slime carrying Dave away and tossing her over the bone walls that surrounded my domain.

Slimey! Bad!

Dave attempted to climb over my newly constructed bone fence, only to be blocked at every turn by the five-hundred-gallon slime. The creature's cores vibrated so violently that the blue goo turned red.

Huh, that's new.

Dave let out an annoyed growl, the creature trying to return to its bed, only to be blocked by Slimey at every turn.

In response, Dave swiped at Slimey, who spat acid into the reptile-woman's face, causing her to roar in anger before charging through my fence!

SLIMEY! LET THEM BACK IN HERE! STOP DESTROYING MY FORTIFICATIONS! I yelled, ordering the two to stop. In response, all I heard was the chorus of a hundred voices, unified in a singular purpose, shouting four words.

'NO! YOU! ARE! MINE!'

Ah... Okay. Fair enough. I'll just be right here on the floor while you two work that out.

Wait. No! Why am I sitting in silence?! I'm the boss here!

The pair of monsters were attacking each other now, Slimey attempting to dissolve Dave as the monster flailed around, completely unfamiliar with its humanoid body.

STOP! I ordered, sending out my mental command that washed over Slimey. The creature shook violently but finally froze.

Dave walked past, the lumbering, depressed, muscular woman awkward in her steps. It also probably didn't help that Slimey, although frozen, had several tentacles of ooze attached to Dave, trying to slow down the monster who was clearly keen on getting back to bed.

Slimey was unhappy, but it'd have to make do while I tried to figure out what was going on.

But first things first!

After about ten minutes, Dave's unmentionables were now covered in the name of modesty, the overgrown muscle-gator woman sporting chest bindings and underwear made entirely of spiderwebs.

Dave wasn't very impressed; in fact, it kept scratching at the bindings, breaking them over and over again. But thanks to repeated scolding, multiple rebindings, and some paralytic venom from Spooderman, Dave eventually learned to keep covered.

Slimey, on the other hand, was eager to get into its nun clothes, attempting to take on a humanoid shape. It filled out the clothes but failed to stabilize its form, the slime changing colors from blue to red, to purple, then orange—something I didn't know it could do.

I considered taking away its dress, but given the outburst and behavior, I couldn't help but feel worried for my life.

Plus, Slimey's thoughts were concerning, the only word being broadcast over and over again with fury and rage: *'MINE! MINE! MINE! MINE!'* as I rode around on my skeleton Hector's head.

What have I created?

Turning my attention back to Dave, who was munching loudly on a monster core, I observed the creature and its stats.

In its evolved state, it had lost most of its mana, instead gaining health points and several skills, along with something called Human Potential...

Why, though?

Its blighted, pus-ridden body was gone, so that was cool. But what had happened to make the crocotaur evolve into a human-like species?

Did it have something to do with me?

Or did it have something to do with the elf corpse it ate?

I'd heard of monsters gaining sapience before, but that was typically reserved for nature spirits or undead—creatures either heavily involved with humans or influenced greatly by them, a process that took years.

But there were no humans here, so why was Dave... human-like?

I didn't know. Another question added to my growing list of mysteries.

Dave.

The lizard-woman turned to me, her hair a mess with a rat dangling out of her mouth.

'Hm? Foob?' Dave sent back before chomping enthusiastically, devouring the rat while a slime cleaned up the blood splatter.

Dave opened its viscera-covered mouth, saying something to me, talking even as a slime landed on her head, cleaning up the gore it detected.

Still, despite having no air with the slime on its head, it kept talking. And talking. And talking, with air bubbles filling the blue goo on its head.

This idiot must breathe through gills or something.

Eventually, the slime slid away, allowing Dave to speak clearly, but there was a slight problem...

I can't hear!

UGH! ENOUGH OF THIS BODY! I WANT A HUMAN BODY TOO! IT'S NOT FAIR! WHY DOES THIS DEPRESSED-LOOKING DOLT GET ONE BUT NOT ME?!

My rubber casing shook in anger. Just when I was getting excited about being able to converse with someone!

AAAAAAAAAGHHHHHHHHHHHH.

Okay. I've had enough. Time to start the next quest chain.

Create a Mana Core!
The mana core is the heartbeat of all dungeons!
WARNING! Crafting a mana core will attract rivals!

I'd been gaining new functions and abilities as I progressed through the quest chain. Maybe the cure to my condition lay in progress? While I was worried about being under siege, after a week of moving up and down the sewers and occasionally returning to the catacombs, it was a somewhat safe assumption that I was in a secure spot.

There didn't seem to be any other notable monsters nearby, and my traps—pitfalls, pulleys, and snares—helped ease my mind a bit. Oh! And something I liked to call *THE MACE* also contributed to my peace.

Basically, *THE MACE* was a collection of rocks, swords, and bones fastened together and suspended on the ceiling next to the pipe leading up to the catacombs.

Attached to a tripwire, anything that attempted to walk through would immediately be impaled and smashed by the mace. But considering my method of getting to the catacombs was sticking to the walls, the trap was safe to all but my foes and intruders. :3

I decided to create the mana core, willing it into existence.

An odd feeling pressed down on me, like I was being squeezed, deflated as mana left my body and formed a ball of energy in the space I had designated as the core's location.

The sphere of mana was akin to a star, at least from what I remembered stars looking like from my old high school memories. It burned with energy, illuminating the darkness, casting away the shadows, and bringing light into a lightless place.

Ah, is this what Thomas Edison and Nikola Tesla felt when they discovered electricity?

I didn't know, but what I did know was that I was feeling oddly giddy as the core pulsed and reacted to my pylons. They extended my senses and cleared away a large portion of the fog of war.

Quest Complete: Create a Mana Core!
The HEART of your dungeon is now active!

Protect it with your life!
Unlocked: Champion Designation!
Incoming Quest!
Designate a Champion! 0/1
Every facility has a manager—a champion. These champions help enforce your will and desires, gaining unique abilities and a stronger bond with their master.
Reward: New Quest Chain
2 Minions Eligible for Champion Designation!
Name: Slimey
Level: 14
Species: Holy Super Slime
Name: Dave
Level: 01
Species: ???

Chapter 20

Memories of Her...

Hmmm.

Between Slimey and Dave, it was obvious that I would choose Slimey as my champion, right? After all, the slime was my first companion and minion—my steadfast, albeit overly zealous, friend.

However...

I was worried. While Slimey was fiercely loyal to me, it also somewhat terrified me with its jealousy. I wasn't sure what Slimey would become if our... "relationship" deepened, according to the system screen. In fact, I was on the metaphorical fence.

I could take the time to promote a different monster to gain that level of competence and become my champion, but I had a sinking feeling that if I didn't appoint Slimey, I would die—especially since I was being held by the slime that had sneakily taken me off Hector's head with a tentacle and wrapped my body in its jelly.

Am I being held hostage? I feel like I'm being held hostage...

Sigh.

Minion, Slimey has been designated as Champion!

I relented, selecting Slimey as my champion.

Suddenly, an inexplicable feeling emerged in my gut—like a leash or rope constricting around my core, an invisible line connecting me to my minion. It seemed to grow thicker and stronger until it became visible in my mind's eye. The emotions transmitted between me and my newly christened apostle intensified, awakening and undergoing a metamorphosis as my entire being seemed to be probed.

I wasn't sure what was happening, but what I did know was that my entire life flashed before my eyes. Memories once dormant, faces once lost—all came rushing back as the images of my past life, first in my own world and then in this one, sped through me.

They were fleeting, with any attempt to halt the stream or focus on any one particular memory being blocked by some unknown force— like a light in my eye that wouldn't allow me to focus. I was stuck, my mind a victim to the tide of a lifetime of memories that were my own yet not. It was like a screenplay of someone else's life, playing on fast-forward.

And then, I saw something that jolted me from the motion picture. An image my mind fixated on, forcing the reel of my life to come to a crawl.

Images. Of Hector, Chloe. And... Ana? Who? A woman. Someone I had spent a life with, a friend? No, a lover? Memories of someone I had forgotten.

"Please. Stop."

Memories of a caring, fierce warrior who fought by my side—sword and shield in hand—since Adam had sent me to this world. Her wild hair, golden-brown; perfect sapphire eyes that twinkled with intellect; and a radiant smile... *Who... Why? How could I...?*

"Please. Stop."

I could see us at a campfire, at the foot of a mountain, the Demon Lord's castle looming in the distance. The cold wind forced us to huddle together for warmth.

There was hesitation, fear, and doubt in the air, but also desire. Desire for each other, rooted in...

Love.

Trust.

We had both been sent here—that was our mutual bond. Our proof of having existed in another world was each other, and the memories we shared.

I could smell the faint scent of Oris lilacs, the perfume she liked, the touch of her soft skin, the warmth of her wet lips as her mouth sealed onto mine, and...

"Please... stop."

The memories shifted. The cozy campfire was replaced by a darkened chamber. Chloe and Hector lay dead, my army in shambles, my weapon shattered, and in my arms...

"Please..."

So much blood.

"Please..."

I could see that same face, staring blankly. The light of intellect was gone, blonde hair was matted with viscera, and her warm lips leaked crimson ichor...

"Don't leave me... Please don't go..."

A quivering voice, one of despair.

Was it mine? I... can't... I can't remember. The memory shifted again, this time with Barbaroll standing above me, the one-horned Demon Lord smirking, its black eyes shaped like crescents as it mocked my pain and ran me through with a crimson spear.

Pain... So much pain...

I could see my hands—blood-stained, dented claws wrapped in wrought silver—reaching out, gripping the shaft of the spear embedded in me, pulling myself closer. A voice, filled with rage, reached out to the one who killed... *Who? Someone dear. Someone... I... I can't... I can't remember! I can't! Why can't I?!*

"Please! Don't! Don't go... please..."

And just like that, the ordeal ended, leaving me alone in the darkness, grasping and reaching out for memories that were no longer there—trying to piece together the jigsaw of my life.

I was alone. The only survivor of an ordeal who couldn't even remember the names or faces of my dearest comrades.

My greatest failure. My greatest shame.

Hundreds of years later, I persisted while they all faded, lost to the annals of time on a mission for an uncaring god.

And I had forgotten them. A hundred years of isolation. Loneliness. Madness. Filth.

I... Who... Why am I spacing out suddenly?

I turned my attention to Slimey, observing the monster as notification after notification flooded my mind.

Name: Slimey
Title: Hiro's Champion
Level: 14
Species: Holy Super Slime
HP: 2050/2050
MP: 400/400
Skills:
Physical Resistance Lvl.04
Slashing Resistance Lvl.03
Striking Resistance Lvl.03
Cold Resistance Lvl.02

Acid Resistance Lvl. MAXED
Shape Change Lvl.01
Mend Lvl.01
Dissolve Lvl.06
Bubble Blow Lvl.01
Slime Bullet Lvl.02
Foam Lvl.02
Solidification Lvl.05
Bounce Lvl.04
Blend Lvl.01
Mimic Lvl.02
Duplicate Lvl.01
Constrict Lvl.01
Cleanse Lvl.05
Holy Imbue Lvl.01

The slime wiggled, its status updating to gain a multitude of my resistances and some skills, a part of myself imprinting on the monster.

Slimey began to move and shift, its cores glowing with iridescent light, blinding to my senses as they merged.

Before long, I found myself held in the blue arms of a golden-haired woman with sapphire eyes. She held me close, and the blue skin on her body shifted into a delicate light pink—so familiar, yet so... painful.

'No one will ever hurt you again,' a voice spoke, gentle and kind— words I understood, words I could hear, words I didn't know I needed to hear.

How can you be so sure?

'I will make sure of it,' Slimey said, holding me close to her dress, her eyes shaking with fury. *'No one shall take you away from me.'*

Quest Complete: Designate a Champion! 1/1
+500 EXP
Level Up!

Chapter 21

New Skill!

Dungeon System Interface!
Name: Hiro Dungeon
Level: 02
HP: 8000/8000
MP: 0983/1500
DEVOTION: 100
EXP: 130/1000
Tamed Monsters: 08/30
Pylons: 5/5
Unlocked: Minion Synchronization!
Dungeon Skills
Domain Expansion: 0/1
Sustained
MP Cost: 500

Radiate your will and designate a nearby area as part of your domain. If there are other competing claims to the area, the strongest will prove victorious.

Designate Minion Lvl.01: 0/10
MP Cost: 20 (Per Minion)

Creatures you target must make a wisdom saving throw against you. Upon failing, the creature is forcibly placed under your command.

Minion Synchronization: Lvl.01
Cooldown: 12 Hours

Synchronize your senses with a loyal minion to take control of the target for sixty seconds. Duration scales with skill level, and effectiveness scales with the bond.

AWWWWW HECK YEAH! NEW SKILL! NEW SKILL! GREAT SKILL! I couldn't help but feel ecstatic about the new skill I'd obtained. Besides my numbers going up, I had gained something I could actually use—something that wasn't as useless as **Summon Rock** or **Bubble Blow**!

Incoming Quest!
Synchronize With a Minion!

Perhaps sensing my ecstatic emotions, Slimey rubbed my rubber head, its hand smearing cleaning solution across my yellow body.

'Lord Hiro, what's wrong? Is something the matter, darling?' Slimey's voice appeared in my mind with a suave, oddly mature tone as it lifted me up. Its sapphire eyes stared at me in reverence.

Even though I knew they were fake... Even though I knew this was a monster...

Even though I knew...

What did I know? Nothing. And the absence of that knowledge oddly gave me comfort.

Nothing. Just a skill. I mentally shook myself from my thoughts as Slimey cradled me in her arms and squeezed me against her liquid body.

'Will you show me, darling?'

Sure. Despite my earlier dismissal, I couldn't help but respond with slight enthusiasm, eager to test out my new skill.

I turned my attention to Hector, my skeleton minion standing nearby, and poured my will into activating the skill.

And then...

Huh?

I'm... I'm big?

Peeking through the orbs of energy that served as Hector's eyes, I stared at my bony hands, my exposed fingers. Even though there was no skin, no flesh, I could see it.

Skin. My palms. My body.

Even though it wasn't real, for a moment—just a split second—I felt real again. Like I was... human.

I moved around, giggling internally with glee. Running in place, twirling my arms, spinning my head round and round—

And then it stopped. My consciousness snapped back into my rubber container.

Minion Synchronization Cooldown: 11:59:00

Great... I let out a squeak, the sound carrying my sigh with it.

Quest Complete: Synchronize With a Minion!
Incoming Quest!

'I'm sorry, Lord Hiro! I have made you suffer! I shall repent at once!' Slimey exclaimed, tearing off her arm with a fervor that made

me wince. She began to unclothe, shedding parts of her liquid skin as the slime cried cleaning fluid from its eyes.

Whoa! STOP! STOP!

'Please! My actions have caused you suffering! Please, punish me at once, Lord Hiro!' She begged, slamming her head against the floor, deforming her jelly and splattering globs of it all over the surrounding area.

Uhhhhh.

'Lord Hiro, your burdens are my burdens. Please, order me to fulfill your wishes so that you may be happy!'

Uhhhhh.

Embarrassingly, an indiscernible amount of time passed, Slimey and I locked in silence, neither of us moving.

Errrrr... HOW THE HECK AM I SUPPOSED TO REACT TO THIS?!

I didn't know, but Slimey was adamant about being punished. So, I sent them on cleaning duty, sending them away while I cleared my mind and tried to process everything that had happened.

'For your glory, I shall commit my tasks, Lord Hiro!'

The slime kept her head to the floor, dragging her face as she went on her way.

I turned my attention to Dave (or was it Davelette), who was sprawled out—the large croco-girl? Crocodile? Crocotaurus? I really need a better naming convention.

Anyway, the large beast-woman was lying on her bed of hardened silk.

I sent an order, attempting to rouse the muscular monster, but she simply batted at the air and turned away.

Great.

A zealot desperate to appease me on one end, and a lazy bum who ignored me on the other.

These were my strongest monsters...

I turned my attention to Hector and Chloe, the two skeletons who couldn't be healed unless given chaos energy or leveled up.

Probably time to add a new addition to that roster. But first, let me deal with this blinking notification.

Defend Your Mana Core!
The heart of your dungeon is new and weak. It must be given time to grow and strengthen!
Defend your heart for at least three days!
Reward: + Minion Capacity Increase
Unlocked: Dungeon Management Panel

What?! DEFEND?!

Dungeon Management Panel!
{Inactive} Dungeon Heart Lvl.01
HP: 850/850 (Weakened)

More micromanagement... Ugh. I wish I could have an assistant take care of all this.

Suddenly, a pulse—a strange feeling washed over me, wrapping around my being to coat my rubber body.

You have been marked!

Huh?

AW CRAP!

Suddenly, at the edge of my domain, monsters—skeletons, slimes, spiders—creatures pouring out of the tunnels in mass from every direction!

Battle stations! BATTLE STATIONS! GET UP! GET UP, YOU LAZY CROC!

Chapter 22

Sitting Duck

*A*ttack! *Attack! We're under attack!*

Mustering my minions for war, pandemonium broke out. My slimes, spiders, and two skeletons fought against the horde clambering through my traps and fortifications.

Monster against monster, my upgraded cleaning slimes attacking and melting creatures stuck in silk traps, clambering over bone walls, or trying to use the green water below to assault me.

Fortunately, I had planned for such a contingency and had created a neatly patterned web of silk to catch any lurkers in the sludge.

Still, their numbers were amassing, growing in size, while I, on the other hand, had limited defenders.

Oh man, I shouldn't have sent Slimey off to clean!

'LORD HIRO?! HOW DARE YOU, UNWORTHY SCUM, TREAD UPON HIS SACRED GROUND! I WILL DISSOLVE YOUR FLESH AND FEED YOUR CARCASS TO THE SEWERS BELOW!'

Ah. There's Slimey.

Go! Get them! DEFEND ME, MINIONS!

Slimey entered the fray like an angry blue tidal wave, a holy water nymph displaying her fury to the intruders who dared to step foot onto my domain.

The mass of enemy skeletons was immediately dissolved, purged from the floor with holy energy, while anything else that dared to get in Slimey's way was caught in her body and turned into a bubbling cleaning solution.

At least from one front, the other two sides were swarming with creatures, their numbers including monsters I didn't even know existed on this floor!

Dave! DAVE! DAVE, GET UP, YOU DAMN LAZY OVERGROWN GATOR! GET UP! WE'RE BEING INVADED!

The large croc-girl lazily rose out of bed, her hair a mess. Scratching her back, the monster's green eyes darted over to me, looking at me for a moment before yawning and rolling back over.

OH, COME ON! DO I NOT HAVE ENOUGH GYM BADGES?! WAKE UP!

I began to squeak angrily, pinging Dave repeatedly with my **Squeaker-Location** until she started groaning and huffing.

Sensing my frustrations—or perhaps having had enough of Dave's behavior—Slimey suddenly broke away from the conflict, moving to encircle me before reforming her body and reaching out. She picked up Dave's bed, along with the croc herself.

'LORD HIRO GAVE YOU AN ORDER!' Slimey screamed, throwing the lizard-girl towards a horde of skeletons climbing over one of my bone fences.

Dave landed in a heap, rolling and knocking over several monsters, while the lizard-girl let out a confused and bewildered whine that vibrated through my body before she began to get attacked by our enemies.

Fortunately, Dave wasn't a complete dunce. The ten-foot-tall monster girl stood up, shrugging off the attacks with ease before unleashing a roar of fury.

About time!

With one tunnel occupied, I turned my attention to the other fronts, watching as my traps worked to entrap, snare, and slow the enemy's advance.

An ounce of prevention was worth a pound of cure!

But there was still the problem of their numbers...

Oooooh, I should have moved into that catacomb chamber!

Suddenly, Slimey began to bubble and shift, her health pool rapidly shrinking, much to my alarm. But my concern quickly turned to astonishment.

She split into three smaller versions of herself—one wearing the nun outfit that was now oversized on her, and the other two naked.

The naked ones took off, racing towards the other tunnels to lead my defenders, while Slimey scooped me into her arms and held me close, her oversized sleeves draping over me like a blanket.

'Be not afraid, Lord Darling. None shall hurt you whilst your most loyal servant still stands.' Slimey cuddled me close in her miniaturized form.

Oddly, instead of comfort, I felt a strange sense of danger—not from the monsters, no, but rather from my champion herself. Her voice sent a tingle down my metaphysical spine.

Clink.

Huh?

Suddenly, something black was around my rubber neck—a band of some kind that clicked audibly into place.

Slimey... What is this? I scrutinized the shackle around my neck that ended with it attached to Slimey's wrist.

'A symbol of our ironclad bond, Lord Hiro. I even cleaned it for you.'

That's... beside the point. Slimey... these are handcuffs. Where did you get handcuffs from?

'Oh, I found them whilst cleaning! Humans apparently give circles to their companions to represent their bonds! And it fits so well around your neck, darling!' Slimey laughed, brandishing a wicked smile as the death rattles of various creatures echoed through my territory.

Around Slimey and me, the invaders were being eviscerated—Slimey's copies making short work of the under-leveled hordes, with Dave thrashing around and smashing everything nearby with its large tail.

It made for an odd scene, to say the least, one made no less peculiar by the Slime with menacing eyes holding me close to its body as it laughed maniacally.

After cleaning up the battlefield, it was time to inspect and repair the traps while analyzing my losses.

Three slimes and four spiders were gone, with Chloe and Hector having nearly been destroyed. But thanks to the experience earned from defending the base, both had leveled up, repairing their white bodies.

Peace to the fallen.

My fighting force was strong—stronger than any monster I'd encountered thus far. But how long would that luck hold? I didn't know. And it had only been thanks to my spider minions that we had managed to minimize the casualties.

Slimey and Dave's actions aside, the spider silk now at my disposal had played a pivotal part in our defense.

I wasn't quite sure how I remembered to build the traps I did—only that the blueprints came to mind. Blueprints that were helpful in building web snares, spike traps, walls, and pits.

Speaking of pits, riding atop my now-reformed Slimey, I made my way to one such pit.

A large hole had been dug into the sewer ground, with swords planted blade-up at the bottom.

In it, a multitude of creatures I'd seen a few times in my past life but hadn't encountered before as a rubber duck—capruxas, they were called. Four-legged monsters the size of a small dog mixed with a lizard. They were green, with bulbous eyes, and their heads sprouted little black horns, crowning their skulls, which featured a sharp, powerful beak.

A few of them were still squirming around, impaled but still alive, gravity having failed to do its job in piercing their strong hides fully.

Slimey quickly corrected that, earning a level in the process.

Not all pits, however, were murder holes. In other areas, I had devised a snare system made from bricks for weights, bones, and spider silk. These weren't intended to capture creatures like slimes or spiders, but to halt troop advances—potentially drafting them into my army.

Or capturing a wayward human, if one could be so lucky.

I made my way to one such hole, eyeing the capruxas within. My knowledge of the little green lizards wasn't the best, but as far as I remembered, they were like snapping turtles—albeit ones that could grow to be upwards of ten to twenty feet and liked to consume minerals.

But that begged the question: *where had they come from? Why hadn't I seen them before?*

Granted, a large portion of my floor still hadn't been explored, but with all my monster slaying and collecting, I should have come across at least one or two by now...

In any case, another fine addition to my collection, I supposed.

I reached out, my consciousness brushing against the minds of the capruxas trapped in the pit, squirming around.

You. Are. Mine! I commanded, expecting the same result I'd gotten from dominating so many other monsters, yet oddly... this time it was different. There was resistance, like I was fighting against something—like the feeling I got when I dominated the spiders.

Could it be that there was another dungeon core nearby? Were these its minions? Was that what had marked me? Was it angry that I had intruded on its domain?

Again, so many questions were unanswered, and it warranted a deeper investigation.

I tried dominating the trio of capruxas again, this time putting more of my will into it. Their minds folded, and three additional monsters joined my army.

You have tamed a new minion!
What is this creature's name?

Kappybara. Obviously, with the other two named Cappy 1 and Cappy 2, respectively.

With their strong beaks, they would no doubt be useful in expanding my territory—breaking walls, excavating new paths, perhaps even opening the crumbled exit leading out of the catacombs.

Possibilities. Possibilities.

But first, I needed to replenish my army, level them up, and prepare for the coming swarms. If there was another dungeon core nearby directing this attack, it would no doubt be hard at work gathering monsters for another go at me.

Which was fine. My minions could use the experience, after all.

My only concern so far was whether that dungeon core possessed a champion like I did—whether it had monsters under its command that were a cut above the average minion.

If so, it would be a losing situation, if ever there was one. No. We needed to prepare.

I gave my order to Slimey, who eagerly obliged, almost frantic to fulfill my commands.

If another dungeon core wanted war, so be it. After all, it had done a poor job of keeping the sewers clean. Now it was my turn to take over, and I would be sure to clear out the filth.

Observing the rubber duck, a large spider with yellow eyes lingered at the far edge of its "domain," clinging to the shadows alongside a dozen red-eyed tarantuals that watched as the bath toy directed its champion.

Rubbing its feelers together, the yellow-eyed spider emitted a command, broadcasted on a frequency undetectable by the human ear. It was an order to be relayed back to its queen.

The yellow-eyed spider was an evolved monster—two steps above the blind tarantuals the rubber duck had stolen from the Matriarch. Yet, despite its size, it wasn't strong. On the contrary, it was quite weak. Its abilities were not focused on combat, but on probing, scouting, and commanding.

The red-eyed spiders quickly dispersed, moving silently through the shadows to carry out their task. Their mission: to ensure that, if attacked, at least one would make it back to their queen.

Chapter 23

A Peek at What Lies in the Shadows

A day passed with sporadic attacks happening intermittently, likely just probes, given the varied angles of invasion and the monsters' movements along the edges of my domain. They seemed focused on testing my fortifications, cutting through my tripwires and setting off my pitfalls.

While this was a problem, it did give me some breathing room—at least they weren't pressing deeper into my territory, which gave me the opportunity to level up my army and reinforce my defenses.

With the attacks being relatively low in intensity, I had Slimey catch the ruffians—mostly spiders—and drag them back for my other minions to finish off.

The goal was to level up Hector and Chloe, as well as my spiders, hoping for an evolution.

Hector had already reached level nine, while Chloe was at eight. Spooderman was at level six, and my new reptile excavator—tasked with digging a tunnel—was at level five.

For the moment, I focused on Hector, mainly because I wanted to use **Minion Synchronization** on him.

Though Hector didn't possess muscles or ligaments, he was still able to swing a sword hard enough to deal significant damage, thanks to the magic that empowered him.

It was my hope that leveling him up would unlock further potential, allowing me to utilize his body for the war effort.

So, I had Slimey deposit monsters, which Hector immediately skewered with a spear made entirely of metal, gleaming in its immaculate cleanliness, scrubbed free of any rust.

Like all things should be, Slimey efficiently dissolved the monster remains, keeping my domain spotless.

Minion, Hector has reached the level cap!

Suddenly, the blue orbs that constituted Hector's eyes flickered out, and the skeleton collapsed into a pile of bones.

Great... Do all monsters go through this when they evolve? Hmm... What would happen if I maxed out Slimey before evolving her?

'Hiro, darling, if you wish, I can duplicate myself and hunt down those misguided and unenlightened cretins who fail to recognize your bountiful grace.' Her voice was affectionate as she lovingly stroked my rubber head. *'I can reach the level cap if you so desire, my lord darling.'*

Wait, can you read my thoughts?

'Of course not, my lord. We are bound by a sacred union. Your goals are my goals. It is only natural that your most loyal, humble, and obedient servant knows what you desire.'

Riiiiiight.

...

...

...

I wasn't sure how comfortable I was with Slimey being in my head.

'Worry not, master! I shall strive to be as non-invasive as possible!' Slimey quickly reassured me, pulling me into a tight hug.

Uhhhh, yeah... somehow, I didn't feel like the master here, especially with this collar around my neck.

'Do... you not like my gift, Lord Hiro?'

Suddenly, Slimey's color shifted, the creature's pale pink skin turned blue before fading into yellow.

Uhhh.

'Do.

You.

Not.

Like.

it?'

Slimey asked again, but this time, her voice turned menacing, her eyes widening as she glared at me.

Uhhhhh. Nooo. It's lovely. The best gift I've ever been given.

'You've been given other gifts? Who is giving you gifts?' Slimey asked, hovering dangerously close, her eyes nearly touching my rubber shell. *'Can I see them?'*

Uhhhhh. Nooo, the only gift I've gotten is the one from you. The only one I need. So, of course, it's the best! I sent back, watching as Slimey's color shifted back to blue.

'Oh, lovely, darling! I'm glad you like it!'

Yup! Yup! Great. Slimey, let's get back to work.

'Of course, my lord. I am here to fulfill your every desire.'

Great. I turned my attention back to the pile of bones when suddenly, a notification appeared.

Minion, Hector is trying to advance to Skeleton Rogue!

Oh?

Unfortunately, the requirements have not been met!

Oh.

Skeleton Rogue Requirements:
Pounds of Bones: 0/40
Weapons (Daggers): 0/2

Huh. Looks like I can't pick a class for the skeleton. Do they choose their own class?

So, I just need to gather more bones—and two daggers. Simple enough. I should have a few daggers in my inventory.

I ordered Dave over. The large gator reluctantly obeyed me for once, moving to collect bones, which it nonchalantly dropped on top of Hector.

Congratulations! The requirements for Skeleton Rogue have been met!

Suddenly, Hector's status changed, a white glow swirling over the pile of bones.

Moving on, Slimey and I went about patrolling my territory, resetting traps, catching ruffians, and feeding them to my other minions.

While the idea of having Slimey reach max level and evolve was appealing, it actually terrified me. So instead, we focused on raising my tarantual spiders and Chloe, my other skeleton, who was undergoing the same metamorphosis that Hector was.

Except...

One small hiccup.

Minion, Chloe is trying to advance to Skeleton Mage!

Ooooh.

Unfortunately, the requirements have not been met!

Awww.

Skeleton Mage Requirements:
Pounds of Bones: 0/20
Arcane Focus: 0/1

Crap.

A magic user would be a powerful addition to my forces...

But an arcane focus... From what little remained of my knowledge, I knew that mages needed a focus or something similar to conduct their magic—something physical through which they could channel their power, to avoid exploding or ruining their magic circuits.

Funny that the skeleton named after the magician of our party would choose mage as their vocation, while Hector chose rogue.

Coincidence? Or were they influenced by my memories?

Whatever the case, I was left with a conundrum: *What constituted an arcane focus? And where would I find one?*

I didn't know. From what I could recall, they were typically gemstones mounted on staffs... then again, there was that one demon wizard who used a book.

What was his name? Zack? Zac? Zatch? Zatch Kell?

Anyway, would a gemstone suffice?

Man, I wish I had an encyclopedia or something. Chloe was always good with random facts and knowled—Can I help you, Slimey?

'Who are you thinking about, darling?'

A companion of mine.

'A female one?'

Suddenly, an odd chill descended along my rubber duck spine. *Uhhhhhh.* Somehow, I felt like I was in danger.

I doubled down.

Yes, a companion of mine from ages past. From my former life. I sent, after all, I was the mastermind here! Why was I afraid?!

Slimey opened its mouth, forming sharp teeth that solidified thanks to its skill, creating a terrifying visage.

Ah… that's why.

'Tell me more about this companion, my darling!'

Uhhhhh. Screw it.

Yes, she was a companion of mine.

I decided to regale Slimey with my tale, or at least, what little I remembered of it.

But just as I was about to, a sinister feeling washed over me—a burst of mana as my consciousness picked up the presence of a monster I had yet to encounter.

A red-eyed spider.

The tarantual was twice the size of my spiders, with beady red eyes and large appendages that ended in razor-sharp, scythe-like talons.

And it wasn't alone.

Ah, about time the actual army showed up.

Let's see what we're dealing with.

Like a tidal wave, they came—at least two dozen of them—smashing through my bone walls, climbing around my traps, and slashing through the webs that coated the roofs.

DAVE!

For once, the croco-girl stood at attention at my command, glaring at the intruders and charging toward the monsters.

Slimey! Support! Let's get in there!

'*Yes, my lord.*'

Riding atop Slimey, I joined the fray. There wasn't much I could do in my rubber duck form, so instead, I took control of Dave.

The first time I had done so, it was a jarring experience—an overwhelming sense of fatigue washed over me as my mind overlapped with hers.

It was different from taking over Hector. Dave was all muscle—strong, nearly overflowing with life force. The opposite of Hector, who was cold, unfeeling, and had no sense of touch or direction. And the sense of sight... it was different. Not to mention having a tail!

Of course, the only thing on Dave's mind was sleep, along with an odd sense of... longing?

Synchronizing with Dave, I moved my massive body forward, charging into the crowd of red-eyed tarantuals.

I slammed down with my talons, squashing the bugs, ignoring their claws as they scraped against my scaly body.

Unlike their hardened appendages and the front end where their mandibles lay, the spiders' bodies themselves were very squishy—at least their bulbous backs were.

Tearing through them, I could feel their exoskeletons crumbling in my palms. Sweeping them away with my tail, I could feel their guts spill across the floor—and the pain! The pain of their sharp teeth and talons piercing my skin!

The carnage was... exhilarating.

Nothing I had known so far came close to finally being able to stretch, to finally being able to fight! To speak! TO ROAR!

And then it ended, my body back in my shell, leaving Dave to handle the rest of these upgraded minions.

Leave one alive, I ordered, having Slimey return me to my dungeon heart.

I observed the conflict, watching as Dave crushed the enemy vanguard. Although she was taking damage, it was nothing Slimey couldn't heal.

Before long, there was only one red-eyed tarantual remaining, held aloft with the creature snapping wildly despite its legs being smashed and broken.

I ordered Dave to gingerly bring the monster to me, to hold it aloft as I reached out, my will touching the creature and pricking against the will of the master it served.

It hadn't occurred to me until recently, but I realized that if I could steal one of the enemy dungeon core's minions... then I could order that minion to show me where my foe was.

However, unlike the lower-level monsters, the bond this red-eyed spider had was stronger, more concrete—a will that fought back against my intrusion.

Then it happened. My consciousness rapidly stretched, moving at insane speeds as I momentarily shifted, my mind now within a being that saw through a hundred eyes.

I was... a matriarch. A leader. A mother. A horror entrenched in the depths of the castle.

A being that had grown too large and whose sole purpose now was to direct the brood and produce more.

To expand.

But to do so, I needed food. Nourishment. More than what the low-level monsters scurrying beneath my talons could offer.

Through a hundred eyes, I peered into the abyss, sweeping my gaze across my lair, my brood—the thousands of spiders crawling around a cavern filled with glowing gems and kennels stuffed with capruxas.

My livestock.

And then I was back, the enormity of what I was dealing with crashing down on me.

Ah... crap.

Suddenly, a furious roar—a shriek—sounded out from the depths of the abyss surrounding my domain. A cry that spoke with hatred, fueled by the desire to destroy that which had invaded it.

Hey, but on the plus side, gems for Chloe!

Chapter 24

Fatal Funnel

S creams.
The echoes of fury bounced off my cavern walls, the sheer anger vibrating my rubber body as the tarantual matriarch reacted poorly to my mind intrusion.

Oops.

The entire sewers rumbled, the brick and mortar that had stood the test of time for hundreds of years violently shaking, dust and crumbs of the structures falling all over my territory.

They were coming—an army. I couldn't see them, but I knew, instinctively, that before long, a thousand spiders would be upon me, flooding my territory.

AHHHHH! THIS IS THE WORST! WHAT DO I DO? WHAT DO I DO? WHAT DO I DO?!

Okay. Calm down. Let's balance this out. Decide on a plan of action. Staying entrenched is completely out of the question. The spiders can crawl on any surface. The waterway is out of the question because of the fish down there, and I'll be DAMNED IF I TOUCH THAT SEWER GUNK!

Should I attack? Launch a counteroffensive?

Twenty against hundreds... that would be suicide!

Guess it's time for Operation Alamo...

SLIMEY!

'Yes, Lord Hiro?'

Operation Alamo! Prepare to move out! We make for the catacombs! All units, prepare to march!

'Yes, my lord! YOU CRETINS! GET TO WORK! LORD HIRO HAS GIVEN US ORDERS!'

A new plan. Well, a contingency plan that involved retreating to a fortified secondary location in case everything went bad.

Unlike my pylons, which I could deconstruct at will, my dungeon heart couldn't be destroyed on a whim. But! I could move it. The issue, however, was that when I did, it paused the timer for the quest, adding more time to the quest itself until I reconstructed my pylons.

Still, it didn't matter too much, so long as I could move it.

I ordered Slimey to take hold of all my stockpiled weapons. The slime expanded her form back into a blob, absorbing the steel, comatose skeletons, and various supplies scavenged from the sewers, with strict instructions not to dissolve. Thankfully, with her new levels, Slimey was able to turn off her innate holy attribute against my minions, allowing them to be absorbed.

Dave carried my other slimes, the vast majority of the creatures sticking to the bed she strapped to her muscular back, while her hands held my mana heart.

Moving quickly and with purpose, my menagerie of creatures made its way to the sewer pipes—the ones leading upwards to the catacombs—where we quickly made our way back into the chamber that had been sealed off.

Thankfully, there weren't many skeletons or much resistance to deal with, and we arrived just in time as the Spider Matriarch's minions reached my now abandoned domain.

I quickly destroyed my pylons, disbanding my territory in the process before staking a new claim.

Sadly, I wasn't refunded the mana expenditure from my previous claim, leaving me manaless. But it didn't matter; the battlefield had been shifted, and now the odds were a bit more in my favor.

The catacomb chamber had only two entrances, but with one of them blocked, there was only one way in. And that way was through a long tunnel—a fatal funnel, as Hector would call it—that was riddled with traps, pitfalls, and strings set up by my minions in between fortifying my previous location.

Fortunately, the plan was simple, albeit risky.

All it required was Slimey blocking the singular entrance with its body, creating an impassable wall of dissolving slime.

A coward's tactic? Perhaps.

But there was no way I was going to confront a hundred spiders head-on with defeat guaranteed.

I ordered Dave to set the dungeon heart in the center of the chamber as I reestablished my domain.

My senses immediately spread out, encompassing the nearby hallways and even the blocked passage at my flank.

I could see them—the six-legged arachnids, the monsters—a tidal wave composed of hundreds of spiders, all directed in my direction.

Slimey!

'At once, my lord!'

Slimey quickly moved, her gelatinous mass filling the cavern entrance and solidifying.

But that wasn't the end of my plan. To simply sit and wait?

No.

Slimey, like many of my slimes, possessed Slime Bullet, a skill that allowed my minion to fire fluid from her body at high speed, turning her own mass into violent projectiles.

And with her body filling the entire circumference of the only entrance to my new domain...

Heh.

Slime go... brrrrrrr.

The ravenous hordes of arachnids were turned into chunks, the only ones surviving being the vanguard red-eyed spiders at the forefront.

Yet they too eventually fell. While resistant to physical damage, each bullet fired by Slimey was infused with her holy body, allowing the attacks to punch through the armored arachnids.

DIE BUGS! DIE! DIE! DIE! AHAHAHAHHAA! HAVE A NICE CUP OF LIBER-TEA!

Ehem.

Weird. Where did that come from?

Anyway, after CTR-ALT-DELETE-ing the first few hundred spiders, the tidal wave of arachnids suddenly halted their advance, turning around and fleeing back into the pipes toward the sewers.

And it was a good thing too.

Having Slimey use **Slime Bullet** actually cost her health points— each shot fired meant another bit of herself lost.

Standing at a thousand and twenty-six health points, Slimey had fired well over a thousand rounds of slime from her body, leaving my champion at half health, with her form a bit smaller than usual.

With the enemy beaten back, it was time to deploy the cleanup crews. After all, a clean home is a happy home, and no one wants bug guts coating their hallways.

Sending out my minions, I had my spiders collect the chitin from their larger cousins, and the slimes mopped up the green goo. Dave, on the other hand, was allowed free roam to munch on the still-twitching bug carcasses.

'dID I dO Gweed Lawd HirO?' Her words were slurred and discombobulated, as if she were drunk, but with the effort she'd put in beating back our enemies. I knew it was just a symptom of her diminished health pool.

Yes, you did very well, Slimey. I'm proud of you.

At my words, Slimey's form suddenly unsolidified and turned into a large, vibrating pink puddle that splashed onto the floor.

'Huehuehuehue.' Slimey wiggled happily. *'I livF to surve mAsHter!'*

Riiight.

Moving on, I turned my attention to the pile of hardened chitin at my side just as a new notification hit my mind, my interface lighting up.

Minion, Hector has evolved from Minor Skeleton to Skeleton Rogue!

Suddenly, the pile of bones deposited beside me began to shift, the skeletal remains rising to stand with twin daggers in its hands.

Oddly, the skeleton crossed the daggers over its chest before bowing a bit more personality than I was used to from the undead.

Suspicious, I reached out, probing its mind. Yet, unlike my other monsters, there was still no consciousness to speak of. Instead, there was a feeling—like something warm buried beneath the coldness of undeath.

Disappointing, to say the least. And here I was, hoping for another guy to talk to.

I opened my minion manager, sorting my minions by strength first to better organize what I was looking at, hiding the others under my control so I could focus specifically on my heavy hitters—my A-Team.

Minion Registry
Slimey: Holy Super Slime Lvl.14
Title: Hiro's Champion
HP: 1026/2050
MP: 185/400
Dave: (???) Lvl.02
HP: 550/550
MP: 40/40
Spooderman: Lesser Tarantual Lvl.06
HP: 90/90
MP: 150/150
Hector: Skeleton Rogue Lvl.01
HP: 100/100
MP: 10/10
Chloe: Minor Skeleton Lvl.10
HP: 100/100
MP: 0/0

Oh! Reviewing Hector's skills, I realized the rogue wasn't very tanky, but what he lacked in health and mana points, he more than made up for in skills.

Which was good. My roster now included a thief-type monster—something I could use to... procure useful goods.

And what could be more useful right now than one of those many gems kept in the cavern of the Spider Matriarch?

A bold plan? Perhaps. But the key to augmenting my forces lay in acquiring new resources and materials. If there wasn't enough experience for my minions to grow, then I just needed to equip them with proper gear to strengthen their weaknesses.

I turned my attention back to the neatly stacked chitin plates, ripped from the carcasses of the dead arachnids, and to Slimey, who was still wiggling happily while the muscular croc-girl munched loudly on bug meat.

An idea began to form in my mind—one of an armored gator and an armored Slimey.

Imagine, Slimey and Dave—draped in armor! The two monster girls, impervious to enemy attacks! OR AN ENTIRE ARMY OF SLIMES! ARMORED SLIMES! ARMORED BUGS! ARMORED SKELETONS! A MASS OF HARDENED MONSTERS MARCHING THROUGH THE WORLD AND PURIFYING THE UNCLEAN!

Without realizing it, I began to squeak loudly, my **Squeaker-Location** sounding more like a twisted, diabolical laugh.

Wait. Am I a villain?

No, my thoughts of conquest are just to build a nice, clean utopia. Nothing wrong with that. Right? Right. Right! I'm totally right.

Oh, speaking of conquest, here's more spiders offering their armor to me now!

I quickly recalled my spiders and slimes, ordering Slimey to position for round two as I noticed a new type of spider on the field.

It was yellow-eyed, larger than the red-eyed ones, with heavier plating. But more than that, what drew my ire the most were the gems encrusted in its legs.

Hmmm.

An odd sense of foreboding began to take hold of me—something screamed danger.

There were three of them, marching at the forefront of the pack as Slimey solidified, their heavy footsteps clacking against the catacomb floor.

Slimey opened fire, her slime bolts smashing against their hardened carapaces, but unlike the red-eyed spiders, their armor held up as they marched.

AH! CRAP!

Then, they stopped. The trio of spiders raised their front legs and dug them into the ground, the gems encrusted in their bodies starting to glow.

Wait... Alarm bells began to ring in my mind, all my senses screaming danger as the enemy spiders began gathering mana! *THEY WERE MAGICIANS! MAGIC SPIDERS?! ARE YOU KIDDING ME?!*

Slimey! Disengage! Return! I ordered, but it was too late. Like field artillery, the trio of arachnids launched their salvo—a massive burst of mana that punched through my Champion, shattering her core.

SLIMEY!

Chapter 25

Gambit

Wrapped in spider silk, I sat in the mandibles of a large spider. One of the yellow-eyed ones, to be exact, at least from what I surmised from my constant squeaking.

My forces had been routed and defeated, my strongest champion laid low as I was brought, still squeaking, into a winding series of tunnels and caverns that eventually led to a massive chamber.

I was alone. No ally or friend, deep in enemy territory, without a single saving grace.

At least, to the enemy, anyway.

Pinging my surroundings, I picked up the leader of my assailants—a massive green and yellow bug, entrenched in a cavern wall with dozens of spiders clinging to its jagged, engorged body.

All around me were arachnids—an entire audience with variants I had already encountered, save for the two hulking spiders that stood even above the yellow-eyed arachnids.

One was fuzzy and blue, the monster staring at me with eight blue eyes. A phase spider of some kind, from what I could recall of my memories. The other was brown and gray, massive, almost the size of the Matriarch, with iron plates clacking with every minor movement.

A guardian variant of some kind, no doubt.

Suddenly, I was dropped on the floor, my body rolling across the cavern and letting out squeaks as the spiders knelt in reverence to their queen.

'Youssssss,' the Matriarch hissed, its voice echoing through my mind with her mandibles clanking as her steel-like forward-facing appendages struck the floor.

It can speak?!

'Dare to intruddde on my domain.'

"Squeak."

'Enter the mind of your superiorrr.'

"Squeak."

'Violate me and attempt to usurp my controlll.'

"Squeak."

'Now you are a king with no subjectsss. A sovereign with no nation. Another slave in my collectionnn. Another livestock.'

"Squeak. Squeak."

'I shall feast on you. And the treasure you brought. A fine addition to my collection.'

"Squeak. Squeak."

I turned my attention to my dungeon heart, the sphere joining the collection of other spheres that sat near the sovereign spider— trophies from other dungeons.

Ah... crap.

I was rolled across the floor, a yellow spider pushing me until I was before the Matriarch, which reached its massive head down and gently picked me up in its mandibles, where it began to suck on me.

"Squeeeeak."

Ah... so this is happening.

Almost immediately, I could feel my health and mana points draining, the vitality in my body leaving its rubbery shell, making me feel droopy.

Suddenly, the sucking ceased, my body covered in acidic drool.

Ick.

'*D-Delicioussss!*' the Matriarch suddenly moaned, its hundred eyes blinking in unison with the cavern rumbling.

Suck. Suck. Suck. Suck.

The sucking resumed, this time so vigorously that it felt as though my soul was being pulled out of my shell.

Well, it's good to know I'm delicious.

Now, you may be asking yourself, "Well, Hiro, how did you get into this predicament? Or why aren't you dominating the spider?"

Simple, really.

To answer your second question first, it's because I was unsure if I could. The mind of the Matriarch was tough, connected to the minds of the hundreds of thousands of arachnids under its command. There was no telling how it would react if I tried to invade its mind or what the spiders would do.

No, I would wait. Bide my time for the perfect opportunity to strike.

And to answer your first question:

I allowed myself to be taken.

After Slimey had taken a direct hit, the battle became a chaotic mess. Still, it didn't mean she was out of the fight—just severely injured with her mind fracturing.

Under my orders, Slimey retreated, falling back as more blasts of energy tore her being apart.

With the damage sustained from the constant use of slime bullet and the enemy attacks, Slimey could no longer hold her form and dissipated, her cores clacking to the ground with no goop to hold her together.

With the main obstacle to their advance gone, the swarm of arachnids marched on my domain, a horde baying for my rubber body. Yet, I couldn't leave Slimey behind. I couldn't have her be subject to the mercy of my enemies.

It was time for plan C. Operation Dunkirk.

I ordered Dave and most of my army to the front, not to hold the enemy off, but to rescue Slimey, fighting off the hordes with my lesser slimes firing slime shots to stem the tide long enough to gather my fallen champion.

With Slimey's cores wrapped in her dress, Dave fled, crawling into the exit that had been dug out by my capruxas at the other end of the chamber, along with Hector and several of my loyal subordinates, to retreat and fight another day.

But they needed time to flee—a distraction—and what better juicy morsel than the leader of an enemy army?

So, I and the lesser monsters under my command stood our ground, a final line of defenders.

I took a gamble, relying on the memories of old that surfaced. Combining what I saw of the Matriarch when I was in her mind, the knowledge I held of arachnids, and what I'd come to learn from my own tarantuals.

Spiders don't eat by munching. Not in the sense we know it. They use their mandibles to inject victims with acid, slowly turning their bodies into jellified goop that they then consume. The caveat of all this is that I have acid immunity!

I CAN'T BE MELTED!

Soooo, instead, I sat in the mandibles of the queen, the monster injecting me with poison and sucking on me, covering me in its sticky green bile.

Suck. Suck. Suck. Suck.

Gross. I'll make sure to make a mop out of your carcass.

Minion Registry
Slimey: Holy Super Slime Lvl.14
Title: Hiro's Champion
{CRITICAL CONDITION}
HP: 0122/2050
MP: 015/400
Dave: (???) Lvl.02
HP: 441/550
MP: 21/40
Spooderman: Lesser Tarantual Lvl.06
HP: 72/90
MP: 081/150
Hector: Skeleton Rogue Lvl.01
HP: 097/100
MP: 00/10
Chloe: Minor Skeleton Lvl.10
HP: 100/100
MP: 0/0

I opened my minion menu, eyeing the condition Slimey was in. I had ordered Dave to retreat to an upper level, taking with her my subordinates who survived.

Fortunately, despite being so far away from my retainers, I could still see what they were doing using one simple trick.

As I sat there, under the crushing pressure of the Matriarch, I reached out, activating **Minion Synchronization**—a skill that cost no mana.

Suddenly, my consciousness shifted, my mind now in the body of Hector.

I had one minute.

'Mast... r Hi...ro,' Slimey wept, my champion immediately recognizing my presence as my menagerie of monsters turned to the skeleton housing my spirit.

I do not have much time, I sent back, my spooky blue eyes gazing upon the small cluster of orbs clutched tightly to Dave's bloody chest. A sense of guilt took me, a sinking feeling sparking in the back of my mind as I gazed upon my injured companions.

Still, time was of the essence. There was work to be done.

Heed my orders, followers of Hiro. Hunt, recover, and grow stronger. Work together so that we may end the tarantual threat that has slain so many of our companions.

Although they were monsters, I would be remiss to say I wasn't attached to them, because I was. These creatures were akin to children under my guidance and care. Children who were devoutly loyal to my whim and reason. At least, when they listen. And as their guardian, I owed it to them to take care of them, to see that they were at least well taken care of if they were to fight on my behalf.

'mAssterrr,' Slimey oozed, its mind weak and wobbly, breaking up into a chorus of voices.

Rest. You have done well. I'm proud of you. I'm proud of you al—

And then I was back in my rubber shell, stuck between the iron pincers of the Spider Matriarch that wiggled with joy, enjoying the treat that was me.

Suck. Suck. Suck. Suck.

*Good. It looks like it can't detect when I use **Minion Synchronization**. Hehehehehe.*

I let out a squeak, pinging my nearby surroundings once more as I plotted how I was going to take over this kingdom of arachnids, ripe for conquest.

Chapter 26

It's Time for My Training Arc!

Skill Level Up!
Minion Synchronization Lvl.03!
Dungeon Skills
Domain Expansion: 0/1
Sustained
MP Cost: 500

Radiate your will and designate a nearby area as part of your domain. If there are other competing claims to the area, the strongest will prove victorious.

Designate Minion Lvl.01: 0/10
MP Cost: 20 (Per Minion)

Creatures you target must make a wisdom-saving throw against you. Upon failing, the creature is forcibly placed under your command.

Minion Synchronization: Lvl.03
Cooldown: 12 Hours

Synchronize your senses with a loyal minion to take control of the target for three minutes. Duration scales with skill level, and effectiveness scales with the bond.

Back in my rubber body, I felt a sense of giddiness as my skill leveled up.

Suck. Suck. Suck. Suck.

For days, weeks, months—every twelfth hour on the dot—I took control of Hector. The only reprieve I had from the acid-covered mandibles wrapped around my body, sucking on me as if I were a lollipop.

In my captivity, the matron spider had become... enraptured with me. Not like how Slimey was, but more like how a child enjoys their favorite candy or a baby with their binky.

Come to think of it, do babies in this world have binkies? I couldn't recall, but the analogy still stands.

Suck. Suck. Suck. Suck.

As time passed, I was regenerating faster than she could suck me off. Not that she was trying to destroy me. I had acid immunity, not piercing immunity, so I was still completely at the mercy of the Spider Matriarch.

One wrong move, and she could pierce my body with her steel-like mandibles.

So, I bided my time. Observing, silently, planning, plotting, training. Occasionally being made to involuntarily squeak as she squeezed me randomly.

Of course, I wasn't the only one improving my skills.

From my confinement, I directed my minions—my army in waiting—carving out my future kingdom in the halls of the Demon Lord's castle.

While I couldn't subjugate new minions given my captivity, I instead focused on those warriors I had. The veterans.

Minion Synchronization... Ready!

I willed the ability to activate, my subconscious supplanting itself into my minion of choice.

Into Hector.

I stood upright, my mind now viewing the world through the spiritual eyes of my skeletal minion.

I was a six-foot skeleton now, one wearing old metal armor, vintage leathers, wrapped in torn cloth stolen from the buried bodies of the damned.

'My lord!'

Flexing my broken gauntlet, my army turned to me, each monster bowing as Slimey demanded a show of fealty.

Even Dave was brought to heel, the large gator too slow and being blasted by Slimey's new skill, **Ellight**. A light magic skill, her spell struck the back of Dave's knees, bringing the monster down quickly to her knees.

'Lord Hiro Darling! You've returned! Every moment away was agony to my core!' Slimey exclaimed, bowing.

What is our status? I asked, the sounds of clashing echoing out in the distance, pricking my undead senses.

'Your army is engaged against gnolls, my lord. Nothing we can't handle,' she replied, as Dave grumbled, the latter unhappy with her treatment.

I opened my system, eyeing the spiders and slimes still under my command that had grown substantially thanks to the presence of higher-tier monsters.

Infected gnolls, blighted rat swarms, sickly goblins, skeletons, and even zombies. They flooded the upper catacombs, the undead biome radiating with the sickness of death. New monsters to be conquered and tamed, but that would be for the future. For now, they would serve the purpose of nourishment for my military.

Fortunately, Slimey was the antithesis of all things undead, making short work of the disgusting abominations that patrolled this stratum.

I pivoted, heading off to the sounds of battle, where a small cluster of gnolls were engaged against my slimes and spiders.

My blind tarantuals had grown eyes and evolved since my capture, getting bigger while my slimes conjoined into two larger slimes. At the forefront, Kappybara led the charge, the now-large capruxa sprouting horns that it used to gore a flailing gnoll.

Tightening my skeletal fingers around my steel daggers, coated in blue holy slime, I entered the fray.

Daggers weren't my preferred weapon of choice, but any warrior versed in the art of warfare makes do. And if there was one thing I was good at, well... It was warfare.

I dove into the crowd of gnolls, slashing and cutting, my weapons digging into the meat of the feral monsters that snarled at me as their flesh sizzled.

In a flash, I dispatched one, my dagger in the creature's temple as I ducked beneath an overhead claw.

I spun, crouching low, slashing the tendons of my assailant, the furry brown monster smashing onto the floor.

The gnoll shrieked, scratching at the ground as the monster attempted to scramble away, but it was pinned under the weight of my armor. Well, Hector's armor, as I sat upon the monster and inserted my daggers into its skull.

The last gnoll was quickly dispatched by my other minions: the slimes, spiders, and capruxa working in unison to bring down much stronger prey.

In all, the ordeal took no more than a minute.

Not my best time, but certainly not my worst.

Day in and day out, this was my training—to familiarize myself.

Getting used to a body so that I could rescue myself. Hector was a decent minion, but ultimately still a skeleton—one that didn't possess the talent for warfare that I did.

Unguided, Hector was lithe but not fast, its movements slightly sluggish compared to my direct control. But under my puppeteering, Hector transformed from a dull blade to a surgeon's scalpel.

And it was with that scalpel that I would carve my way out of the clutches of my enemies.

'Lord Hiro! So graceful! So magnificent! Your skill, astounding as usual, my lord!' Slimey exclaimed, kowtowing before my vessel of choice.

Arise, Slimey. Flattery will get you nowhere with me. There are more monsters to be culled, more levels to be earned, I admonished firmly, a slight odd sensation of clarity pricking my mind.

'Oh, lord! I mean not to offend! You are the greatest warrior known to the world, and your ascension is my only goal, master! I merely speak the truth!' Slimey persisted, her head raised with a crazed madness in her eyes. *'Please! Give the order to march on our enemies and free you from the unclean and unworthy!'*

Sigh... This again.

While the devotion was touching, it was also unsettling.

No. We must bide our time. This is the last I will tell you of this. Do not pester me further. The slime turned red, her skin billowing steam from the frustration building.

'My apologies, Lord Hiro! It was not my intention to be a pest! Please! Allow me to repent by crushing one of my cores!' She spit out

one of her cores and held it aloft, offering the sticky, slime-covered orb was offered up to me.

No. If you are truly sorry, aid your fellow comrades. Every moment you delay with these displays is another moment I must spend as a prisoner.

Something seemed to shift in Slimey, her usually wide eyes somehow getting even wider before she splattered her head against the floor.

'I UNDERSTAND, MY LORD!'

Oh... crap.

Suddenly, my worldview shifted, the duration of my skill at its end, with my senses cut off and dampened drastically.

Now, back in my rubber body, I let out a low, quiet squeak.

It wasn't really that bad when I thought about it. Actually, I was quite safe! Although I was akin to an unending lollipop in the maw of a massive spider, I was still protected, its own army of spiders shielding me from any threats.

The trade-off, however, was that the entire place was disgusting and filled with webs, my own form covered in sticky, acidic drool. Every moment in this accursed kingdom of webs infuriated me as I observed these filthy monsters living in squalor.

In short, it was disgusting. And I would not stand for such filth. No, they would be cleansed. Made to bend the knee and brought to heel to clean, and if they would not... then they would be eliminated and turned into immaculate sculptures and suits of armor.

This, I swore. It would only take time, however, as I squeaked and eyed the blue phase spider with gemstones on its body.

As with anything, it's always good to have a backup plan. That's why the alphabet was invented, after all.

Chapter 27

Infiltration

Skill Level Up
Minion Synchronization Lvl.08!
Dungeon Skills
Domain Expansion: 0/1
Sustained
MP Cost: 500

Radiate your will and designate a nearby area as part of your domain. If there are other competing claims to the area, the strongest will prove victorious.

Designate Minion Lvl.01: 0/10
MP Cost: 20 (Per Minion)

Creatures you target must make a wisdom-saving throw against you. Upon failing, the creature is forcibly placed under your command.

Minion Synchronization: Lvl.08
Cooldown: 12 Hours

Synchronize your senses with a loyal minion to take control of the target for eight minutes. Duration scales with skill level, and effectiveness scales with the bond.

Suck. Suck. Suck. Suck.

Once more, the familiar level-up notification flashed across my screen as I sat in the jaws of the Matriarch.

Roughly two months had passed since my captivity began, and in those two months, something had occurred that I hadn't accounted for.

I was tasty.

Suck. Suck. Suck. Suck.

TOO TASTY!

Through these past months, the Spider Matriarch had been sucking on my body every second of the day! It had become so bad that, during my routine squeaks, I could see the spider queen herself was significantly withered, the once hulking mass of chitin and bug meat now nothing more than a hollowed and starving shell of her once menacing stature!

Apparently, I was addictive, and any attempt from the other spiders to feed or offer food to the queen was met with disdain, the matron even laser-eyeing one of her yellow-eyed commanders!

So now a new plan was in play—my patience rewarded.

One to capitalize on the queen's weakened mind and addiction to my rubber body...

Wow, that sounded incredibly lewd.

Suck. Suck. Suck. Suck.

In any case, exploiting an enemy's weakness is Warfare 101! I just needed to pick my moment. From my constant scans of the surroundings, I knew the egg chamber was roughly thirty meters wide and a hundred meters tall—enough to accommodate the gigantic spider.

However, the tunnels leading out of the chamber actually connected to a single corridor that led back to the rest of the lower catacombs and sewers.

A potential kill zone.

My initial tactic in combating the bug menace had been a success—at least until the heavier spiders showed up, introducing a problem that my army faced: a severe lack of magical firepower.

Thankfully, I had the remedy.

And it lay in Hector's class and the gemstones coating the walls.

There were two ways out of this mess.

Either I dominated the phase spider, and by some grace, it wrestled me from the jaws of its maker and teleported me out,

Or the queen was slain during an all-out assault.

Suck. Suck. Suck. Suck.

Of course, I also factored in dominating the phase spider during the ensuing chaos, but I'd rather not leave my soldiers to die and be pursued by endless bugs.

So, the queen had to die. I was unsure if I could dominate her even in her current state. Rather than be at the mercy of the massive bug and her army, if I failed, I would even the playing field.

And it started with Hector.

Minion Synchronization... Ready!

Suck. Suck. Suck. Suck.

It was time.

I reached out, my consciousness supplanted in my skeleton once more.

Hector's bones shifted, the skeleton shivering like a well-oiled engine, no creaks in its joints thanks to the slime coating parts of his skeletal frame.

Eight minutes.

In and out.

That's how much time I had to infiltrate and retrieve a gemstone.

The thing to note about all undead is that they were all pretty unnoticeable thanks to their undead trait. With no life force to speak of, undead were able to move about virtually invisible unless in large quantities. The one thing setting most undead back from their potential as ruthless and effective killers was that they were all bloodthirsty, unfocused, sluggish. At least the lower-tier ones were.

But take away those negatives?

A scary thought. A recipe for a nightmare.

One that I would now become.

Name: Hector

Level: 13

Species: Skeleton Rogue

HP: 1300/1300

MP: 20/20

Skills:

Undead

Inconspicuous

Acrobatic

Play Dead Lvl.01

Souls Vision Lvl.01

Concealment Lvl.04

Trap Finding Lvl.01

Detect Prized Possession Lvl.02

Pilfer Lvl.02

Dash Lvl.03
Swift Step Lvl.03
Uncanny Dodge Lvl.02
Scarlet Kisses Lvl.03
Critical Damage Lvl.01

After one last system check, I piloted Hector's now naked body and was off, not wasting a single second as I trespassed into the Spider Monarch's domain.

Activating Hector's newfound concealment ability, I combined every element of stealth I had at my disposal to intrude unseen.

My body was now light, and the area around me warped. My skeletal form almost appeared wavy, even to myself, like a distortion caused by a gust of wind—perceivable, but at the same time, not.

Moving rapidly, visions of my time as a hero plagued my mind. More specifically, visions of me and Hector. Not the skeleton, but my companion of old.

Memories of the perverted master assassin, the days we would sneak into bars, steal money from nobles, and infiltrate the women's sauna.

Of course, the infiltrations always involved me trying to stop him, which would result in a cat-and-mouse chase, both of us getting caught and beaten up by Chloe and...

Hmm. An odd sensation—a name just out of reach, on the tip of my metaphorical tongue.

I dispelled my thoughts, continuing with the mission. Each step filled with purpose, I avoided the webs that could alert my captors.

Seven minutes left.

I crept quickly, but silently. The slime on my naked bones muffling any sound caused by my swift movements.

Six minutes left.

Damn, the pathway took longer than I thought. Then again, it had been two months since I was last carried through these cavern halls as a prisoner.

Now, I was a delver, a thief in the abyss, entering enemy territory to pilfer from my enemy's coffers.

Just like old times.

"Screk?"

Suddenly, I stopped, my body locked mid-pose as a spider shifted, looking in my direction.

Crap.

Thanks to Hector's acquired soul vision, I could see the energies of the spiders in the dark, allowing me to avoid the bulk of the monsters—either scurrying or idling about—with the concealment skills I possessed making me invisible.

Yet... this tarantual was staring at me. It was a red-eyed one, a tier two spider. Had I tripped a web? Had I accidentally triggered a trap I wasn't aware of? Or did it see through my skills?

No, of course not. Thankfully, **Trap Finding** registered the webs as a type of trap, alerting me if I triggered one. Still, it was staring at me. Almost as if aware I was there in the dark.

A moment passed, then another. Each second fading by, another one wasted.

As deep as I was, if it spotted me and alerted the others...

I held my metaphorical breath, a staring contest ensuing between me and the small spider that held me captive.

Then it moved, scurrying away.

I pushed forward. Nearly there, my skeletal eyes picked up the massive core of the Spider Matriarch sequestered at the far end of the corridor. Taking care to avoid the webbing at the entrance, I glided through, bypassing the hundreds of blind tarantuals that scurried about, my vision momentarily settling on my rubber body held captive.

Tsk! Every fiber of my soul wanted to stab the monstrosity, to be cleaned, to be free! TO ENACT VENGEANCE FOR COVERING ME IN ICK!

But that wasn't my objective.

Five minutes left. I acted quickly, heading toward the glowing gem piles and crystals, confident in my ability to remain unseen and avoid the hundreds of spiders scurrying about.

Suck. Suck. Suck. Suck.

In the chamber, I reached down, grabbing several small glowing crystals and pocketing them into a pouch crafted from the fabrics looted from various coffins littering the catacombs.

Four minutes left.

I turned to leave, observing the queen's champions—the phase spider and the knight—both unmoving despite my intrusion.

Then my undead gaze spotted the piles of dungeon cores. The beady hearts of defeated dungeons, all held captive by the sovereign arachnid, enraptured by my taste.

A risk, I know.

But... what if I could fashion a weapon from one? Dungeon cores were highly prized artifacts after all, and they made great conductors of magical energy. If I had a monster capable of using one...

The decision made, I shifted, stepping lightly behind the large blue phase spider, which stood oblivious to my presence. I was so close—too close. The furry hairs and encrusted gems on the arachnid were visible to my eyes.

Ick.

I reached out, grabbing one of the cores as I inwardly cringed. I could hear the Matriarch's sucking—the subtle *'suck, suck, suck, suck'* repeating over and over again.

Ugh!

I grabbed hold of a core, the little sphere of energy pulsing for a moment as it reacted to my touch.

Suddenly! An intrusion! The core attempted to dominate Hector! To remove my will!

I could feel the dungeon core's mind—not words or intelligence, but something cold and unfeeling, like a gush of ice-cold water smashing against my face nonstop. Each splash of mental pressure attempting to breach my defenses.

If I were just a monster, I would undoubtedly have lost Hector, yet I possessed something it did not. Something it couldn't replicate.

Human will.

And I would not lose to some two-bit defeated dungeon core.

I grabbed the core fully, a visible shine of light occurring as its advances were rebuffed.

YES!

Suck. Suck. Suck. Suc—

Suddenly, the cavern rumbled, and a sudden silence coated the entire chamber.

NO!

The Matriarch shifted, every spider that had been moving now stopping dead in their tracks to focus on one thing.

The intruder.

Me.

Ah, quack.

Chapter 28

Phase One

No—NO! Nonononononononoo!

Ducking (no pun intended), dodging, and weaving, I scrambled my way out of the cavern of spiders.

Upon being spotted, I was beset by horrors, the spiders swarming me all at once, with dozens of the creatures spewing webbing at me.

Uncanny Dodge activated, my skeletal body automatically shifting to avoid the attacks before I leapt over the armored, segmented appendage that tried to skewer me.

The queen remained immobile, aware of my presence but uncaring. Sadly, this attitude didn't extend to her honor guards. Her juggernaut immediately rushed me with its armored legs, while her magician teleported away to fire bolts of mana.

I hit the ground with the grace of a ninja ballerina, the juggernaut acting as an unwilling shield to the magical attack that smashed into its carapace.

Three minutes left.

It roared, and the juggernaut turned its body, taking off after me down the corridor with a hundred tiny spiders scurrying close behind.

To any outsider looking in, it was obvious I was screwed, but I had a plan—one that involved using the heavily armored spider to my advantage.

In front of me, a hundred critters blocked my path. An immobile wall I could not get through. Behind me, a giant juggernaut charged me with power that was sure to crush Hector and anything else foolish enough to get in its way.

An immovable wall of spiders and an unstoppable heavy object. Who would win?

Let's test it.

I slowed my advance, just as I was about to be smooshed between the two sides, and leapt, grabbing hold of the charging behemoth that sailed on by with my skeletal fingers.

In that instant, the wall of chitin proved not to be so immobile, collapsing immediately from the force of the juggernaut ramming into it. Bug guts quickly coated the cavern, the juggernaut only stopping when it finally hit the cavern wall.

But my path was clear now, a trail of insect genocide left in my wake.

Two minutes left.

I wasted no time, leaping off the juggernaut half-buried in the wall. I moved like a thief in the night, clutching my "acquisitions" that I had risked so much for.

Two minutes, two minutes, less than two minutes! The time kept ticking in my mind, every ounce of willpower I possessed funneled into placing one foot in front of the other as quickly as I could.

Every so often, a spider would leap out to attack, but unlike the original invasion and attacks I'd experienced previously, these spiders were uncoordinated, wild—no strategy to slow my advance, save for their last swarm that ended in failure.

I was nearly home free; I could see the entrance, the exit of the Spider Matriarch's domain.

One minute left.

Before I could finish the thought—

Huh?

Suddenly, I was flying. My body spun, tumbling through the air before crashing onto the smooth, stained floor of the sewer path.

CRAP!

It took me a moment to realize I'd been cut in half. The phase spider had appeared out of thin air, ambushing me with a single swipe of its clawed appendage, bisecting my spine.

My head refocused, my legs still running—until they hit a wall and collapsed. The spider crawled over me, hissing, its mandibles opening to crush my skull!

But what kind of Hiro would I be without a backup strategy?

Suddenly, the tension of the flowing sewer liquid broke, and a muscular, scaled monster leaped out of the green sludge with a roar. Dave smashed into the spider, its talons sinking into the blue creature's skull, catching it completely unaware.

Immediately, the blue monster attempted to teleport, to flee. It visibly blurred and pulsed with power, but thanks to the claws embedded in its skull, the skill failed. The spider crashed to the floor.

Take it alive! I ordered just as my timer ran out and my consciousness snapped back into the body of my rubber self.

The Matriarch's brood was in a bit of a tizzy, with a hundred tiny spiders scurrying about in panic. The queen, however, remained immobile, still sucking on me despite the carnage inflicted on her army.

Man... am I really that tasty? Maybe this is why Slimey is always holding me in its body.

I opened my minion registry.

Minion Registry
Slimey: Holy Super Slime Lvl.15
Title: Hiro's Champion
HP: 2350/2350
MP: 500/500
Dave: (???) Lvl.06
HP: 839/850
MP: 50/50
Spooderman: Red-Eyed Tarantual Lvl.10
HP: 190/190
MP: 150/150
Hector: Skeleton Rogue Lvl.13
HP: 0891/1300
MP: 03/20
Chloe: Minor Skeleton Lvl.10
HP: 100/100
MP: 0/0

With my prizes in tow, my army scurried off, phase one of my plan a success. An enemy officer was held hostage, and the commander's mind was left befuddled.

Oddly, a sense of giddiness took hold of me—one I hadn't felt in a while. A sublime feeling of having completed a mission successfully.

But this was only phase one of a multi-step operation.

I had dealt an unexpected and crippling blow to the enemy. Yet, despite the losses sustained, the Spider Kingdom still had hundreds, if not thousands, of troops hidden in the various caverns. The queen's armored and mage divisions remained intact, and her champion—though injured by the phase spider's attack—was still functional.

All these would be purged soon enough, as I bided my time, listening to the chorus of a thousand angry feet skittering against the floor.

ELSEWHERE, IN A BRIGHTLY LIT CAVE FILLED WITH BOOKS AND SKELETONS...

"Hmmmm." The red-haired man with cat ears, wearing a pink bathrobe, let out a sound as he scratched his back with the arm of a skeleton whose fingers moved back and forth.

In front of him stood a golden ornate mirror, sequestered between two massive bookshelves. The mirror showed him thousands of stories—various moving images of people in different stages of talking, fighting, or dying.

However, there was one story in particular that interested him the most: a still image of an acid-covered rubber duck.

"Well, look at him go! He's certainly making a go of things," Junith said, the Paladin of Death, as she took off her cat-eared helmet to shake free her bundled-up hair, caked in blood. She walked to a nearby couch, her blood-stained black greaves clinking with each movement, before she splayed out and stretched.

"I concur," said the Bookkeeper, scratching his chin as his massive white cat leapt off a bookshelf to land on his shoulder. "It may seem as though intervention isn't needed."

"Aw, but where's the fun in that!" an excited voice exclaimed from across the room, emanating from a pink-haired cat latched onto a skeleton sweeping the floor. "We should totally help him out! Give him some ULTRA skills! Undo his curse! Drop a cache of legendary weapons into his slime—oh! OH! OH! Or better yet! Let's send a dragon—NYAH!"

The pink cat's excited rambling was cut off by a skull lobbed at her head, sending the cat flying off its skeletal perch.

"Liza, why are you here?" The Bookkeeper groaned; the primordial god's left eye twitching.

"For the tea!"

"Tea?"

"You know! Entertainment!" Liza replied, shapeshifting into a cat woman with pink hair, golden eyes, and a bushy tail that swished back and forth as she hugged the red-haired man.

"Of course..." The archivist sighed, pinching the bridge of his nose. "Don't you have some mortals to trick into signing pacts or magical girls to make?"

"Eh, why do you hate me so? All I want to do is love you!" Liza exclaimed, rubbing her head against the scowling god. "Plus, I've got Luna and Artemis creating a new batch of Mystic Sailors for me."

"Typical lazy bum," Junith sneered. "Have everyone do your work for you."

"Of course! That's what middle management is for, you workaholic!" Liza shot back, sticking her tongue out.

Suddenly, the Bookkeeper snapped his fingers, and the two cat women vanished from his presence.

"Hmmm. Red."

"Yes, sir." A pillar of shadows manifested, revealing a pale, handsome man with crimson eyes, dressed in a business suit reminiscent of old-fashioned Earth attire. He stepped out of the darkness.

"What is Three-One-Eight doing?"

The crimson-eyed steward blinked, the gears in his undead mind churning.

"Are you referring to the one called Truck-kun?" Red asked, raising a brow.

"Ah, yeah," the red-haired man said, clapping his hands. The image shifted to a large red truck running a man over. "Bring him here. I may have a job for him."

Chapter 29

The Gang's All Back

Compatible Magic Catalyst Detected!

Inhabiting Hector once more, I stood amidst my crowd of monsters as a familiar blue spider screeched and moaned in the background of my army's hideout.

It was a small cove, located not too far from the Spider Monarch's territory and the upper strata. A cave dug into the earth by my capruxas and spiders, working in tandem to break and churn the rock until it could fit the totality of my army.

My forward operating base and staging area. A home, until we could assert dominance over the lower strata.

Placing the dungeon core on Chloe's bones, the item immediately resonated with my comatose minion. The core cried out—a ghastly sound akin to a banshee's wail—as shadows oozed out of the sphere in mass.

From Hector's soul vision, I could tell it was mana—a large quantity attempting to escape before it stopped mid-air, almost as if it were caught by an unseen force, before it was forcefully absorbed by Chloe.

Suddenly, a white light flooded my senses, an energy that washed over my very bones.

Minion, Chloe has evolved from Minor Skeleton to Skeleton Orb Mage!

The light faded, revealing a small white skeleton standing upright, with a red gem embedded in its spine and mythical runes carved along its skeletal frame.

Huh. It looked like it had skipped an evolutionary step. The dungeon core had proven to be more than enough for the evolutionary process, creating a class I'd never heard of.

Name: Chloe
Level: 01
Species: Skeleton Orb Mage
HP: 50/50
MP: 370/370
Skills:
Undead
Innate Phylactery
Spontaneous Caster
Mana Surge
Recorder
Mage Armor Lvl.01
False Life Lvl.01
Souls Vision Lvl.02
Telekinesis Lvl.02
Minor Illusion Lvl.01
True Strike Lvl.01
Ray of Sickness Lvl.01
Fire Bolt Lvl.01

Shocking Grasp Lvl.01
Chilling Touch Lvl.01
Impalement Lvl.01
Dust Blast Lvl.01
Decaying Touch Lvl.01
Bone Cage Lvl.01
Magick Bolt Lvl.01
Fire Infusion Lvl.01
Cold Infusion Lvl.01
Lightning Infusion Lvl.01
Necrotic Infusion Lvl.01
Fester Lvl.01
Levitate Lvl.01
Magic Chant Lvl.01
Gem Missile Lvl.01
Curse Lvl.01
Cause Fear Lvl.01
Mote of Light Lvl.01
Spark Lvl.01
Blunt Barrier Lvl.01
Bone Wall Lvl.01
Nightmare Lvl.01
Aura of Decay Lvl.01
Reverse Life Lvl.01

Oh! OH WOW! WHY DO YOU HAVE SO MANY SKILLS?! Phylactery? DID I GET A MINI LICH?!

Chloe bowed, the undead magician recognizing my presence in Hector.

Interesting. Yeah, I can definitely work with this!

Although exceptionally squishy with a low health pool, making Chloe a glass cannon, what she lacked in defensive properties, she more than made up for in skills and utility.

The stereotypical spellcaster. But more than that, I could already see the potential! The versatility unlike any other creature in my army!

I turned my attention to my monsters.

Dave, the crocodile girl clad head to toe in chitin and bones, armor held together by webs. My tank and warrior.

Slimey, my champion, my holy slime in her priestess outfit, with chitin plate armor over her body. My healer, who was glaring angrily at the skeleton mage, with the words *Look at me* playing over and over in the slime's mind so loudly that she didn't need to transmit them directly.

Spooderman and the others, each up-armored in bone or bug armor—my army.

It felt a bit redundant to stack chitin atop chitin, but better safe than sorry.

And then finally to myself—well, Hector. I looked down at my skeletal hands, wearing aged gauntlets. The metal, picked clean of rust, was still worn from the effects of time.

The gang's all back together, huh...

Slimey shivered, the slime woman suddenly hugging me, taking extra care not to inflict holy damage on Hector's body as a sense of melancholy struck me. I had... other companions. People besides Chloe and Hector. But... for whatever reason, I couldn't remember them.

I took a moment, turning to my army.

And then I saw them—my comrades, my friends. The people who had put their trust in me. The people I lost. Their faces all blurred, all lost to time. But I could see them, recognize them as they stood in rank and file between my minions. Specters, ghosts who had been invisibly haunting me all this time... each asking,

What did I do with their sacrifices?

And my answer, silence, as the apparitions faded away.

Did the world know what happened here? Did they know what happened to their champions? Chloe's grandfather, Hector's sister. Did they wait at their homes, spending the rest of their lives staring out windows, at roads, eyes looking up at the same sky, wondering what happened to the five hundred who died under my command?

But, well over two hundred years had passed. And even those left behind were long gone. No one to remember the tales of Ravenhawk Hector and Annihilator Chloe.

Everything was gone now... except for me and my sins.

Had I been stronger? Had I been faster? More tactical? Cautious?

Perhaps I would have never lost the ones I cared about.

I think that's why I challenged Barborall in the first place. Why I took up the mantle of "Hero." To protect them and this world I had come to love.

At least... I like to think that was the reason, Adam's plan aside. But... for the life of me, I can't remember the true reason I embarked on this journey.

No... I remember.

My fists clenched at my sides.

Even as much as I say I don't, I can remember.

It was for power. Recognition. The ecstasy of a job well done.

That was my muse.

In my previous life, I had nothing. A dead-end job in corporate hell. But here... endless possibilities.

And while everyone fought for each other, bled and cried to save their world, I deluded them all into entrusting their future with me. Pushing forward when I should have retreated. Inspiring everyone with false speeches and idioms. A con man sacrificing the brave to build a ladder for my own selfish ascension.

For my own selfish glory.

And what did I have to show for it?

A home of dust and ash. Cobwebs in corridors that held no warmth, and rivers that stunk of death and decay. Why was I still here? What was my purpose?

Was this Adam's punishment for my hubris?

Wouldn't it just... be easier to fade away?

No... If I did, then everyone that died would simply fade away... even if I couldn't remember their faces, even if I couldn't remember their names, I still remembered their deeds.

The good they did, the essence of what they were.

Heroes. Each and every one of them, as they deserved to be remembered. At least in the utopia I'll bring, there will be a nice and clean monument for those forgotten. Pine-scented, maybe.

Or maybe I'm just going insane. Or... am I already insane?

I just...

Two Minutes Remaining...

My timer blinked at the side of my vision, reminding me that I was running out of time.

Slimey, I called to my Champion while my mind was still here, before I slipped back into that cloudiness.

'*Yes, Lord Hiro?*'

Take Chloe and make sure she levels up. Have one of the slimes coat her body and weave her armor. She is now of great importance and vital to my operations.

Slimey's eye twitched at the word importance, the pinkish skin she imitated flickering a shade of yellow for a moment.

'Understood, my lord. Your will shall be done,' Slimey replied. Despite her face smiling at me, it felt as though the slime had grown four times as big, hovering over me with an aura that threatened to choke out my life.

And play nice, I added. Not to rub salt on the wound, but to ensure Chloe wasn't being tortured. Not that the skeleton could feel pain or anything, but the idea of my minion being abused made me sad.

'Of course, master,' she grumbled.

Dave.

The crocotaur girl looked up, bags clearly visible under her eyes as she yawned but held the phase spider in her arms, which had long since lost the strength to flee.

Good job, I sent. The green-haired giant seemed to shrink a little bit, hugging the defeated blue spider in her arms like a toy.

I decided to cancel my skill early, transferring back into my rubber shell to bide my time.

Suck. Suck. Suck. Suck.

Soon. Soon. Soon. The words kept appearing in my mind. Desires to clean, to purge, but most importantly, even as my mind darkened and the fog set back in, a desire to remind the world of the sacrifices made here and to turn this decrepit ruin into a mausoleum fit for my friends.

Suck. Suck. Suck. Suck.

Just a little more time.

Chapter 30

Down With the Queen!

One Month Later...

S uck. Suck. Suck. Suck.

In the maw of the Matriarch, I squeaked, pinging the cavernous surroundings now devoid of spiders. During my time of captivity, the queen laid no new eggs, fed none of her brood—her one and only purpose in life now devolved to sucking on my rubber body.

Her kingdom was now in despair. Her subjects were starving, dead, or docile, with most of her livestock of capruxas eaten by her minions.

Despite that, the mind of the matron spider wasn't broken. At least, not in the manner I wanted it.

In the month since Chloe's evolution, there had been a bug uprising—a small revolt—one to steal me away from the queen's jaws, to break her addiction, to rid her of the parasite that was me.

Yet that was quickly put down by the sovereign arachnid's large appendages and magical prowess, proving to me that the oversized bug was not to be taken lightly, even in her weakened and deprived state.

The battle had lasted mere seconds. The queen unleashed beams of mana from each of her hundred eyeballs. On top of her laser eyes, she also spewed acid, melting her own minions as she conjured dozens of magical sigils to shock, freeze, and set flame to the rebellion.

They never stood a chance.

Thankfully, with my acid immunity, I remained unharmed throughout the ordeal. The enemy numbers dwindled, and valuable intel was gained from being so close to the action.

Suck. Suck. Suck. Suck.

And now, with only her juggernaut and the few hundred loyalists that remained docile to her will, it was finally time.

I reached out, my mind delivering but a single command in the air that spoke one word.

Attack.

After what felt like an eternity, a purple smoke began to creep into the cavern, a poisonous smog that was by no means natural.

The queen shifted, reacting to the magical energy but paying no mind as she continued sucking.

Fun fact: spiders, like most insects, breathe oxygen. But they are the only ones that breathe simultaneously with lungs and a trachea, intaking air from the bottom of their bodies.

A bottom that touched the floor. *EHEHEHEHEHEE.*

Outside the Spider Monarch's domain, at the entrance of the cave, Chloe stood in a silk-spun gown, the skeletal mage emitting smog from its core as Dave, Hector, and my slimes worked in unison to generate a wind current using makeshift fans.

It was... comical, and perhaps not the most effective way to start an attack, but it worked.

And that's all that mattered.

I let out a squeak, my rubber sound pinging my surroundings as the various spiders skittered about in a mad frenzy.

They knew. Despite their queen's uncaring pacifism, the spiders still possessed self-preservation skills, and in their endeavor to save themselves, they scrambled out of the caves.

Just as planned.

Slimey was up, leading my slimes, acting as the vanguard with Chloe preparing a spell to cut the suffocating spiders' avenue of escape. With my pseudo machine gunners lined up, a torrent of death was unleashed, cutting the arachnids down mercilessly and whittling their numbers until the armored spiders appeared.

This wasn't going to be like last time.

I reached out, my consciousness hopping from my shell into slime-covered Hector as Chloe chanted, her body glowing with sigils before releasing her spell.

Fire Bolt.

With a simple spark, the smog ignited, and the entire cave exploded with flames that consumed every creature within.

Now, as Hector, I took off, racing into the flame-coated tunnel. Daggers in hand, I charged at the armored arachnids forming a phalanx, the insects unleashing magical attacks in my direction despite being on fire.

A testament to their devotion to their monarch? Perhaps. But it wouldn't matter as I removed their stain from the world.

I deftly dodged, shifting left and right, Hector's uncanny dodge ability augmenting my movements to avoid the magical attacks.

There was a millisecond delay—close calls where I'd almost get hit—but after months of piloting the skeleton, I finally knew how to account for the delay.

Avoiding a mana blast, I bounced off a nearby wall, using the shockwave of the explosion as a springboard to land on an artillery bug's head.

My daggers plunged into its head—one knife in its eye socket, the other in its maw. With one slick twist of my wrists, I popped its armored casing open to expose its brain.

Then I leapt, the bug phalanx distracted, attempting to intercept me—only for their injured companion's exposed brain to be crushed under Dave's fist.

Dave was behind me now, the ten-foot-tall crocodile girl leaping into the fray as I broke through the enemy ranks.

A phalanx bug charged at her, lifting its armored appendages, forcing Dave to catch both legs with her muscular arms bulging. As she engaged in a contest of strength, another phalanx bug charged, its arm cracking her chitin armor but inadvertently releasing an ooze.

Suddenly, slime shot out of the armor, entering her assailant's mouth.

The spider began to spasm, screech, and gurgle as the cleaning slime forced its way down the monster's throat, before solidifying and bursting the bug's organs from the inside out.

Dave let out a roar, stepping forward as Slimey healed her injuries, the crocotaurus lifting the armored arachnid with ease.

"DIE!" Dave screamed, the first I'd ever heard her speak. The green-haired giantess ripped the armored bug's arms off, spewing green ick everywhere before she began to beat the poor monster to death in a fit of rage with her new spindly weapons.

FORWARD! I commanded as my army charged through the smoldering flames.

Carving our way through, it wasn't long before we entered the queen's chambers.

DODGE! I ordered, and my monsters scattered immediately as the queen fired laser beams from her eyes while the juggernaut charged.

Six minutes. That's how much time I had.

Eyeing the queen, both she and my body remained unscathed from the smog explosion, no doubt protected by her magical power. The juggernaut, on the other hand, was looking crispy—an oversized brown bug, blackened and burnt all over, with wounds still sizzling.

Keep your distance and keep moving! Don't bunch up! I dictated, narrowly avoiding a beam of energy that shaved off part of my lower ribcage and disintegrated a slime.

My minions were flooding in now, the plan being to engage the juggernaut before taking on the monarch herself.

First, we needed to restrict its movements, which is where the slimes coating my body came in. Unlike the other blue slimes, these purified creatures weren't my minions but draftees, and they would serve the purpose I needed them for.

I grabbed one of the gelatinous masses adorning my body—the creature attempting to dissolve flesh off bones that didn't exist—and hurled it at the juggernaut's joints as it was being harassed by my spiders and Dave.

Immediately, the sentient ooze went to work, sticking and grabbing. The creatures couldn't be shaken off due to their porous nature and ability to cling to anything.

It wasn't much, but every bit helped as the juggernaut began to buck, smashing and pulverizing the cavern floor.

Next, my spiders danced around, spewing webs that entrapped the slimes, binding them to the joints of the Spider Monarch's champion to further bog the Titan down.

Slimey then entered the chambers, her body immediately turning crimson as her eyes went wide.

'YOU DARE?! YOU DARE?! YOU DARE DEFILE MY LORD HUSBAND WITH YOUR PERVERTED UNCLEAN MOUTH?!' she screamed, a sudden flux of rage-filled energy detonating from my champion's body. *'I HOPE YOU'VE ENJOYED YOUR FREE TRIAL OF LIFE, BECAUSE IT JUST GOT CANCELED!'*

Oh boy...

Chloe!

As Slimey immediately shot off to retrieve me, a barrier of force energy erupted from the cavern floor, intercepting the holy priestess, who splattered against the invisible wall.

'MY LORD!' my companion cried as a multitude of beams disintegrated my champion.

Or they would have, if not for the barrier of blue magic that blocked the attack.

This is where Chloe came in.

Name: Chloe

Level: 06

Species: Skeleton Orb Mage

HP: 90/90

MP: 374/490

Skills:

Undead

Innate Phylactery

Spontaneous Caster

Mana Surge

Recorder

Mage Armor Lvl.01

False Life Lvl.01

Souls Vision Lvl.02

Telekinesis Lvl.03

Minor Illusion Lvl.01

True Strike Lvl.01

Ray of Sickness Lvl.02

Fire Bolt Lvl.03

Shocking Grasp Lvl.01

Chilling Touch Lvl.01

Impalement Lvl.01

Dust Blast Lvl.01

Decaying Touch Lvl.01

Bone Cage Lvl.02

Magick Bolt Lvl.03

Fire Infusion Lvl.02

Cold Infusion Lvl.02

Lightning Infusion Lvl.02

Necrotic Infusion Lvl.01

Fester Lvl.01

Levitate Lvl.01

Magic Chant Lvl.03

Gem Missile Lvl.01

Curse Lvl.01

Cause Fear Lvl.01

Mote of Light Lvl.01

Spark Lvl.02

Blunt Barrier Lvl.01

Force Barrier Lvl.04

Mana Barrier Lvl.06

Bone Wall Lvl.01

Nightmare Lvl.01
Aura of Decay Lvl.01
Reverse Life Lvl.01
Emit Smog Lvl.02
Emit Force Lvl.01

Unlike other skills, magic spells and abilities grew as long as they were used. One could always level up and gain new spells, but without application, the spells would never reach their full potential.

So, for a month straight, I had Chloe leveling up, practicing certain spells, spamming them day in and day out just for this singular moment—

To keep Slimey in check and to spell-guard against the sovereign arachnid's attacks.

Four minutes.

CALM YOURSELF! I barked with authority, chastising Slimey, who immediately changed colors from red to pink, then to purple, her psyche undergoing various emotional shifts.

Go! Protect Chloe! I ordered as the juggernaut turned its attention to the spellcaster.

Then, my capruxas came charging into the chambers, each one now swollen to the size of an earth bull, with a red-eyed spider riding them. On their large, curved horns were thick ropes of webs, one end connected to the capruxas, with the other ends held in the mandibles of the spiders.

The trio of green monsters encircled the juggernaut, the spiders firing strong blasts of webbing that carried the rope, striking their target.

My other spiders went to work, adding their webs to the mix, with Dave herself leaping in front of the titan and smacking it with **Iron Tail.**

The juggernaut grunted, raising its forward leg, which was then enveloped by Slimey, the monster expanding her form to encompass the entire appendage while my green pigs brought down the walking tank.

Two minutes.

Chloe dispelled the force barrier, allowing me through, as the juggernaut suddenly found itself wrapped in ropes, webs, and slimes, its head being repeatedly headbutted by Dave.

Well, well, well... a queen with no subjects, I returned the words to the massive spider holding my body hostage.

Chapter 31

Regicide?

*S*uck. *Suck. Suck. Suck.*

The Spider Matriarch stared at me; the large, shriveled creature indifferent to the struggles of her last surviving brood.

Suck. Suck. Suck. Suck.

Pitiful. The once proud and intimidating monstrosity was now a shell of its former self. The queen shifted, easily wiggling her way out of the hole that once encased her in the wall to rise from the ground.

My hands clenched, an odd sensation bubbling up in my core as I eyed the monstrosity and prepared for the battle to come.

What was this excitement? What was this anticipation? This slight underlying feeling of disappointment at having envisioned a grand battle against the large spider at her peak.

Was I always such a battle junkie? Did I crave conflict so much that it sent a shock of ecstasy through my body as I carved through my enemies?

Yes.

I shot off, avoiding the eye beams as magical sigils lit up the air.

Lightning, ice, fire. The queen's anima magic compelling the laws of nature to bend to her will. But I was piloting an undead, a being of darkness. Hector's own natural body was resistant to the magicka as Chloe unleashed her **Aura of Decay**, dampening all anima-type magic in the chamber.

From my memories, magic spells fell into one of three categories:

Anima—the forces of nature. Earth, wind, water, and fire. Elemental magicka, one could say, influenced by direct control and mastery gained from countless hours of study or raw talent.

Holy—divinity and faith. Spells that utilized the direct power of a patron or one's own willpower to bestow blessings and favors. Miracles born from enlightenment, steadfast order.

And lastly, Dark—spells that relied on the spirit and strength of the soul of the user, and an absence of faith and control. Usually what one could call chaos.

Naturally, anima beat light, while light beat dark, and dark beat anima—a variable magic triangle that balanced each other out, with anima magicka battles contingent on the elements used.

Aura of Decay greatly dampened the queen's magic barrage, with some spells even fizzling out before they reached their intended target.

Of course, this wasn't because Chloe was so powerful or anything, but rather because of how famished the Matriarch was, her control greatly disrupted by her malnutrition.

Another boon for me.

I shifted and weaved, avoiding the attacks as they narrowly struck my body or splashed harmlessly on the ground. The queen lifted a forward-facing leg, still possessing enough strength to maneuver her heavy-plated arm and lash out.

But it was slow, lethargic. My body merely sidestepped the massive appendage, reaching out to plant a knife in the tendon while my other hand moved toward my rubber body and activated Pilfer.

One minute.

Suddenly, I felt a heavy weight in my hands, my yellow-shelled body displacing from the maw of the spider to Hector's bony hand, finally freeing me.

Immediately, there was a visceral reaction.

The queen's eyes quivered, her mandibles slamming shut with an audible squish that sent acid splattering.

I retreated, my rubber ducky body in hand, as the sovereign seemed to freeze, almost as if it couldn't believe its lollipop was taken.

But I wasn't a lollipop! I was a grown man! A human! Not a thing to be sucked on!

The queen began to move, shifting, her mandibles clacking repeatedly with a loud sucking sound as she inhaled air before a shrill scream flooded the chamber.

Ohhhh, quack.

Suddenly, the Matriarch was off—a newfound, never-before-seen strength invigorating the massive arachnid as it propelled its legs forward.

It brushed past me—or should I say, through me. Hector's body made the "colorful children's building blocks" death sound as I was immediately disassembled from the impact of her carapace.

Minion, Capi 3 has perished!

The familiar notification hit my screen, inflicting a pang of guilt in my mind.

One of my capruxas had died, crushed under the weight of the armored arachnid.

Seek cover! SCATTER! I ordered as dozens of glyphs materialized in the air.

'GIVE IT BACK! GIVE IT BACK MY PRECIOUSSSSSSSS!' The Matriarch screamed, unleashing a hailstorm of magic bolts that fired indiscriminately in an uncontrollable tide.

Dave raced into the barrage, the chitin-armored croc-girl taking multiple hits as she dove to pick up Hector's skull and my body. Slimey covered her, the holy slime healing Dave's injuries as she gathered us all up.

Suddenly, my consciousness swapped—my mind leaving my decapitated skeleton and returning to my duck body.

Chloe retreated, the skeletal mage removing its core to invoke a spherical barrier of magic, exhausting its mana points to protect my other minions.

Then it stopped. The rain of magic ceased as the matron spider shuddered, its body releasing steam as if it had overheated.

Now! THIS IS OUR CHANCE! Dave and Slimey rushed the queen as my other minions charged.

Legs! GO FOR THE LEGS! BREAK HER KNEECAPS! I ordered, squeaking rapidly to make sure I didn't miss a moment. Of course, spiders don't have kneecaps, but you get the idea.

Dave roared, driving her fist into the bend of one of the massive legs. The croco-girl ripped out the tendons in a show of brute force with her claws. Slimey, on the other hand, focused on pinning down the queen's movements, firing blasts of **Ellight** at the titan's joints and weak spots, picking up nearby slimes and hurling them at her open injuries.

Suddenly, a snapping sound. The Matriarch's body slammed into the ground with an audible thud. Two of her legs broke, the malnutrition, coupled with the lack of muscular support, unable to sustain the weight of her massive abdomen. She shifted her weight, faint magical sigils appearing in the air, but they were immediately dispelled by Chloe, who used her remaining mana to blast away the sovereign's swan song.

'*YOU! COME BACK TO ME!*' the queen roared, its eyes charging up an attack as I ordered Dave to bring me face-to-face with the queen. Of course, not before gouging several of the demonic spider's eyes out and putting an end to her attack.

Well, well, well. I began, the spider queen letting out low-sounding clacks. *How the mighty have fallen.*

'*Pleaase...*' she begged weakly, her remaining eyes focusing on me.

Please what?

'*Give...*'

Give you what? Mercy? Why would I give you mercy after you killed so many of my minions?! Why would I—

'*Me your delicious boddddy back...*' the Matriarch let out meekly.

Oh...

'*YOU DARE—*' Suddenly, Slimey was on the move, the holy slime preparing an attack, only to be stopped by Chloe dropping a magical barrier on her.

Injured and her army wiped out, the spider queen was now at my complete mercy.

Against my better judgment, I ordered Dave to insert me into the queen's mouth, much to Slimey's disgruntlement.

'*NO! NOOOOOO!*' Slimey began to rage, all my minions attempting to restrain her as the spider began sucking on me.

'MMM! MMM! So tassssty!' The sovereign wept.

I reached out, probing the queen's mind. The only thing on her arachnid brain was: *'suck, suck, suck.'*

You. Are. Mine. My first attempt at dominating a higher-level being.

Suck. Suck. Suck.

The spider, of course, ignored my intrusion.

YOU! ARE! MINE! I sent again, this time more forcefully.

Suck. Suck. Suck.

Seriously?

I continued to probe the spider, feeling around and realizing that she had magic protecting her mind. No doubt, this was erected after my first incursion into her brain.

So, it was time for a different tactic. I ordered Dave to take me from its mandibles.

Of course, the queen refused to let go. *'NOOOO! NOOOOO!'*

So, Dave simply broke her mandibles, prying me out of her grasp, leaving the Spider Matriarch weeping on the scorched floor.

Man... I kinda feel bad.

But if I couldn't dominate the monster, then... there would be no other choice.

'Gibb! Gib Bak!'

Not until you deactivate your magic, I sent, the Matriarch shuddering from my touch as it stopped its begging.

'Gib,' the spider pleaded, a mist rising off of its carapace.

Submit to me. My mind intruded into hers once more, this time with no protections guarding it.

Immediately, memories hit me. The spider, originally one of thousands of bugs made to protect a treasury. I could see it—a vast armory, filled with... with...

MY WEAPONS! MY GEAR! TROPHIES TAKEN FROM MY COMPANIONS OF OLD!

That bastard Barborall!

The memories shifted, showing me thousands of spiders dead, the armory being ransacked and attacked.

In the chaos of battle, I became the spider, a singular order in my mind: to protect the treasures at all costs before the connection was severed. On beady legs, I crawled, grabbing the nearest ticket I could before fleeing.

Suddenly, I was back in my body, my mind flooding with notifications.

You have tamed a new minion!
Overwrite the creature's name?

It has a name?

Magicka Spider Monarch Ayahkanomuthell

Yeaaah, that's too long. Ayaka seems good.

Name: Ayaka
Level: 33
Species: Malnourished Magicka Spider Matriarch
{ADDICTED}
HP: 00112/21560
MP: 021/970
Skills:
Rune Gesture
Spin Silk Lvl.10

Paralytic Bite Lvl.05
Pounce Lvl.10
Poisoner Lvl.10
Blend Lvl.05
Dark Vision Lvl.05
Magic Vision Lvl.05
Bile Spit Lvl.05
Resonate Silk Lvl.03
Magic Chant Lvl. MAXED
Magic Circulate Lvl.08
Ice Spear Lvl.03
Glacial Shot Lvl.03
Flame Bolt Lvl.04
Lightning Bolt Lvl.03
Flamethrower Lvl.02
Blunt Barrier Lvl.04
Commander Lvl.02
Egg Incubator Lvl.09
Mana Charge Lvl.03
War Cry Lvl.03

Addicted and malnourished—two stats my newly acquired boss monster had. Of course, when I got the boss as a playable character, it was already nerfed.

But it wouldn't be for long.

'Giiiiiiib,' the queen whined, asking for my rubber body.

I sat in Dave's hands, the croco-girl holding me just out of reach of the Spider Monarch.

No.

At my reply, the spider paled, shifting as its broken mandibles reached out, trying to snatch me up.

Sit.

The spider hit the ground, its massive body slamming into the floor.

'No! Y-You! You promised!'

I lied.

'NOOOOOOOOOOO!' It cried, the mighty monster throwing a fit as Slimey let out a cackle that echoed through everyone's minds.

Chapter 32

Moving On Up!

N uzzled in Slimey's hands, I had Dave sift through the dungeon cores that the queen held as trophies.

In the corner of the chamber, Ayaka and her juggernaut stood, the creature now docile and under the control of its queen, who was recovering from her injuries.

The juggernaut wasn't slaved to me, but rather to its queen. However, as long as Ayaka obeyed me, so too would her minions. Still, it didn't seem to mind too much. In fact, it ignored me, more intent on protecting its queen from me and my army that now occupied its home.

Dud after dud. Most of the dungeon hearts and cores were either depleted or cracked, not a single one usable for the purpose of creating another orb mage like Chloe.

It... may also not have helped that my smog explosion had damaged the cores.

Sigh...

At least my mana heart was okay.

After subjugating the queen, I immediately went to work setting up my new domain.

Pylons were crafted; guards posted. Whatever pockets remained of the queen's guards were recalled under Ayaka's orders and eliminated.

Cruel?

Perhaps. But I wouldn't chance it. It was a kindness on its own that I allowed Ayaka's juggernaut to exist. Mainly as an experiment, but also because the six-legged tank would be instrumental in helping me deal with Ayaka's withdrawals.

Can spiders get withdrawals? I wasn't sure if they could, but I'd need all the support I could get if I was going to deal with a twenty-foot-tall magical arachnid.

Hmm.

Hey. I looked at Ayaka and she shifted. *Where is your treasure?*

A moment of silence, the injured arachnid moping.

Hey!

'*So mean to me...*' Ayaka replied. '*You've taken everything from me, and yet you still want more?!*'

Slimey spun her head so fast her facial features blurred, doing a partial 360 until she corrected her gaze to leer at the giant spider.

'*Trash! You are property of Lord Hiro! Everything you own, everything you are, now belongs to our God!*' she spat, her body changing colors rapidly from pinkish human skin to bubbling red. '*Know your place!*'

Well, calling me a god was a bit much.

Ayaka's juggernaut shifted, the monster eyeing me.

'*I-I-I'll t-tell you if you just... g-give me a taste.*' Ayaka's forward legs fidgeted and touched tips, reminding me of one of those cheesy animes with a cute girl.

Except, this wasn't an anime, and the cute girl was replaced by a massive, armored spider.

'A l-little taste?'

No.

'P-Plplwse?'

No.

'B-Bu—'

No. Most of my army is being used to feed you. You're going to sit there and behave.

Ayaka splooted, the spider more akin to a scolded dog than a massive creature capable of killing everything in this cavern.

Now tell me what I want to know.

Sequestered inside the hole that Ayaka normally blocked with her body, it wasn't long before I was staring at the defeated matron's treasure.

A silver pendant, encrusted with faint magical gems—the only thing she could escape with as a small blind spider. One that I was more than intimately familiar with.

The Amulet of Siros Saccus, also known as the Warlord's Armory. A storage device used by one of my companions of old. Eyeing the device, I could tell from the faint magical aura that its power had waned, but it still seemed to be active, albeit empty.

Still, it was an unexpected boon—one that left me with unanswered questions.

Where was this treasury? What happened to my gear? And more importantly, who had attacked the Demon Lord's castle?

Questions that needed answers.

Ayaka!

'*Y-Y-Yes?*' The spider replied, shivering.

Where is the treasury this came from? I asked. The queen bug hesitated, reluctant to speak, but ultimately bent to my will after I promised her... a little "taste."

Of course, I was lying. But if there was a chance to recover any of my gear...

Still, a new problem arose. While Ayaka could explain and remember where the treasury was, I didn't know the inner workings of the Demon Lord's domain and was unfamiliar with the terrain after a hundred or so years.

Did I say one problem? Because I really meant two.

I needed a guide to find the treasury, and the only one who knew its location was too fat to fit through the caves! Maybe I should just starve the spider some more. Shave off its legs...

Ayaka, you don't need your legs to survive, right?

The giant spider skittered back a bit, her juggernaut lowering itself into a charging position as Slimey brandished a wicked smile.

Arrrgh, why does life have to be so difficult?!

'*C-C-Can I have my suck now? Just a t-taste?*' Ayaka asked, much to Slimey's gross displeasure.

No. I denied her, and the spider made odd chittering sounds, as if in sorrow. *Ughhhhhhh.*

Okay, think, rubber duck. Think.

First things first, I need to re-establish my domain completely. Get everything up and running with my dungeon heart growing again. Then, I need to rebuild my armed forces, construct new defenses, and clean up all the dead bugs!

A laundry list of tasks to complete.

But for now, I would use the monarch's chambers as my new fort, complete these quests, and level up a bit before moving on to scour the upper levels. Now that I had Zorkwen's storage device—wait... Zorkwen?

Suddenly, an image of an imposing, bronze-skinned man wielding a massive hammer flashed through my mind. A comrade I had forgotten—one who had stood with me during the raid on the Demon Lord's domain.

I could see him now: the smiling, bearded man, his last words urging us to push forward as he held off one of the Demon Lord's generals.

Seeing his amulet here... it didn't take a rocket scientist to figure out what happened to the half-giant, giving me an answer to a question I didn't want to know, but one I needed answered.

Dave.

The muscular reptile woman paused in her munching of spider guts to cock her head at me.

How would you like a new name?

The green-haired woman shrugged, nonchalantly resuming her feast, with no care in the world save for eating and sleeping. But considering her size—almost matching Zorkwen's—I thought this was a fitting tribute to the fallen comrade, lest I forget again.

Target: Minion, Dave
Overwrite the creature's name?

My minion manager updated, "Davette" now replacing her old name.

I ordered Slimey to hand the amulet to Davette, a reward for the work well done. Now, Davette could carry her bed, armor, and other gear—convenient for her, but also a great way to transport any other items I might need.

Actually, speaking of transport...

There was a certain blue spider I had trapped somewhere. That would be the perfect solution to my problem.

Davette! I ordered, my thoughts solidifying with purpose. *Go! Fetch me my blue bug!*

Before long, a familiar sight appeared: the blue phase spider, tangled in webs, bones, and various rocks, was dragged in. It couldn't shift or move so long as it was bound like this.

Command it to serve me. Have it take me to the armory.

The spider let out a low-frequency whine, one that echoed in my rubber body. The vibrations were strong, barely perceptible to others, but clear to me.

'I... *can't,*' Ayaka groaned, her voice dripping with frustration.

And why not?

'The treasury is guarded against... teleportation...'

Of course it was. Why wouldn't it be?

The hard way it is then... I sighed.

Pylon Created!
You have successfully expanded your domain!
Defend Your Mana Core!
The heart of your dungeon is new and weak. It must be given time to grow and strengthen!
Defend your heart for at least three days!
Reward: + Minion Capacity Increase

With my last pylon in place, my consciousness expanded, and my field of view grew as the fog of war lifted in the nearby area. My quest timer picked up right where it left off.

Excellent. I was back on track.

Another day, and my quest would be clear, and my minion capacity would be increased—something I'd undoubtedly need if I were going to storm the upper levels.

Despite my recent training success, many of the battles had been stacked in our favor, deliberate incursions that carried little risk, where I kited stronger monsters and ambushed them.

But this new stratum was filled with infected gnolls, blighted rat swarms, sickly goblins, skeletons, and even zombies—lower-tier monsters that were a step up from spiders and slimes.

If any evolved forms were lurking—goblin mages, blood wilters, or gods forbid, a living armor—my army could suffer catastrophic losses.

An idea flitted through my mind: turn Ayaka into a spider-making factory, creating loyal fodder for the cause. But that idea would cost time and resources. And more importantly, the thought of creating a factory of procreating spiders didn't sit well with me. Not out of any moral reason, mind you, but because of how disgusting it would be—and the maintenance involved.

Ick.

For now, I would have Ayaka serve as my Mana Heart Guardian. She'd be sequestered in my chambers while the rest of my army scouted and scoured the upper strata for the treasury.

From what I could recall, the castle itself had been built into a mountain—a hundred or so floors I would have to navigate before I ever made it to the surface. But that was fine. If there was one thing I had in abundance, it was time. With no new threats knocking at my door, my path to ascension was clear.

It was time to move on up.

Chapter 33

My Life is Just an RTS Game!

Sitting on a stone throne fashioned from dissolved stalagmites, today, like most days, I eyed my minions.

Below my rubber duck body was a slime in the shape of a woman wearing a priestess outfit, her lap doubling as my seat cushion. Around my neck and the slime's wrist was a handcuff—a countermeasure to prevent me from being duck-napped.

Or... at least that's what I chose to tell myself.

To my left was a muscular, ten-foot-tall humanoid crocodile woman with green hair and armored scales. She yawned and closed her eyes, the narcoleptic reptilian falling asleep upright.

To my right was a bleach-white skeleton, one wearing chitin plates and a fine robe made of spider silk that matched the color of its body.

And finally, in front of me was an armored magic spider, twenty feet tall and in the middle of molting as it kowtowed to me, pleading for a taste.

'Please, my lord! I beseech thee! Allow me but a simple taste of your body!' Ayaka pleaded, its skin shedding in various places. *'EVERY day is agony!'*

No. I sent to the spider amid withdrawal, the arachnid yearning to indulge herself but unable to pounce on me due to her being under my command.

'Such insolence!' Slimey chastised, her body turning a reddish hue as her serrated teeth came out. *'Filthy bug! To THINK you deserve to touch our lord! Be thankful you can gaze upon him at all!'*

I could feel Slimey's bloodlust... her desire to kill and tear apart the spider matriarch.

Now, now... Settle down.

Dungeon System Interface!
Name: Hiro Dungeon
Level: 02
HP: 8000/8000
MP: 0683/1500
DEVOTION: 100
EXP: 130/1000
Tamed Monsters: 27/30
Pylons: 5/5
SKILL LIST
Bubble Blow Lvl.01
MP Cost: 5

Create a bubble of charged mana. When it pops, it releases a light burst of magic.

Squirt Water Lvl.01
MP Cost: 5

Create and squirt water from your beak.

Summon Rock Lvl.01
MP Cost: 10

Summon a small rock. That's it. It summons a rock.

Purify Lvl.05
MP Cost: 20

Gathering light mana, attempt to cleanse an object or creature of curses, poison or disease. Effectiveness scales by level.

Squeaker-Location Lvl.03
MP Cost: 1

With a squeak, send out a pulse to map your surroundings and form a vivid image in your mind.

Impart Instruction Lvl.01

Teach skills and share experience with minions or selected creatures.

Dungeon Skills
Domain Expansion: 0/1
Sustained
MP Cost: 500

Radiate your will and designate a nearby area as part of your domain. If there are other competing claims to the area, the strongest will prove victorious.

Designate Minion Lvl.01: 0/10
MP Cost: 20 (Per Minion)

Creatures you target must make a wisdom-saving throw against you. Upon failing, the creature is forcibly placed under your command.

Minion Synchronization: Lvl.08
Cooldown: 12 Hours

Synchronize your senses with a loyal minion to take control of the target for eight minutes. Duration scales with skill level, and effectiveness scales with the bond.

Minion Registry
Slimey: Holy Super Slime Lvl.15
Title: Hiro's Champion
HP: 2550/2550
MP: 550/550
Davette Zorin: (???) Lvl.08
HP: 955/955
MP: 50/50
Spooderman: Red-Eyed Tarantual Lvl.13
HP: 200/200
MP: 160/160
Hector: Skeleton Rogue Lvl.15
HP: 1300/1300
MP: 25/25
Chloe: Skeleton Orb Mage Lvl.06
HP: 90/90
MP: 490/490
Ayaka: Malnourished Magicka Spider Matriarch Lvl.33
{ADDICTED}
HP: 18200/21560
MP: 321/970

I turned my attention to my mana heart, the pulsating orb radiating magic as it hung behind my throne.

Within a minute, my quest would finally complete, increasing my minion capacity.

Growing the size of my army...

Skittering into the throne room, a lowly spider entered and reported to me via taps and spindly arm gestures that the defenses had been finished being set up. It's behavior... kinda cute, the minion dancing around like one of those little jumping spiders.

Good.

Quest Complete: Defend Your Mana Core!
Dungeon Heart Matured!

A series of notifications hit my mind.

Minion Capacity Increased to 40!
Dungeon Management Panel
{Active} Dungeon Heart Lvl.01
HP: 1000/1000
Manacyst Production
Manacyst Culture: 0/2

Suddenly, a flood of power enveloped me, a feeling of strength and solidification that reinforced my sense of self. I began to feel a rhythmic thump, like a heartbeat, one in time with the pulsating core behind me.

Incoming Quest!
Establish a Manacyst Culture!
Reward: New Construction Options!

Huh...

Guess I really am a dungeon core, huh?

Manacyst crystals were mana condensed and given form, usually in the shape of crystals that hung on the walls of dungeons.

From what knowledge I retained about dungeons, they were part of a planet's magic recycling system—a way to gather mana in mana-rich environments and create monsters to redistribute the energy via dungeon breaks and invasions.

They could also be used for experience or crafting magical tools.

Redistributing mana, growing monsters... This looked to be my new purpose in life.

Nah.

Unlike the fractured dungeon cores that sat beneath my throne, I possessed one key trait that set me apart from my defeated cousins:

I was mobile.

This meant I wasn't limited to the scope of a dungeon cave or just another crevice in this world.

Oh, and I guess I also possessed human will and intelligence...

So, with these factors combined, who's to say I had to stay here? Because I didn't. After all, there was a whole wide world above that was just waiting to be cleaned.

Hmmm. For now, I would continue to follow these quests, as long as they unlocked functions and power. I didn't want to get too locked in or trapped, especially since staying in one place for too long was surely a death sentence.

A human had managed to delve into the Demon Lord's castle and find me, meaning there would no doubt be more on the way.

How much time did I have to prepare? I didn't know, but if they returned, I would need to be ready. And part of that readiness was securing the home front.

I turned my attention to the pit near my throne, the gaggle of monsters bound in webs and wiggling about.

New additions waiting to be added to my collection.

Seven blighted goblins, two gnolls, and a skeleton.

I dominated them all, rooting around in their minds for any useful information.

Of course, the skeleton was useless—a clean slate with no intelligence—while the furry brown gnolls only had an insatiable desire to consume everything. In fact, the feeling of wanting to eat and devour was almost akin to my own thoughts of wanting to clean!

But I suppressed it, disciplining myself to tolerate the filth as I moved on to dominate the goblins, who were busy letting out muffled screams.

Now, this... was different.

Due to their ability to communicate in their goblin language, I had attempted to talk with them when they had first been plucked from the upper strata and brought into my chambers, but alas, all they did was scream and cry.

'SILENCE, YOU CRETINS! YOU ARE IN THE PRESENCE OF LORD HIRO!'

It probably didn't help that Slimey kept yelling at them as they were brought before me.

Reaching out, my mind probed the goblins one by one.

Unlike all of the monsters prior, I could feel personalities, vivid memories, and strings of terrified intelligence that fought against my will.

Still, they, like all others, succumbed. Their pitiful cries eased as they became loyal soldiers assimilated into the swelling ranks of my army. Did I feel bad? Oddly, no. Not that I didn't want to, mind you, I did. However, I just... didn't. Was I changing? Maybe. I was about the business of domination after all, but there was a part of me that felt as though I was crossing the line when dominating an intelligent being... almost asking, *what right did I have?*

Conquest. The reality was conquest.

You have tamed a new minion!
What is this creature's name?

Gnoll 1 and Gnoll 2. Goblin 1, 2, 3, 4, 5, 6, 7, and Skeleton 2, of course.

No names given.

Forty monsters under my command, a sizable force no doubt, but one comprised mostly of weaklings.

Weaklings... When did I start referring to them as such?

I turned my attention to the far corner of the chamber, willing the dungeon management panel open to craft a manacyst culture.

Suddenly, I was outside of my body, a top-down view of my domain as if I were a bird flying overhead. I could see the entirety of my kingdom, every monster under my command highlighted in green, while every creature not under my control was marked in red.

Perhaps most interesting was the fact that I could see the manacyst culture—not physically, but as a holographic 3D-rendition of the item, with a message asking me where I wanted to place it.

This...

THIS IS EXACTLY LIKE AN RTS!

Chapter 34

Goals

Placing my manacyst cultures around my domain, it wasn't long before bluish stalagmites began to grow, the mana already being siphoned from the air and condensing into crystals.

Quest Complete: Establish a Manacyst Culture!
New Construction Options Available!
Dungeon Management Panel
{Active} Dungeon Heart Lvl.01
HP: 1000/1000
Manacyst: 0
Anima: 0
Holy: 0
Dark: 0
Manacyst Production
Manacyst Culture: 0/2
Construction Options...
Dark Gestator
REQ: 100 Dark Manacysts
Graveyard

REQ: 50 Dark Manacysts, 10 Anima Manacysts
Guardian Room
REQ: Any 50 Manacysts
Composter
REQ: 20 Dark Manacysts
Incoming Quest!
Construct a New Building!
Reward: +1000 EXP

Interesting. From my estimate, it would take a month before I could afford most things; however, the composter would take only a few weeks to get started.

Reading the description, the building did as advertised—it composted, turning dead matter into manacysts. Meaning, I could expedite the process by simply hunting down monsters and tossing their bodies into the compost.

From my math, it would take about thirteen days, give or take. But having a composter would help
Davette be less chunky and ease the cleanup process after every massacre.

Hmm. I focused on the damaged dungeon cores, the failed dungeons that had been conquered by the Spider Queen. There were more than fifteen, meaning there was a good chance that other dungeons were operating in the Demon Lord's manor—probably somewhere higher or far below. But considering the number of monsters out and about, the chances were high that I had competition.

Not that it mattered much. So long as I retained my core group, I could plunder my cousins and take their manacysts for myself—that is, of course, if the adventurers hadn't purged them already.

In the meantime, with new disciplines at hand, it was time to arm and equip them, as well as level up my army.

Davette, I called, ordering the crocodile to use her storage device to equip my pus-riddled goblins with chitin armor and weapons.

Under Slimey's green glare, the goblins all took a knee, bowing to me like knights showing deference to their king. In a way, it was somewhat comical—a rubber duck king and his slime bishop, surrounded by a menagerie of monster subjects. Still, I couldn't let myself be distracted. There was work to be done: a throne room to be scrubbed, and a treasury still to be sought after.

I turned my attention to Hector, my skeleton rogue. A few more levels, and the skeleton would be on the verge of leveling up again, granting me a more powerful undead. I suppose now would be a good time to venture out as I waited for the manacysts to grow.

Slimey.

'*Y-Yes, Lord Darling Hiro!*'

Gather the scouting party! We have a treasury to find!

'*Of course, my lord!*' she replied, smiling ear to ear before her gaze turned to the goblins, who shirked back from her divine presence.

Before long, I had an honor guard that consisted of seven chitin-armored goblins along with Hector, Chloe, Slimey, and Davette. For the time being, the rest of my army would remain at base, assisting Ayaka in gathering her full strength while hunting monsters to be added into the compost.

ELSEWHERE...

In a distant land, far from the clutches of the winding Demon Lord's castle, a scarred man stood staring out the window of a run-down inn, his eyes focused on the platoon of monsters marching through the decrepit city streets.

"Paladin Lhikan," a woman said with a knock, announcing her presence to the man before opening the door with fresh clothes in her hand. "Up and about today, I see. How was today's training?"

Lhikan sighed, turning to face the nurse practitioner. "Fine as usual, Joy, thanks for asking."

"Are you sure? You don't have to play tough with me; I'm your physician," Nurse Joy said, gesturing for the man to give her his sweat-stained shirt. "It's been three months since your return from the Demon Lord's castle, but everyone can see that you're bothered."

Lhikan shook his head, taking off his shirt to reveal a body covered in numerous scars, several new ones near his heart.

"It's..." he gritted his teeth. The seasoned veteran paused, thinking back on the failed expedition as he turned his head toward the holy symbol of their church that hung on the nearby wall. "I should be leading the expedition. Not sitting back here idling about."

"You were poisoned by demonic miasma and run through by a monster. It's a miracle you survived, let alone made it back," Joy replied, taking the stinking shirt before handing the paladin a new tunic. "Besides, with the intel you gathered, Paladin Commander Danse and his knights should be able to handle anything the dungeon there can throw at them."

"I pray you are right," Lhikan said, narrowing his eyes and clenching his fists. "I just... Natalie and the others. I feel responsible for their deaths and wish to be there to give them a proper funeral."

Nurse Joy stood to the side, her arms folded.

"You were given an impossible task—one that by all accounts was deemed to fail."

"Because it was supposed to!" the knight hissed, his eyes flashing gold. "Those cowards hated Natalie. They feared what she could become as a true healer, so they gave her an impossible task. These cretins don't care about defeating the Demon Lord! All they care about is maintaining the status quo and building up their own power. And now that they know that the Hero's legacy dwells within the old fortress, they'll no doubt use that power to propagate their reach rather than destroy the enemies of humanity."

"Then do something about it." Nurse Joy shrugged.

"Tsk! What would you have me do? I have no alms, no gear, and am under constant surveillance by Nidhiki's goons."

"Oh, I'm sure something can be figured out. After all, it's not like they have a map to Hero's Folly, seeing as the only one was destroyed. Oh, and I think a person familiar with the route has a better chance at beating them to the prize than someone with a general direction," Nurse Joy said, smirking as she laid the basket of linens on the bed, making a loud metallic chink sound. "At two after night's peak, all of the guards will suddenly fall asleep."

Lhikan blinked, his eyes darting from the woman to the basket.

"If Krekka or Nidhiki find out—"

"They won't. Plus, Prior Dume and I can take care of ourselves, and if they do..." Nurse Joy pulled out a kunai from her sleeve, twirling the weapon in her fingers. "It wouldn't matter anyway."

"Thank you." Lhikan said.

"Don't thank me, L. You may very well die," Joy said before blowing a kiss and leaving the rustic room.

His mind flashed back to that fateful night in the catacombs.

He turned back to the window beside him, eyeing the streets of Minstrel, a city once teeming with life, commerce, and blue skies.

Now, the city was infested with monsters, an occupation force under the Demoness Bellona that had turned the city of thirty-three thousand into a large cattle farm.

The Lord Regent had fled, returning to the capital, taking with them the entire garrison force along with Cardinal Krekka's forces that had been stationed in their cathedral, effectively abandoning the city to the mercy of the Demoness invasion.

Bellona announced that there would be no wholesale slaughter, so long as the citizenry bent the knee. But in lieu of that, the people lived in fear, made to form lines to donate blood to the monsters that now patrolled the streets, some even plucked from their homes to satiate the needs of the inhumans.

Enough was enough.

Lhikan would make a difference. Fortunately, he had plenty of comrades that remained in the city who felt the same way.

Tonight's the night, he mentally affirmed with great resolve, removing the sheets from the basket that covered his armor and arms. *Tonight, I take my steps to avenge you.*

Chapter 35

STAMPEDE?!

Scurrying my way through the catacombs of the Demon Lord's castle, the resistance my squad encountered was... minuscule, to say the least. Thanks to Slimey's innate holy properties, anything and everything undead or heavily saturated with the darkness attribute didn't stand a chance.

Blight goblins fled in terror, undead simply dissolved, and the gnolls, completely infatuated with their hunger, threw themselves into Slimey's gelatinous mass.

All in all, a good spring cleaning. While this went on, I decided to have the slimes remaining under my command follow me, cleaning up the bodies, webs, and dust in the wake of our carnage, each slime spreading the good word of Ajax, my personal lord and savior.

Of course, I also had my goblins stop and organize the tombs and coffins left in disarray, using a few of them as impromptu trash cans to be taken out later!

Ahhh. How nice. How pristine.

After an hour of exploring, it took me a moment to realize I'd only traveled a few yards into the upper strata. My surroundings looked mighty familiar but clean.

Ah... quacks.

I... may have... gotten a bit off mission.

Heck.

'Look, my lord! Look at how spotless I've polished this coffin!' Slimey sent, the slime girl smearing her hand over a dusty coffin and sucking up the dirt.

Yes! Very good! I'm very proud of you!

Slimey changed colors, her form wiggling and collapsing into a bright pink puddle as Davette carried me on its head, picking up a bone to gnaw on.

Hmmm. Sparkles.

Suddenly, vibrations! Skittering down the tunnel, my monsters all turned as a swarm of unknowns came charging in our direction.

Squeak! I yelped, pinging the assailants that consisted not of undead, BUT UNICORNS?!

WHAT?!

The stampede of muscular horned monsters charged, galloping their way through the catacombs. My squeaks came out rapidly as I pinged the attackers, and Slimey quickly took me into her arms.

Quack! SPEAR WALL! SPEAR WALL! I hollered, my untrained blighted goblins running around in blind panic.

"ROOOOOOOOOOOOOOOOOAR!" Seeing the looming threat, Davette spun, leaping to the forefront. The gator-girl raised her arms and caught the first unicorn with her body before the rest of the stampede overran her and my goblins unfortunate enough to be in their path.

Farewell, goblins one through seven. Your deaths will not be in vain!

Anger began to surge within me. Despite being goblins, they were still my minions!

CHLOE! ***FORCE WALL, NOW!***

My orb skeleton went to work, creating a wall of force energy before hitting it with an Emit Force spell. The two combined, forming a wall of moving force that slammed into the crowd of unicorns.

Still, that wasn't enough to halt their trajectory. With their horns, they pierced through, their magical appendages breaking apart the barrier. Chloe immediately fired another one.

This time, it worked. The lead unicorns were stopped, the monsters rearing on their hind legs as their momentum was killed.

COUNTER ATTACK! My cleaning crew engaged as Hector appeared from behind me.

Suddenly, the corridor began to fill with magic. The unicorns fired bolts of mana, and Chloe held aloft a mana barrier to intercept the attacks.

Immediately, Slimey and my slimes returned fire, the corridor now becoming filled with bolts of energy and slime.

A literal fantasy firefight.

Outmanned and outgunned, my forces began to retreat, using the nearby pillars and coffins as cover as Chloe maintained her mana barrier. Still, despite the overwhelming show of force, we were not out-skilled.

I reached out, taking control of Hector. The skeleton rogue shivered as my consciousness entered its body.

Chloe touched my shoulder, conferring buffs to my skeletal body as my bones clenched around the daggers.

Mage Armor.
Lightning Infusion.
False Life.
Concealment.

With stacking buffs, I shot forward, racing through the barrage of magic bolts to engage the unicorns, while Davette let out a frustrated roar.

I charged the four-legged beasts from the front, and Davette attacked from behind, the two of us working in tandem to eliminate the threat.

I quickly entered melee range, my daggers slicing into the unicorns' flesh, but did little to bypass the thick muscle beneath their skin.

Tsk. Too shallow!

The lead unicorn bucked, kicking off its hind legs to unleash a blast of magical power at me.

Uncanny Dodge activated, and my skeletal form sidestepped, narrowly avoiding the blast. Using Swift Step, I weaved through the crowd of unicorns, closing the distance with each passing moment.

With a flick of a wrist and a twist of my daggers, I nicked each beast, my lightning infused weapons leaving behind a mark on their tough skin as Davette picked up one of the creatures by the hindlegs, using it as an impromptu weapon.

Now! I sent, Chloe dispelling the lightning infusion to activate its secondary effect: **Chain Lightning**.

Unlike fire and ice infusions, which displayed immediate effects when their target was struck, the lightning infusion relied on a delayed function for its damage.

Upon the spell's activation, the small cuts and nicks began to glow, the marks left behind resonating with one another before a large bolt of lightning shot through the crowd.

Of course, it wasn't enough to put them down, but it paralyzed them, stunning the four-legged beasts long enough for me to insert my daggers into their bloodshot eyes.

Before long, I was standing above a group of dead unicorns, their rainbow-colored blood staining the floor, their long, forked tongues sticking out of their maws.

Despite the surprise attack, my squad had survived, albeit with eight fewer members than I would have liked. One of my slimes took a direct hit to its core, shattering it, while all seven of my goblins had been crushed underfoot.

Davette was wounded, with green blood leaking from cracked scales, but otherwise, he was fine, thankfully.

Tsk.

Where the hell did these unicorns come from?! And who had sent them?! I didn't know, but it was time to find out.

With the last surviving unicorn kicking and screaming as Davette pinned it down, I had Slimey bring me close to tend to Davette while I made the unicorn mine.

You. Are. Mine. I claimed, probing the brown-furred unicorn.

Immediately, I felt pushback, resistance—a similar feeling to when I had dominated the spider matriarch's minions. Except this was different. Less warm, more cold. The same feeling I had when I picked up an active dungeon core as Hector.

The dungeon core's iron grip didn't last long. I unmade that lock, shattering the hold it had on its minion and supplanting its will with my own.

You have tamed a new minion!

What is this creature's name?

Buttstalion, obviously.

Name: Buttstalion
Level: 07
Species: Unicorn
HP: 231/550
MP: 020/200
Skills:
Stampeder
Mana Charge Lvl.03
Gallop Lvl.05
Mana Bolt Lvl.03
Detoxify Lvl.02
Cure Lvl.02
Purify Lvl.01
Mana Blast Lvl.02
Magic Resist Lvl.02
Muscle Reinforcement Lvl.02

Suddenly, a flash—my mind flooding with the creature's memories.

In them, I saw a pasture, a large open field, one sequestered by high walls and tall trees. An underground woodland paradise filled with monsters, trees, and copious amounts of dangerous plant life that would be hazardous to any who intruded.

I also saw a familiar object: a mana heart, similar to my own, except this one was green, encrusted with bark, with a large plant-like figure in the shape of a woman humming as she fed a 2,000-pound rune bear a berry.

I was back, and the location of my competitor was revealed to me.

I see... Recounting the details of the information obtained, I knew exactly what I was dealing with.

A dryad—a spirit-type creature residing in old trees and given shape by large concentrations of anima magic in the air.

The champion of the dungeon core, no doubt, and considering the fact it was surrounded by a flock of massive rune bears...

For those not in the know, a rune bear is like a black bear if you took that bear and sized it up three times, gave it claws like a wolverine, anima magic resistance, and then gave it the bite force of a great white shark.

In summation, basically Davette—but on steroids.

Fortunately, I had a plan. I knew exactly how to make short work of the dryad and how to kill every single bear, poisonous monster, and barb in one fell swoop.

But in the meantime, I turned my attention to the deceased equines below me, a sudden idea popping into my head as I eyed a broken spear that lay nearby and the dust that coated the floor.

I ordered my arachnids out, summoning my squad of spiders through Ayaka's phase spider, which dropped off new troops before disappearing.

My own personal dropship.

Get to work. The arachnids immediately went to work webbing up the dead unicorns and dragging them off for later use, while my slimes cleaned up the blood.

With a heavy heart, I turned my attention to my dead goblins, the monsters having died in my service.

Davette, take these bodies to be buried, I ordered, stopping the ten-foot-tall monster in the midst of attempting to eat one of the corpses. The croc-girl looked at me with an inquisitive expression but ultimately followed my instructions.

This unprovoked attack would not go unpunished. Fortunately, dealing with them would only take a moment of my time.

Chapter 36

Let 'em Cook

Moving in the opposite direction of where my original path lay, Slimey held me in its body as we sat atop my newly acquired unicorn, which led me to its home.

Behind me, Chloe and my primary squad—my monsters—marched through the darkness, preparing to begin our "assault" on the Dryad Heart.

I'm sorry, did I say assault? I meant extermination.

Turning a corner, it wasn't long before my surroundings began to shift from catacombs covered in dust to tunnels filled with flora, roots, and new monsters.

Not many, mind you—mostly deerlings, bipedal humanoid beastmen with the heads of deer, and large reptiles that were akin to crocodiles but smaller and more smooth-like. Kind of like a gecko, but if the gecko were the size of a wiener dog and could spit acid.

Weak monsters that didn't last long under the scrutiny of Davette's hungry maw and Slimey's serrated smile.

Before long, I was standing before a cave, pinging my surroundings, which were flush with green plant life teeming with anima mana.

Perfect.

From what I could discern, it was exactly like my pilfered memories—the vast underground woodland so majestic and beautiful, teeming with life in an impossibly dark place. A small beacon of hope in an otherwise bleak and dreary world.

Chloe.

The orb mage shifted.

Burn it down.

At my command, Chloe began Operation Verdun.

A simple plan, similar to my assault on Ayaka's nest.

Immediately, Chloe began emitting smog, the flammable mixture spreading into the spacious dry forest as I had Slimey expand.

My champion formed a sphere to block the exit, leaving only one opening for the poison to flow.

Squeaking, I could make out the monsters inside stirring, reacting to the intrusion.

Yet, it would be too late.

The moment the chaos mana came in contact with anima mana, the latter would become infected, corrupted, and bogged down by its aversion to its opposite on the mana triangle, helping to spread the contagion. The only way to purify the chaos infection was holy mana.

Ordering Chloe to back out of the entrance, I had Slimey form a hole to let her out before sealing it up again.

With the flammable smoke inside the enemy's domain, I had Slimey collapse the entrance, using her porous body to seep into the cracks of the archway and bring it down.

Satisfied that the exit was sealed, I waited.

'My lord, the smog is seeping out now.'

Excellent. Slimey, use your body to cover the debris. Make sure the force of the detonation doesn't blow the entrance clear.

'Of course, my darling. Anything for you!' she replied, eager to appease and be of use.

She quickly moved, splattering herself against the collapsed tunnel while forming an appendage to keep me aloft.

Chloe. **Firebolt**.

Chloe lit the match, the smog sparking and traveling through the debris to reach the forest inside.

I didn't need to see or hear to be able to feel it—the vibrations of the explosion shaking the tunnel system and Slimey, her body wiggling as debris hit her and rubber-banded back into the exit.

Excellent.

With my limited sight and sound, I could make out the screams of various monsters inside. The panic and cries of dying creatures that had dared to try and attack my minions!

Suddenly, another explosion—this time, one so volatile that the force created shifted the entire cavern, with dust and other bits falling on me. Fortunately, Slimey was quick to clean me.

Chloe Lvl.06 → Lvl.07

Chloe Lvl.07 → Lvl.08

Chloe Lvl.08 → Lvl.09

Chloe Lvl.09 → Lvl.10

Chloe Lvl.10 → Lvl.11

Chloe Lvl.11 → Lvl.12

Chloe Lvl.12 → Lvl.13

Chloe Lvl.13 → Lvl.14

Chloe Lvl.14 → Lvl.15
Chloe Lvl.15 → Lvl.16
Chloe Lvl.16 → Lvl.17
Chloe Lvl.17 → Lvl.18
Chloe Lvl.18 → Lvl.19
Chloe Lvl.19 → Lvl.20

Huh... neat.

Minion, Chloe has reached the level cap!

Suddenly, Chloe collapsed, her bones falling into a pile with her robe falling gently to the floor.
Wait. No!

Name: Chloe
Level: 20
Species: Skeleton Orb Mage
HP: 395/395
MP: 1500/1500
Skills:
Undead
Innate Phylactery
Spontaneous Caster
Mana Surge
Recorder
Mage Armor Lvl.01
False Life Lvl.01
Souls Vision Lvl.05
Telekinesis Lvl.03
Minor Illusion Lvl.01
True Strike Lvl.01

Ray of Sickness Lvl.02
Fire Bolt Lvl.03
Shocking Grasp Lvl.01
Chilling Touch Lvl.01
Impalement Lvl.01
Dust Blast Lvl.01
Decaying Touch Lvl.01
Bone Cage Lvl.02
Magick Bolt Lvl.03
Fire Infusion Lvl.02
Cold Infusion Lvl.02
Lightning Infusion Lvl.02
Necrotic Infusion Lvl.01
Fester Lvl.01
Levitate Lvl.01
Magic Chant Lvl.03
Gem Missile Lvl.01
Curse Lvl.01
Cause Fear Lvl.01
Mote of Light Lvl.01
Spark Lvl.02
Blunt Barrier Lvl.01
Force Barrier Lvl.04
Mana Barrier Lvl.06
Bone Wall Lvl.01
Nightmare Lvl.01
Aura of Decay Lvl.01
Reverse Life Lvl.01
Emit Smog Lvl.02
Emit Force Lvl.01
Raise Dead Lvl.01

Doom Strike Lvl.01
Acid Spray Lvl.01
Force Bind Lvl.01
Force Siphon Lvl.01
Next Page →

I closed the skill menu, focusing instead of the requirements needed for her next evolution.

Minion, Chloe is trying to advance to Hellcaller Dullahan!
Unfortunately, the requirements have not been met!
Hellcaller Dullahan Requirements:
Pounds of Bones: 0/200
Complete Skeleton: 0/3
Equine Skeleton: 0/1
A+ Grade Magic Catalyst: 1/1
Kill 500 Life Forms: 2989/500
Kill 200 Life Forms using Flame Magic: 1903/200

Ignoring the screams of monsters dying, I focused on the requirements.

Equine? What the hell is an equine? Why would Chloe choose to evolve into something that required materials I didn't have?

"SHREEEEEEEEEEEEEE!" The death throes of a monster.

Hmmm. Equine... What's a word similar to equine?

"SHREEEEEEEEEEEEEEE!"

Equestrian? Equestrian is like... a horse rider, right?

Am I supposed to find a horse rider? No, that's dumb.

"AWOOOOOOOOOOOO!"

I need a horse skeleton. OH! WAIT! I HAVE PLENTY OF THOSE!

Ignoring the vibrations and constant death wails, I pondered what my next actions should be.

With my main DPS (damage-per-second) dealer down, I decided to retreat, calling forth Ayaka's phase spider to teleport in and bundle Chloe up in the web before taking her back to base.

Once I had her advance to another class, I would return to collect my spoils from my firebomb.

Moving back into the catacombs, I decided to do some material gathering, much to Slimey's unhappiness. Oddly, as we went to work hunting down the skeletons fleeing from us, I could feel a simmering anger in the slime, like a heated pot of water threatening to boil over.

Did I do something wrong? I wasn't sure, but Slimey was pure red, the gelatinous priestess's skin crimson like blood.

Slimey?

'Yes, Lord Darling?' She looked down at me with a wicked grin filled with serrated teeth.

Uh... is... everything okay? I asked, sensing a bit of... pensiveness from the slime.

'Oh, nothing is wrong, my lord,' she replied, squeezing me slightly in her arms.

Ah... okay... Why are you squeezing me tighter?

'It's just...'

Ah, here we go.

'You focus on leveling everyone but me. Am I not your champion, my lord?' Slimey asked, enveloping my body with her form, my rubber duck shell floating until being propelled out of Slimey's mouth to stare directly into her eyes.

Right... uhm...

'Am I not your champion, darling? Am I not the pinnacle to which all your subjects should look to for inspiration? To be your greatest and BEST WARRIOR? To be YOUR ONLY CONFIDANT?'

Biting! Biting! BITING! YOU'RE BITING ME!

'RIGHT, LORD HIRO?' Slimey asked, her eyes filled with deranged madness.

UUHHHHHHH. YEAH! YUP, OF COURSE! LESS TEETH! LESS TEETH! PLEASE DEAR GOD, LESS TEETH!

Slimey's features distorted, a slight ripple before I was back in her hands and the slime smiled at me.

Someone, help! I pleaded silently, eyeing my minions, who all were suddenly busy admiring the nearby architecture.

TRAITORS!

'I'm so glad you feel the same, my lord darling. Truly, we were meant to be!' Slimey said, the familiar iron shackle appearing around my neck and her wrists. *'Let's get to work immediately!'*

Right... Uh. Let me get Chloe done fir—TEETH! TEETHTEETH! WAIT A MOMENT!

Slimey closed her jaw, either from the power of my command or her willingness to pause, compelling her to stop.

Let me get Chloe set up and I PROMISE! I'll help you evolve!

'D-Do you promise?'

YES! Just give me time! I swear!

Slimey changed colors, swapping from red to her usual blue before donning the humanoid pink.

Before long, I was dragged back into my territory, the bones carried in Davette's storage device dropping into a hole dug into the ground by Ayaka as the large arachnid visibly molted.

'P-Pweese may I—' Ayaka began.

No.

Ayaka scurried away, the large bug's mandibles rubbing against each other to release a loud whine before she sat in the corner and splooted out. Her juggernaut laid beside her, giving the sad bug company.

Man... if only my other minions were as obedient and less scary.

Hmm, I could probably use my **Purify** skill to detoxify the large arachnid, come to think of it...

Nah. Better to let her stew after my many months of captivity.

I turned my attention back to the pit I dubbed my evolution hole. Sitting in Slimey's hand, I observed as Chloe slept beneath the pile of bones and carcasses being thrown in by Davette.

Seeing as I had no use for the unicorns other than their hairs and horns, already pulled out by my spiders, I had Davette throw them in to help facilitate Chloe's evolution.

After all, the evolution screen didn't state what kinds of bones were needed.

And now we wait... In the meantime, I would have to figure out how to make Slimey grow.

Fortunately, I had a plan for that as a notification hit my screen.

Chapter 37

Laundry List

Milestone Achieved: By your orders, 10000 creatures have been slain!

*H*uh... *neat. I guess the enemy dungeon is still burning. Ten thousand dead, huh?* A mortifying event, yet strangely... I felt nothing.

+10000 EXP!
Level Up!
Level Up!
Level Up!

Suddenly, I could feel an influx of strength hit me. My core seemed to solidify, my senses growing sharper and my body heavier.

Milestone Achieved: Reach Level 5!
Minion Capacity Increased to 50!
You have earned a new skill!
Water Affinity Detected!
Generating Skill...

Obtained: Water Jet Lvl.01

NEAT!

I opened my dungeon interface, eyeing my new stats and skill.

Dungeon System Interface!
Name: Hiro Dungeon
Level: 05
HP: 10000/10000
MP: 3000/3000
DEVOTION: 100
EXP: 3130/8000
Tamed Monsters: 36/50
Pylons: 5/5
SKILL LIST
Bubble Blow Lvl.01
MP Cost: 5

Create a bubble of charged mana. When it pops, it releases a light burst of magic.

Squirt Water Lvl.01
MP Cost: 5

Create and squirt water from your beak.

Water Jet Lvl.01
MP Cost: 20

Shoot a high-pressure stream of water from your beak.

Summon Rock Lvl.01
MP Cost: 10

Summon a small rock. That's it. It summons a rock.

Purify Lvl.05
MP Cost: 20

Gathering light mana, attempt to cleanse an object or creature of curses, poison or disease. Effectiveness scales by level.

Squeaker-Location Lvl.03
MP Cost: 1

With a squeak, send out a pulse to map your surroundings and form a vivid image in your mind.

Impart Instruction Lvl.01

Teach skills and share experience with minions or selected creatures.

Turning to Slimey, I immediately used **Impart Instruction**, dumping all of my newly gathered experience into the slime, who shuddered as she held me.

'L-L-Lord Hiro! I can feel you inside me!'

My mind shut off momentarily.

Siiiiiiiiiiiiigh.

Of course, the experience given was only enough to level Slimey up once, but it seemed sufficient to placate her as she dissolved into a pink puddle.

'More! MORE! MORRRRE! I WANT MORE OF YOUR LOVE!'

OR NOT?!

Suddenly, I was hoisted into the air as Slimey resumed her human form, her eyes staring at me with heart-shaped pupils.

Ah... quack.

'MORE! MY LORD, I WANT MORE OF YOUR BLESSING!'

Whoa! Stop! You're shaking me! SQUEEZING ME!

'*GIVE IT TO ME!*' Slimey screamed, her voice filling my entire head as she opened her mouth, revealing serrated teeth.

SETTLE DOWN! I snapped, my mental command freezing her in place.

She quickly kowtowed, bowing, the slime holding me aloft as her face hit the floor so hard it splattered and deformed.

'*Forgive me, my lord! I did not mean to offend!*' Slimey shrieked, her voice in my mind breaking before she peeled her face off the floor to gaze at me, cleaning liquid flowing from her face. '*Punish me, my lord! TAKE ONE OF MY CORES AND CRUSH IT IN YOUR MIGHTY MAW AS COMPENSATION FOR MY INSOLENCE!*'

Slimey spit out a core, offering it to me on her tongue slick with goo.

Ehh, I'll pass. We want you to get stronger, not weaker...

'*Yes, of course, my lord,*' she acknowledged, swallowing the orb.

Be patient, I sent, the latter coddling me close as she wiggled her way onto the throne, holding me in her arms.

Using my slimes and capruxas to shape my throne room and the burial ground for my deceased goblins, I pondered my options as I waited for Chloe to evolve.

Should I make an experience run to a higher stratum?

Start cleaning up the enemy dungeon now?

Or should I explore the sewer and catacombs more?

I decided to focus on renovating my domain. Once I had my composters up and running, it would be a small task to establish a functioning kingdom.

Minion, Chloe has evolved from Skeleton Orb Mage to Animusflam Dullahan!
Stage 1 of 3

Huh?

My interface lit up, the pit of bones and carcasses glowing with a rainbow hue as Chloe's status appeared, showcasing a slew of new abilities.

Anima abilities! And spells! The skeleton somehow being augmented—

Then it hit me, the unicorns!

Unicorns were beings created from high concentrations of anima mana, their very essence infused with anima!

Meaning...

Meaning...

MATERIALS USED AFFECTED MINION EVOLUTION!

Of course, it made sense! How could I have been so dumb?!

Suddenly, an idea popped into my head as I watched the defeated dungeon cores being batted around by Spooderman and another spider.

Slimey, are you hungry?

I beckoned my spiders over, ordering them to bring their toys.

Spooderman skittered up to my throne, holding a cracked core like an offering, which I had Slimey absorb.

Slimey suddenly began to rapidly change colors, her body vibrating violently.

Oh no. Wait!

I felt an intrusion—a cold will reaching through my bond with Slimey to caress my mind.

Thunder, clouds. A clear image of a sky darkened by lightning and torrential rain.

The phenomenon didn't last long, fortunately, and Slimey suddenly leveled up, gaining a new skill that didn't seem normal for a slime.

Obtained: Electric Discharge Lvl.01
Obtained: Lightning Body

Huh. Unexpected, but neat. It wasn't unheard of to obtain abilities and skills from cores, but usually, they took a lot of introspection and understanding of the core to do so—like a book that needed to be transcribed.

At least, for normal folk.

For those who had a system like Ly—... me, we didn't need to do that. We could simply absorb the cores, which seemed to be the case with monsters.

How are you feeling, Slimey? I asked, the priestess shuddering as her features deformed, sparking with electricity that arced into my body.

'I'm fine, my lord,' Slimey replied, her cores visibly shifting.

Interesting. I reached out, probing the damaged cores, testing a hypothesis.

One core, encrusted with crystals, gave me images of earth and rock, crystals spanning a cavern.

Another, this one covered in bone-like chitin, showed me a cold coffin, broken with undead bones rising out.

And finally, the last core—this one was different. A pervasive feeling touched my mind, something disgusting and horrid, every part of my being wanting to simultaneously cry and vomit. It showed me sewers and sludge, a putridness that made me sick to my non-existent stomach.

I involuntarily squeaked, bits of black water spilling from my mouth as my body shook violently.

FILTHY, FILTHY, FILTHY!

Suddenly, the orb was obliterated, pulverized by Slimey, who blasted the core with holy mana before taking me into her arms and scrubbing me with her cleaning liquid.

Aaaaaaah. That's better.

Recollecting my thoughts, an idea came to me.

Davette, I called out to the croco-girl lying on her side upon her bed of silk.

Davette...

Nothing.

'Daaaaavette.'

'Hnnnnng,' Davette replied, grunting but not moving, the gator girl curling into herself to hug her tail.

Aww.

Slimey stretched out, her form turning red, her gelatinous body elongating to latch onto Davette.

'RESPOND WHEN LORD HIRO TELLS YOU TO!' Slimey screamed, dragging Davette out of bed as she began to scream.

'NO! NO! JUST FIVE MORE MINUTES!' Davette replied, the muscular woman digging her claws into the earth as Slimey dragged her toward the throne by her ankles and tail.

Here, eat this, I redirected her attention, Davette twisting her body to look up at me with a frown.

Slimey threw the rocky core at the lizard, the orb bouncing off the yawning creature's head.

Davette scratched her back, the slouching woman picking up the core and taking a massive bite out of the crystal with a mighty *CRUNCH!*

Before long, the entire core was gone, Davette letting out a yawn before slowly closing her eyes and falling asleep while standing up.

Seriously?

Then, without warning, Davette began to glow, her scales shifting, transforming, giving off a rainbow-like clear pattern in certain areas of her body.

Obtained: Mana Reflection Lvl.01
Obtained: Crystal Scales
Obtained: Crystal Dagger Lvl.01

Nice!

Judging from the abilities, it seemed the core had given Davette harder scales, transforming her appearance slightly with crystal spikes forming on her tail.

As for the last core, I decided to save it for now, as it seemed to correlate with undead.

Maybe Hector could use it?

I turned my focus to the skeleton, who walked into my throne room along with several spiders carrying bundled-up monsters.

Hector bent the knee, bowing to me unprompted, which I found odd. Was he gaining sentience? Autonomy? Or had Slimey's constant demands for me to be worshipped finally rubbed off?

Whatever the case, I focused on the offering presented by this hunt.

Sixteen goblins, two gnolls, and three skeletons.

Six of the goblins went to feed Ayaka, three to my army, and the rest were conscripted into my army, though they would need armor and weapons. I, of course, refrained from naming them, attempting to put a barrier between me and these monsters with rudimentary sentience.

Hmm. Where are all these goblins coming from?

Wait, hold up. One thing at a time, Hiro! I still had a clean-up operation to handle regarding the dryad, as well as locating the treasury, appeasing Slimey, evolving Chloe, and—of course—finding something for my unicorn to eat!

Buttstallion was milling about, drinking from a pool of water I had set up, the basin dug by a Capruxa, filled with sewer water carried in by slimes, and purified with my purify skill and a cleaning slime.

The problem now was its diet. Davette was keen to eat anything that moved. My capruxas fed on minerals in the dirt, while my spiders and goblins were left to eat what they caught or what remained.

But this big magical horse? It was an herbivore.

Aaaaannd I may have firebombed its only source of food...

Great.

Okay, there was no sense in sitting around and speculating. It was time to confirm the kill and reap my spoils.

Chapter 38

An Old Friend

I gathered a group of soldiers. My squad consisted of Slimey, Davette, Hector, Kappybara, the skeletons under my command, and Buttstallion. For now, I planned on leaving the goblins behind, ordering them to secure traps and fortifications beside Spooderman.

While I could bring them along, the only purpose the goblins served in their current state was food and cannon fodder—something made painfully clear during their poor performance in the unicorn stampede.

No, I needed to train them, teach them tactics in warfare and battle if they were going to be of any use.

I turned my attention to the mausoleum, entire teams of spiders and slimes working to install the coffins. Could I be using my minions for something more productive? Perhaps, but my minions deserved a proper burial. And what better place than my throne room, where they would be with me always?

As I prepared to order Slime and my detachment to leave, Ayaka approached. The giant spider lowered herself several feet in front of my throne.

'My lord, I, Ayaka, humbly ask to approach your throne,' the spider sent, her molting bits being cleaned up by my cleaning slimes.

Okay, that's new.

'Sure, whatever,' I accepted dismissively.

'Lord Hiro has deigned to allow you within his presence. You may approach.' Slimey's gaze was one of disgust as she looked down at the massive spider queen skittering toward the throne.

Actually, come to think of it, when did my throne get so high up?

Somehow, my throne had managed to rise into a pillar with stairs leading downward. What was once just a spot for me to be centralized in the chamber had now transformed into an actual throne room!

AND I WAS SO HIGH UP!

'State your request,' Slimey demanded, her tone authoritative, like a queen addressing her subject.

'Lord Hiro, Lady Slimey—'

Lady?

'I would request a bigger role in your army, that my silk be used to fashion clothes and armor for our soldiers. My Queen-Silk would make an excellent fabric for your body—'

'Denied,' Slimey said without hesitation.

Ayaka lowered her head, beginning to skitter off.

No, wait! Hold up! I'm the one giving orders here! I commanded Ayaka to stop.

That was actually a good idea. While I had the giant spider sequestered in my home base, I could spin up some garments for

Davette and the goblins. Maybe even teach a goblin to sew? To make a proper outfit out of spider silk.

An interesting idea. Begin immediately. I sent, much to Slimey's displeasure, who flashed a green hue.

'And... perhaps... i-i-if I do a good job' Ayaka said, shifting to one side, her massive body leaning slightly as her mandibles clacked together like a shy schoolgirl.

Maybe, I sent, the giant arachnid scurrying off to her knight with excitement.

Of course, I would never actually feed her addiction—especially if either of us wanted to remain alive while Slimey's hands gripped my neck.

Riding in Slimey's hands, who sat atop Buttstallion, I made my way back to the enemy dungeon's territory. Pausing at the collapsed entrance, I let out a squeak and pinged the area, observing that the rock formation had shifted slightly. No doubt a creature or being had attempted to escape, but failed.

Kappy. The large green lizard-like boar started biting at the rock with its beak.

And now we wait.

Maybe I should gather a thousand slimes or something and try to combine them with Slimey? My thoughts drifted, mainly focusing on how I would train the goblins and how to deal with Ayaka's addiction. I could use Purify on her, but that would probably take a significant amount of time. Plus, given her anima constitution, she'd likely be resistant to the skill.

After a few moments, Kappybara had dug out the rock and ore, some of the bits still slightly warm from the explosion.

With the entrance clear, I sent a mental command to Ayaka, instructing her phase spider to teleport in and teleport Kappy out to work on other projects.

Let's go, I signaled, initiating our march forward.

Entering the enemy dungeon, what had once been a lush and flourishing underground garden was now reduced to nothing but ash, charcoal, and burnt scraps. Charred carcasses littered the field, wilted flora lay in ruin, and the rock and stone that constituted the ceiling were marred by ash.

We moved slowly but cautiously. Davette, with her new crystal scales, was at the forefront, rubbing and admiring them, almost entranced by their beauty.

At my sides, Hector and the skeletons under his command followed, each one carrying a slime and spider on their bony frames.

Man, wouldn't it be nice to have Ayaka's juggernaut with us? I lamented. Alas, her phase spider could only teleport items it could physically carry.

Anyway, we continued, moving at a brisk pace, with me letting out occasional squeaks.

The damage was extensive, to say the least. Chloe's attack had created a cascading explosion that wiped out the forest and every living thing within the dungeon's territory.

I could feel the dark mana lingering in the air, clinging to the ash. Whatever traces of anima mana that remained had been infected and overtaken by its counter element.

Marching forward, I sent another ping, taking in the shriveled grass and burnt dirt.

We were in a field. Or, what used to be a field.

Desolation lay in the wake of my attack. Nothing remained on the grassland except for a large crater, with floating debris from the mana overcharge and the hole in the ceiling above.

Overkill? Definitely. I hadn't intended to cause this much damage, but it was for the best. Given the extent of the enemy territory, a full-on assault would've been a losing battle. Diplomacy, of course, was out of the question—they had attacked me first.

'I'm sensing movement,' Slimey said, and my squad shifted and spread out.

Hold.

My next ping picked up movement: a humanoid shape poking its head out from an opening in the crater.

Great... and here I thought it would be easy.

Move slowly, I ordered, my army making its way toward the hole in the earth via the floating debris and chunks of earth.

Quacks...

Reaching it, I realized that this opening was part of a larger tunnel system, one made visible by the explosion.

I pinged the tunnel, the corridor stretching for some distance before encountering what appeared to be a humanoid figure.

Hmmm. Was that a scout? Or the dungeon guardian?

I didn't know, but it wasn't moving. I sent out a few more quacks, each ping showing me the same humanoid figure with its hands raised, its mouth open, its body in a position that suggested it was running away.

The heck?

We needed to get closer.

Entering the tunnel, it wasn't long before my menagerie was sequestered in a lavish underground garden, one littered with...

Statues. Dozens—no, hundreds of statues—resembling various types of creatures, including spiders, skeletons, minotaurs, treasure mimics, cockatrices, and even...

Humans.

Odd. Scanning the underground garden, untouched by the flames above, I realized I was within a trophy room of some kind, with each statue giving off faint magical residue.

These creatures... these monsters and humans... THEY WERE ALIVE!

I recognized the effects immediately: petrification, a type of anima magic that combined dark mana with anima, twisting the two energies to achieve a... quacks, what did Chloe call it?

A... sym... symbiosis? A parallel state where the dark mana didn't infect the anima mana. A feat unachievable by most spellcasters, save for one creature in particular.

A gorgon.

This didn't make sense... The champion was a dryad, not a gorgon!

Or maybe I had seen Buttstalion's memory wrong?

I pinged my surroundings again.

No. It was definitely a dryad. So, what the quack was—

No.

Time seemed to freeze, my mind going blank as I focused on a statue of a young man with cat ears. One I recognized—a teen, maybe no older than sixteen, whose feminine face was twisted in fear.

Alexio.

A catboy journeyman blacksmith, one serving under Zorkwen as his adopted son and second. Alexio was a talented craftsman, quick with his hands, fast on his feet. The boy often handled the repairs of all our armor and gear, as well as the maintenance of our mounts.

'Are you okay, my lord?' Slimey asked, sensing my distress.

I... I'm not—

Suddenly, movement—a vibration traveling across the ground and into Slimey, where it reached me.

Huh?!

I quacked, sending a ping, my **Squeaker-Location** picking up something impossibly large in the garden moving.

Oh... quack.

It was the dryad, burned, broken, and glaring at me. The lithe feminoid was furious at the sight of me. Yet, that wasn't what made me choke on my own squeaker.

No.

What made me begin to panic was THE HUNDRED-FOOT-TALL SNAKE IT WAS RIDING!

Chapter 39

NOPE!

The Gorgonus-Hydra. A six-headed monster whose heads each contained massive mouths that formed eyeballs when closed.

A mythical creature, one I'd only heard of in rumors—tall tales from old mercenaries and rumor mills.

Similar to a gazer or an evil eye, the gorgonus possessed the ability to petrify, except instead of one eye capable of turning anything to stone, there were six, each connected to sharp teeth that let out a visceral shriek.

Haha.

Run.

On command, my army turned and fled, but not before having Davette grab a certain felinoid frozen in place.

Behind me, I could feel a gathering of energy, a powerful influx of mana, as the gorgonus shut its mouths and activated its gaze.

Ah... quacks.

This was it. I had messed up, and now I would be yet another statue in this monster's garden.

Maybe I should have Slimey strike a pose? Wouldn't that be funny?

Would I dream? Would I retain my thoughts as I remained petrified?

Hmm. Actually, when I thought about it, not much would change, considering I already couldn't move.

I probably wouldn't be able to squeak, but I could probably still give commands.

Then it happened—the earth vibrating from the force of the monster moving. The gorgonus shut its maw, its eyes targeting Davette, who brought up our rear, and hit her crystal body fully with all six eyes.

Davette! NO! NOOOOOOOOOoooooo?

A twist of fate. Instead of Davette being turned into stone, she merely stood there, looking up at the monster that was frozen in place.

Huh?

The gorgonus... IT HAD BEEN TURNED TO STONE!

Ha! AHhaahahahahaha!

I let out a squeak, pinging the area as the dryad dismounted its petrified snake and took off in a panic, its trump card defeated in a stroke of bad luck.

Get her!

Buttstalion took off, my army racing through the garden of statues after the fleeing monster.

Several unicorns with bulbous growths emerged, charred survivors from Chloe's explosion, attempting to intercept us. But Slimey wasn't having it.

Shifting her body, Slimey leapt off Buttstalion and expanded, slamming down on the unicorns as they charged.

Immediately, they were engulfed. The massive slime showcased her true size, enveloping the horde as they tried to gallop and cast spells.

A simple electric discharge put an end to their struggles.

Fortunately, I was unaffected by the lightning, but just in case, Slimey had tossed me into the air. My body rotated before landing back onto the slime.

Go! Don't let it escape!

Slimey reformed her shape, latching onto Buttstalion as Davette threw the frozen Alexios at the dryad.

WAIT! NO! DAVETTE, YOU IDIOT!

The catboy statue flew, striking the green creature on the back of the head.

Thankfully, Slimey's goopy body shot out tendrils, catching the statue just before it hit the ground.

Ah! Slimey! You're the best! You're actually the best! I sent, the slime turning bright pink and melting.

NO, WAIT! STOP! DON'T MELT! DON'T MELT!

Fortunately, Slimey managed to resume her blob form, pulling in the statue she had absorbed into her body.

As for the dryad, it was lying on the floor, crawling away with golden ichor leaking from its head.

Slimey reached out, multiple tentacles latching onto the green humanoid as it attempted to flee. The dryad flailed in futility as Slimey held her aloft.

I think I recall this hentai.

A quick electrocution stilled the dryad's movements, allowing the guardian to be captured by Slimey.

With the last resistance of the dungeon snuffed out, I summoned Ayaka's phase spider. The creature took both Alexios and the dryad with it.

I pinged Alexios as the phase spider crawled over him. This... this teen was proof of my past. If there was a way to cure him, to save him, then I would find it.

Alexios hadn't been part of the assault force, but rather our support team—a dedicated group focused on logistics and upkeep. If he was here, then it was only natural that the support group had been decimated as well.

Still, that was only speculation.

The real answers lay in the mind of Alexios... if he still had a mind left. Oddly, the thought of unfreezing the felinoid gave me comfort, the thought that I wasn't alone in this cycle of torment...

Just wait, my comrade.

The spider teleported out, leaving me with an odd feeling in my core. Still, there was work to be done. Always more work.

A dungeon core, waiting to be absorbed by Slimey for new abilities.

Marching unopposed, I surveyed the stone garden, seeing, hoping, almost praying to find another comrade of mine.

Nothing. None of the humanoids I found bore any resemblance to anyone I knew. It was a jarring experience, but it was what it was. There were quite a number of monsters, though—some much higher tier than I'd come across in this rubber life, like a wyvern, a minotaur, and oddly, and perhaps more surprisingly, a demon.

She was almost six feet tall, oddly familiar looking with her curved horns and scowl. Her body was adorned with jewelry, making her resemble a noblewoman.

A sudden urge began to well up inside me—anger, hatred.

Without waiting for my command, Slimey shot her hand out, tipping over the statue and shattering it against the cavern floor.

Ah. Much better.

Moving through the remaining garden, it wasn't long before my army reached the encrusted dungeon heart. The large pool of mana pulsed rapidly as we neared.

At its side, the core of the dungeon was wrapped around a large, inhuman weapon.

I pinged the weapon, the item immediately recognizable in my mind.

Sjúrður.

The Dragon Slayer. A two-handed black blade, buried deep in the ground.

Slimey and I approached the core, the orb manifesting energy as the weapon shook, rising from the ground.

I attempted to reach out—more of a gesture of my humanity, I guess—and try to offer the core a chance to surrender.

Instead, what I was met with was the same feeling I felt from all other cores: a cold indifference. No sign of sentience.

The orb shuddered, rising, and the Dragon Slayer looked almost as beautiful as I remembered it in battle.

A last defense, no doubt. Futile, if any—

Slimey was suddenly beheaded, the weapon slicing through her jelly neck and nearly bisecting Davette if not for the croc deflecting the blade with her claws.

AW QUACKS!

The greatsword flew into the air, picking up speed and boomeranging back around.

Davette! The croco-girl shifted, moving to intercept, this time putting both her arms together to catch the blade with her flesh.

NO, WAIT!

I activated **Water Jet**, blasting Davette's legs out from under her with a stream of black water just as the Sjúrður cut off her hands.

The blade continued to fly, and Davette let out a scream as I racked my mind, searching for a way to stop the weapon from coming back around.

Blast it! I ordered, my slimes unlatching from their skeleton mounts and firing at the legendary weapon.

Buttstalion! Heal Davette! Slimey! Full salvo!

The room began to coat with slime, hundreds of bolts flying into the air and striking the weapon that didn't slow down.

AHHHHHHH! How the heck do I stop it?!

Suddenly the weapon changed course, aiming in my direction!

Aim for the core! Aim for the core!

The weapon hit me on the head, bouncing off with a clang, my slash resistance holding up but not before nicking my head.

Ow?!

'MY LORD!' Slimey screamed, her body spreading out and unloading a massive barrage at the blade.

Knock it down! My spiders joined the assault to pile onto the weapon.

AHHH IT'S COMING BACK AROUND!

Suddenly Davette leaped off the ground, intercepting the blade's handle with her mouth.

The gator girl hit the ground, her bloodied stumps digging into the earth as she savagely banged the weapon against the cavern floor.

NOW! HIT IT!

My entire army opened fire, webs and slime, the entire barrage binding the weapon to the floor to kill its momentum.

Target the core!

Davette unlatched from the weapon, unleashing a roar before biting down on the core.

Oddly, her teeth only managed to scrape the orb, the Dungeon Core being significantly stronger than I'd thought it'd be.

The Sjúrður began to wiggle violently, the core attempting to lift the blade once more.

Ah. Wait. Ayaka!

'Yes, my lord?'

PREPARE FOR A GUEST!

I reached out, the spider matriarch sending her phase spider over to me that latched on to the blade.

BYE BYE!

The spider took the core and weapon away, bringing it back to the one thing that possessed enough power to take it out.

With the weapon away, it was time to destroy the heart and put an end to this fiasco.

Together with my army, I fired bolt after bolt at the enemy heart, breaking the chitinous shell that surrounded it to expose the pulsating mana below.

Before long, the beating heart stopped beating, the sphere deflating and striking the ground with a loud thud.

A stillness struck the air, a tangible shift in the cavern as the territory became ungoverned.

Hmmm. I wonder. My attention settled on the deflated heart on the floor, a number of crystals on the ground.

A mischievous feeling nestled in my core.

It was time to engage in the time-honored tradition of all adventurers.

Looting!

Chapter 40

A Time-Honored Tradition

With Davette sitting on the floor, staring at her regenerating arm stubs, my minions and I got to work.

Facilities, facilities, facilities—it was time to search for them.

Slimey quickly gathered the manacyst crystals that had come from the mana heart, storing them in her body, while Buttstalion went to work healing Davette.

The stallion lowered its head, its horn touching Davette's shoulder to transfer healing mana into the reptile.

I contacted Ayaka, requesting a sit... sitrep? What's a sitrep? I requested an update on the Dragon Slayer situation.

'All goooooooooowd,' came the response from the giant arachnid, who sounded almost drunk.

Huh? Is everything okay?

'Y-Yup! All good, Lord Hiro!'

Hmmmm. Suspicious. But for now, I would let it go until the ransacking was complete. Oh, and finding Davette's cut-off hands, which were somewhere around here.

Those were important too.

Slimey duplicated herself, allowing the main body to walk me through the statue garden while the other two halves roamed around in search of loot.

We spent some time in the garden, mostly me cataloging each and every petrified monster.

Wyverns.

Minotaurs.

Gorgonus.

Kobolds and humanoids of various species.

All of these boss monsters...

If I could cure and dominate them...

An army-in-waiting.

Why were there a bunch of boss monsters frozen down here?

My attention shifted to the shattered demoness. Maybe a falling out? It wasn't unheard of for demons to fight each other—killing each other was practically all they did. At least... until Barborall showed up.

Then they became a unified front. The demons, once mindless in their bloodshed, evolved into a hierarchy and pledged their loyalty to the one they called lord.

Hundreds of demons bent the knee, answering his summons, and the Demon Lord Barborall amassed an army unlike any seen in this world.

Maybe, after my defeat, there was a coup? An uprising, now that there was no Hero to stand against the darkness? No foe or army left to challenge them, so they descended upon each other?

Speculation.

That's all I had.

But... maybe I could find some clues with Alexios.

If I could cure him, then I'd have all the answers I needed. Of course, only if his mind was still intact.

'*Your eminence,*' Slimey Numbers 2 and 3 bowed before the minified Slimey that held me in its arms.

'*Speak,*' Slimey Number 1 replied, almost like a separate entity.

'*We've located the facilities.*'

The trio of slimes merged their forms, shifting back into the tall Slimey.

Before long, we were in a tunnel leading to a series of chambers—chambers filled with deflated organic material and manacysts of various types.

Unlike my blue crystal cultures, these manacysts were greenish and surrounded by beds of grass. Anima mana, no doubt—a good addition to my collection that would hopefully expand my building options.

Collect it. Collect it all. Slimey quickly obeyed, with a snoozing Davette being dragged over by Buttstalion for her storage device.

We spent a few more minutes scouting the chambers and garden, finding little else of use besides a few manacyst clusters and a colorful stone I thought was neat.

There wasn't anything special about the rock—it was just colorful. Oh, and really smooth.

After checking on the sleeping Davette, whose hands had been reattached, my army and I returned home—this time as successful conquerors, with spoils of war.

Entering my throne room, I saw Ayaka hunched over in a corner, her massive arachnid form turned away, her head buried against the wall.

Ayaka?

Suck. Suck. Suck. Suck.

A sudden sucking sound hit my senses, and my core flared up in anger as Ayaka continued to ignore my calls for her attention.

Ayaka!

The juggernaut at her side backed away as Slimey and I approached the massive arachnid, who was sucking on the Dragon Slayer.

What the—

More specifically, the spider monarch was sucking up the black ichor that coated the sword—a black mold that had somehow appeared and grown on the legendary weapon.

But more than that, THE ENEMY CORE WAS STILL FUNCTIONAL!

The blade was shifting violently, still attempting to move despite Ayaka's iron grip holding it in place.

Suck. Suck. Suck. Suck.

Great. Well, at least now we can try to pry the core off the sword...

I sent Slimey ahead, my holy slime attempting to wrap around the dungeon core to detach it from the blade. However, there was just one problem...

AYAKA KEPT TURNING AWAY!

BAD AYAKA! GIVE US THE CORE!

SUCK! SUCK! SUCK! SUCK!

Ayaka began sucking more violently, spinning in circles to flee from Slimey, her massive arachnid form more like a dog with something in its mouth that it didn't want to let go of.

Ayaka!

Suck. Suck. Suck. Suck.

ARRRRRRRGH!

Suck. Suck. Suck. Suck.

Ayaka! I am ordering you to give me that core!

The arachnid shuddered, momentarily halting as its body vibrated violently. But it still managed to turn away, not before smashing Slimey over the head with the massive blade.

Suck. Suck. Suck. Suck.

That's it! Everyone, out here now!

I summoned all forty of my minions—slimes, spiders, skeletons, and goblins—my entire army pouring out with one command in mind:

SEIZE HER!

At my order, every monster I had charged, goblins with their nets and ropes, spiders with their silk, and even my tiny slimes going to work binding her legs.

'*NO!*

NOOOOOOOOOOOOOOOOOOOOOOOOOOOOOOOOOOOOOOO!'
Ayaka screamed, desperately attempting to buck and run. Fortunately, her Juggernaut stepped up, the massive armored bug stepping atop its queen, pinning her down with its armored appendages.

'*TRAAAITORRRR!'* Ayaka wailed as every monster descended upon her.

Suck. Suck. Suck. Suck.

After safely extracting the core, I left Ayaka to continue sucking on the sword, the mighty monarch now lying in a corner with the legendary weapon still stuck in its mouth.

With the dungeon core in hand, Slimey immediately began to absorb it, gaining a new ability along with valuable experience.

Obtained: Telekinesis Lvl.01

Nice.

With that taken care of, I decided to let Ayaka continue sucking on the sword for the time being—something to calm her down—while I focused on dividing the loot from my latest venture.

Davette emptied the storage device, dropping the crystals beside my mana heart. The gems quickly dissolved into vapor, flowing into the beating heart and adding to my ever-growing stores.

Dungeon Management Panel
{Active} Dungeon Heart Lvl.01
HP: 1000/1000
Manacyst: 370
Anima: 296
Holy: 9
Dark: 55
Manacyst Production
Manacyst Culture: 2/2

Quite a hefty haul... I think?

Construction Options...
Dark Gestator
REQ: 100 Dark Manacysts
Graveyard
REQ: 50 Dark Manacysts, 10 Anima Manacysts
Guardian Room

REQ: Any 50 Manacysts
Composter
REQ: 20 Dark Manacysts

Lots of anima manacysts, but not enough dark energy. I could create a graveyard to summon new minions, I supposed.

Hmm, a Guardian Room perhaps? It would make sense, given that Ayaka was permanently stuck in this room, and I had no immediate use for the surplus yet.

Yeah, a Guardian Room it is.

I selected the option, my consciousness lifting from my shell as my point of view shifted to a bird's-eye view of my territory.

From above, I saw the layout of Ayaka's original nest, the chambers scattered throughout. A few of my goblins were using one as a living space, while my spiders had claimed another.

Interesting... I wondered if I could eventually create living quarters for the goblins, or perhaps even workshops. Maybe Alexios could start a forge and arm my goblins and skeletons—*heh, that'd be fun.*

In due time, Hiro.

After selecting my throne room as the Guardian Room, a subtle shift took place. Unlike other chambers in my domain that were highlighted blue, this one now pulsed with a yellow hue. An influx of mana filled the air, though there wasn't an obvious physical change—just an intangible shift as unseen energy flooded into the room.

Guardian Selection Available!

Of course, I choose Ayaka, the bug shifting uncomfortably in place with no other noticeable changes.

Hmm. Is that it? Bit disappointing—

Obtained: Summon Guardian
SKILL LIST
Bubble Blow Lvl.01
MP Cost: 5

Create a bubble of charged mana. When it pops, it releases a light burst of magic.

Squirt Water Lvl.01
MP Cost: 5

Create and squirt water from your beak.

Water Jet Lvl.01
MP Cost: 20

Shoot a high-pressure stream of water from your beak.

Summon Rock Lvl.01
MP Cost: 10

Summon a small rock. That's it. It summons a rock.

Purify Lvl.05
MP Cost: 20

Gathering light mana, attempt to cleanse an object or creature of curses, poison or disease. Effectiveness scales by level.

Squeaker-Location Lvl.03
MP Cost: 1

With a squeak, send out a pulse to map your surroundings and form a vivid image in your mind.

Impart Instruction Lvl.01

Teach skills and share experience with minions or selected creatures.

Summon Guardian

Once per day, you may summon a designated guardian to your location.

Ha... haha. AHAHAHAHA—Ehem...

The possibilities! OH, THE POSSIBILITIES!

Quest Complete: Construct a New Building!
+1000 EXP
Incoming Quest!
Level Up Mana Heart!

A new option appeared on my dungeon menu: an option to level up my mana heart, requiring a thousand manacysts.

Guess I need those composters.

I built them in a chamber once used to house Ayaka's spider eggs, now a cave holding all the carcasses of my enemies, including a certain squirming dryad.

Pits opened up in the earth—dark, crystalline-filled holes that reeked of undeath.

Moving on, I had my goblins toss all the leftover bodies of dead goblins and spiders into the composters until they were marked as full, with a "processing" symbol above them.

Alright. So... what's next on my to-do list?

Notes:

- Locate Treasury.

- Dominate the Dryad.

- Train goblins.

- Take the Dragon Slayer from Ayaka.

- Find a cure for Alexios.

- Find a cure for the monster garden.

- Dominate the monsters in the garden.

- Clean out the sewers and surrounding area.

- Breach the surface of the Demon Lord's castle.

- Dominate the world.

- Fight God.

Not exactly in that order, but this was what I had on my shortlist:

A rubber duck and his monster army versus the world.

I turned my attention to the injured dryad squirming around, the monster being held down and tickled by my goblins, who found it fun to torture.

Slimey. Bring the dryad before me. It's time we welcome another into our fold.

The slime changed colors to an odd orange, vibrating slightly before setting me up on my throne and doing as ordered.

Chapter 41

Goblin

S *ubmit to me.*

'Nyet!' The dryad spat, glaring up at me with green eyes, half of her face and body deformed from the explosion that had claimed her kingdom.

You. Are. Mine!

"Poshel ty!"

Mine!

"YA nikogda ne ustuplyu!"

SUBMIT TO ME!

"YA ispol'zuyu tvoy trup, chtoby vyrastit' iz nego rozy!"

Alright... That's not working. Time for a new strategy, I guess.

Submit to me, please?

The dryad gave me an annoyed look, continuing to stare me down.

Hey, at least I'm being polite. I guess I don't have enough gym badges or something.

"Idi ubey sebya—"

Slimey shot off then, snatching the dryad up off the floor. She elongated and warped herself around the dryad, emulating a gorgon. *'HOW DARE YOU DENY THE GIFT OF SERVITUDE LORD HIRO HAS DEIGNED TO BESTOW UPON YOU!'* Slimey screamed, her mouth unhinging to reveal serrated teeth that encircled the dryad's head. *'IF YOU WON'T SUBMIT, YOU HAVE NO PLACE UNDER OUR LORD'S GLORY!'*

Slimey. That's enough.

The slime retracted her mouth, her head snapping in my direction.

Let her go.

Slimey shifted to a green color momentarily but did as ordered.

Good girl, I praised, and Slimey suddenly turned pink before wrapping around my body and resuming her humanoid form on the throne.

'My lord, why not throw it into the composter? Surely, we'd get more use from this riffraff than if we were to accept it into our ranks,' Slimey offered, glaring at the dryad with disgust.

We have a use for her, Slimey.

'But—'

That's enough.

'Yes, Lord Hiro. My apologies for my insolence. Would you like to crush one of my cor—'

Siiiiiiiiiiiiigh.

Turning my attention back to the dryad, the former enemy guardian was proving a tough nut to crack.

Bound in webs and slimes, my monsters were constantly dissolving the creature to prevent it from regenerating. Considering the state of its injuries and how spry it was, I could only imagine what it would be like at full strength.

A considerable threat.

Fine, I sent. *If you won't submit, torture it is then.*

"Khm?" The dryad replied as a pair of goblins entered my throne room.

Off you go.

"Zhdat'!" The dryad screamed, dragged off by the goblins to be tickled until she broke. "ZHDAAAAAAAAT'!"

Bye bye.

With that taken care of for the time being, I focused my gaze on the loud clang that rang through my domain, followed by a sobbing sound.

'It's all gone!' Ayaka screamed, dropping the legendary sword, now picked clean of the black substance that came from my body. *'Gone! Gone! GONE!'*

Hmm. Now that I think about it, that black stuff is just the water I shot out... Is there something inside me that's making that goo?

I opened up my system menu as the spider began to shake and stomp.

Now that I think about it, the water squirt got less and less black the more I used it. Maybe there's—

'LOOOOOORD HIRO!' Ayaka cried.

The spider suddenly appeared beside my throne, kowtowing to me.

'Lord Hiro! Please! You must give me more! Just a taste! A small taste! A little itty-bitty taste!' Ayaka pleaded. *'I'll do anything you ask of me!'*

And we're back to this again.

'Pathetic,' Slimey replied.

Recover from your injuries and regain your strength. Do this, and I'll reward you.

'Y-Y-You promise?'

Of course. When have I ever lied?

Ayaka let out a chittering sound, wanting to refute but holding her tongue.

Now, behave. I ordered her back to her corner as more dead goblins were dragged in by Hector and the hunting squad.

Speaking of goblins, with twenty of them under my command, it was time to form a troop. There were enough of them for a lance or a platoon, but not enough for a company.

Organizing them into an effective unit wouldn't be too hard but getting them armed properly and trained would be.

Hmm.

Looking over the inventory of weaponry neatly stacked in a corridor of my chambers, I had roughly twelve spears, twenty swords, nine hand axes, fifteen kite shields in various stages of disrepair, and five bucklers. There was also a great shield, but it was doubtful any one of my goblins would be able to wield it.

I focused on the spears.

Fortunately, they were made of metal, allowing for a usable weapon that wasn't rotting wood.

Training a bunch of sickly goblins into spearmen didn't seem like such a bad time-waster.

However, the problem lay in the quality of the troop. I'd trained peasants before, turned villagers into warriors, and recruits into veterans. Inspired them to protect their families, homes, and country.

But goblins? And blighted ones at that? They had no allegiances or thoughts really, other than to eat, sleep, and kill.

Or that was until I took these goblins under my command.

Much like Slimey, I could feel beyond the veil of their shell—their desires, wants, and needs. But most of all, I could feel their pain from their blight.

It was dull, but there, underneath the gnawing hunger and desire to kill, a lingering torment that was more of an inconvenience to the goblin consciously but something that affected its health.

Hmm.

I sent for a goblin as Hector and the other skeletons moved the food bundles away.

Speaking of teaching...

Slimey.

'*Yes, darling?*'

How would you like to learn some swordplay?

'*L-L-Learn from you?!*' Slimey suddenly turned yellow. '*IT WOULD BE MY HONOR, LORD HIRO!*'

Try using **Telekinesis** *to summon the Dragon Slayer,* I commanded, and Slimey reached out with her hand, only for the blade to remain unmoving.

Unsatisfied with the result, Slimey began to turn red, her mana bar visibly lowering as she activated the skill repeatedly.

It's okay if it doesn't work.

'*I've got this, my lord! Please believe in me!*'

Of course, I believe in youuuuu—Aw, great.

Slimey deflated again, turning into a hot pink puddle on my throne, her body vibrating rapidly.

I swear, I'm never going to get anything done at this rate.

Pus-ridden and covered in ick, a naked goblin stood before me, quivering under Slimey's and Buttstalion's gaze.

I could see its fear, its doubt—a cannibalistic creature worried that it had been chosen to be consumed.

I didn't know much about goblin culture, but I did know that when food supplies got bad, they drew sticks to see who would be eaten to preserve the rest of the pack.

'How dare you stand before our lord? KNEEL!' Slimey snapped, and the goblin immediately hit the floor, kowtowing.

Slimey.

'Yes, my love?'

Screaming is a poor form of education. In the future, see to it that you take a gentler tone when speaking to the uneducated.

'Y-Yes. As you wish, my lord.'

I turned my attention to the quivering goblin.

Be calm, I sent, the creature going wide-eyed as I addressed it directly.

The shivering stopped.

Now approach.

The goblin stood up, its head low, walking slowly up to the stairs of my throne, where it stopped.

I activated **Purify**, casting the energy over the goblin, who began to glow and scream. Adding to the experiment, I had Buttstalion cast **Detoxify** while Slimey used **Mend**.

A three-pronged attack. Unlike the formerly known "Dave," the goblin didn't have the benefit of evolution.

Plus, I wanted to test if I could purify and alleviate the monster's symptoms.

The monster's screams bounced off the chamber walls, its cries alerting all of my goblins, who came out to help.

They formed a loose gathering, each goblin slack-jawed as they eyed their companion glowing with power.

Focusing on the goblin, its brackish skin began to lighten, going from brown to green, the pus and spores boiling off its body to be replaced with new green skin.

Before long, the goblin began to shake and shudder, black blood pouring out of every orifice before the ick was replaced with crimson red.

Blighted Goblin 12 → Goblin 12

The goblin stood in awe of its own condition, staring at its arms and body as its cohorts let out audible gasps.

On top of losing its blighted status, the goblin gained an increase in maximum health points, mana points, and even a new ability—**Endurance.**

Next. The goblins snapped out of their stupor to stare at me.

'You heard our lord! STEP UP!' Slimey snarled, sending pure killing intent across the room.

Immediately, three volunteered, stepping in unison at the command to be the next in line to be cured.

I could feel it—their eagerness. The monsters were a step above their kin by virtue of their will.

I grinned inwardly. Maybe there was hope yet to create a professional fighting force.

THE HIRO IS A RUBBER DUCK

Chapter 42

Goblin Bosses

*T*hrust!

At my command, two rows of five shot out their spears, the weapons scraping against the shields held by the goblins beside them.

A pseudo-phalanx, a formation of ten goblins holding spears and ten goblins holding shields. The spears were too long for any of the goblins to wield one-handed with a kite shield, so instead, they were taught to work in pairs.

One spearman. One shieldman. Splitting the focus of one task into two so that the goblins could accomplish the needed objectives.

The goblins took to the training surprisingly easily, following my instructions to the best of their ability, thanks to my Impart Instruction skill.

I could visualize what I wanted, think of actions, attacks and techniques, then transmit them to the goblins eager to follow my lead.

All in all, a good day for everyone.

Well, almost everyone. Slimey, on the other hand...

She was having trouble lifting the Dragon Slayer.

The massive black blade was stuck in the ground as Davette pointed and laughed at the slime's efforts.

'Having trouble?' Davette teased, a rare moment where the gator girl "spoke."

Slimey shot a glare at the gator-girl.

Slimey.

'Yes, my lord?' Slimey asked, appearing beside me almost instantly, her eyes big and round.

How about we focus on leveling up **Telekinesis** *first?*

'Of course, my lord.' Slimey replied, using the skill on my body to lift me and bring me into her hands.

Ah... Not quite what I meant...

Moving back to organizing the goblins, I began splitting them up, creating two ten-goblin squads, each led by a commander.

Goblin 12 and Goblin 15, renamed Gobeldee and Gobeldo, respectively.

These two would be captains of their squads, leaders who would facilitate the needs and upkeep of their units and arms.

Although I'd led armies in the past, micromanaging everything wasn't something I particularly enjoyed doing. Which is why I employed commanders, strategists, and tacticians—people who handled the minor tasks for me so I could focus on the big picture of fighting a war.

It would be some time before I had suitable officers, though, so in the meantime, I would focus on spear drills and techniques. I'd have them build cohesion as a unit and develop Gobeldee and Gobeldo as leaders.

To cement their statuses as leaders above the others, I ordered them to my throne, where they both took a knee under Slimey's gaze.

I reached out, giving them both one thousand experience from my own pool.

Both goblins began to shake, their bodies flooding with power as their levels went up and they hit their level cap of ten.

Unlike the other monsters under my command, the goblins had no skills or abilities—nothing that set them apart from the others. In fact, skeletons had more abilities. Fortunately, that would soon change.

Both goblins underwent a visible evolution, growing slightly bigger with thicker muscles. Instead of short, child-sized monsters, they now stood the height of an average thirteen-year-old.

Goblin → Goblin Boss

Both goblins gained the skill **War Cry**, as well as an ability called **Rally**. Leadership skills that I would sorely need and test out.

The pair fell to their knees, heads planted into the cavern floor as tears fell from their green eyes.

I could feel their reverence, their devotion. Their hands and heads raised up to gaze at my throne, as if praying to their God.

+10 Devotion

Huh?

I could feel a strange energy welling up within me, a lightness that bubbled before settling down.

Weird.

Verrrrry weird.

Slimey was one thing, but having more devotees...

I can't say I'm particularly a fan of it. I wasn't a god, nor was I a hero, yet these monsters all turned to me with devotion in their hearts. I could feel their eagerness to please me, their willingness to do anything I commanded.

Was this what the Demon Lord felt as he unleashed his hordes? I won't say it's not an intoxicating feeling because it was. Is.

The goblins in the back were kneeling as well, following their newly appointed leaders in their display of devotion.

'Praise be to Lord Hiro!' Slimey joined in, holding me aloft as the entire crowd of goblins fervently cheered in response.

"PRAIZ TA LORD HIRO!"

Great... This is a cult. I've actually formed a cult...

Siiiiiiiiiiiiigh. I didn't like this at all, not at all... but if it gets me closer to dominating the world?

Then I would play the role.

ELSEWHERE...

Under the blighted purple sky, Lhikan moved quietly yet swiftly through the dense jungle, each step taking him one step closer to his destination.

Pausing for a moment, Lhikan eyed the symbols carved into the nearby trees—way signs left behind by Zak'naufen, typically unseen by the human eye.

Typically.

Thankfully, the traitorous elf had been useful during the journey, granting Lhikan and the others the ability to read drowthraki way signs, ensuring they wouldn't get lost.

Lhikan brushed his gloved hand against the rough tree bark, an odd buzzing feeling erupting in his palm.

Heading left ahead.

He adjusted his gas mask, checking the box attached to his hip.

Six hours of air left.

"How much further?" a man asked, one of the paladins clad in hazard gear.

"Five days at our current pace," Lhikan replied, turning his gaze to Marcus and the twelve others following him. "We're at least two weeks ahead of the army, but we need to keep moving."

Marcus reached out, grabbing Lhikan by the shoulder just as the man began to turn.

"Wait a moment," Marcus said, halting his friend.

"What?" Lhikan replied, eyeing the man through the red lens of his gas mask.

"We should take a moment to rest. We're a good two weeks ahead; it would do no harm to slow down."

Lhikan scanned his group of volunteers and clergymen, men and women abandoned by their church and country. They were people who had doubts but followed him because of the hope he promised them.

"No," Lhikan replied firmly. "Every moment delayed is another that the enemy gains ground. By now, word of my escape has probably reached Danse's ears, with Krekka ordering them to force march. Next checkpoint is half a day's walk; we keep moving until then, Sergeant."

Marcus grimaced but obeyed, falling in line behind his old friend.

"So, are you ever going to teach me how to read drowthraki waysigns?" Marcus asked, brushing aside a vine that nearly caught his boot.

"I told you before, no."

"Aw c'mon, why not?" Marcus pressed, stepping around thick vines that nearly tripped him.

Lhikan grunted. "Because it's not something that can be taught. You need a drowthraki elf to give you the ability."

"You still never told me how you managed to find a drowthraki."

"I didn't," Lhikan replied curtly.

Marcus shook his head with a sigh.

"Okay, fine. Keep your secrets. Just trying to make small talk."

"Less talking, more walking," Lhikan ordered, pushing ahead.

"Aye, aye, Paladin."

Through the jungle they marched, the air silent except for their steps and the distant sound of the jungle.

When they finally broke through the dense foliage, Marcus and the others gasped.

Beyond the jungle lay a rainbow meadow, a vibrant biome of colorful reeds and flowing streams, a small slice of paradise nestled in the heart of blighted venom.

"H-How?" Marcus asked as Lhikan entered the pocket of dense anima magic, taking off his gas mask.

"That," Lhikan said, pointing to a glimmering blade lodged in a concrete structure, an unnatural sight amidst the wilderness.

"Is... Is that—" Marcus began, his eyes widening as he and the other knights approached the blade.

"Excalibur?" Lhikan replied, taking a seat on a log next to an old campsite. "Yes."

"THIS! THIS IS INCREDIBLE!" Marcus exclaimed, dropping to his knees in front of the blade. The other apostates began to examine the weapon, untouched by rust or decay.

Marcus turned to Lhikan, who remained unmoved.

"This is an incredible find! Why did you not report this to Prior Dume?!"

"And have Krekka's cronies deface this landmark? To desecrate this resting place?" Lhikan replied.

Marcus looked down, realizing a face peeked at him from beneath the glass.

"WHA?!" he exclaimed, scrambling backward, his feet scraping against the glass flooring.

"Everyone, meet Ravenhawk Hector. Ravenhawk Hector, everyone," Lhikan said, gesturing to the perfectly preserved corpse beneath the glass.

Ravenhawk Hector, one of the Legendary Six. Master spy under Queen Liliana's command and companion of The Hero.

Marcus quickly scrambled off the glass, his jaw agape as he stared at the roguish-looking figure below.

"Is he... dead?"

"As a doorknob," Lhikan replied, his gaze shifting to the two men trying to pull the legendary weapon from the stone. "Don't bother; it's magically bound to the earth."

The two knights exchanged glances but attempted to pull the blade anyway. It didn't budge.

"This is a magnificent find!" Tipsy, a gnome, observed through the lenses of a mechanical contraption perched on her head.

A non-human among the group, Tipsy was responsible for maintaining their rebreathers. Though paid in coin, her dedication to the mission was unwavering.

"Hmmm, the algorithm for the spell is extremely complex," she reported. "I can see rune traces for 'purify' and 'chosen.'"

"Can you decode and deactivate it?" Marcus asked.

"No," Lhikan interjected, drawing everyone's attention to him.

"He's right," Tipsy added. "This is in an ancient language. The encryption is constantly shifting, with at least fifty—no, a hundred lines and an access code of sixty, with a one in sesvigintillion possible combinations."

"Meaning?" a knight named Zach asked.

"Meaning a number with eighty-one zeros behind it."

Marcus started counting on his fingers, stopping when all of his hands were palm up.

"That's like a billion possible combinations!"

Tipsy turned to him, the lenses of her contraption closing as though imitating a blink.

"Sure. Let's go with that," she said dryly. "Anyway, it's impossible to crack unless you fulfill the requirements to unlock the blade."

"And what are those requirements?"

"To be the Hero," Lhikan said, his eyes closing as he recalled the time he and Natalie spent at this campsite with their companions.

Ivanc and Natalie, both transcribing the runes etched on the enchanted glass coffin.

Zak'naufen stringing his bow while Krota discussed the customs of cannibalism from his culture.

And Morty, Edward Richthofen, Sammy Maxis, Takeo Masekai, Sergei Ravenov, Nikolai Belinski, John Dempsey—drinking, playing card games, and taking a rare moment to breathe.

At that point in their journey, they had still been twelve. Every threat they faced was destroyed by their teamwork, with no sacrifices yet made.

Sacrifices that went unrecognized by their Church.

"Garrus," Marcus snapped his fingers, summoning the beastman scribe. "Work with Tipsy to document everything. I want a full record of this grave site—the effects of the blade, the inscription on the glass casket."

"Yes, Sir."

The two non-humans quickly went to work as Lhikan opened his eyes, staring at the blue sky—only visible thanks to the legendary sword.

Soon, Natalie. I'll make sure your efforts weren't in vain.

Chapter 43

Ambush

S tanding in a cave illuminated by the faint glow of crystals, Gobeldee barked an order as his chitin-clad defenders clashed against Gobledo's raiders.

"LEF! LEF YOU IDGITS! SHOR UP DA FLAK!" Gobeldee screamed, directing the goblins on his left to adjust their shields.

Gobledo's forces slammed into Gobeldee's phalanx, his group of ten desperately trying to hold off the invaders attempting to breach the throne chamber.

"Hol! HOL!" Gobeldee shouted, his voice rising as he directed his goblins from the rear.

Suddenly, an axe latched onto a shield—one of Gobledo's goblins gripping a hand axe and pulling with all its might.

"SCREE?!"

Gobledee's goblin tried to stop it, aiming to knock the dull axe head off, but was struck in the eye by a rock.

The goblin's shield lowered, just enough for its attacker to reach up and bop it on the head.

'Enough.'

At the words, every goblin froze, spinning and snapping to attention at the champion of their nest.

"Mistress Slimmay!" Gobeldee took a knee, his squad following suit, mirroring his actions as Gobledo's goblins did the same, their heads lowered in respect.

Slimey looked down at the goblins, their bug-like armor clanking softly as they knelt. To her, they were only a step above skeletons and spiders—not much more, if she was honest.

If it were up to her, she'd do away with them entirely. Her lord needed only her.

But, for now, they served piously, and Slimey would tolerate them.

'Enough training for today,' she said, her voice carrying the weight of command. *'By Lord Hiro's decree, you are to take the remainder of the day to relax.'*

The goblins flinched as something clattered to the floor, the sound echoing in the cavernous space.

'By cleaning.'

Gobledee dared to raise his head, his eyes locking onto the spears with unicorn hairs tied to their ends.

"Cleaning?"

Minion, Chloe has entered Phase 2: Coalescing Mana!
Stage 2 of 3

Uuuuuuuuuugh, this is taking so long! Why can't you just evolve instantly like a Pok—**TRADEMARK REDACTED DUE TO LEGAL REASONS**?!

A few days had passed since the creation of my new goblin army—days spent training them and researching new technologies.

What kind of technologies? Oh, well, I'm glad you asked!

Brooms! Brushes! AND HORSE ROPE! All made from the remains of the unicorns before they were tossed into the composters.

And speaking of composters, they were beginning to churn out copious amounts of manacysts thanks to all the bodies thrown into them.

I still had a stockpile of bodies that needed to be disposed of, but at least my stores of manacysts had doubled.

Still, no new buildings to unlock, so for now, I had my capruxas—who apparently could walk on any hard surface—create new rooms for future expansion.

With all my minions assigned to their tasks, I split my focus to two other urgent matters: reversing the petrification effects on Alexios and figuring out the mystery of the black ink I kept producing.

As for Alexios? Well, there was nothing I could do... not that I knew of anyway. I was a weapon master, not a mage or cleric, after all. Even though I understood the basics of magecraft, every magic spell I knew came from my system.

Sigh. Maybe I should have listened to Chloe's lectures.

Still, I had Slimey, my pseudo-cleric. If I could evolve her, maybe she'd gain something useful...

Can I help you?

Slimey appeared from behind my throne, her form hovering as she gave me a wide, expectant grin.

'Were you thinking about me, Lord Darling?'

No.

Slimey wiggled in the air, her form deflating before suddenly expanding, her body turning red.

'Why not? Are you thinking about other women? ARE—'

I ignored her tantrum and focused back on the problem at hand: the black ink.

What was it? Why did Ayaka like it? And why was I producing it? After a few preliminary tests—**Squirt Water**, **Water Jet**, and **Bubble Blow**—it seemed that the more I used my water skills, the less black substance I produced.

Ayaka was completely enamored with it, even turning into a juggernaut as she scraped her massive face across the floor to lick up every drop.

Yet, the more concerning aspect was that the liquid I secreted grew mold if left untreated. Or, in Ayaka's case, eaten.

Hrrrrrn... This was making me uncomfortable. *What was this black stuff? Where did it come from?* None of my skills showed any modifications... So, what was causing this acidic effect? It wasn't blight, but it was poisonous ink, deadly to everything except Ayaka, who seemed to eat it like candy.

Hrrrrrn... Okay, now I'm uncomfortable.

Feeling my agitation, Slimey wrapped herself around me, lifting me in her hands.

'Is there something wrong, my lord?'

I sighed deeply. *Hmm... trying to figure out what this black ink is.*

'Oh, those are secretions from the toxic mold inside your body.'

Huh. I froze. *Wait, what?! Toxic... mold... inside me?!*

Slimey nodded, her expression sweet. *'Yes, my lord. You've got mold inside you. It's probably why the ink is poisonous.'*

I have mold in my body?! I involuntarily squeaked and immediately spit up a small bit of the black ink.

NO! NONONONONONONO!

'MY LORD—'

NOOOOOOOOOOOOOOO—CLEAN ME! CLEAN IT OUT! GET IT OUT! GET IT OUT OF ME!

Slimey's body turned bright pink.

'M-M-My lord? Y-You want me inside you?'

SLIMEY, I SWEAR TO AJAX AND MR. CLEAN I WILL FIND A WAY TO FLY YOU INTO THE STRATOSPHERE AND DROP YOU FROM ORBIT!

'A-Are you flirting with me, my lord?'

GET. IT. OUT.

Slimey paused, hesitating, looking at me with confusion.

Well?! WHAT ARE YOU WAITING FOR?!

'My lord...' Slimey's voice trembled. *'I... I... I... forgive me, my lord! To purge the mold is beyond my capabilities.'*

What?!

'I... I...'

An indiscernible amount of time passed as I lost myself in the sheer horror of it all. Thankfully, a nearby goblin sweeping the floor with a broom managed to stir me from my breakdown.

Ha... Hahaha...

I'm full of mold!

I'm full of mold!

I'M FULL OF MOLD!

I'M FULL OF MOLD!

'My lord? A-A-Are you okay, darling?' Slimey asked, her voice soft as she caressed my head, trying to comfort me as my rubbery body shook uncontrollably.

Suddenly, I became aware of every one of my minions staring at me, their eyes wide and curious. The chamber suddenly felt claustrophobic.

Okay. Breathe. Breathe, Hiro. You're okay. You're fine. Just momentarily dirty. Just momentarily dirty. Don't think about it. Don't think about it. Just don't think about it. Yup. Yeah. Not thinking about it...

I CAN'T STOP THINKING ABOUT IT!

MOLD?!

MOLD!

GAAAAAAAAAAAAAAAAAAH!

Composting Complete!

Oh hey, that's done.

Dungeon Management Panel
{Active} Dungeon Heart Lvl.01
HP: 1000/1000
Manacyst: 784
Anima: 673
Holy: 17
Dark: 84
Manacyst Production
Manacyst Culture: 2/2

Almost there. I just needed two hundred and sixteen more manacysts until I could evolve my mana heart.

Gah! I need something to distract my mind.

Slimey!

'Yes, my lord?!'

We're going treasure hunting.

"GET BACK! NOW!" Lhikan barked, cleaving his sword through a ball-like mass of squirming tentacles that screeched as it died.

"What are these things?!"

"HELP!"

"MARCUS!"

"Two more on the left!"

Lhikan pivoted, his blade cutting down another squealing tentacle.

Mimics. Not the typical treasure mimics, but wild ones—creatures that didn't possess shape-shifting capabilities to ambush prey but instead hunted in packs with feral tenacity.

"MY LEG! IT'S GOT MY LEG! IT'S GOT MY LEG!" Marcus screamed through his gas mask. "DON'T LET IT TAKE MY BUTT VIRGINITY!"

Lhikan gritted his teeth, throwing his blade at a pair of tentacles attempting to drag Marcus into the unknown.

The sword severed the appendages, allowing Marcus to scramble away as Tipsy began firing iron pellets from a contraption she called a "gun."

"Thank you, thank you, THANK YOU!" Marcus exclaimed, his mask repeatedly pressing against Lhikan's boot.

"On your feet!" Lhikan barked, yanking his friend up as a ten-foot-tall mimic crawled out of the shadows of the nearby cove. "AN ALPHA! WATCH OUT!"

"I offer up this contract to invoke the lord's blessings that dance within the air—Holyinu!" Garrus chanted, the beastman holding his palm open where sigils and golden runes danced.

A blade of holy mana formed, targeting the alpha, which spun and slapped the magic out of the air with a barbed tentacle before charging the mage.

"Oh no," Garrus let out, as the alpha mimic opened its mouth to scream and brandish rows of serrated teeth.

"STOP IT!" Lhikan barked, the entire cohort under his command shifting as the monster raced through their lines.

The Alpha leaped, targeting Garrus, the church scribe going slack-jawed as his life flashed before his eyes. Was this it? Would he be—

Garrus didn't get to finish his thought as he was crushed underfoot, the alpha mimic's weight alone killing the mage before its tentacles penetrated his body and began ripping the beastman apart.

"DAMN IT!" Lhikan roared, drawing his spare blade from his back and rushing the monster. Silvery steel came out of his sheath, the weapon cutting off a barbed appendage as he sidestepped and sliced.

The alpha spun, all the tendrils adorning its body lashing out at Lhikan, who leapt over them with a roar.

"SCREEEEEEEEEEEEEEEEEEEEEEEE!"

Lhikan's blade was now in the mimic's head, the monster violently bucking to dislodge the paladin, who placed his armored boot in the monster's maw for purchase.

The monster immediately bit down, denting Lhikan's sabaton, but not before he drew his dagger and stabbed the monster in its eye.

With Lhikan occupying the creature's attention, Tipsy and Marcus flanked the Alpha, the paladin using his greatsword to cut off the monster's foreleg, whilst Tipsy used her size and agility to deftly avoid the tentacles and draw close.

"Keep its mouth open!" Tipsy yelled as the horror fell on its side with a scream.

Tipsy reached into her bag of holding, producing an orb-like flask as she slid next to Lhikan. Acting quickly, the little gnome tossed the alchemical mixture into the screeching maw held open by the paladin's boot and gauntlet.

"GET AWAY! GET AWAY!" Tipsy yelled, Lhikan and the others backing off as the Alpha let out a low whine before its head was suddenly detonated, showering the surroundings in blue blood.

Suddenly, the sounds of battle stopped, the tiny balls of squirming tentacles halting their ambush and fleeing.

Lhikan wiped the blue blood off his gas mask, huffing as he eyed his dented boot and sat down on the black grass beneath him, allowing the adrenaline in his veins to ebb away.

"Damn it... damn it! DAMN THAT SUCKED!" Marcus exclaimed, kicking the carcass of a dead mimic, sending it flying.

"Enough!" Lhikan barked, rising to his feet, his eyes scanning the battlefield where three of his men lay dead. "Scavenge our dead and wounded, collect Garrus, Jon, and Rita, and be prepared to move."

Lhikan began to walk off to retrieve his thrown sword, but not before he was stopped by a certain gnome.

"Sir, you're hurt," Tipsy said, Lhikan looking down at his thigh, which was leaking blood.

"HEALER!" Marcus snapped, calling up two of the priestesses who followed them to treat the injured paladin. "We should take a moment to rest, set up cam—"

"No," Lhikan replied, eyeing the two priestesses who were healing his leg with efficiency that paled in comparison to Natalie's. "We are a day away from the Demon Lord's castle. Every moment exposed out in the deadleads is another that increases our chances of being ambushed. Get to work, all of you."

Marcus and Tipsy shared a look but said nothing, leaving the paladin alone as they went to scavenge the field and collect their dead.

Lhikan sighed, pressing his thumb into the center of his palm and closing it into a fist.

Chapter 44

My Own Worst Enemy

*M*old.
Mold.
Mold.
Mold.
Mold.
Mold.
The word kept bouncing in my head.
Mold.
'Lord Hiro?'
Mold.
'Lord Hiro?'
Mold. I'm moldy! Slimey! I'm full of mold!

'Yes, you are, sir,' Slimey replied, stroking my head as she carried me through the decrepit hallways of the catacombs. *'But that's okay, I love you anyway, Lord Hiro.'*

ARGHHGH! Screw love! I need a cure! A cure! Wait! AYAKA! She can suck—

Ah... what's this killing intent I'm suddenly feeling?

Slimey! Slimey, calm down!

'Hrrrrrn!' The slime vibrated, her form turning red.

After calming Slimey down, she and I continued our journey, a calm stroll through the catacombs with an army of slimes cleaning behind us.

'*Such a lovely day for a stroll, my lord,*' Slimey said.

Right. Day... in an underground cavern with no sunlight.

I decided to play along, placating the jealous slime's emotions while I figured out my next steps.

Curing my disease, finding the treasury, getting a thousand manacysts, and evolving Chloe.

And, of course, manually evolving Slimey using a tedious plan that involved the use of a very deep hole.

This mold was why Ayaka thought I was so tasty. Now this begged the questions: *why was there mold in me? Where did it come from? Why hadn't I seen this mold anywhere else?*

Why was it so deadly? Why couldn't it be purged?

Questions, questions, questions.

But no answers.

Gah, it's just one thing after another!

Moving through the catacombs, I suddenly felt a shift in the air, a tangible taste that hung suspended in my surroundings.

A dungeon's territory.

Great...

I pinged my surroundings, noticing an ornate archway at the end of my current tunnel.

An exit out of the catacombs, a new biome.

Fall back.

'My lord?'

Retreat.

'Yes, my lord.'

I wouldn't begin an incursion without more firepower.

Chloe was still in stage two of her evolution process, and while I could summon Ayaka to me, I needed her in the throne room to keep the dryad contained.

Just in case she broke free from her hourly tickle tortures.

No. I wouldn't chance it. Not yet. If my last dungeon run was any indicator, I was basically running on luck.

There was also the fact that Davette was out of commission, the large croco-girl regenerating from an experiment of mine.

From my testing, Davette's new scales reflected magical effects to a certain extent, returning magical effects to the target as long as the spell was non-lethal.

However, this also applied to healing skills as well, with Slimey's Enlight bolts penetrating the monster's scales while Mend simply bounced off.

A bit annoying. But after more testing, it was shown that Davette's scales eventually lost their reflective property the more they reflected, allowing for healing to be used.

I was down three of my strongest: one recovering her spell reflection, one tied up defending my prisoner, and one stuck under a pile of bones evolving.

All I had was Slimey and Hector. And while that was enough for the lower biomes, I wasn't sure what threats lurked above the catacombs.

Yet.

Stepping out of the enemy domain, I called up Hector, my assassin bending the knee as it responded to my summon.

I reached out, taking control of Hector, with the rest of my minions on standby to provide support.

Looking through the eyes of the undead rogue, I shot off through the archway, my eight-minute timer already counting down.

Stepping into the next room, I could see that the biome had changed, the walls and flooring of cobblestone replaced by white marble, cracked and stained by the passing of time.

However, despite the weathered appearance of my surroundings, I recognized them immediately as the same tile and walling as the floor Ayaka had fled from in her memories.

The treasury was nearby.

However, considering my last dungeon core encounter just so happened to be grown around the Dragon Slayer, it was a safe assumption that the core in this area was probably the same.

Stepping lightly, I could feel the gaze of another on my back, a foreign will reaching out to touch my mind only to be rebuffed by my control.

Great. It knew I was here. Still, I wouldn't be dissuaded by its gaze. I had an objective, after all, and I needed to find it.

Opening one of the many rotting wooden doors that littered the space, I moved cautiously with my daggers raised, eyeing the storeroom I entered.

Wine barrels, rows upon rows of them, with the containers long since fallen into disrepair. Judging from the layout, I had now entered the castle proper, as any base typically kept the alcohol close at hand.

Now the question remained: *where exactly in the castle was I? Presumably near the kitchens or dining room, maybe?*

Walking through what I presumed was the basement level of the castle, there was oddly a scarcity of monsters. In fact, there were none! However, despite the lack of aggressors, I could still feel the dungeon core's presence—the mastermind of this strata watching every movement I made, completely aware that I was intruding into its space.

So now that begged the question:

Why hadn't it sent enemies after me? What was it waiting for?

Hard to say.

I pressed on, exiting the wine storeroom and climbing a set of stairs that led into a massive chamber I recognized immediately.

The arena...

A massive coliseum with rows upon rows of benches and seats, a place once used for the entertainment of demons.

I looked up, eyeing the hole in the ceiling, the trap door that led unsuspecting victims into the sandpit floor.

As I stepped into the arena, my bones rattled as mirages and echoes of the past played out around me.

Scenes of battle, dozens of monstrosities, hundreds of voices. Cheers and screams, monsters demanding blood as my companions of old collected ourselves to stand against the chimera, hydra, and twin-headed gorecyclops.

Walking into the open, I stood at the center of the sandpit, my undead eyes scanning the decrepit landscape, filled with bones of monstrosities once slain by my hand.

I could see them—the echoes of the past, images of that battle playing out before my eyes, visions of myself wielding my holy blade, dubbed "Excalibur."

Not the actual Excalibur of Arthurian legend, mind you, but a blade I personally crafted with the help of my friends. A weapon infused with the strength of our friendship.

Cringe? Probably. But... it was something made with the combined efforts of those who put their trust in me. A weapon that resonated with the wielder's strength of emotion and commitment. A holy armament that could only be used by those who had a hand in its creation.

Hmm. I wonder where that sword is now?

A couple of hundred years had passed, with no one left alive to power the blade. No doubt the strength of the weapon had long since faded into oblivion, becoming no more than a useless piece of expensive metal.

Suddenly, movement—a strange shift in the atmosphere of the arena.

The sands began to shift, move, a cold wind blowing as the sand swirled, forming what appeared to be a humanoid shape.

Power. I could feel it. An influx of mana condensed to form a man in armor with jet-black hair, his body adorned with armor fashioned of enchanted magi-gold and antimuonium. The silver trim of his claw-shaped gauntlets held a blade that was all but unfamiliar to me.

My jaw unwillingly dropped; my undead eyes quivering as I eyed...

Myself.

OH SH—

Suddenly, my worldview was spinning, my skull decapitated from my skeletal body and sent flying. My instincts kicked in, plucking my head out of the air and backpedaling, avoiding the return swipe that broke open my ribcage.

Quacks!

Duck!

My knees gave out, avoiding the sword jab that shaved the top half of my skull.

I shot forward, not to attack, but to dodge, scurrying through the legs of my sand copy to perform a tactical maneuver known as running away.

AYAKA!

'*Yes, my lord?*' Ayaka sent back as the blade speared the back of my ribcage, stopping me in my tracks, my feet sweeping the sand on the floor.

TELEPORT! TELEPORT *HECTOR OUT RIGHT NOW!*

My field of vision began to shift, my body held aloft as my mirror image brandished my body into the open air like a sacrifice.

AYAKAAYAKAYAKAKSKDBkwpapalYT!

Suddenly, a magnificent blue bug appeared out of thin air, the phase spider latching onto my body as mana began to condense below me.

TELEPORTTELEPORTTELEPORT!

Suddenly, the world erupted in white, my back being blasted open as my consciousness shifted.

Chapter 45

Oops... I Died!

A setback.

Not... the biggest one, but a substantial one, nonetheless.

Hector was injured, nearly unrepairable, but thankfully his skull was still intact.

Meaning, given time, he would recover. If Chloe were here, she could heal him with a chaos spell, but seeing as SHE WAS STILL LAZING ABOUT, that option was lost to me.

Grrrr. GAAAAAAAAAAAAAAAAAAAH.

What the hell was the meaning of this?!

Why was there a copy of me?!

No, wait. Stop. Let's think.

Why is there a copy of me?

It was obviously a mirage spell of some kind, a high-tier skill that formed an imitation of me... right?

Right?

Mana Heart Upgrade Available!

Brooding in my lair, a notification lit up, interrupting my thoughts.

Ah. A thousand manacysts. Lovely.

I immediately selected the upgrade function for my mana heart, sitting there for a moment and watching as my dark and anima supplies dropped to zero.

A moment passed, then another, with no discernible change.

Huh... IamEEEEEEEEZZZZZ?!

Suddenly, a pulse of energy akin to lightning struck my body, my internals seeming to go into an overcharge state as Slimey's and Ayaka's mana pools shot up.

Ah.

I was abruptly yanked out of my body, my mind in RTS mode again, looking down at my minions and my rooms. I could see faint lines, bluish strands of energy that connected from my mana heart to Slimey and Ayaka, the beating structure augmenting them both.

Huh... neat.

Incoming Quest!
Domain Expansion!
Construct Additional Pylons: 0/8
Construct Manacyst Cultures: 0/5
Reward: +Minion Capacity Increase

Well, this will be interesting.

I returned to my shell, a number of construction options appearing in my mind as my mana heart swelled and pulsed, increasing my territory by a vast margin that included part of the sewer and catacombs as well as—

Huh... So that's where the goblins are coming from.

Not too far from my throne room, two floors up, was a den of goblins, an intricate set of tunnels that had the misfortune of being in my expansion.

Seeing them with my RTS vision, they didn't seem to be aware that their home had been annexed.

Looking at them, there were roughly about a hundred blighted goblins in total, a few variants in their lot like goblin bosses, hobgoblins, and what appeared to be an old, red-skinned rare variant orc, the leader of the pack, carrying with it a club.

I reached out, caressing the mind of the blighted muscular orc boss that sat on a throne of bones and goblin carcasses.

Shag-Ulkr sat on his throne of bones, the old orc boss dozing off slightly.

Hello.

"Hrrn?"

This is your God speaking.

"Hn??" Shag-Ulkr sat up, the red-skinned orc furrowing his brow at the intrusion.

"Skrre?" A nearby goblin looked up, wondering what was wrong with their leader.

You wish to serrrve Lord Hiro! You wiiiiiish to serve the rubber duck!

"Hrng. What is this? Who is this?! Show YOURSELF!" Shag screamed, rising from his throne. His inward thoughts seemed to match his outward bellows word for word.

Hello, I am Hiro, and your home is on my land, I would—

"Yous land?" The orc blinked, his agitation rising. "YOUS LAND?! THIS IS SHAG'S LAND! NOT YOUS! RAAAAGH!"

Whoa, whoa, PAL, let's calm down here.

"CAM! CAM! I SHOW YOUS CAM! I AM DA CAMIST IN DA WORLD!" Shag-Ulkr began to rage, the orc's red skin heating up with energy.

HIRO

Well...

That didn't work...

BLOODBATH IT IS!

I kid. But it would be easier to exterminate them. *Sigh.* Guess I'll need to pay an in-person trip to this Shag fellow. In the meantime, while I waited for my pylons to be built, there was an arena I needed to investigate further.

With Hector out of commission, I decided to use a different skeleton—a regular, unaugmented one—to perform my scouting.

There were telltale differences between inhabiting a skeleton rogue and a regular skeleton, most notably that I was... less limber? If that makes sense for a skeleton without muscles. But I could feel it: a millisecond disconnect between my thoughts and actions that was noticeable to me.

I allowed myself a full thirty seconds to adjust before taking off, entering the domain of the enemy once more.

Upon stepping onto the sandpit, the winds began to blow once more. The sands shifted to form the image of a familiar black-haired swordsman.

I took a moment to observe the clone. Mirror-me entered into a low crouch, clawed gauntlet outstretched, blade held at shoulder height.

Form one: **Blink Strike**. A skill that fired off the ground with explosive speed to skewer the user's target. An undodgeable attack... for those unprepared. Fortunately, I wasn't—

Minion, Skeleton 5 has perished!

Ah...

I died.

Whoops.

...

Well, that went about as expected...

'*How was the scouting, my lord?*' Slimey asked, spinning my body in circles in her palm with **Telekinesis**.

Fantastic, I replied—not in a sarcastic manner, but sincerely!

Back in my rubber body, I pondered over the results of my last battle, specifically the crucial clue that had washed away my fears.

Blink Strike.

I could see it. As fast as mirror-me was, the fact that I could track his movements confirmed it was just a copy. A good one, but an imitation. The strike held no mana, no magical power—just... movement.

It became evident to me that what I was up against was some form of tangible mirage, something akin to Chloe's (old Chloe, not the new one) spell called Doppelganger, which she used to distract enemies and combine chant spells. Except, unlike her spell that vanished the moment it took damage, I had a sneaking suspicion this clone wouldn't.

Great.

Well, there was still twelve hours until I could test my theory. I wasn't too keen on sacrificing minions, but at least the skeletons don't have a soul or ego.

With twelve hours to kill, I considered a visit to my new tenants.

Slimey.

'Yes, Lord Hiro?'

Let's go for a walk. Oh, and take Davette with you.

Chapter 46

Short Life

Sitting within his den of filth and rotting blight corpses, Shag-Ulkr growled, his mood sour despite the disembodied goblin leg in his mouth.

"B-Bosssk! Wha' iz wrong?" one of Shag's warband asked, the small yet brave creature attempting to placate the irate beast.

"Wrong? Nothin's wrong, ya git! Get me some more grub, Geple!" Shag-Ulkr snapped, throwing the goblin leg at the puny goblin boss named Geple. "An' make it Uni meat!"

The goblin quickly fled, taking with it a group of its kin.

"Grrrr..." Shag-Ulkr let out, smashing the side of his throne in a fit of rage. "Who does he think he is, tellin' me what to do?"

Shag-Ulkr slouched in his chair, the nine-foot-tall orc resting his hand on a weathered knuckle beneath the light of a glowstone.

"I'm gettin' too old for this stress," Shag-Ulkr grumbled, his eyes drifting across his audience chamber, where dozens of goblins milled about.

'Then how about we help you get some rest?' a silky voice reached out, caressing his mind.

"WHO?! WHOG?!" Shag-Ulkr stood up, bloodshot eyes wide with rage at the taunt.

"Me." From the shadows, a human appeared—one wearing nothing but a black dress. No armor. No weapons. Just a yellow thing in her hands as she approached with a wide smile.

Shag-Ulkr licked his lips. It had been a while since he'd last seen a human. Never mind tasted one! But for one to walk into his lair— and a beaut at that!

The orc rose from his throne, a wolfish grin spreading across his face as his body welled with hunger and lust.

"Disgusting," the human grimaced, casting her green eyes on Shag-Ulkr with a look that made him feel...

Shag-Ulkr froze. Something was wrong.

The old orc clenched his jaw, his fingers tightening into fists. He hated being looked down upon, and this... this woman!

"Wha' do you want? Where's Geple?"

"Wrapped up," the woman replied, causing Shag-Ulkr's annoyance to rise.

"Ya got some nerve, humie, comin' in here alone."

"Oh, but I'm not alone." The woman's voice was calm as she spoke, and a group of upright goblins... no, these were goblins, HIS goblins!

Shag-Ulkr's eyes widened. The green-skinned, bug-armored goblins were a far cry from his own warband.

"What is dis?" Shag-Ulkr hissed, his underlings rising and making noise at the green-skinned goblins, who stood in a neat formation with spears and shields raised.

One of his warband charged, rushing the woman with lust in its eyes. The blighted goblin let out a howl as it leapt into the air.

The woman turned her head, her smile widening to impossible lengths, and her jaw unhinging.

A scream rang out but was abruptly cut off as the goblin disappeared.

The woman closed her eyes, dabbing her mouth with a satisfied expression. The entire cave fell silent.

"Y-Yous no humie! What is dis?!" Shag-Ulkr growled, the panic setting in.

"This is your subjugation. By decree of Lord Hiro, the land you tread upon is now under new management."

"What?!" Shag-Ulkr roared.

"You will be given one chance to bend the knee. Failure to submit will be met with your organs being harvested and turned into compost to build the foundation of Lord Hiro's empire," the woman said, her calm smile never faltering as she stared Shag-Ulkr down.

"Submit? SUBMIT?!" Shag-Ulkr's skin began to glow. "Yous come into my home, turn my gits against me, and DEMAND I SUBMIT?!"

"Alive or dead, either way you will serve. Do not reject my lord Hiro's kindness," the woman replied.

Shag-Ulkr's nose scrunched, his anger at an all-time high as the woman remained unphased by his shouts.

"I AM SHAG-ULKR!" The orc roared, drawing all the goblins in his home, who began to chant his name.

"SHAG!"

"SHAG!"

"SHAAG!"

"SHAG!"

Shag-Ulkr let out a war cry, his bloodlust filling the air as several goblins came out, carrying makeshift armor made of assorted metal and materials. The entire cave shook with the sound of thumping feet, metal clashing on metal, and anything else the goblins under Shag's command could use to make noise.

"I am Shag-Ulkr, and I submit to no one!" the orc spat, his goblins strapping him into his war suit and handing him his beating stick.

"Fertilizer it is then." The woman's form began to shift and wiggle, her skin changing color from pink to blue as she opened her mouth to reveal rows of sharp, inhuman teeth.

She took a step forward—almost—but froze in place.

"Shag-Ulkr, was it?"

"Dat iz me!" he replied proudly.

"Would you consider yourself a king?"

"What's dat?" the orc asked, never having heard the term before.

"Rephrase. Would you say you are the leader of your people?"

"Ain't no people here! Only gits and me! I am chief!"

The woman maintained her placid expression.

"Then as Chief, how would you like to fight my Chief? An honorable duel, one chief to the next. Winner gets everything."

Shag-Ulkr turned his head sideways, the orc towering over her, holding a yellow thing in his hand.

"Ain't nothing yous got I want."

"Treasure. Food. And..." The woman licked her lips. "Me."

The orc's muscles tightened, his carnal instincts nearly taking over. But he reined them in. After all, he was the gitzziest of the gits. The strongest of the warband, and the oldest too!

"Fine, tiny woman," Shag-Ulkr huffed. "Bring your chief. I will fight like gummies do! With honor!"

"SHAG!"

"SHAG!"

"SHAG!"

"SHAG!"

The blighted brood under Shag's control whipped into a frenzy, chanting their leader's name over and over.

Suddenly, the woman's skin turned red. Her eyes were wide with such bloodlust that even Shag instinctively took a step back, the goblins falling silent.

The woman closed her eyes, her soft smile returning as a green-skinned woman with shiny scales sluggishly walked into view.

Shag balked at the chieftain, brandishing a smile at a challenge he would relish!

He readied his beating stick, preparing to do battle.

However, the scaled woman didn't step forward to face him. Instead, the soft-skinned woman stepped forward, placing the yellow thing in her hands on the floor.

"What's this then?" Shag-Ulkr asked, poking the yellow item with his stick.

"Why don't you take a close look and find out? Maybe if your eye gets close enough, it can recognize greatness."

Shag-Ulkr crouched down, cocking his head at the unmoving item with its unblinking eyes. He poked it again, the yellow object letting out a high-pitched squeak as the woman vibrated violently in place.

"What's this puny—"

And that was the final moment of Shag-Ulkr. The orc leader was reduced to a bubbling mess of black goo, surrounded by screams from his panicked goblins.

One and done. The yellow item unleashed its attack, blinding and melting the red-skinned monster.

"Congratulations," the woman said, her form expanding as the blighted goblins cried in terror. "You have all been selected to serve Lord Hiro. Please resist."

Chapter 47

Oopsy!

HIRO
One Moment Prior...

The orc screamed as my attack hit him, my acid splashing into his face. The red-skinned monster clawed at his face, only spreading the ink around.

Within moments, the orc was nothing more than a puddle, the creature's innate regeneration unable to keep up with the rate at which my acid burned through his flesh and bones.

'Congratulations. You have been selected to serve Lord Hiro. Please resist,' Slimey said before unleashing her true form, her body moving to collect the screaming monsters.

Ah... whoops. Well... there goes that minion... heck! HECK! I WANTED HIM! HE WAS A SHINY TYPE! A SHINY! ARRRRRRGH! WHY COULDN'T YOU HAVE A FOCUS SASH?!

Quacks... Well, what was done was done, I thought, the bubbling acid on the ground gestating an odd kind of growth.

Concerning... very concerning... ehk! Gross.

Make sure none of them escape! But don't kill them! I ordered as Davette moved to block the cave entrance with her body.

Slimey slithered across the floor, a great blue tidal wave laughing as it swept up the terrified goblins.

"ME CAN'T SWIM! ME CAN'T—gurgufjlidcjktea!" one goblin screamed, sinking into Slimey's body.

"Drowny, no!" another goblin cried, calling out for its friend.

'DON'T WORRY! YOU'LL BE JOINING HIM TOO!' The slime woman smiled, her body forming large teeth that chomped in taunt.

"NOOOOOOOOOOOOOOOOO!"

I left her and the spiders to the task of capturing the goblins, Slimey snatching them while the spiders rolled their screaming bodies into bundles as I kept quacking to observe the puddle.

Hmmm. This... may be a problem.

The puddle was settling down, hardening, forming into mold that began to grow at a quack pace.

Oddly, the mold was growing rapidly—too rapidly—feeding off the fleshy remains of the orc and using them as a catalyst to grow.

Hrnnnnnn. Problem! Problem! Problem! AYAKA!

'Yes, Lord Hiro?' Ayaka sent, her voice echoing in my mind over Slimey's deranged laughter.

Get over here. Now.

Suddenly, the space around me began to distort, a bubbling of mana wrapping around me like a tether.

Davette stood beside me, the mino-croc scratching her back with a lazy look as she picked me up. A rare moment of unprompted action from the reptile woman.

Yes? Can I help you, Davette? The croc-girl blinked at me.

'So...'

So?

'How are you going to fit the spider in here?' Davette asked, holding me close so I could perceive her words and looking up at the low ceiling that her head almost touched.

Ah... Ah, wait. Wait, wait, wait!

ABORT! ABORT! ABORT!

The air shifted, a portal opening up above me with Ayaka's titanic claws peeking through.

NO! GO BACK IN! GO BACK IN!

"RaaaHG!" Davette let out, the bulky mass of Ayaka pushing down on her as the remaining goblins were crushed underneath the weight of the massive arachnid.

AH! IT'S TOO TIGHT! TOO TIGHT!

Ayaka and Davette were smooshed into me, my rubber form squished against the cavern wall, my body letting out a low, soft "squeeeeeeeak."

Three hours... That's how long it took to bring Kabbybara and my other capruxas to dig us out.

But we were free. Well, Davette and I. Ayaka was busy licking up my black goo.

Great. My strongest monster is addicted to mold... In a way, this worked out, seeing as everything else died nearly instantly to the black gunk. Ayaka had unknowingly become a kind of waste disposal.

When I thought about it, this mold could be the chief compound for a catastrophic disaster!

Hmm. I should probably go and trace every place I've fired my gunk at... if it was molding this quickly...

Putting that to the side, I collected the bundled-up goblins, which numbered about two hundred total. Two hundred sticky, blighted goblins that reeked of death and decay.

Some were old, some were young, some had hair and others didn't. But one thing they all had in common was that they were all gross.

Moving them into my expanded throne room, I took a moment to try and decide how exactly I wanted to play this.

With two hundred wiggling goblins stuck to the walls of my main chambers, the plan had gone awfully awry.

Originally, I was just going to beat the goblin leader and have him make the others submit to me. And now, I had beaten the boss, but the unexpected consequence was that... well... he was dead!

Great, guess I'll just try and CP30 this...

'Lord Hiro.'

I should get bigger quarters...

'Lord Hiro.'

Hm?

'Your subjects are ready.'

Ah, yes. My two hundred captives.

Sigh. The treasury was still not located, but I suppose it didn't matter too much. After all, a couple of hundred years had passed, and whatever was left would probably still be there waiting for me.

Well, I've got eight hours to kill before my next pylon construction and rematch with mirror me. Time to be productive.

One by one, I had my skeletons bring me a bundled-up goblin, the terrified creature brought before my throne, where Slimey, me, and Buttstalion were.

I reached out, my mind touching the goblin's that was filled with panic.

Be not afraid. You will be cured. I penetrated its mind, the monster going rigid at my intrusion.

What followed next was a series of screams, tears, and black ooze pouring out of the goblin, with the spider silk it was wrapped in turning black. Once cured, I had one of my armored goblins cut the silk binding the recently cured and allowed it to process its new body for a moment. The goblin stood there, tears in its eyes, before it bowed to me and began calling me "bosk!" which I assumed was goblin for boss.

Right. Over there to the left. The goblin fervently heeded my direction, a devotion point adding to my grand total.

Huh... great.

One by one, the blighted were cured, and with each goblin freed of their affliction, I gained another fervent follower.

Devotion: 345
Skill Level Up!
Purify Lvl.08!

Devotion was great, but it didn't guarantee anything in terms of loyalty or commitment to my cause.

Fortunately, I had those loyal to me—my own personal pseudo-knight order in chitin armor that stood over the captives.

It also helped that I had a massive armored arachnid that was getting anxious without its queen, who was still stuck in the goblin's home, munching happily on mold.

Hmm. A Knight Order... Now that I think about it, it wouldn't be too bad to teach and have an order of soldiers versed in my tactics.

Twenty goblins. Twenty potential commanders whose loyalty was certain. Two hundred goblins, ten goblins per commander. I could turn my trusted into sergeants, have them learn skills and techniques, then teach them to the others. A method of training I employed on peasants called cascade training.

Train ten. Those ten trained ten. So on and so forth, until you had an army of trained soldiers.

Of course... effectiveness varied as it continued to go on, but that's why repetitiveness played a huge factor in the level of soldiering.

Suddenly, an image... a man in fatigues. A man who was... me?!

Barking orders, standing in a forest with a knife in hand, my mouth moving as a crowd of people hung on every word I said.

Odd. When was this?

I could see myself, a man wearing an insignia of a yellow bar pinned to my collar.

My eyes, they were tired. Done. The words coming out were lies I told to delude these youth of various ages to fight.

I... was a soldier? No... I was something else. Doing something that wasn't... honorable despite the uniform I wore.

In fact, the uniform was just a disguise.

But what did it matter? Today was my last day in that humid jungle. The day I would go home, collect my check, and start a new life.

The memory faded; the images gone.

'Lord Hiro?' Slimey asked, stroking my head. *'Is everything okay?'*

Hm? What was I doing? Oh, right!

Training. Training! I was planning on training my soldiers. Well, two hundred goblins with big mouths to feed and in need of housing, clothing, and arms.

Now they were my responsibility. Buttstalion was easy to feed as the unicorn fed on the remains of its former home, but as for the goblins... well... as carnivorous cannibals, eating one another wasn't unheard of, but I'd rather not have my army feeding on their own.

Then again, there were other goblins out there. Other dens not found, asking to be turned into food.

A short-term solution to a long-term problem.

No. There were two hundred and fifty-three mouths to feed.

I needed a more... efficient solution. My brain told me to turn Ayaka into a spider meat producer, but that, too, didn't sit well...

Hrrrrrn. What do, what do, what do?

'My lord. You are so cute when you're thinking.'

Huh? Sure. Right.

'What troubles you, my lord?"

Trying to figure out how to feed my new army.

'We could cut off the lizard girl's tail and feed it to them. She regenerates.'

Davette snapped towards the throne, the green-haired muscular crocotaurus clutching her tail with an angry look.

Yeah... no. We're monsters, not barbarians. We need a long-term plan to feed everyone.

'Fine. Why not feed them manacysts?'

Huh?

'We are creatures born of mana. We can survive off mana alone if need be.'

The upkeep would require a LOT more mana cultures... or, throwing enough monsters into the composters to produce feed.

Good work, Slimey, I praised, the slime turning bright pink as I directed Gobledo and Gobledee to step forward.

The two armored goblins bent the knee, heads held low.

From this point, you two have been promoted to lieutenants.

'Thank you, lord!' the two thought respectfully.

Good. You can repay your gratitude with service. Now... Listen closely.

Chapter 48

Army Training

Gobledo sat in the corner of his cave, a private room given to him by the lord to befit his station as commander.

The goblin boss stared at his suit of chitin, web, and bone—the armor a gift from the Great Yellow One. He, one of only twenty, had received this glorious gift.

However, unlike the rest of the trusted, Gobledo had a pristine iron helmet to complement his armor and a cape made of fine spider silk woven by the Grand Guardian.

Gobledo bowed, saying a prayer before donning his armor, fastening it in place before taking up his sword—another gift from the Yellow One, which sat in an iron scabbard.

He turned and walked out of his cave, entering the pristine and smooth tunnel system that was once part of the Spider Matriarch's nest.

With constant excavation and lots of slimes moving about, what was once a jagged corridor was now a smooth, evenly sized square hallway lit by glow stones.

From the parallel room, Gobledeee, the two making eye contact before nodding and walking in step through the tunnel.

Before long, the pair reached a large room—a place the Yellow One had dubbed the "DFAC."

Dining Facilities Administration Center, as explained by the Great Yellow One.

A large chamber with neatly aligned entrances coating the walls.

Inside the chamber, dozens of tables—each meticulously chiseled out of stone by slimes, spiders, and the large lizards known as capruxas.

Gobledo walked over to a nearby counter, a trustee goblin behind the table giving a haphazard salute, as taught by the lord.

The two commanders returned the salute, a custom they both found odd, but by their lord's order, they gave it their all.

Standing there, a spider from a nearby entrance walked in with a bundle of crystals.

Dinner, food for both goblins. It wasn't actually the most tasteful thing, but by the lord's order, they graciously accepted the manacysts.

After lunch, the pair entered the throne room where Lady Slimey sat, the Champion of the Yellow One, perched on the throne with her usual soft smile. In her hands, their lord—the rubber being— gazed unblinking, staring down Gobledo and Gobledee.

The twin goblins rapidly approached the throne, walking through the centerline of the crowd of armored goblins kneeling before their lord.

"Our lord!" The pair cried out, bowing to the throne.

Slinking from the stone chair, Lady Slimey descended from above, now towering over the pair of goblins, who couldn't help but shiver.

Not only was the Champion very beautiful, but she was also very temperamental. One wrong move... and Gobledee and Gobledo understood that she would have them fed to the composters like so many of the new kin had been.

Gobledo suppressed his goblin urges, the fear he felt from the woman's touch on his chin more than enough to clamp down on his spore production.

Not to mention, the Great Yellow One was right there! Right in front of him!

"Rise, lieutenants," Slimey said, her voice intruding into their minds. "Our training begins now."

HIRO

Twenty screams. Twenty thrusts. Twenty goblins in my chambers, all moving in concert. Another training session. My days were filled with organizing my army.

Oh, and dying over and over again.

Between training the first twenty and Gobledee and Gobledo in sword techniques, I would dominate skeletons—sacrificial pawns that I would use to fight my mirror self.

Now, with my skeletal skull currently flying once more, you may be wondering: Why am I constantly getting myself decapitated?

The answer?

Simple.

I plucked my skull out of the air, pivoting on my bony foot to jab at my doppelganger with a knife.

Shadow Clone Me reacted swiftly, bringing his sword back to lean right and knock the weapon out of my hand.

A disarming technique, one I knew quite well, that used the base of the blade to dig into an opponent's fleshy wrist.

The problem was, however, I had no flesh. Combined with the lack of power in the maneuver, I simply dropped my dagger out of my right hand and caught it with my skull in my left hand.

Immediately, the clone backed away, retreating just as the knife between my teeth nicked his armor, cutting through it like butter.

Yeah. My original armor wouldn't be caught lacking against a regular iron dagger. But the results of this bout told me two things:

One, the defensive power of the clone was low, and two, the doppelganger possessed a sense of self-preservation.

The doppelganger shot off the floor once more, attempting another Blink Strike. But this time, I was actually prepared. Unable to fully see the attack, I relied on the seconds before he built up—the split moment when the clone took the stance—before preemptively dodging.

I couldn't react when it happened, so I needed to counter just as the attack began.

Simple enough, right?

Wrong.

The blade shaved a bit of my skull as I side-stepped right, slashing the arm and cutting through it with my dagger before attempting a pickaxe maneuver aimed at my stupidly chiseled jaw.

The doppelganger reacted swiftly, raising his left hand, the gauntlet catching my wrist.

Ah... quacks. Alright, cue Dark So—

Minion, Skeleton 8 has perished!

Back in my rubber shell, Slimey gently stroked my head as my vision returned, the Dragon Slayer floating in a circle around the throne.

Ugh...

'Welcome back, my lord. How was today's training session?'

Great, I replied sarcastically, casting my attention on the twenty goblins in my chambers doing spear drills.

'That's wonderful, Lord Hiro! Please! Tell me all about it!'

No, I... I began but stopped as Slimey's radiant smile seemed to cause the background behind her to distort. The cavern walls became a forest, with flames from a campfire reflecting off...

As quickly as it came, it disappeared, and the background behind Slimey returned to what I knew it was.

What was that? What did I just see? Questions began to rise, but just as quickly as they did, my mind seemed to avoid them.

'My lord? Is everything okay, darling?' Slimey asked, sensing my distress, her skin tone shifting to an orangey-yellow hue.

Yes. It's fine. Are you ready to learn sword techniques? I sent, avoiding the question, not wanting to delve into my champion's inquiry.

'O-O-OF COURSE! It would be my honor to learn from you, my lord!' Slimey replied exuberantly, lifting my mood as I eyed my pylon counter.

Pylon Created!
Pylon Cooldown: 3:59:54

Three hours until my next pylon creation, eleven hours before my next attempt at fighting my doppelganger. It seemed that the more pylons I created, the longer the timer between each one became.

I turned my attention to my minions. Chloe was still on the mend in her hole, Davette was sleeping, curled up and hugging her tail, while Ayaka was busy being... Well, actually, I wasn't sure what she was doing.

The massive arachnid was just sitting there in the corner of the throne room, doing... nothing? Almost as if catatonic.

Her Juggernaut, on the other hand, was pacing back and forth—the armored bug more active than usual.

I opened up Ayaka's menu, noticing nothing unusual.

'My lord?'

Hm?

'Shall we begin training? I am very much eager to be soaked with your knowledge.'

Why... Why are you saying it like that? >__>

The slime wiggled in response, smiling at me.

Let's just get this done.

As Slimey descended from the throne with me on her head, Gobeldee barked out an order. The goblin lieutenant called the twenty troops to halt their maneuvers.

Like a well-oiled machine, the Trustees snapped to attention, straightening their posture and splitting off into two sides of the cave, forming an honor guard flanking Slimey and me.

Give us space, I ordered. The entire group simultaneously took several steps back.

It had taken a few days and a couple dozen fumbles, but after repeated—*Ehem...* motivational speeches from Slimey and my goblin officers, the twenty were now a well-oiled machine.

But not battle-tested. Yet.

With space given, Slimey stood within the chamber with me on her head.

Slimey. Imperial Form One, I ordered.

The slime stood straight, her hand reaching out to wrap around the handle of the impossibly massive blade. It had taken days of constant use, and thanks to the mana given from my mana heart, Slimey was able to maintain **Telekinesis** 24/7.

Next, I willed the image of specific footwork to the forefront of my mind—what I wanted Slimey to imitate.

The slime moved in accordance with my will. Her center of mass lowered, feet spaced, and the blade held at her side, near her hip, striking a stance known as the plug guard stance where I was from.

And then... we began to dance.

Lifting, striking, thrusting, slashing. Slimey used **Telekinesis** on the Dragon Slayer to reenact my memories of a friend.

The original owner of the Dragon Slayer: a black-armored knight who was nothing short of a raging berserker. Gaining his trust had been hard, but getting him to fight for me? That had been much easier.

Glory was... an odd one. He didn't talk much, but he hated demons. So, point him in the right direction and he became unstoppable.

At least, that was the impression I had as I focused on his weapon.

I recalled his fighting style: wild, obtuse, and all-out offense with little regard for his own safety. For a normal human, it was a suicidal technique that would leave the user dead from the injuries sustained. Injuries that Glory should've never survived. Yet, his sheer tenacity always saw him through.

Slimey, on the other hand, had the benefit of not being human. Her cores constantly shifted beneath her "skin." And with her ability to heal herself, any damage done to her became negligible.

What she really needed was armor.

Hmm... Maybe the treasury would have something we can use.

ELSEWHERE...

"Finally," Lhikan said, standing at the entrance of the Demon Lord's castle.

Chapter 49

Peace Was Never an Option?

Quest Complete: Domain Expansion!
Minion Capacity Increased to 20!
Incoming Quest!
New Construction Options Available!

Another day, another quest. All six of my new pylons line the walls of my throne room like pillars holding up my ceiling. I even decorated them with webs!

At each pillar, a pair of goblins stands at the base—Slimey's idea to instill discipline and boost morale among the troops.

The room seemed to have grown now that I think about it. Like... very big. There's even an indoor balcony.

Wait.

WHY IS THERE A BALCONY?! AND WHY IS MY THRONE FOUR FLIGHTS HIGH?!

'Is something wrong, my lord?' Slimey asked, her face broadcasting a radiant smile that made my mind go blank for a moment.

Errr... no. Actually... Slimey.

'Yes, my love?'

Alright, time to handle this tactically.

Uh, why is my throne so high?

'Because you are above all, my lord,' Slimey replied, as if it were the most obvious thing.

Right... but a four-story-high throne? Seems a bit excessive.

'If it were up to me, my lord, I'd have your throne touch the very sky itself, with the stars as your backdrop and everything under your rightful domain bending the knee.'

Riiiiight... okay. Cool. But isn't this like... a major inconvenience for anyone attempting to talk to me?

'Anyone allowed in your presence should be honored that you deign to allow them within our chambers at all, Lord Darling Hiro.'

Uh... Right.

Maybe I'd been so preoccupied with fighting my clone, training soldiers, and setting up my manacyst farms that I hadn't noticed my throne room expanding.

Man, was I that out of it? Maybe I need a naaaaaaa—Whoops! Almost turned on power-saving mode.

Slimey continued to stroke my head, just another day in my darkest dungeon.

Man... I wish I had legs to stretch... Sigh.

Maybe I should take control of Davette again, get the feel of actual muscles and ligaments...

Hmm. Wouldn't it be interesting to take control of Slimey? Or Ayaka, for that matter. Heh.

Land-sculpting Available!

Hm?

Design Your Space!
Use manacysts to landscape rooms within your dungeon to empower minions.
Reward: Supercysts

Huh... neat.

Construction Options...
Dark Gestator
REQ: 100 Dark Manacysts
Graveyard
REQ: 50 Dark Manacysts, 10 Anima Manacysts
Land-sculpting Presets...
Catacomb
REQ: 500 Dark Manacysts
Aqualife
REQ: 200 Anima Manacysts, 300 Dark Manacysts, 10 Holy Manacysts
Meadow
REQ: 550 Anima Manacysts

Ahhh. So expensive! With ten manacyst cultures, I was basically making only twenty manacysts every day! AND THIS DUNGEON LANDSCAPING THING WANTED CLOSE TO A THOUSAND?!

WHAT KIND OF SCAM WAS THIS?!

A SCAM! A SCAM! I'm barely feeding my army as it is, if not for the composters! And even then, that's with round-the-clock hunting!

'Lord Hiro, are you okay?'

Sigh...

I wasn't okay. So... it was a good thing I was always busy doing something.

According to intel extracted from various goblins, the goblin cove led by the red-skinned orc was only one of dozens of goblin coves.

Each led by a goblin boss, each one in their own territory, with every goblin doing their best to avoid the various dungeon cores scattered throughout the castle.

I focused my attention on the large etchings carved into the floor of my chamber by my capruxa and spiders. The spiders handled the line art with their silk, and the capruxas dug the earth.

The maps were ever-expanding, each one representing a different floor of the Demon Lord's castle currently being scouted by my minions.

On the maps, there were pieces of chitin, daggers, and glowstones. The chitin represented monster clusters, the glowstones' potential resources, and the daggers indicated goblin lairs.

I reached out to my recon team, with Gobeldee leading a squad-sized element to negotiate with a goblin band at the edge of my territory.

Go, I sent, with Gobeldee moving out of my sphere of influence and into the misty black where my consciousness ended.

As beings capable of speech, I decided to try dialogue with these creatures rather than subjugation. A carrot-and-stick approach.

Fear was a powerful motivator, but more often than not, fear led to resentment and hatred—two things that would undermine the foundation I was aiming to build.

So, I would offer an olive branch, offer to cure these wayward lambs, and supply them with "fancys," as Gobeldee called them, along with training. Fancys being armor, weapons, and the training to conscript them into my growing army.

GOBLEDEE

At the entrance of a goblin dugout, nearly naked save for the various spider-silk items, Gobeldee took a breath as he felt the touch of his lord and master.

His first mission, his first real task from the Great Yellow One—Gobeldee would not fail. To do so would tarnish the station he had been given, something he cherished. Before he was Gobeldee, he was just a lost being, one with no other purpose than to procreate and consume, an aimless, run-of-the-mill goblin. But the lord saw past that and gave him purpose, purified him, gave him a name and enlightenment that cast away the cloudiness that once plagued his mind with the urge to eat and consume.

He would not betray these gifts from the lord.

It was time.

Gobledee took up the rotting wooden stake wrapped in spider silk and goblin fat that hung from his spider-silk belt. He placed the wooden piece on the ground and picked up two stones, rubbing them together just as he'd been taught to produce a spark.

All eyes were on him now, the other goblins breathing down his neck as he did his best to replicate what he'd been taught during the lord's lessons.

With mounting pressure on his back to perform, Gobledee struck the stones, a spark forming on the first try that caught the silk-wrapped stick on fire.

"Oooh," the others in his consort let out, allowing Gobledee a moment of reprieve as his squad collectively admired the illuminating flames.

With renewed vigor, Gobledee wrapped his three-fingered hand around the torch, standing tall. He then took out the hollowed-out unicorn horn at his side and blew into it as instructed.

"OOOOOOOOOOOOOOOOOOOOOOOOOOOOOOOOOOO OOOOOOH!"

At the cry of the war horn, the eight goblins behind Gobledee stood rigid, clanking their arms in unison, tightening up in formation as they readied their spears and shields.

One moment.

Two.

Satisfied that they wouldn't come under attack, Gobledee ordered his squad in. The unit marched into the dugout, with their semi-naked leader leading the way.

Inside, Gobledee stood proud, walking past the blighted goblins within who had come out to inspect the noise.

Blinded by the light of the flames, many of the sickly goblins shied away, unable to make sense of the sudden light, while those that remained...

They stood in awe of Gobledee, not because of his muscular, well-fed body or silk wrappings, but because of his smooth green skin that was on display for all to see.

Marching unopposed, Gobledee quickly made it into the heart of the goblin lair, he and his soldiers surrounded by dozens of the diseased ones, as the lord called them, or the unclean, as Lady Slimey referred to them.

It was his mission to purify them, to guide them into the light.

"WAT IZ DIS?" A voice boomed, ricocheting off the walls to strike at Gobledee's heart.

Orc Fear. A skill some of the higher variants of goblins acquired that allowed them to bend their lessers to their will.

Gobledee clenched his jaw, taking a moment to observe the two dozen or so goblins led by a green-skinned humanoid who was a giant compared to the goblins—an orc with a massive club in its hands.

"By da decrees of the lord! I, Gobledee, lieutenant of the Great Yellow One, offer ya to join DA ranks of da cleaned!" Gobledee shouted, his heart racing as he resisted the Orc Fear. "To be free of disease! To be clean! To be strong!"

The orc approached from the crowd, pushing away several of his underlings to tower over Gobledee by a full head.

"Yous say yous strong?" the orc said, his skin riddled with pustules and black blight, kept at bay by his regeneration. "Stronger 'ten me?"

Gobledee's hand clenched around his torch, his other hand resting on the hilt of his blade strapped to his waist.

The orc licked his lips, eyeing Gobledee's squadmates and their armor. "Yous got fancys. Me want fancys."

"Submit to the Great Yellow One, get fancys!" Gobledee stated, the crowd of sickly goblins inching closer to his unit.

"Suhmit? Neva!" The orc spat, his maw opening and spewing rancid breath over Gobledee. "Dis be me space! ME! My gits! No one takes from me! Gib me yous fancys!"

Suddenly, the orc lifted his club, preparing to strike, to smash this puny git that dared to enter his territory. Yet, as he went to do so, Gobledee and his consort dropped to one knee in unison, almost as if in prayer, as a green shadow flew over their heads.

"ARRRRGHKKKLCKAS!" the orc let out, screaming as Davette bit into his neck, dragging the orc across the ground and into the shadows.

HIRO

"Wesa failed," Gobledee sent back, the orc leader unable to be persuaded.

Which was fine.

The thing about the carrot-and-stick policy was that if the carrot failed, there was always the stick—the stick, of course, being Davette. And while I didn't want to rule by fear and force the goblins into servitude, exterminating a few of the rotten apples would serve as an example to the other dens of what happened to those who attacked my soldiers.

The plan was relatively simple: decimate a few goblin lairs, kill their leaders, scatter the survivors, let them spread the fear of my army to the other dens, and then force a dialogue for negotiation.

Of course, those who bent the knee would be welcomed into the fold, but those who resisted... well, if they couldn't be persuaded, I had... other uses for them. Especially their body fats, bones, and skin, which made excellent leather once dried. Hehe...

Man... Am I a bad guy?

No. Of course not! Everything I do, I do for a better world!

Yup... A better world, right, Slimey?

'*Yes. Of course, my lord!*' Slimey affirmed, not even knowing what I was talking about as maniacal laughter echoed in my mind.

Chapter 50

Cult of Duck

HIRO

I shifted to the side, dodging the blink strike aimed at my head. Sword in hand, I lifted my blade and severed the arm of my attacker before coming back down with my sword, the weapon's edge aimed at evil me's clavicle.

The blade came down, the doppelganger's eyes widening. The man pivoted, dodging the blade, my attack shaving the enemy's hair just shy of nicking his nose.

TSK!

His left hand shot out, attempting to grab my skull, my head already moving just barely out of reach as I retreated and struck a stance.

My doppelganger paused, eyeing its severed hand regenerating at a visible pace before its left hand went up, gathering mana to its palm.

Phase 2.

I kicked off the sandy floor, rolling left, dodging the blast of mana that kicked up dirt.

I gripped my sword, racing forward, shifting left, shifting right, avoiding the mana bursts that were a far cry from my peak self.

Pitiful.

I closed the distance, my form shifting into blink strike and kicking off the ground.

The doppelganger shifted, avoiding the attack easily, his own dodge mirroring mine with his left hand coming up with mana.

Gotcha.

I dug my heel into the earth, pivoting, changing my depowered blink strike into a slash that dug into my evil clone's bicep.

Minion, Skeleton 52 has perished!

Tsk! TOO SHALLOW!

'How was the training, my lord?' Slimey asked enthusiastically. *'You lasted one minute and thirteen seconds! Twelve seconds longer than last time! A new record!'*

Sigh... please don't be so jubilant about my defeat.

Now back in my rubber body, it took a moment for my consciousness to reset, to settle in my rubber body with my point of view encapsulating my entire dung...

Slimey.

'Yes, darling?'

Can... Can you explain to me why there is a twenty-foot-tall statue of myself in the middle of my THRONE ROOM?! And... WHY ARE THERE GOBLINS WORSHIPING IT INSTEAD OF RELAXING FOR THE NEXT CAMPAIGN?!

'Ah! I knew you would be just as excited as I!'

Excited?! I don't want them worshiping me! I need them!

Suddenly, a light—an armored goblin in the center of the crowd glowing white.

+5 Devotion

Huh.

The light left the goblin, transferring to the statue, my devotion points rising in the process.

The goblin wandered off to the side, rejoining its cheering brethren.

Great. It's a shrine. My goblins built a shrine.

In my honor, no less...

Should I let this play out?

See what came of this?

Hmmm. I'm not too thrilled with my rubbery likeness being worshiped...

'Aren't you just thrilled, my lord?' Slimey exclaimed, cradling me in her palms as she began to descend from the fourteen-flight throne. *'I had it made in your honor!'*

You did that?

'Of course!' The Slime beamed a radiant smile at me, her pink imitation skin peeling away to reveal her blue form.

Well, the goblins were lacking in extracurricular activities. Maybe a bit of religion would help them.

Do I feel bad about lying to them? Of course, but if it keeps my minions in line and loyal...

"DA GRET YELLOW ONE DESCENDS!" A goblin screamed, the entire cohort, a mix of thralled and conscripted worshiping minions, turning to face Slimey and me descending from the throne.

"DA YELLOW ONE!" The crowd barked in unison, jubilation and excitement spreading like wildfire.

Great... I'm the Yellow One now...

Alright! I sent, attempting to project my voice to every goblin in the crowd.

"DA YELLOW ONE SPEAKS!" A goblin cried.

Alright. Settle down. Settle down, folks.

The crowd rapidly went mute, Gobledo standing on the sidelines and giving a signal to the troops.

Almost instantly, the goblins shifted, forming rows, the armored cadre moving in unified discipline to kneel as one.

The conscripted balked but quickly followed suit, haphazardly scrambling to imitate the trusted.

Maybe I could get used to this.

An ecstatic feeling crept up within, bubbling in my core.

Is this why demons do the things they do?

Very annoying. I'd have to guard against this darkness, no doubt, lest I lose myself.

I looked over my goblin horde, my trustees and conscripted. Tthe conscripts, of course, being the survivors of exterminated goblin lairs.

Over the course of the last two days, my "negotiation" teams had been hard at work, Gobledo and Gobledee working their way through nearly a dozen goblin dens with Davette and Hector.

There were casualties, of course—losses for the cause. Those warriors, given names and entombed in my throne room along with their armor and arms. A sacred memorial.

'My lord, would you like to address your subjects?' Slimey asked.

Subjects? Sigh... fine, might as well play the part.

HEAR YEE! HEAR YEE! The goblins quivering with anticipation as my mind caressed theirs.

Thank you all for your hard work!

Those simple words were enough to move them to tears.

+5 Devotion

+3 Devotion

+6 Devotion

+3 Devotion

+2 Devotion

+4 Devotion

+5 Devotion

+4 Devotion

+5 Devotion

Aaaaaagh!

A hundred notifications hit my mind, a massive stream of feelings and numbers compounding atop one another that was quickly adding up.

Well... quack. I wonder when I'll be able to use this devotion thing...

Anyway, moving my attention back to my monsters, I continued my speech, this time reaching out to all my thralls: spiders, slimes, goblins, skeletons, gnolls, and capruxas.

Thank you for your hard work. Thank you for your efforts in creating a home for our family.

Slimey vibrated at my words.

Look to your left.

The horde of monsters looked collectively to their left.

Look to your right.

The horde of monsters shifted their heads to the right.

These are your family. We are family. Every step you take, every blade you swing, is done in the service of our family. Our familia. This home of ours, a foundation for the future.

I could feel it, a hundred eyes, a hundred minds focused on me and every word I spoke.

Ah... I missed this feeling.

I continued my speech.

You must strive to protect your family. Strive to protect your home. Strive to purify and clean the world!

"Clean!"

"Clean!"

"Clean!"

"Clean!"

"KLEEN!"

The goblins began to chant, their voices one as Slimey held me aloft.

"CLEAN!" One goblin screamed, tearing off his silk clothes as he roared fervently, tears falling down his little green face.

+9 Devotion
Congratulations!

Huh?

Thanks to the devotion of those worshiping you, you have gained access to the first tier of the divinity function.

HUH?!

What would you like to name your religion?

HUH!

Confirm Name: HUH!

No!

What would you like to name your religion?

Sigh... This again.
"Clean!"
"Clean!"
"Clean!"
"Clean!"
The goblins continued to chant.

Confirm Name: Cleaners

Sure, why not? Short, simple, and easy.

Religion Founded: Cleaners!
Active Members: 248

Well... great. I've created a cult. An actual cult of devoted followers...

You have 685 devotion points available to spend!

Oh?

RELIGION FEATURES
Emit Mending Energy
30 Uses (Per Hour)

With the prayers of your devoted followers, use the power of your servants to have a designated shrine emit mending energy.

Holy Barrier
300 Uses (Per Hour)

With the prayers of your devoted followers, use the power of your servants to have a designated shrine emit a holy barrier of immense strength.

Bless
500 Uses (Per Subject)

With the prayers of your devoted followers, use the power of your servants to bless a designated follower, increasing their experience gains, strength, and skill mastery for a limited time.

B-Bless?! BLESS! That was a powerful skill! One that even Chloe wasn't able to learn, forcing us to attend and visit churches during our travels to maximize learning gains.

Awww yeah. AWWWWWWW YEAH!

'Isn't it lovely, my lord? Look at how they worship you!' Slimey beamed.

Yup. "Lovely" is certainly a word to describe this! I replied maliciously.

ELSEWHERE... IN A DISTANT REALM

The Bookkeeper stroked his beard, the red-haired man in his signature pink bathrobe observing the moving image of armored goblins marching through a tunnel in disciplined formation, while another image showed scores of monsters bowing in reverence to a certain rubber bath toy.

"Hn. I would have used skeletons instead," the Bookkeeper commented, his arms crossed and gold eyes shifting from the goblins to the human paladin covered in monster gore. "Well, this will be fun."

"What will be fun?"

"GAH! NYX BELOW! Seriously, woman! Stop doing that!" The Bookkeeper spat, turning to his giggling pink-haired companion of old.

"Oh, you know you like it when I surprise you!" Liza quipped, the woman transforming into a floating pink-haired cat. "Keeps ya on your feet!"

The Bookkeeper sighed, punching his nose. "Liza. How is it that after three hundred years of continued existence, you perpetually elect to ignore the fact that I hate being jumpscared?"

"It's only because you hate it that I keep doing it, boo boo." Liza giggled, floating away as the Bookkeeper's cat hissed at her. "Gotta keep your guard up, Aaaaaaadam. Never know what's lurking around the corner after all."

"Yes, yes," the Bookkeeper hissed, waving the goddess off. "Don't you have that NFD project going on on Earth and a bunch of sailor soldiers to indoctrinate? Why are you bothering me?"

"First off, they're called N. F. T.s, and secondly, they're called Mystic Sailors to avoid copyright."

The Bookkeeper pinched the bridge of his nose, a headache forming as the white cat on his shoulder breathed fire at Liza.

"Liza... Since when do you care about copyright? You're a goddess."

"Since you created the extra-dimensional IRS!" The pink cat snapped. "Seriously! Who asked you to do that?! Who?!"

"Alright, here we go," the Bookkeeper sighed, snapping his fingers and dispelling the mirror. "What did you expect me to do?! There were hundreds of guardians out of work and they needed something to do!"

"NOT CREATE SPACE I.R.S! Do you know how much they hound me?!"

The Bookkeeper slumped his shoulders. "Please leave."

A red-eyed, pale-skinned butler manifested, waving his hand and opening a portal that began to tug at the pink cat.

"Nooo! No, wait, NYAH! I want to know what's going on with the duck!" Liza exclaimed, the cat holding on to a desk for dear life as the sucking suction began to pick her up. "Did he find out yet?!"

"Nope. Now out you go."

"NYAAAAAAAAH!" The cat let out, cartwheeling into the portal.

Chapter 51

First Contact

*S*erve *me,* I commanded, reaching out to the dryad bound in tight silk, her green form suspended in a cave with her arms and legs tightly tied to restrict movement.

'*Nyet!*' her thoughts refuted.

Fine, whatever. I can use anima manacysts.

I opened up my dungeon manager, spending a bit of my manacysts to create a composter in front of the suspended monster. The earth shifted, opening up with serrated teeth chomping, causing the green-eyed dryad to widen her eyes in alarm.

Davette.

At my signal, the sleepy croco-girl entered, in her arms, a dead unicorn—one of the survivors of the massacre that had been caught, killed, and now, used to serve as an example. She tossed the corpse into the pit, the composter happily munching, with rainbow-colored blood splattering over Slimey and the dryad.

I opened up several more composters, surrounding the dryad with the pits. Davette pulled in several bodies from out of the hallway, a mix of gnolls, goblins, and spiders. Most of the bodies were gnolls, after uncovering a den of feral creatures.

Like sarlacc pits, the composters produced fleshy red tentacles, latching onto the dead bodies and dragging them into their maws.

I focused on the dryad.

I'll give you some time to consider the offer. Slimey spun around to face me, Davette shutting the bone cage door behind us.

'*My lord?*'

Yes?

'*Why do you insist on conscripting that worthless tree hugger into our family?*'

Because she has a purpose. A strong addition to our resources.'

'*Of... course,*' she nodded, her form briefly shifting to a yellow color.

Sigh.

Do not be jealous, Slimey. You alone are my champion. My first minion. You need not fear.

At my words, the slime turned bright pink, hugging me close as we passed a group of goblins cleaning—one sweeping the floor while the other used a slime attached to a spear to mop.

Suddenly, we stopped. Slimey vibrated in place, all color draining from her body to leave behind a dull grey, marred by her red cores.

'*Hero... Please...*'

Huh? A voice, one that came out as a slight whimper, echoed through the recesses of my mind—a plea filled with desperation.

The quack?

And just as quickly as it had come, it was gone. Slimey and I resumed our walk once more.

Slimey.

'Yes, my lord?'

What was that?

'What was what, my lord?'

That... You turned grey.

'I have no idea what you're referring to, my lord,' Slimey replied, smiling up at me.

Right...

Weird. My mind began to ponder what that was. Unfortunately, I didn't have too long to think about it, as a notification hit my mind.

Minion, Goblin 18 has perished!
Minion, Goblin 45 has perished!
Min—

What?

WHAT?!

WHAT'S GOING ON?!

Opening my minion menu, I scrolled down, catching the last name just as it blipped away.

Goblin 46! Gobeldee's replacement team—one of three goblin teams assembled to provide relief and support for Gobledo and Gobledee in the field. Now, they were being picked off!

What's the meaning of this?! Goblin 47! Respond! I sent, attempting to contact the team leader.

Screams. My trustee was dying, the connection severed.

'My lord?' Slimey began. *'What's wrong?*

WE'RE UNDER ATTACK! I bellowed, reaching out to the other teams in the area, ordering a retreat.

ELSEWHERE...

Lhikan grimaced, flinging the dead armored goblin against a nearby wall. The green-skinned creature crashed with a sickening thud as his party caught up to him.

"Oh good, you caught them!" Marcus exclaimed, catching his breath.

"Yeah... the runner didn't get far," Lhikan muttered, frowning as he eyed the phalanx of goblins that had tried to ambush him after he chased down a fleeing goblin. The creature had been about to alert its horde.

"Weird," Tipsy said, the gnome standing over a dead goblin. Its silk garments remained untouched, and its skin was unmarred by blight.

"Alright. Let's prepare to head out!" Lhikan barked, flicking the green blood off his blade and signaling his soldiers to move.

"No, wait!" Tipsy shouted, halting the blood-covered paladins in their tracks.

"What? What's wrong?" Marcus asked, raising an eyebrow.

"These goblins... they shouldn't be here," Tipsy said, her voice filled with concern, even through the robotic filter of her pink-lensed gas mask.

"Okay? And?" Marcus replied with a shrug. "Lots of monsters crop up in places they shouldn't. Besides, these are gobl—"

"No," Lhikan interrupted, cutting off the sergeant. "These goblins... they're armored and organized. Displaying a clear ranking structure."

"Are you sure?" Marcus asked, his steel boot kicking the corpse of one of the goblins. "They didn't last long."

"When I ambushed the first goblin, the others didn't scatter. They retreated," Lhikan said, nudging the dented shield of his first victim. "They lured me into an ambush with reinforcements, standing their ground."

At the senior paladin's words, the scribes and knights exchanged uneasy glances. Tactics. It was unheard of from goblins unless they were being led—or controlled—by something far more powerful.

Marcus cocked his head. "Is it a demon?"

"Doubtful," Lhikan replied, his gauntlet tightening into a fist. "We would have felt its presence by now. No, it's something else. Maybe an evolved variant... or something else elevating these goblins' performance."

"Sir, didn't you say that blight ran rampant through this entire castle?" Tipsy asked, pulling out her mana reader. The dial on the gauge was already pointing at DANGER, lowering only slightly as she swept it over the goblins' corpses. "These goblins are clean. Barely any traces of blight. In fact, they're giving off some holy energy."

"Impossible!" Marcus exclaimed, his eyes blowing wide. The scribes crowded around the gnome to get a better look.

"The reader doesn't lie, Marc," Tipsy said.

"Well, maybe it's broken!" the paladin countered.

"Impossible! I made it myself and maintain all my gear!" Tipsy shot back, offended. "Are you calling my work shoddy, spoon-ear?"

"Cut it out, you two," Lhikan intervened, his voice cold. "We've got work to do, and two dungeons to get through if we're going to reach the artifact."

Reluctantly, the pair fell in line, and the group moved deeper into the castle's bowels.

As they walked, Lhikan's pace slowed, his eyes scanning the walls. The air had shifted. Something was off.

"What is it?" Marcus asked, signaling the group to halt.

Lhikan clenched his jaw, his gaze narrowing.

"The last time I was here, these hallways were crawling with webs and swarming with gnolls and skeletons. Tarantuals hid behind every corner... but now, nothing. It's too quiet."

"Please don't tell me you're being paranoid," Marcus groaned.

"Quiet," Lhikan continued, unperturbed. "Too quiet."

Marcus sighed. "What do you suggest, sir? Should we turn back?"

"No," Lhikan said firmly. "Within the week, Danse and his army will clear the roadblocks we left behind, including the landslide. We need to push forward. But we'll do it cautiously. I want no more losses from here on out." He signaled for two knights to move to the front, shields raised. "Joshua, Kyle, you two lead. Tipsy, stay by my side. Marcus, cover our retreat."

"Aye, sir."

Tipsy's eyes went wide as she spotted something. Her gaze locked on a blue slime slinking across the floor.

"CATCH THAT!" the gnome yelled, pointing at the blue orb.

"What? WAIT!" Lhikan snapped, grabbing the excited gnome by her backpack as she tried to rush past him. "What part of 'stay by my side' don't you understand?!"

"THAT SLIME! CATCH IT!" Tipsy screeched, her arms flailing as she struggled in Lhikan's grip.

Lhikan turned to the creature, raising an eyebrow. "What's so special about a slime?"

"THAT'S A CLEANING SLIME!" Tipsy hollered.

Silence fell over the group, every set of eyes locked on the gnome.

"... And?" Marcus asked, blinking.

"YOU IDIOTS! IT'S A CLEANING SLIME! AN UNMUTATED MONSTER IN A BLIGHTED AREA!" Tipsy exclaimed, her voice laced with panic. "There hasn't been a natural sighting of an unmutated slime in YEARS! They're an endangered species!"

"Stop," Lhikan said sharply.

"What are you—"

"I SAID STOP!" Lhikan barked, cutting off the gnome. "Need I remind you of our mission? We can't afford to waste time trying to capture monsters for experiments."

"But—"

"No," Lhikan said, his tone final. "If it's still around when we're heading back, we'll take it with us."

The gnome deflated, but Lhikan's orders were clear.

"Let's keep moving," he commanded, and the soldiers filed forward, careful to sidestep the blue slime.

With their lightstones raised, the group pressed on at a slow, deliberate pace. Tipsy walked between the soldiers, checking their filtration boxes. Eventually, they reached a well-lit area, the walls now illuminated by glowstones.

"You were right," Marcus muttered, rubbing a hand over the pristine tomb in front of them. "This place is too clean. Too clean for somewhere that's supposed to be abandoned. And these glowstone fixtures... they aren't natural."

"Still think I'm paranoid, sergeant?" Lhikan asked, scanning the area.

"Jesse," Lhikan added, turning to one of the scribes who moonlighted as a rogue. "Scout for traps."

"Right on, sir," Jesse replied, slinking ahead. He moved low to the ground, eyes darting back and forth until they settled on something that shouldn't have been there.

"What is it?" Marcus asked as Jesse returned.

"Tripwire... made of spider silk," Jesse reported, pointing to a thin, nearly invisible wire. "It's connected to some kind of spike trap—bones whittled down and attached to each wall."

Lhikan grimaced. Traps weren't unusual in old ruins, but newly crafted ones suggested something was still living in the place. Something with intelligence.

"Can you disarm it?" Lhikan asked.

"Yeah, no problem," Jesse replied, setting to work.

But just as he neared the tripwire, disaster struck.

"AGH!" Jesse cried out, his leg sinking into the floor.

"AMBUSH!" Lhikan shouted, drawing his sword as stones, slime, and webs began to fly through the air.

Chapter 52

Fatal Error

"**A**MBUSH!" Lhikan yelled, racing forward, moving in unison to pull Jesse out of the hole where his leg was stuck.

"AGH!" Jesse cried, two paladins moving to shield Lhikan as he stopped pulling at Jesse and inspected the trap.

A punji trap, a typical orthodoxy trap made of sharpened spikes attached to two rollers that spun the moment someone's limb fell between them, entrapping the victim and causing more damage if someone attempted to pull them out.

Lhikan frowned before his fist broke the large bones that held the trap together, freeing Jesse.

"Goblins!" Marcus yelled, Lhikan pulling Jesse out of the trap.

Lhikan raised his head, his eyes widening at the sight of a formation of armored goblins marching in his direction.

"Great," he hissed, pulling Jesse, who was bleeding profusely. The rogue attempted to stem the blood gushing from the various holes in his thigh.

"Artery! It nicked! Nicked my artery!" Jesse cried as Lhikan dragged him while his knights guarded them.

"HEALER!" Lhikan barked, a stone bouncing off his helmet as he laid the rogue on the ground and attempted to apply pressure to the injuries.

Two scribes quickly approached, one gasping as she laid her hands on the gushing blood and began praying.

"We have to heal him here! You need to protect us!" Simone exclaimed, the church scribe wrapping a cloth above Jesse's injury and tightening it to stem the loss of life force. "Keep pressure! This is going to hurt!"

"GAH! DAMN IT!" Jesse barked as the scribe tightened the tourniquet.

"Cover us!" Lhikan ordered, his gauntlets quickly soaking in blood.

Marcus and Tipsy led the vanguard, the latter brandishing her blunderbuss, which punched a hole through the ranks of the enemy shield wall.

With a boom, Marcus shot forward, riding the momentum of Tipsy's attack. The goblins were peppered with iron balls and thrown into confusion as the paladin roared.

Cleaving through the enemy's frontline, Marcus splattered blood as he slashed through them, his eyes focusing on a taller goblin wearing a helmet and barking orders to the second wave.

A commander?! Marcus's eyes went wide, the revelation cementing his fears about the enemy's tactical organization.

The goblins reinforcing the frontline tightened their formation, raising their spears. The monsters shifted into a spear wall and began marching as a war horn sounded, followed by howls.

"GNOLLS!" Marcus barked, Titus and Marth joining him. The two knights raised their shields to ward off the claws of four vicious attackers snarling at their flanks.

"SPIDERS!" Tipsy called out, firing at the ceiling with her flintlocks. The skittering creatures traveled over the heads of the armored goblins and began spitting webs at the adventurers.

"Buy us time!" Lhikan spat, Jesse's pained cries momentarily overshadowing the sounds of clashing.

"YES, SIR!" Marcus, Titus, and Marth shouted in unison, the trio of knightly paladins holding the line.

Marcus leaned left, dodging a web bolt, his eyes focused on the commander as Tipsy produced a gadget that shot flames at the ceiling, driving away the spiders.

Ambush, multi-pronged attack, multiple monster types! There's definitely a demon here! Marcus affirmed, a sinking feeling in his gut.

"Oh Divinity, grant me strength!" Marcus roared, divine energy arcing across his blade, the weapon a beacon in the darkness.

With a swipe, his sword released a wave of holy energy. The arc of white mana slashed through the enemy's decrepit shields, with the goblins standing no chance against the divine attack.

Goblins weren't much of a threat when it came down to it; however, their numbers, the tight corridors, and the use of armor and traps left Marcus on edge. If there were commanders, there was a possibility of spellcasters—or worse, evolved beings—which meant every second spent fighting was another second used to wear down their strength.

The commander ducked the wave of mana and rushed forward, screaming in fury as its comrades fell.

Readying his blade, Marcus grinned and welcomed the attack. The commander was devoid of any protection.

Saves me the trouble.

The goblin unsheathed its sword, rushing Marcus, who slashed at the goblin, only for the creature to deflect the attack.

Huh?

Marcus kicked off the ground, dodging to avoid the blade that scraped against his armor.

What?

Marcus clenched his jaw, eyeing the goblin. The monster struck a short guard sword stance that...

Wait. THAT'S THE IMPERIAL FORM ONE!

A typical sword guard, where the hilt is held near the user's waist with the blade facing at an angle toward the attacker. It's a balanced stance, great for defense but also used to chain into other sword forms.

Every swordsman worth their salt was taught this form. Now, the question on Marcus' mind was: who taught this disgusting goblin?

Titus and Marth dispatched the four gnolls, joining Marcus. The trio stared down the goblin, which was all alone except for the two spiders that survived being immolated.

The goblin quivered under the glare of the three paladins, the monster fighting its instincts to run as Marcus calmly approached it.

"I commend your courage, green thing," Marcus said, bearing down on the goblin. "But the only good goblin is a dead goblin."

"ScRE!" the goblin cried, rushing Marcus.

"So, let's make a good goblin," Marcus said, cutting the monster down unceremoniously.

The creature hit the floor, its weapon clattering with a dull sound.

"We're clear!" Marcus turned and barked, moving to step away, but he paused.

Looking down at his boot, he saw a three-fingered hand latched onto it.

"Hmm?"

"ScreEk," the goblin let out, leaking copious amounts of green blood but still alive.

"Huh, guess I cut too shallow." Marcus lifted his blade, the edge hovering over the monster's neck before dropping it, ending the small creature. "Well, whatev—"

"SQUEAK!"

Marcus paused. The pulse of a faint magical sound wave rolled over him, one filled with... despair?

It caught him off guard, every human turning as Lhikan rose to his feet.

CLANG.

Suddenly, the sound of metal bashing against something echoed.

CLANG.

"Did anyone else feel that?" Titus asked, looking around.

CLANG.

"What's that sound?" Marth asked, readying his bloodied mace.

CLANG.

"More goblins, probably," Marcus said, his anxiety rising.

CLANG.

"How are we on healing?!" Marcus called out.

CLANG.

"Almost do—" Scribe Simone called out, but she stopped, a scraping sound echoing through the tight corridor.

All eyes turned to the end of the tunnel, an ominous sensation emanating from the darkness.

"Shields!" Marcus called, just as something massive flew out of the darkness.

"GAH!" Titus and Marth were sent flying, hitting the ground with a loud thud, while Marcus ducked beneath the massive spinning blade.

"FALL BACK!" Lhikan spat, picking up Jesse. The sound of armored footsteps, skittering, and bloodlust echoed through the hallway.

"SQUEAK!"

Marcus went to help the two paladins, his eyes going wide at the body that was missing its head.

What? No!

Marth was gone, but Titus was still alive.

"Titus! On your feet!" Marcus barked, grabbing the injured paladin. The pair fled the way they came.

"You okay?" Marcus asked, turning to Titus, the man clutching his shield arm, the shield bent out of shape.

"Think my arm is broken. What in six hells was that?" Titus huffed.

"Something's—"

Suddenly, an influx of mana surged.

Marcus shifted, eyes wide, his blade scraping against a large, green-scaled humanoid with a blue spider on its back soaring past.

"TITUS!" Marcus exclaimed, reaching out to save the man who had been snatched up by the monster. Just as he did, he was struck by a bolt of light mana in the shoulder. "GAH!"

What?

Marcus went wide-eyed, stunned. His mind blanked as he processed that he'd just been hit with a bolt of holy energy.

"Marcus! Come on!" Lhikan said, grabbing him and pulling the paladin to safety as another shrill-sounding SQUEAK echoed behind them.

Bloodlust.

They could feel it. That simple squeak carried with it rage and hatred.

Something was coming. Something fueled by red-hot anger. Something that sent a cold sweat down Marcus's back.

"Let's go! Keep moving!" Lhikan barked.

"What about Titus?!"

"He's gone! We'll come back for him!" Lhikan snapped, pulling the reluctant man away, as a malevolent smile appeared in the shadows.

Chapter 53

Trapping Adventurers

Minion, Gobledee has perished!

My mind focused on the notification, a numbness taking over me as Slimey held the commander's body in her arms.

I had given an order:

To stall the enemy's advance long enough for my soldiers to arrive.

Gobledee had done just that, slowing the enemy's progress from a position not yet scouted by my forces…

"AHHH! AAH! AHK! GET OFF ME!" a human screamed as the armored knight was pinned to a wall by Davette.

I reached out, my mind touching the man's, where I was greeted with fear and alarm, the pounding of his frantic heartbeat audible to my senses.

"OUT! OUT OF MY MIND!"

The man began to scream as my will overlapped his. The knight convulsed and shook as I uttered three words that, in a past life, would have made me sick:

You. Are. Mine!

The man shook, images of his life spilling from his psyche into mine.

Glimpses. Pictures. A city under siege.

Monsters.

A blue sky.

A man... with a family. Two kids and a wife.

Pity? Remorse? I didn't feel them as the man finally seized up and died, the connection severing.

I had a family too, and this human had slaughtered members of my clan without pause.

Find them.

'*Yes, my lord,*' Slimey acknowledged, my entire army taking off in pursuit as several of my skeletons picked up the bodies and dumped them onto the back of Buttstalion.

Take the head too. I ordered as I envisioned the layout of this floor.

We were close to the castle basement. From their direction, they must have either come from the castle or from the adjoining hallway connected on this floor.

But considering my skeletons at the castle basement hadn't been attacked, I knew exactly where they were going.

Ayaka.

'*Y-Yes? What do you need, master?*' the spider replied, sensing my mood.

I relayed my instructions. The plan was simple.

At the rate they were fleeing, they would soon end up at an intersection that either allowed them to go up to the basement or into un-scouted territory. But not before I had my men in place.

Slimey. Let's go. We've got some rodents to exterminate.

'*Of course, my lord,*' Slimey said, placing me on her head as she gripped her black-iron blade and began dragging it across the floor.

Standing in what appeared to have once been a wine storage room, Lhikan and the remaining party members under his command caught their breath.

"Okay, what was that?!" Marcus exclaimed, clutching his shoulder. "Where did those traps come from?! Why were there goblins from an area we cleared?!"

"I don't know," Lhikan said, catching his breath.

"You!" Marcus spat, turning to Jesse, who was switching out his mana battery for his air box. "It was your job to clear them!"

"I DID!" Jesse snapped, the rogue rolling ointment onto his regenerated skin. "They weren't there before! The skeletons that showed up must have planted them!"

"They're skeletons; the amount of fine-tuning required is more than—"

"ENOUGH!" Lhikan barked, taking control. The paladin stood up to glare at the four soldiers left.

In the ensuing retreat, they had lost two more of their party: Christa, the other scribe healer, and Delrio, their hunter. Both had succumbed to spike traps that separated the group before a nimble skeleton appeared, slashing their throats and forcing the group down a different corridor.

Now, they were in uncharted territory inside the Demon Lord's domain.

"You can take your filters off," Tipsy said, placing the box that began to purify and detox the air.

"Are you sure we're safe?" Simone asked, the last remaining cleric glancing around anxiously as she tended to Marcus's injury.

"Marcus?" Tipsy asked.

"The adjoining rooms are empty, and the skeletons and goblins are just waiting at the end of the hall below," Marcus replied, peeking down the stairway where the spiritual glare of a skeleton met his gaze, the monster unmoving. "We're safe, for now."

"Any reason they aren't coming up here?" Jesse inquired.

"No idea. Maybe the ground is sacred or something?" Marcus replied, wincing in pain as Simone gasped. "Or this is another dungeon's territory."

"This! This is holy energy!" Simone said, eyeing the wound seared by divine mana.

"See, and you questioned my equipment," Tipsy quipped, earning a glare from Marcus.

"Senor, what's going on?" Marcus asked, all eyes now on the silver-haired paladin. "This route was supposed to be cleared. A straight shot to the artifact you said belonged down here."

"It was clear," Lhikan growled, stomping on a nearby skull. "Last we were here, there were hundreds of gnolls, thousands of skeletons, and hungry goblins. We already took care of the evolved beings. There shouldn't have been anything else on this way."

Lhikan shook his head, his brow furrowing.

"Yet, they are," Jesse said. "And they're intelligent. Working together. This kind of coordination between monsters isn't something that's normal."

"They're evolving," Tipsy said. "Or something is making them evolve."

"A dungeon core?" Marcus offered, clenching his fist as Simone chanted and slowly mended his injury.

"A dungeon core can evolve monsters quickly. But they don't display combat tactics or work in unison with other creatures," Tipsy said, dropping her large backpack and pulling out a gauntlet made of chitin, web, and bone. "This... the materials are crap, but the craftsmanship is expertly woven. A dungeon core doesn't have the technical know-how to do this. Or create the traps we've been seeing."

"What are you saying?" Simone asked, finally taking off her mask to reveal a freckled face, blonde girl who was maybe no older than twenty.

"A demon," Lhikan answered, everyone turning.

"But you—" Marcus began.

"That's the only explanation I have. Only a demon can inspire this much radical change and growth in monsters."

"Or a number of evolved ones," Tipsy added, sitting atop her purifier. "But evolved ones still don't explain the cooperation between anima and dark monsters. Even with a dungeon core, they still fight each other."

"What's the play here, sir?" Marcus asked, finally taking off his mask to reveal a tanned young man with bright blue eyes.

"We cannot allow Commander Danse and his army to acquire the artifact. If they do, all hope for our world dies once Krekka gets their hands on it."

"So what? You want us to take on a demon?" Marcus asked. "If it has the power of the Hero... we don't stand a chance, even with you at the helm."

"Then leave. All of you. I will see the journey through," Lhikan replied, the reality of the situation settling on the party.

They were baggage, slowing Lhikan down. The group of adventurers was a far cry from his former party. Every stop, every injury, every retreat was due in part to his party members being ambushed or hurt.

Marcus and the others knew it, and so did Lhikan. Their purpose here was to carry supplies, validate his claims, and help him conserve his mana to allow him to get to the artifact.

"We can't do that, sir." Marcus said resolutely.

"I'm not asking, I'm telling you. At this point—LOOK OUT!" Lhikan moved forward, tackling Tipsy off her purifier as a green-scaled creature lunged into the room from the stairwell, taking out the purifier.

"MASKS! MASKS! MASKS!" Marcus barked, the adventurers donning their filters as goblins, skeletons, and spiders rushed the room from every entrance.

"WHERE DID THEY COME FROM?!" Simone shrieked, blasting a skeleton with a bolt of holy mana.

Lhikan looked left and right, taking in the chaos, his eyes settling on the green-scaled monster standing upright to reveal itself as some kind of beastkin.

She had strong muscles and green scales, along with a large, spiked tail that glittered from the reflection of the party's glowstones.

The monster roared, brandishing inhuman teeth, the creature charging Tipsy and Lhikan.

"Get up! Let's go!" Lhikan barked, grabbing the gnome and punching the charging monster in the face, sending the scaly creature careening into the floor.

"There's too many!" Marcus screamed, cutting down a pair of goblins and unleashing a wave of holy mana that disintegrated a group of skeletons.

Jesse rose to his feet, throwing a dagger that took out a goblin attempting to rush Simone.

"Retreat!" Lhikan called out, eyeing the one passage that was clear of the flooding monsters.

"Wait! My bag!" Tipsy cried.

"NO TIME!" Lhikan barked, running with the gnome on his shoulder as Marcus and the others followed him out of the monster swarm.

"More monsters! On our left and right!" Tipsy cried.

"This way!" Marcus said, charging forward, leading the survivors into an expansive arena of dust and bone, a gargantuan entertainment center littered with the bodies of the deceased.

Lhikan looked around, eyeing the sandpit filled with bones but devoid of monsters.

With no threats in sight, Lhikan spun, turning to face their pursuers.

"We'll kite and draw them out here, disperse their numbers, and deal with them as they come!" Lhikan ordered, the survivors fanning out into a wide formation to create an arc around the entrance to intercept the monsters.

Yet... oddly, like before, the creatures paused, refusing to enter into the next room.

The survivors glanced at one another with echoing the confusion that was hidden behind their air masks.

"W-What? Why are they stopping? Why aren't they coming up?" Simone asked, her voice trembling.

"I don't know," Marcus said, eyeing the two goblins in armor interlocking their shields to block the entrance.

Lhikan narrowed his eyes.

"Demon. Definitely a demon," Tipsy said, pulling out a hammer and a screwdriver as her weapons of choice.

Suddenly, an influx, a large gathering of mana picking up as the sand along the ground kicked up.

"Yeah, definitely a demon," Marcus said, turning to face the condensing mana taking shape: a man with black hair and silver armor.

"Ah... This is a trap," Jesse said before being pulled off his feet, a silver blade trimming his hair as he was sent flying from Lhikan tossing him.

"SCATTER!" Lhikan roared, engaging the mysterious knight.

Chapter 54

Execution

"GAH!" Lhikan hissed, his shoulder rocking back from the force of the attack, the silver blade merely an inch from his face.

He quickly activated his rune circuits, his body glowing, his eyes focused on the man who was the splitting image of the grand statue in Lizaria.

"It's a doppelganger!" Tipsy yelled, lifting her flintlock pistol.

The paladin lifted his foot, kicking off the black-haired man as Tipsy opened fire.

A bang sounded as the Hero lifted his blade, parrying the gunshot in a shower of sparks.

"Well…" Tipsy went slack-jawed, wide-eyed and dropping her gun. "Nope."

The gnome turned and ran, the doppelganger shooting off, nearly impaling the small woman if not for Lhikan intervening. He kicked off the ground with explosive speed, distracting the doppelganger.

Tsk!

The doppelganger effortlessly dodged his blade, the man's eyes shifting to glare at Lhikan.

"Damn," Lhikan muttered before he was sent flying.

"SENIOR!" Marcus cried, charging the black-haired man with Jesse. The two warriors activated their mana circuits as Simone finished casting her buff.

"O' divine above, grant thee vigor!" Simone yelled, her body bursting with radiance that empowered Jesse and Marcus.

"KEEP HIM OCCUPIED!" Marcus commanded, Jesse throwing a series of daggers that were easily deflected by their opposition as Marcus closed the distance.

"O' divinity!" Marcus surged with strength, his blade clashing against the doppelganger's, who easily parried both his and Jesse's attacks with a look of indifference.

Lhikan pulled himself out of the crater in the arena, lurching forward. The paladin released his inner rage, supercharging with sparks flying off his body as mana focused on the tip of his blade.

"Thunderous Smite!"

The doppelganger looked up, blocking Lhikan's blade but not the follow-up, the paladin's weapon unleashing a concussive blast.

Jesse and Marcus were sent flying, Lhikan performing a flip in the air before landing on his feet, the sand in the arena kicking up.

Lhikan held his breath, eyeing the dust, waiting, watching, looking for signs of the doppelganger, who was nowhere to be found.

"Everyone okay?!" Lhikan called out, Marcus, Simone, and Jesse giving words of affirmation.

Tipsy had run off, but considering they no longer had their purifier, she was now the least of Lhikan's concerns.

"Damn, that was scary. Is it dead?" Jesse queried, looking around.

"Why does everyone insist on saying death flags?" Marcus groaned, causing Jesse to chuckle.

"Please, it's only a death flag if... if..." Jesse slowly turned his gaze down his body, eyeing the blade poking out of his chest. "Well... I'll be damned."

"JESSE!" Simone screamed as the rogue coughed up blood and fell to the floor, Lhikan moving.

"Stay alert!" Lhikan barked, cutting the black-haired man's head off, killing him instantly.

"Jesse! Jess!" Simone cried, attempting to heal the rogue, who was struggling to breathe.

"We have to get out of here," Marcus said, moving to shift the injured rogue.

"We won't get far. That thing's too fast," Lhikan reported, everyone's gaze turning to the paladin as he struck a stance.

In the distance, despite being previously decapitated, the black-haired man reappeared, his former body gone.

"It's a DOPPELGANGER!" Tipsy cried from across the arena, atop a balcony. "You have to destroy the catalyst summoning it!"

Lhikan narrowed his eyes, his pupils straining as he willed mana to his eyes and activated Mana Vision, observing the tether of mana latched onto the specter.

"Marcus, I need you on your feet. Simone, you'll have to put everything into buffing Marcus," Lhikan instructed, feeling discomfort in his ribs.

One. Maybe two ribs broken...

"W-Wha?" Simone said, looking up as she held Jesse in her arms. "I can't! I need to heal Jesse or he'll—"

"Do it."

At the paladin's words, the scribe went pale.

"Or we all die. Marcus, I need you to buy me time," Lhikan said, his body wafting with holy embers. "Distract it."

"Great. Of course, I'm bait..." Marcus grimaced, striking a stance, eyeing the black-haired man calmly approaching.

"I... I..." Simone stuttered, her voice cracking.

"Simone," Lhikan said.

"B-But! But!"

"SCRIBE SIMONE! DO AS YOU HAVE BEEN ORDERED!" Lhikan snapped, the woman flinching.

"It's okay. D-Do it," Jesse groaned, grabbing the woman's shoulder.

"He's getting closer," Marcus hissed, silently praying, activating all his augments, his body releasing blue energy.

"I'm sorry," Simone squeaked, the girl crying audibly underneath her air filter as she lifted her hands and began chanting, a series of glyphs floating in the air.

One for strength.

One for speed.

One for fortitude.

And lastly, one that cast a magical shield over Marcus.

All of her mana. Gone. A tactical decision by Lhikan, who closed his eyes as Marcus rushed forward.

"O' Lord, hear thy prayer," Lhikan said, channeling divinity, the sound of clashing metal on metal echoing through the arena. "Grant thee succor and strength, display upon the world a miracle from thy hand—"

Marcus screamed, the ground shaking. The paladin was barely keeping up despite his various buffs.

"—Let your grace flow through me, mold me, shape me into an instrument of your divine will," Lhikan recited, runic glyphs floating around his body as he held his glowing sword aloft. "Judgment Blade, Radiance!"

Lhikan's eyes shot open, his pupils brimming with golden energy.

"GET CLEAR!" Lhikan roared, Marcus fleeing as Lhikan swung, unleashing a devastating torrent of divine energy that smashed into the doppelganger.

The arena shook, the force of the divine attack kicking up sand that obscured everyone's vision.

A moment passed, then another. No one moved until the dust settled.

Lhikan huffed, out of breath, standing over a large crater in the earth where a dungeon core had been.

"Remind me not to piss you off," Marcus said, bleeding profusely as he knelt beside Lhikan.

"Won't have to if you do your job," Lhikan replied, steadying his trembling hand. The paladin turned, eyeing Simone, the girl crying over her friend, who was bleeding out. "Take Simone and the others and get out of here."

"What?" Marcus said. "You can't be serious. You want us to leave you? We can still be useful, sir!"

"You're all useless to me without mana, and I can't spend all my time watching after you four. Go. Help Simone."

"Okay, how? Last I checked, the exit is flooded with monsters, and we don't exactly have a purifier anymore."

"I'll cut a path. Carve out the escape route so you can leave," Lhikan said, before handing Marcus the party's rift stone, his lifeline to escape. "We have about five days' supply of air. If we can't retrieve the artifact, use—"

CLANG!

Suddenly, the clashing of metal on metal sounded, every set of able eyes turning to the hallway where the armored goblins stood flanking the entrance like some form of honor guard.

Lhikan clenched his jaw, the old man's arms trembling as he pushed Marcus behind him and stepped forward.

CLANG. CLANG. CLANG.

The sound kept echoing, getting louder and louder with each clang until it was replaced by a loud scraping sound.

Then it stopped, the silhouette of a woman standing in the doorway sending shivers down Marcus's spine.

"Now," a voice echoed. "What's this I hear about you wanting to leave?"

"A-A maiden!" Simone cried, her eyes wide at the priestess with emerald eyes and green hair walking into the arena with a massive blade in hand, dragging across the floor. "PLEASE! Madam Light, my friend! You have to help me heal my friend!"

Marcus eyed Lhikan.

"Commander Danse isn't supposed to be here for another two weeks. What's a Maiden of Light doing here?!" Marcus asked incredulously.

"That's no maiden," Lhikan hissed, his teeth audibly grinding as he eyed the rubber duck on the head of the mysterious woman wearing Natalie's clothes.

"Please! You've got to help Jesse! Madam Ligh—" Simone began to approach the woman, but a quick blast of mana hitting the dirt in front of her stopped the scribe.

"Stop. Don't go near it. It's a shapeling." Lhikan lowered his palm, stepping towards the woman smiling ominously at him as dozens of armored goblins entered the arena.

"Not quite," the woman giggled, her hand covering the smile that contrasted the evil in her eyes. "Would you like to guess again?"

Simone scurried away, grabbing Jesse and dragging him along.

"Ah... this ain't looking good, senior," Marcus muttered, eyeing the monsters that now surrounded them. "What's the plan here?"

"I'm thinking," Lhikan hushed the other, eyeing a skeleton stepping out of the crowd with daggers in its bony hands.

"Well, it's talking to us, maybe we can negotiate with it?" Marcus offered, the man coughing up a bit of blood.

Lhikan grunted, his jaw clenched as a seething rage bubbled within.

"Uh, excuse me!" Marcus began, walking forward. "Hi! I'm—"

"The human who killed Lieutenant Gobledee," the woman said, all smiles, bloodlust rising into the air from the gathered crowd of goblins.

"Uh... right..." Marcus let out, the man at a loss for words as he eyed the massive two-handed weapon. "Well, I'm Marcus Delphi, what's—"

"By order of Lord Hiro, Marcus Delphi, your execution shall commence immediately. Please resist," the woman said, her lips moving to reveal inhuman teeth that made Simone yelp.

Wait, Hiro? Lhikan's eyes went wide as Marcus chuckled nervously.

"Wait, my execution?" Marcus said, barely containing his nervousness. "Surely we—"

The woman shot off, blade in hand, giggling as she seemed to disappear.

"WAIT!" Lhikan barked, reaching out, attempting to move. Yet, try as he might, his body wouldn't obey his orders; pain shot through it, his mana circuits on fire.

"NO!" Simone shrieked, watching both halves of Marcus fall away.

Lhikan clenched his trembling hand, unable to do anything for his soldier as the sound of crying echoed out.

Chapter 55

Captives

"M-Marcus!" Simone cried, reaching out but freezing as the woman, covered in blood, turned towards her with a sinister smile.

"Stop! Please! WAIT!" Lhikan barked as the woman wearing Natalie's clothing brandished her blade towards Simone. "She's just a healer! Leave her alone, she hasn't killed anyone yet!"

"Interesting. Unfortunately, I don't ca—"

The woman paused, her black blade merely a centimeter away from the healer.

"Of course, my lord."

The woman lowered her blade, Lhikan and Simone breathing a sigh of relief as the woman suddenly took on a gentle expression.

"In accordance with my lord's will, as of this moment, you are all prisoners of Lord Hiro," the woman stated, the armored goblins surrounding them beginning to move.

There it is again, Lhikan thought to himself, the second time he'd heard the changeling refer to her master as "Hiro."

"If you resist. You will be killed. If you disobey our lord's orders, you will be killed. If you—"

"No! No! No! You can't take him!" Simone cried, throwing herself over Jesse as the goblins moved in.

"Simone!" Lhikan barked, his skin tingling from the bloodlust radiating off the woman, whose skin seemed to visibly wiggle. "Let them take him."

"But—"

"That is an order," Lhikan said, his eyes drawn to the yellow duck atop his assailant's head.

The woman approached Simone, kneeling down, her slender fingers taking hold of Simone's chin strap on her gas mask.

"You may rest easy, your friend will know no harm under Lord Hiro's protection," the woman said, resting a hand on Jesse's curled-up body.

Simone locked eyes with the woman, whose pupils reflected no light.

Lhikan frowned, feeling the presence of holy mana in the air.

"Cough! Ugh! AAAGH!" Jesse let out.

Impossible. Lhikan's mind dulled, telling him that his eyes were lying to him.

"JESSE!" Simone cried, hugging the man who cried out in pain.

"What's? What's going—Well, hello, beautiful," Jesse said, his eyes wide at the false Maiden of Light. "Who is thi—"

The woman smiled, brandishing rows of sharp teeth.

"Never mind," Jesse finished, eyes wide with shock as he gazed at the corpse lying nearby.

"What are you going to do with us?" Lhikan asked as the goblins surrounded them and forced them to move.

"Whatever Lord Hiro deems is necessary," the woman replied. "Now move. We won't ask again."

He walked forward, stepping over Marcus but not before tripping, sprawling in the dirt as his hands moved frantically across the sand.

"Senior!" Simone cried, rushing over and helping him up to his feet.

"Strike One," the woman replied, Lhikan stopping in front of her.

"Please, you have to know that if we're kept down here, our purifiers will run out of power," Lhikan said. "If that happens, we'll become blighted and die."

The woman cocked her head. Now that Lhikan was face to face with his captor, it suddenly dawned on the old paladin why she looked so familiar!

Lyndis, the Skyshot Huntress!

She was a mirror image of the woman, at least, the statue of the Big Six from Lizaria. In fact, now that he was so close, the weapon she held with the tip in the sand had an inscription that read DRAGON SLAYER.

Lhikan's breath caught in his throat.

"We will take care of that," the woman said.

"Wait!" Lhikan exclaimed, drawing spears that were aimed at him from his captors. "At least, tell me your name. As Commander, I need to know who is in charge of my soldiers' well-being."

"You are testing my patience, human. You will not gain any intel from me," the woman said, her skin starting to visibly shift from human pink to crimson red.

"Are... they going to kill us?" Simone asked, sitting in the darkness of a damp cell with Jesse and Lhikan, the only company they had being a pit in the earth lined with rows of sharp teeth.

"I don't know," Lhikan replied, the gears in his mind turning as he stared at his goblin guards through the prison bars made of bone.

Could he escape? No doubt. But could Simone and Jesse? Short answer: no, especially if he had to fight off the False Maiden. There was also the Tarantual Matriarch and the Tarantual Titan, the two monsters flanking the throne room leading out of these caves.

"Why didn't we fight?" Jesse asked, sitting propped up against a wall, tossing pebbles into the pit, one rock snatched up by a tongue. "Gross."

"You want to go up against an army with no mana, no backup, and no clue what we're facing? Be my guest," Lhikan said, before raising his hand, signaling for silence.

Jesse and Simone's eyes shifted to the paladin, their gazes following the gestures he was making.

'Tipsy is still free,' Lhikan signed, his hand moving in the quiet language of the Ministry, a language introduced by Hiro himself for the deaf but later adopted by the church at large.

'What's the plan?' Jesse replied, signing back quickly.

'We wait. Any day now, Commander Danse and his army will breach these walls. When that happens, we make our move.'

'And? What's our move? Why did we surrender?'

'Because we'd die.'

'We'll die without mana batteries to recharge our packs!'

'I don't think so. These monsters want us alive.'

'To violate us and cook us!' Simone signed, her fingers moving vigorously.

'No. I think Hiro is alive.'

Simone and Jesse froze.

"Oh, great. You've gone senile," Jesse laughed, only to be punched in the shoulder by Simone.

"Ow! Wounded!" He groaned while rubbing the spot.

"Have some respect for the Senior!" Simone hissed.

'Or at least something bearing his name. Maybe his likeness. The woman with the sword, the one wearing Natalie's clothes... she's a copy of The Skyshot Huntress.'

'Of the Big Six?' Jesse replied.

'Yes. And the weapon she's using is—'

"DRAGON SLAYER!" Simone exclaimed, immediately going flush as she recovered from her outburst.

Lhikan turned to the guards at their cell door, who remained unmoving.

'Yes,' Lhikan continued. *'Something is going on here. Something we need to uncover.'*

No. What we need to do is find this artifact and leave, especially before our air runs out!' Jesse refuted.

Lhikan sighed. *'We already did.'*

Simone and Jesse went wide-eyed.

'WELL? WHERE IS IT?!' Jesse demanded.

'The rubber duck,' Lhikan replied simply.

Silence fell over the prison cell.

"Okay, maybe you were right," Simone conceded to Jesse. "I'm sorry for hitting you."

"Apology accepted, lass."

'I'm serious,' Lhikan asserted, brows furrowed.

"Yes. We're aware you're serious, sir," Jesse said before leaning in to whisper in Simone's ear. "Well, our chances of survival just hit zero. Wanna make out before we die?"

Simone looked at Jesse with disgust.

"Well, a simple 'no' would suffice," Jesse shrugged.

"Quiet," Lhikan ordered, the sound of heavy marching drawing closer.

With bated breath, Lhikan and the others fixed their eyes on the door, where a green-skinned humanoid woman with scales stood. Her torso was visible, but her head remained hidden by the door's overhang.

"Hello," the scaled woman slurred awkwardly, crouching down. Her voice was monotonous, almost deadpan, with dark spots under her eyes that contrasted sharply against the rest of her body.

The cage creaked open.

"Follow me," she said, yawning as her fangs glistened in the dim light.

Lhikan and the others obeyed, stepping forward.

"Is it wrong that I want to bang her?" Jesse said, causing Simone to furrow her brow.

"I should have let you die, jerk!" Simone spat, flustered and walking faster to match pace with Lhikan.

"Excuse me, ma'am," Lhikan said, attempting to make conversation with the lizard-woman. "But where are we going?"

The woman grunted but said nothing.

"Smooth, sir," Jesse commented, earning a glare from Lhikan.

"Here, let me handle this... Hello, beautiful miss! My name's Jesse. What's yours?"

The woman turned. "You look tasty."

"Right... Shutting up," Jesse said, retreating.

"Smooth. You handled that well, Jesse."

"Thank you, sir. You know me; I always aim to please."

Walking through the smoothly cleaned and carved caves, it wasn't long before they were brought into the throne room, the massive fourteen-foot-tall throne seating the false Maiden of Light.

Lhikan's eyes shifted left and right, taking in the armored goblins flanking the massive, pulsing pillars lining the walls and the two enormous tarantuals.

"Still want to try running?" Lhikan whispered, tracking the string of goblins moving in formation, carrying the bodies of several dead goblins.

Lhikan and the others observed as the goblins laid out their deceased, placing them into the stone caskets laid out in front of the throne before kneeling.

A goblin in a vestment walked into the room, along with hundreds of its brethren. The slow march of the goblins made Simone and Jesse scrunch into themselves.

The goblin in silk robes stood at the foot of the throne, beside a statue of a rubber duck, as the chamber filled with congregants, flanking Lhikan, Jesse, and Simone.

"Okay, anyone weirded out by this?" Jesse said as the goblins began to chant.

"This!" Simone exclaimed, her alarm bells ringing.

"I feel it too," Lhikan said, gritting his teeth. "This is a funeral."

The priest goblin spoke in their goblin language, saying a few illegible words before the caskets were closed and placed into openings lining the walls, where they joined other caskets.

A moment of silence passed, with even Lhikan, Jesse, and Simone bowing their heads—an act that may have saved their lives.

"Welcome, humans, to Lord Hiro's domain," the woman atop the throne said, her form shifting from Lyndis the Skyshot to a massive blue slime.

Chapter 56

One-on-One With the Godblade

Lhikan gritted his teeth as he stared at the enemy that had consumed Natalie. Every fiber of his being boiled with a demand for revenge for his fallen charge.

Plop...

Natalie... you were supposed to be the hope of the church. Despite his feelings, he held his tongue and gripped his trembling hand, his head held low as he nodded his time.

Plop...

Plop...

Plop...

Jesse and Simone held their breath, watching the massive blue slime slink slowly down all fourteen flights of stairs.

Plop...

Plop...

Plop...

Beside the sound of the slime falling onto each step, silence permeated the space.

Plop...

Plop...

Jesse looked over to Lhikan, brow raised as the slime descended two hundred and twenty floor steps.

Lhikan waved the man off, giving the hand sign for "wait."

Plop...

Plop...

Plop...

Ten full minutes passed before the gelatinous mass walked past the rubber duck statue and stood before the three humans.

It reformed, taking the form of the Heroine Lyndis.

"State your business. Why do you trespass upon Lord Hiro's sacred ground?" the slime demanded, her green eyes glaring down at Lhikan.

Lhikan clenched his jaw, the monster's massive blade striking the floor beside him.

"If you keep glaring at me without answering, I'll rip out your eyes," the False Maiden hissed.

"We... are," Lhikan began, picking his words carefully. "Emissaries of the Church of The Keeper. Here to search... for the power of The Hero. To save our world from the Demon Queen Gisellneia."

The woman blinked, her form distorting as the rubber duck on her head squeaked.

"You mean Demon Lord."

"No, I mean Demon Queen."

"Demon Lord Barborall."

"Demon Queen Gisellneia." The slime lifted her blade, the weapon at Lhikan's throat.

"Tch!" Jesse shifted; his hands balled, freezing as the goblins nearby readied their spears.

"Six feet tall, three red eyes, with large pointy horns."

"She's four feet tall with four red eyes and curved horns. Daughter of Demon Lord Barborall—"

"SQUEAK!"

Suddenly, a pulse of mana—unbelievable killing intent—flooded the chamber, with even the seasoned Paladin Lhikan dodging back.

Simone lay on the ground, passed out, while Jesse was on all fours, the man struggling to keep his head up.

"I will only ask once," the False Maiden said, her massive blade held against Lhikan's throat, her crimson-colored skin releasing steam. "Who is the current Demon Lord of this world?"

"Demon Queen Gisellneia... She is a tyrant whose magical prowess knows no limits! Whose generals have polluted much of the world and whose armies run rampant across each nation!" Lhikan reported, as though his life depended on it, eyeing the rubber duck that seemed to gaze into his soul.

What is this?! This feeling! I've never felt such bloodlust!

Lhikan's skin crawled, the hairs on his body standing on end as he reached for a blade that wasn't there.

A moment passed, and the rubber duck visibly shook.

You.

Then... time seemed to freeze, a voice pricking at Lhikan's mind.

"Hrrrn. Gaaah." Lhikan winced, his psyche caught in some kind of vice, his head pulsing.

How many of you are there? The voice echoed.

Images of his soldiers, the dead piling in his mind before they were replaced by Jesse, Simone, and... Tipsy.

"No!" Lhikan snapped, refusing the touch. Yet it wasn't his to refuse.

Who are you?

Lhikan could feel a foreign presence, something pricking at him. Unraveling him. The memories of his life flashing before his bleeding eyes as a gaze unseen bore down on his life.

'I'm! Lhikan—NO! NO!'

From his childhood at the monastery, to his training as a paladin. Then, to his memories of the Thirteenth Crusade and the battle of the four fronts.

'I AM—'

A memory came to the forefront of his mind. That war-torn battlefield, with Lhikan and a dozen men and women surrounded by thousands of corpses and thousands of monsters.

Out of breath, out of mana, his face bleeding from the copious wounds on his body. The last commander left to defend a monastery already sacrificed to the demon hordes.

'I'm—'

Lhikan stood hopeless. His trembling hands gripping his broken blade.

"O' Lord. Hear thy prayer," a soft voice spoke.

A light, a magnificent light shining on his back, casting away the dark clouds that hung over his head like an executioner's axe.

A young girl. An orphan praying, radiating such divinity that it was as though God Himself had descended upon the world.

'Natalie...' Lhikan groaned, falling to his knees, everything threatening to come undone.

"Stop! Get out! GET OUT OF MY HEAD!" Lhikan roared, discharging mana, the ground cracking from the energy seeping out. *"OUT! OUT!"*

Lhikan went wide-eyed, reaching out, his own mind snapping back at the entity and pulling at the invisible tether that latched onto his mind.

HIROYUKI

"Huh? What is this?" I looked down, eyeing my... MY HANDS! My body! "What the hell?!"

One moment, I had been probing the man for information to confirm the details I already knew thanks to their sign language, and then the next—

"YOU!" a voice roared, turning my attention to the old man charging at me, rushing with a blade in hand.

I dodged back, pivoting, striking a stance and kicking on reflex. The kick caught the man in the abdomen, sending him staggering.

"GET OUT! GET OUT! GET OUT OF MY HEAD!" the man roared, racing at me.

I lashed out, my hand slipping past his guard and snatching the warrior by his throat. The man's feet lifted off the ground from my superior strength.

"What is this?" I hissed, anger and confusion taking root as I surveyed the shadows of our featureless surroundings.

I was in a void of no light. But also, no darkness. The only thing I was aware of was me and this human who had dared to intrude into my home!

"Y-You... Lord Hiroyuki..." the man whispered, almost a whimper, wide-eyed as his tired eyes gazed upon me. "The God Blade."

My name. I...

"Tch."

I don't know why, but I released him, dropping the man who fell onto his knees, then to all fours, sobbing.

"What is this? Some kind of trick? Where am I?!" My mind shook, my surroundings vibrating violently, almost as if reflecting my feelings.

"All our sacrifices... They weren't... They weren't in vain..." the paladin whispered, teeth gnashing. "Natalie!"

My eyes shifted, gazing down at the man.

"Please... Save us," the human pleaded, hand outstretched, palm reaching out to me as I stared at his church insignia on the gauntlet.

A cat face.

"No."

The answer was out of my mouth before I could process his request.

"W-What?"

Color visibly drained from the paladin's face, but I was done with saving worlds and helpless strangers. In the end, all of my suffering had led to nothing.

Even my loss... and the deaths of my companions. Nothing in this world had changed.

From his memories, I saw humans. Lying. Cheating. Stepping over one another to garner power, with those in charge sacrificing innocents to protect their wealth.

Hundreds of years later, humanity had somehow survived my defeat. Had remained strong despite the sacrifices of so many heroes.

So, what... What was the point then? Why did we?! Why did we DIE?!

To protect the wealth of corrupt bastards?!

Just like those damn elves! There were people like them in the human, dwarven, and beastren lands—people with the power to fight! To stand up against tyranny and fight the Demon Lord!

But instead, they cowered! Pumped me with praise and showered me with coin until I was foolhardy enough to believe I could lead the assault on Barborall's castle.

And yes, I was at fault too. I recognize my sins! My weak-mindedness and lust for glory—it blinded me enough so THAT I WAS PLAYED LIKE A GODDAMN FIDDLE!

No! The world was beyond saving! It needed to be cleansed! ALL OF IT! Conquered under my rule. The demons wiped clean! The corrupt purged! Then I would garner my power and topple every damn Church belonging to that bastard who sent me here, before mounting that little girl's head on a spike!

I turned to the paladin who had somehow found himself choking in the grip of my palm.

"Please..." he whispered, a noble soul seeking aid.

"No."

The void shifted, my body breaking into smoke as my senses returned to my rubber duck shell.

Two humans were comatose, the only one still conscious being the old man curled up.

Take them away, I ordered, a bitterness settling in my mind as I realized the humans were in no condition for further interrogation.

'*Take them away,*' Slimey repeated, my goblins moving the two unconscious humans, with Davette dragging off the Paladin named Lhikan.

"Please..." The knight whimpered as he was taken into a tunnel.

Gah. This feeling...

From the sly sign language, I observed from the paladins in their prison, it was evident that more humans were on the way.

And from what I garnered from the one named Lhikan, an army. Six or seven platoons of paladins, scribes, and priests.

Holy warriors, all of which were marching upon my domain.

Tsk.

Damn humans.

Rally the soldiers. Gather the scouts. Our time of mourning is over. We have a castle to take over.

'Yes, *master*,' Slimey said.

Natalie.

An image of a young girl praying.

Gah... What is this?

Slimey.

'Yes, *master*?'

Split yourself. I need your clothes.

'*M-M-My lord! You want me to strip?*'

Not... Not like that you idiot. I have a plan. One to get more information. But I need your mimicking skills.

'O-Of course, my lord. Anything for you, darling,' Slimey said before duplicating herself, transferring her clothes from one slime to another as she followed my instructions.

A moment passed before Slimey took on a familiar humanoid shape—the appearance of a girl named Natalie.

Chapter 57

Interrogating Humans

HIRO

Looking through the undead eyes of Hector, I gazed out at the expansive scenery of trees, mountains, and purple smog that hung in the sky.

Outside... I was... outside.

Well, not quite. I was still inside the Demon Lord's manor, just standing in a gaping hole blown into the side of the rock, exposing the innards of the castle's foundation.

'Is this everything you had hoped for, my lord?' a smaller Slimey asked, standing behind me with my rubber body in her hands.

A sense of melancholy took me as I eyed the lands below that had once been barren.

Now they were teeming with life—purple, corrupted trees covering the land, with blighted smog rising from the forest.

No... I'm... I'm not sure, to be honest, I replied back to Slimey.

I crouched low, rubbing my bony hands over the metal grappling hooks on the floor and bundles of stashed supplies.

Mana stones, weapons, rope, food, and other supplies.

Nicknacks mostly, perhaps the best thing being the steel swords and sets of broken armor.

Remains from the paladins' comrades, perhaps? I didn't know for certain.

Two days had passed with my army on the prowl. My forces spread rapidly through uncharted parts of the castle, capturing, killing, or converting the various denizens within the dungeon.

Ghasts, living armors, carnivorous plants, and even blighted direwolves. Those unable to be reasoned with or talked to were immediately exterminated by Slimey, while those who could think— well, the choice was simple.

Submit or die.

Sadly, most chose to un-alive themselves, feeding my composters.

It didn't take long to find where the humans had come from. Thanks to the trail of stones on the floor left by the adventurer party, it was easy to trace their steps and avoid getting lost in the winding labyrinth.

Now, I stood on the edge. My eyes saw a battle that wasn't there, while my non-existent ears heard screams that tore through my skull.

A hundred years ago, this entire forest had been burned to the ground to deny my soldiers camouflage. Now it had regrown... albeit a shade different than I remembered it.

Collect the supplies and seal this hole. I ordered as my consciousness left Hector and re-entered my shell.

"Please... you have to let us go!" Jesse exclaimed, rattling the bone bars of their prison cell with his boil-covered hands. "Our purifiers are out of mana!"

The goblin guards spun, raising their spears.

"PLEASE!" Jesse screamed, ripping off his filter mask and throwing it at one of the guards.

His pleas fell on deaf ears.

"Damn it!" Jesse snarled, his stomach growling as he backed away from the cell door, spears poking through.

"Are you okay?" Simone asked, speaking to Lhikan, who sat silently in the corner of the cell.

She reached out, her cracked hand touching the paladin, who, unlike her and Jesse, wasn't showing heavy signs of blight yet. But his skin was beginning to turn ashen black, the first stage of blight.

Silence. The man didn't speak.

Simone sat on the floor beside him, her head resting on the old knight's shoulder.

"Is he still not speaking?" Jesse asked, standing over the pair. Simone shook her head lightly. "Damn it."

Jesse sat down on the floor, while Simone used her mana to heal him and stave off the infection. It was a stop-gap measure, as her overall energy would diminish the longer she was affected by the blight, until she had no mana left.

"We'll be dead in days," Jesse groaned.

Suddenly, there was a rattle of the cage, and a taller goblin stood in front of the prison cell, a helmet tucked under its arm.

The prison cell door opened, and the goblin tossed a lump of cooked meat onto the floor.

'*You. Eat,*' the goblin signed, causing Simone and Jesse's jaws to drop at his hands.

"How... How do you know sign language?" Jesse asked, his voice quivering. The goblin cocked its head sideways.

'I don't... understand human,' the goblin slowly replied, almost uncertain. *'Eat. Now.'*

'We need water. Purified water. Mana cells for our purifiers,' Simone signed.

'We have a supply stash! We just need to get to it and we'll come back,' Jesse attempted.

The goblin blinked, taking a moment to process before responding.

'You. Two. Eat. Water soon. Mana rock. Soon.'

Jesse slowly reached out, grabbing the cooked meat, which was covered in dirt. He split the meat, handing the bigger piece to Simone and Lhikan.

'What is it?' Simone asked.

"Better not to ask," Jesse said, biting into the charred meat.

'I am...' The goblin unsheathed his blade, causing Simone to flinch, but she settled as the goblin began writing in the dirt.

"Gobledoo? Gobledee?" Simone read aloud, looking up at the goblin.

'I am. Commander.' The goblin pointed at the word "Gobledoo."
'You. Killed my friend.' The goblin pointed at the word "Gobledee."

Simone and Jesse shared a look.

'We... We're just looking for an artifact to save our world,' Simone signed. "Please help us."

'Stupid human. I don't know your language,' the goblin replied, making Simone flush slightly.

'We were just looking for an artifact to save our world,' Simone signed again. *'We—'*

'*I don't care,*' the goblin interrupted.

'*Are you going to kill us?*' Jesse asked, eyeing the blade at the goblin's hip, the same blade that belonged to Marcus.

'*I want to. But lord says no. You are guests,*' Gobledoo replied. '*But I hate you. We all hate you. You killed my friend.*'

Should I make a run for it? Jesse weighed his options.

"By all means. Go for it," a sweet voice sounded, causing Lhikan to finally look up.

At the entrance of the prison cell, a woman in Maiden of Light robes stood, a soft smile on her face.

"But you won't get far," the woman said, calmly strutting into the prison cell with a bowl of water in her hands. "You may leave us, Lieutenant."

The goblin snapped off a salute, marching out in an orderly manner.

"Nat... NAT!" Lhikan stood up, reaching out to the woman. "Natalie!"

"Sir Lhikan," the woman said, reaching up. Her fingers radiated holy energy that washed over Lhikan. Upon contact, the man's skin began to regain its regular complexion, the speed and severity of how fast her skill acted astonishing Simone and Jesse.

"You... You're..." Lhikan put his palm against the top of Natalie's hand, feeling the touch that had no warmth. "Alive."

Jesse's gaze shifted to the paladin, his jaw clenching as he eyed the tears in the man's eyes.

Ah... Crap.

"For now," the woman named Natalie said before turning to the other two in the cell. "Come, children, let yourselves be cleansed by the light of our lord."

Jesse and Simone hesitated. They knew this woman was no Maiden of Light despite the power she possessed, but then, what choice did they have?

Reluctantly, Jesse went first, accepting the monster's touch, his body shaking as the effects of his blight infection were reversed at a visible speed.

"Dear Lord..." Jesse muttered as Simone approached and was also healed.

"Th-Thank you," Simone let out before she was handed the bowl of pristine, clean water that had been sanctified.

"This... This is insane!" Jesse exclaimed, looking at his hands that were cured of the infection that would have taken weeks to months to resolve, even with expert priests. Yet, this... THIS SLIME!

"Natalie, will Lord Hiroyuki help us?" Lhikan asked, peering into the eyes that reflected no light.

"Lord Hiro has considered your request," Natalie replied, making Simone and Jesse go wide-eyed at the confirmation of Hiro's name. "The answer remains no. Lord Hiro has no further interest in the affairs of humans."

"But! He's human too! He's the hero! Has he defected to the demons?!" Lhikan asked, resulting in the man being slapped.

"Never lump my lord with those disgusting... Lhikan."

Suddenly, the tone of the woman changed. Her head vibrated violently as her skin turned gray, almost like clay. "L-hi-kin. He. You!"

"Natalie?! What's wrong?!"

"He is here!" the woman screamed, her appearance shifting, almost melting. Natalie, the REAL Natalie, was struggling. "The Hero! His soul is trapped in the shell of a rubber duck! HE'S THE DUNGEON CORE!"

Lhikan's jaw dropped.

"I... I don't have much time!" Natalie cried, the slime solidifying. "Lhikan. Thank you. For... everything. For not giving up on me. Hiro's not... a bad person. Please. Don't give up on him. He just... he just wants peace..."

The slime shifted, reforming. The gray color peeled away, and the shape of Natalie blinked several times before looking down at the stunned humans.

"You would be wise to mind your tongue when speaking about Lord Hiro, or I will cut it out," Not-Natalie replied as she stepped out of the prison cell, the door open. "Now, come along, your quarters are ready."

HIRO

Suck. Suck. Suck.

Quest Complete!
Reward: Supercysts
New Construction Options Available!

Sitting atop my throne in Slimey 1's hands, I finally bit the bullet and landscaped new rooms. First, I uprooted my throne, caskets of my fallen, and Mana Heart, ordering my minions to dig out new rooms while I was away on scouting.

The first room was a meadow. Why a meadow? Simple. Trees. Plants. Food. Land to grow resources for my soldiers. A garden taking over what was once my throne room.

Suck. Suck. Suck.

The second one was a catacomb. The room empowered skeletons within and even buffed Graveyard structures to summon new skeletons if I so chose.

Paying the toll for a graveyard and testing it out, it was a neat function, if not for the fact that it ate into my overall minion count.

A decent stop-gap if I was under attack, however. So, I spent a bit of my stockpile and made a place for Hector and Chloe to hang out, when, of course, SHE FINISHED EVOLVING! IT'S BEEN NEARLY A DAMN MONTH NOW!

Anyway, my dungeon had expanded by at least four rooms: the garden entrance, the catacomb, the reception hall (now designated as my guardian room with Ayaka in it), and finally, my mausoleum/throne room.

While I was at it, I had also expanded the doorways and tunnels through the dungeon to allow Ayaka and her Titan to roam freely and exercise. Did I have to? No. But fortunately, Landscaping also had a neat function of deleting what the RTS mode designated as tiles using mana, allowing me to expand the rooms easily.

Sadly, the mana cost was a hundred per five-by-five feet—an exorbitant cost when added up. So, it was an ongoing project along with the training hall, dining room, workshop, and miscellaneous rooms for other buildings that the construction teams were working on.

Suck. Suck. Suck.

Throw in the three rooms created near the prison for my human guests. Well, this grand design thing was an enormous undertaking that had split my attention over the last three days between interrogating the humans, scouting, and building up my defenses.

Suck. Suck. Suck.

Still, it was good to be doing something—progress in motion as—

Suck. Suck. Suck.

I worked towards defending against—

Suck. Suck. Suck.

...

Ayaka.

'*Hm?*' the large spider replied, burying its head into the floor.

Ayaka... look at me.

SUCKSUCKSUCKSUCKSUCK!

DON'T SUCK LOUDER, YOU CRETIN! LOOK AT ME!

'*YOU CUR! LORD HIRO HAS GIVEN YOU AN ORDER!*' the smaller Slimey screamed, firing an electrified shot of slime at the massive arachnid, which began electrocuting the bug.

'*NO! nOz! NOoOoOoOoOoOooOoOO!*'

After much persuasion and physical violence, the spider queen finally turned around, showing me her face and making me wish she hadn't.

Chapter 58

A Mold Issue...

 *old.*
  Mold...

Mold...

MOLD!

WHY IS THERE MOLD EVERYWHERE?!

Gazing at a newly opened room of my dungeon, I was appalled to learn that the entire damn thing was covered in mold!

Where?! How?! WHAT?!

Slurp, slurp, slurp, slurp.

Ayaka continued eating, sipping up the black mold on the floor with a loud chittering sound coming from the crowd of spiders behind me, all of whom seemed eager to eat at the mold.

Interesting...

Slimey held me in her hands, the woman's body wiggling from the proximity of the mold, the only one besides me who seemed appalled by the spectacle.

I focused my attention on the opening at the other end of the cave, one exposed by one of my capruxas that had been chewing up the dirt for an expansion.

The hole had revealed some sort of chamber, one laden with fungus and mushrooms from what my **Squeaker-Location** could pick up, along with various square objects and hanging materials. A room with furnishings, it seemed.

This was supposed to be the stairway to connect my domain to the catacombs, instead of walking through the sewers. Walking out of my throne, traversing the sewers and pipes, then entering the catacombs ate too much of my exploration time.

So, the idea was to make a stairwell. Something to ease the strain on my soldiers...

Suck, suck, slurp, slurp.

Aaaaand of course, no good deed goes unpunished.

Sigh.

This needed to be investigated. So far, the only source of mold was... ick. Me.

Well, until now.

The hole was too small for a goblin or Ayaka to pass through, meaning the only way to investigate would be from Slimey and me.

Sigh.

Slimey.

The slime in a spider dress moved forward, her feet stepping into the black mold and immediately sizzling.

-5 HP

-5 HP

-5 HP

A panel showed up, Slimey's health rapidly decreasing from contact with the mold.

Slimey!

'*Yes, my lord?*' the slime replied, unphased by her rapidly decreasing health points.

GET OUT OF THE MOLD!

'*What for, my lord? Our objective is ahead,*' Slimey replied, standing still, her body slowly dissolving into the black goop below us.

DON'T JUST STAND HERE! WE'RE SINKING! SINKING!

'*Oh... My apologies, my lord. But I don't seem able to move.*'

HELP! HELP! HAAAAALP!

After being fished out along with Slimey's cores by Ayaka's spiders, I sat on what remained of Slimey and pondered my plan of action.

The mold was spreading, growing rapidly, visibly inching closer and closer to the hallway where a dozen of my spiders stood, chittering. Even Ayaka, face down in the mold, was incapable of eating it all on her own.

Great. HOW DO I CONTAIN—*Wait a minute.*

Slurp, slurp, slurp.

The spiders... they were immune to the blight!

Were all of them capable of eating the mold?

Come to think of it, they all seemed hungry...

Was it possible they could eat the mold unharmed?

Ayaka.

'*Hm?*'

Are all your kind able to digest this mold?

Suck, suck, suck.

Ayaka.

SUCKSUCKSUCKSUCK.

ANSWER ME! The spider shuddered as my command forced her to obey.

'Y-Y-Yes. *BUT YOU DON'T NEED THEM TO! I can eat it all faster! J-Just watch!'*

SUCKSUCKSUCKSUCKSUCKSUCKSUCKSUCK.

Right... At this pace, we'll be here till next year.

Get in there, boys! I sent, ordering the rest of my spiders to descend on the mold.

'*NO! WAIT! PLEASE!*' Ayaka screamed.

What? Why?

'*BECAUSE IT'S MINE! ALL MINE! MY PRECIOUS! MINEMINEMINEMINEMINE!*'

Get in there.

'*NOOOOOOOOOOOOOOOO!*'

The swarm of arachnids went to work, gnawing hungrily at the mold, the cavern erupting into a cacophony of sucking sounds.

Great. Wait. It just occurred to me that I... Oh no.

Well, this sucks.

Squeaking over and over again, the lower sewers were... infested. My little test from all those months ago had festered and grown.

Even the few remaining monsters were covered in mold, blighted and twisted. Their forms were perverted and in pain.

Burn it. Burn it all.

That was the only option left to me.

I couldn't stop the tide. I simply didn't have enough spiders. So, I instructed an experimental group of goblins to move forward.

Goblin Archers, armed with arrows and short bows crafted from bone.

Not the most ideal material. It lacked elasticity and the ability to store and release energy. But the elastic spider silk helped, allowing crude arrows to be fired from a short distance.

One crappy arrow? Not much of a threat. But a dozen sharp arrows in a tight corridor?

Definitely an issue. Wrap silk around the arrow and spark a flame using stones?

Well, a fire archer was created.

I ordered the goblins to keep their distance, with one row in charge of lighting the arrows while the other row fired. For now, the only thing that could halt the spread was flames. Or... at least, I thought it would.

'SCHREEEEEEEE!'

Suddenly, a scream—a banshee's shriek that shook the sewer walls, with black smoke striking the ceiling from the roaring flames.

What the— What is that?!

I could feel it—killing intent, albeit oddly restrained, more akin to a dull, blunt weapon striking me heavily. Even my goblins were cowering.

Huh... Well... that's terrifying.

What was that? Was the mold connected to something? An extension of some creature's will?

I reached out, touching the disgusting mold just in case.

Nothing. No sentience. No will or spirit.

The killing intent subsided.

Great... Well...

Nothing is coming to kill me. So... safe?

I'll need to get a hazmat team together. A control—

An image.

Flames.

Men and women in yellow suits. Tubes—known as flamethrowers—in hand, torching tents in a wooden environment.

A cigarette in my mouth, my body clad in camouflage fatigues as I put on black glasses that reflected the flames.

I blinked. The memory faded. A sickly sensation settled in my mind, quickly subsiding...

Eh.

Gobledo. The goblin broke formation and kneeled beside me.

'My lord!' Gobledo exclaimed through our connection, head lowered.

As of this moment, you have been elevated to the rank of Captain, Head of Purification.

From this moment, your role will be to purify my domain. Select two to raise as your lieutenants.

'Yes, my lord! Thank you for me rank!' Its mind flooded with my instructions on what to do.

It would take some work, but eventually, we'd get there.

I needed to level up my goblins. Fortunately, I had the bodies of those adventurers—three in total, who were excellent sources of experience.

The goblin bosses were stronger than my regular goblins, but against humans... they still wouldn't stand a chance.

From my goblin followers, I had fourteen goblin bosses total, out of the hundreds of goblins.

Sadly, no orcs. But that would have to change.

Skill and constant training alone would only get them so far; strength and power would ultimately be the deciding factor. In fact, I should upgrade all my minions now that I think about it.

Oddly, Ayaka was close to leveling up, the bug suddenly leaping up two levels, almost as if she had killed something strong or consumed a...

Oh no.

You! YOU! AYAKA!

MINION AYAKA HAS HIT LEVEL CAP!

NOOOOOOOOOOOOO!

Name: Ayaka
Level: 40
Species: Hibernating Magicka Spider Matriarch
{ADDICTED}
HP: 25560/25560
MP: 1000/1000
Skills:
Rune Gesture
Spin Silk Lvl.10
Paralytic Bite Lvl.05
Pounce Lvl.10
Poisoner Lvl.10
Blend Lvl.06
Dark Vision Lvl.05
Magic Vision Lvl.05
Bile Spit Lvl.05
Resonate Silk Lvl.03
Magic Chant Lvl.MAXED

Magic Circulate Lvl.08
Ice Spear Lvl.03
Glacial Shot Lvl.03
Flame Bolt Lvl.04
Lightning Bolt Lvl.03
Flamethrower Lvl.02
Blunt Barrier Lvl.04
Commander Lvl.03
Egg Incubator Lvl.09
Mana Charge Lvl.03
War Cry Lvl.04

I focused on my domain, a massive spool of web forming around a stupid glowing bug, splattered out on the floor with a leg sticking out of its mouth.

YOU! YOU! SLIMEY! TAKE ME HOME NOW! I'M GOING TO KILL HER!

Invincible...

Ayaka's web had hardened into an invincible-like substance that prevented any physical or magical damage. Even Davette's claws couldn't dent the web.

WAKE UP! WAKE UP! WAKE UP! WAKE! UP! YOU STUPID UGLY FATASS BUG! I WAS SAVING THOSE BODIES! YOU'RE LIKE A DOG! BUT A BAD DOG! A VERY BAD DOG! AAAAAAGH!

Okay...

Slimey.

'Yes, my lord?'

Remind me to kill Ayaka later.

'Of course, my lord,' Slimey replied, wiggling around. *'Shall it be death by electrocution, immolation, drowning, or crushing, my lord? We can also spear her to death if you so choose... There are several options I have considered for this inevitable day.'*

Right. Hmm. Drowning seems like the way to go. Actually, it would be more productive to waterboard her, wouldn't it?

'Spiders don't breathe through their mouths, my lord. May I recommend tying her up and having Gobledo and his men lower her into the bubbling sewer water below?' the pink slime suggested, wiggling happily.

Hmm. Excellent choice. Maybe skewer her and roast her over a fire even?

'OH! I'm so happy that you're finally making the choice to be rid of that cancer in our lives!'

Alright. Settle down. How are our guests doing? I queried, casting my attention over to the three prisoners isolated in their bedrooms.

The furnishings were sparse: a bed made of silk and bone, a composter for their bodily wastes, and a stone table scavenged from the castle basement above.

Every day, I had Slimey's clone bring them food and water, using the time there to gauge their reaction to the blight as well as interrogate them for everything they knew, in the form of something they were familiar with.

Surprisingly, the senior paladin had been most cooperative, telling Slimey the size of the enemy troops, the commander's name, time until arrival, and even proposed strategies on how to defeat them.

Which, all things considered, seemed odd. There was definitely more to the story, but I wanted to butter them up just enough that they would feel comfortable answering me when I asked for more... personal information.

Personal... for me.

From the memories, I had a glimpse of the state of the world. But... I had no real concept or idea of the full picture.

That would soon change.

'Nearly there, my lord. The old one is eager to talk with my other self and seems to enjoy my company. The female priest is weary but cooperative, while the human male is a degenerate that I would recommend executing posthaste,' Slimey reported, recalling how the man had slapped her rear, as some sort of "jiggle physics" test, and tripped, landing between her chest and resulting in copious burn wounds.

No. If we kill him now, it would demoralize the others. The rule of interrogation is making the enemy believe you're on their side—that you don't enjoy what you're doing but you have to, and you can help them. If they believe they won't get out of here alive, they'll shut down.

'Ah... I see. Very insightful, my lord. Truly, your genius is unmatched, darling.'

Right. Let's just focus on each task one at a time and find this treasury. We have less than a week left to prepare entertainment for our guests.

'Of course, my lord,' Slimey replied, bouncing happily.

Chapter 59

Bombshell

Empty.

Sitting in the palms of a miniature Slimey, who had yet to fully recover, I squeaked, confirming what I already knew.

The treasury was completely empty.

I had hoped upon hope that something would remain, but within the broken-down and desolate vault, nothing was left—not even cobwebs amongst the ruined pillars and shattered displays.

Sigh. At least the armory was located next to the treasury, cutting my run time short and scratching another quest off my list. Well, a personal quest.

I still had the system quest, which was telling me to create an add-on for my mana heart, something called a mutator.

Problem was, the DAMN THING COST TEN THOUSAND MANA CYSTS! WITH FOUR ZEROS! Did the system think I was made of manacysts? How the heck was I supposed to upgrade under these conditions?! Did every dungeon have to do this? If so, it was a wonder anything got done at all!

Ehem.

Anyway, I did get a few new construction options. Mainly, some things to alleviate the bloat of manacyst cost increases.

Dungeon Management Panel
{Active} Dungeon Heart Lvl.02
HP: 1000/1000
Manacyst: 1275
Anima: 773
Holy: 23
Dark: 479
Manacyst Production
Manacyst Culture: 20/20
Construction Options...
Dark Manacyst Culture
REQ: 50 Dark Manacysts
Anima Manacyst Culture
REQ: 50 Anima Manacysts
Dark Gestator
REQ: 100 Dark Manacysts
Graveyard
REQ: 50 Dark Manacysts, 10 Anima Manacysts
Guardian Room
REQ: Any 50 Manacysts
Composter
REQ: 20 Dark Manacysts
T2: Dark Manacyst Farm
REQ: 500 Dark Manacysts
T2: Summoning Pit
REQ: 500 Dark Manacysts, 3 Dark Supercysts
T2: Forced Strengthening Pit

REQ: 200 Dark Manacysts, 200 Anima Manacysts, 200 Holy Manacyst, Any 1 Supercyst

Looking over my dungeon manager, it seemed as though my composting had paid dividends, giving me access to anima-type construction options.

More importantly, the anima cultures could be used to build up my meadow.

There was also a new "recommended" tab on my screen, something that caught my focus, but ultimately, I discarded it.

Gestators were... ugly and hard to look at. Ya know those eggs from that one movie with the face wrappers and the extraterrestrials versus the hunters?

Yeah, pretty much those things. I had made one to test it out but immediately destroyed it on account of how gross, sickly, and vile it looked.

Shooting myself in the foot?

Perhaps.

Did I care?

No.

I was trying to clean the place! Not pervert it! Anything unclean like that deserved to be destroyed!

Eem. Anyway, moving on.

I HAD WEAPONS AND ARMOR NOW!

The armory was fully stocked! We're talking steel plate, iron mail, chainmail, bronze swords, copper spears! The room lined with rows upon rows of weaponry untouched by time.

All I had to do?

Knock down the door.

Thanks to Davette, who was finally being useful for once, my military was able to breach the vault, kicking down the entrance to reveal the treasure trove inside.

Odd that the armory was so locked up, there were even faint magical traces on the doorway that were no doubt remnants of some kind of barrier.

There were even traps, trip wires, and pressure plates physically set up and left behind.

The treasury didn't have that, but the armory did... which was weird.

Still, my entire army had dozens of new suits of armor and weaponry. Proper arms for a proper war.

Most of the armor didn't fit my regular goblins, though, and it was a little big on the goblin bosses. *But if it were equipped to an orc?*

A game changer.

There were even suits of heavy armor in here!

But, despite the discovery, a question plagued my mind.

Why?

After pondering for too long and searching every nook and cranny for a hidden secret, I sadly found none.

But Davette now had a set of steel armor, Slimey also had a suit for herself, and I equipped Hector with better daggers.

With better-conditioned weapons and gear, I started organizing my goblins into squads. Sergeants, goblin bosses leading each squad that reported to one of two Lieutenants, who then reported to Captain Gobledo, who then reported to me.

Well, Slimey, who had begun delegating tasks with my approval, while I tried to figure out ambush points, trap areas, and plot out the defense to balance a war on two fronts.

Mold from below, humans from above.

It turns out, burning the mold in the sewers only kept the infestation at a barely manageable level. It was still spreading, albeit in the opposite direction, but still.

There was also the issue of toxic smoke, several goblins being infected by the poison produced by burning mold, with some even being consumed by mold spores.

Soldiers mercifully purged.

So, I was forced to switch to skeletons, the monsters immune to toxic mold inhalation but unable to be used for anything else once they began their jobs.

Acceptable losses. Each skeleton consumed by mold was replaced with another raised from my graveyards.

Tch.

We aren't ready. Three days left until the enemy invasion, and we just weren't ready.

Having to split my attention like this was dangerous, especially against devious humans. My map of the entire domicile also wasn't complete, and many hallways were left unexplored.

Areas where enemies could come through.

Or... maybe we were ready, and I was just being too cautious?

No. Never. There was no such thing as being too cautious when it came to war.

Slimey.

'Yes, my lord?'

Connect to your other half, it's time to have a chat with our guests.

Lhikan paced around his cage, rubbing his trembling hand to try and steady it.

The bone door opened, and Natalie entered the room with a soft smile on her face. In her hands, she held a familiar rubber duck, while an armored green-scaled woman, who he had come to learn was named Davette, escorted her in.

"Lord Hiro," Lhikan dropped to one knee. "I greet thee."

Natalie blinked.

"Rise, Sir Lhikan," Natalie said, placing a hand on the paladin's shoulder and helping him to his feet.

"Ah, thank you. How... how may I be of assistance... my lord?" Lhikan said carefully.

Silence settled.

"Tell me about the outside world," Natalie said, strolling through the room.

"The outside world?"

"Your home. Where you're from, Senior Paladin," the woman said, picking up a bowl of tainted sewer sludge and purifying it into actual drinkable water.

"I've told you this before. Sixteen times already," Lhikan said, taking the bowl as his eyes latched onto the rubber duck orbiting around the woman.

"Indulge me, one last time. Please?" the woman urged, her voice so alike Natalie's it made Lhikan's jaw clench.

"Bastonia. A city east of the Eldorum Lake."

"That's located in the Miserni region of Lizerneen, yes? Formally a fishing village on the Eldorum River?" Lhikan replied with the exact same response he had given the last five times.

"Yes."

The door closed, then Natalie and the lizard guard were gone.

This process repeated. Hour after hour. No rhythm to when his captors would return. And when they did, sometimes it was the same question, other times not.

"That's located in the Miserni region of Lizerneen, yes? Formally a fishing village on the Eldorum River?"

Lhikan blinked, standing at attention at another repeat.

"As... I've said before, the Eldorum River is now the Eldorum Lake," Lhikan said, tracking the woman placing items around him as the heavily armored lizard lady passed out on his bed. "Why don't we skip this and get to what you really want to know?"

The woman with Natalie's cadence raised a brow.

"Oh? And what would that be?"

"What became of the world you left behind?" Lhikan said, staring directly at the rubber duck.

"My lord has some insight into the machinations of current society. Thanks to your memories, remember?" the woman said, her form visibly wiggling—a sign that she was displeased.

Lhikan decided to chance it. A gamble.

"You are only aware of what you saw," Lhikan countered. "Not what I know."

"Oh, and what is it you know?" The slime in disguise asked, almost seeming to tower over the paladin with bloodlust in her eyes.

Lhikan raised his head and met the gaze that held no light.

"What happened to Lyndis Skyshot and your original team that survived?" Lhikan doubled down.

"What happened to your wife and the child she had?"

Chapter 60

Kill Yourself

"What happened to your wife and the child she had?" As the words left Lhikan's mouth, he regretted them immediately.

"DO NOT SPEAK OF HER!"

Uncontrollable bloodlust flooded the space. Lhikan was on the back foot, his hands instinctively shifting to a non-existent sword handle as the lizard girl stirred awake.

Lhikan's jaw dropped, his eyes wide. He didn't even have a moment to process his mistake before he was lifted into the air by the black-haired man.

Natalie's form had shifted, her soft and delicate features morphing into the sharp, angular visage of a man.

Rage.

All Lhikan could see through the fingers gripping his face was the pure, unadulterated fury contorting the face glaring at him.

Unlike the doppelganger, this was real. Real emotion. The face twisted into the expression of a demon willing to destroy anything it gazed upon.

Unfortunately, that gaze was fixed on Lhikan.

"Speak your last words carefully," the slime in the form of Hiroyuki hissed, his grip tightening around Lhikan's jaw as Hiro's fingertips began to de-solidify.

"I... I... When word of your party's defeat broke out through the ranks..." Lhikan stammered, his fingers unable to find purchase on the slimy arm holding him. "Queen Lidica herself led a counterattack, a spearhead straight into the Demon Lord's throne where she lost her life!"

The pressure around Lhikan's face intensified, a faint sizzling sound as the paladin began to burn from prolonged contact with the slime.

"Die."

"I SWEAR IT!" Lhikan gasped, his voice desperate. "Lady Lyndis's body was successfully recovered at the cost of most of the royal guard!"

Suddenly, Lhikan was released, hitting the floor with a grunt.

"Revivify," Hiroyuki muttered, eyes wide in disbelief. "Revivify..."

"Yes," Lhikan gasped. "At the cost of her life. Queen Lidica sacrificed herself and many retainers to save her friend, to give us another fighting chance with the last system user left alive."

"Child... You... You said there was a child..." the hero muttered, his face melting off as his form struggled to maintain itself.

"Lady Lyndis... She gave birth to twins: a warrior who grew up to found a lineage of expert tradesmen and warriors, and a chaste magician who remained pure until she died. Men and women who were pivotal in halting Barborall's second and third invasions and inciting Gisellneia's rebellion."

Lhikan caught his breath, the First Hero standing over him, causing the paladin to hesitate.

"Continue," the man ordered, his skin boiling with energy.

"But... after the second invasion, both sides suffered heavily. No one gained ground for centuries until the Hero Clan suddenly disappeared, paving the way for the fifth invasion that plagues our world today."

"So, everyone who could validate your claims is conveniently gone? Is that it?!" the hero spat, lifting Lhikan into the air once more. "You expect me to believe that?!"

"It's true! For two thousand years, the Hero Clan has persevered!"

The man's eyes went wide, his form shaking, visibly vibrating as if struck by some mighty revelation.

"Two thousand years?"

"Yes! You've been buried for two thousand years!" Lhikan exclaimed, his feet scraping against the ground.

"Oh? And how is it this knowledge has been preserved for so long?" the hero demanded, his left-hand cackling with lightning.

"BECAUSE NATALIE IS YOUR DESCENDANT!" Lhikan snapped, causing Hiro's grip to slacken, the man blinking. "Every member of the Hiro Clan is born gifted. More powerful than anyone else. Each one destined, in some way, to accomplish feats unobtainable to us lessers! Each one inheriting a mission to reclaim their birthright! None of them can use the system like you and Lady Lyndis can, but they were promised access if they could!"

Lhikan hit the ground once more, catching his breath and rolling his jaw, his head held low so as not to draw any further ire.

"My lord." Suddenly, a new mouth sprang up on the hero, sprouting a feminine voice. "Why don't we execute one of his comrades? Torture them to coax the truth out of him?"

"No! I swear I speak no falsities!" Lhikan exclaimed, crawling across the floor to grab hold of the man's leg, turning to leave.

"Then swear it on your oath."

Lhikan froze at the demand.

"SWEAR IT!"

"I SWEAR ON MY OATH AS A PALADIN OF DESTINA! My words are true! If you must kill someone, then kill me! I led them here!"

Lhikan's body gave off a white shine, his words activating an ancient pact.

The hero glared down at the man, no words spoken, only an insatiable bloodlust that made Lhikan nervous.

The paladin closed his eyes, accepting his fate. Moments passed in silence.

"What was Natalie to you?"

Lhikan opened his eyes, blinking several times before his brow furrowed at the unexpected question, his gaze staring at the pair of feet before him.

"A daughter. A savior. I was against her coming here. But the Church allowed it, fearing the threat she posed. It was my duty as guardian to protect her. And I failed," Lhikan said earnestly, his hand trembling. A new emotion flared up that made his palm clench into a fist.

"Are you angry?"

"I am," Lhikan hissed.

"Do you want... revenge?"

"I..." Lhikan looked up, meeting the gaze of the man who was once known as the Godblade.

"Do you want revenge?"

"Revenge?"

"I have seen your memories, Lhikan. Your pain. Your anger. Your inability to change the establishment that holds the world in its sway. You're desperately clinging to a child half your age for salvation."

Lhikan clenched his jaw at the stinging words.

"You are a failure. A man without hope. One without friends or meaningful allies. A once-respected knight, long since past his prime and sent to die." The man seemed to tower over Lhikan, who trembled. Every word that caressed his ears was akin to honeydew, bearing no falsities. "But you still have a place in the future."

"A place... in the future?"

"Paladin of Destina, do you want revenge?"

Lhikan dry-swallowed, brow furrowed, his heart somehow beating in his ears.

What is this feeling?

"I... I do," Lhikan whispered softly. Was it wrong? Perhaps. Did he care? No.

Without warning, a shift. Something seemed to change in the atmosphere of the room. Even the lizard girl was awake and observing the pair.

"Then, would you join my cause? Raise your blade in my name? Dispose of the enemies that stand in my way? Do all that is required to uproot the corruption that has taken the world? The real corruption. Not the demons. Not the monsters. But the humans. The monarchs and nobles? The leaders who perpetuate stagnation?"

Lhikan blinked. This... This was his chance!

"I would!" Lhikan replied earnestly, his head down, bowing to the man.

Suddenly, a dagger fell to the floor beside Lhikan—an ordinary iron weapon dropped by a skeleton.

"Then kill yourself."

What?

Lhikan froze, stuck in his position, pondering the command. The paladin raised his head, locking eyes with Hiro.

"Did I stutter?" Hiroyuki said indifferently. "You said you were willing to do anything. Was that a lie, noble knight?"

The paladin blinked; the hero's savage grin was akin to a demon.

Was he being played? Lhikan didn't know, but the purity and rage he'd been shown wasn't something that could be faked. No, this... This was the real thing.

"With your death, you will become the steppingstone for me to ascend. For me to rise from my imprisonment and wage war against the world to save its future." The black-haired man now stood behind Lhikan. "Make your choice. The future, or your life."

Lhikan closed his eyes, his head held low. Thoughts of Krekka and his thralls that held the church in their palms filled his mind. The nobles that abandoned the common folk and the knights who sold their honor for women and coin pulling at his raging sense of justice.

He made his choice.

"If my death can shape the world for the better..." Lhikan said, grabbing the dagger. He held it aloft and eyed his reflection in the dim glowstone light. "Then so be it."

Lhikan turned the blade to his chest, and with no hesitation, he thrust it toward himself. His eyes were shut as he embraced his sacrifice for his home, his world...

Or... he would have, had it not been for the invisible force that caught his hands.

Telekinesis!

Lhikan opened his eyes, the tip of the blade pricking his skin and drawing a thin line of blood.

"Congratulations, Paladin Lhikan. You passed," the hero commended. "I welcome you within the esteemed ranks of the Cleaners."

HIRO

"Thank you, Lord Hiroyuki," the paladin said, bowing as the bone door shut to the prison cage.

Possessing Slimey, I walked away, maintaining my stoic posture and expression until I was well out of sight.

WHAT WAS THAT?! WHAT WAS I EVEN SAYING?! OH, THAT WAS SO CRINGEWORTHY! WAGE WAR TO SAVE THE WORLD?! OFFERING REVENGE?! I HAVE GRANDKIDS?! I HAVE GREAT-GREAT-GREAT-GREAT-GREAT-GREAT-GREAT GRANDKIDS?! WHAT DO YOU EVEN CALL TWO THOUSAND YEARS' WORTH OF GENERATIONS?! WAIT! LYNDIS SURVIVED?! SHE WAS PREGNANT?! BUT WE ONLY HAD LOVELY TIME ONCE, AND I... I...

I... Lyndis.

The memory of Lyndis sprang up in my mind.

As much as I didn't want it to, as much as I ran from her memory, it plagued my mind like a shadow—a part of my past I pretended didn't exist. There were gaps, here and there. But her image, her voice, her touch, and fiery nature were always there.

Even if I wished otherwise... Slimey was proof of that.

I stood in the hallway, minions going about their daily chores as I pondered the paladin's words.

Revivify could absolutely return a person from death's clutches, though only if they had died recently, and if the appropriate cost was paid. Seeing how a calamity-tier Priestess, such as Queen Lidica, lost her life to pay for my failure...

My face was buried in my hands—an urge I hadn't felt in... centuries. Correction... two millennia.

I wanted to cry.

Yet my eyes held no tear ducts. My hands held no warmth. And my body was merely on loan.

Two thousand years... Not hundreds. That was how long I was down in these damn halls!

Two thousand years of isolation...

I wasn't sure what was worse: knowing that Lyndis had survived and dying thinking I had died, or that my children grew without me, never knowing their father.

Did she wait for me? Did she tell our children our tales? Things I wish I wasn't asking, but I was. There was also a... a sense of pride knowing my progeny grew to become so renowned. But it was... bittersweet.

Was Adam so cruel to send a descendant of mine to die in search of promised power? Was this all a test? A game of his?

No... The system couldn't be inherited. Couldn't be passed on. It was tied to our souls. Lyndis knew this. There was no way that she would tell any... *Wait.*

Lyndis knew this. If the paladin was led to believe it, it was passed on to each member of my bloodline that the system was transferable.

She knew this, yet she still sent them... passed it along to charge our descendants to search for me.

"You never gave up on me... Ah. Ahhah. AhahahaHAHAHAH! AAAHHHHH!" The laughter-turned-scream escaped my mouth before I knew it, a roar that bounced off the walls before my body turned into a puddle, my consciousness back in the shell of my rubber self.

"Lord Hiro," Slimey said, picking me up off the floor.

Yeah?

"Would you like me to wash you?"

Yeah... I would very much like that, I replied, my mind seeming to get murkier, less clairvoyant. The fog resettled as my thoughts shifted, not on my small, isolated corner of the world, but on my ascension and plans of conquest.

I WANT YOU
TO REVIEW

Thank you for reading a MoonQuill original novel. More exciting stories can be found at www.moonquill.com.

We would greatly appreciate it if you would take a moment to leave a review. Each one helps the author and supports their ability to continue writing fantastic books for everyone to enjoy!

If you're looking for more great books to read, join our mailing list by scanning the QR code below. You'll get 4 books for free!